**Praise for *New York Times* bestselling author
Heather Graham**

"An incredible storyteller."
—*Los Angeles Daily News*

"Graham is the queen of romantic suspense."
—*RT Book Reviews*

"Intricate, fast-paced, and intense, this riveting
thriller blends romance and suspense in perfect
combination and keeps readers guessing and
the tension taut until the very end."
—*Library Journal* on *Flawless*

**Praise for *New York Times* bestselling author
B.J. Daniels**

"B.J. Daniels is a sharpshooter; her books hit the
target every time."
—#1 *New York Times* bestselling author
Linda Lael Miller

"Daniels is a perennial favorite on the romantic
suspense front, and I might go as far as to label
her the cowboy whisperer."
—*BookPage*

New York Times and *USA TODAY* bestselling author **Heather Graham** has written more than two hundred novels. She is pleased to have been published in over twenty-five languages, with sixty million books in print. Heather is a proud recipient of the Silver Bullet from Thriller Writers and was awarded the prestigious Thriller Master Award in 2016. She is also a recipient of Lifetime Achievement Awards from RWA and *The Strand*, and is the founder of The Slush Pile Players, an author band and theatrical group. An avid scuba diver, ballroom dancer and mother of five, she still enjoys her South Florida home, but also loves to travel. Heather is grateful every day for a career she loves so very much. For more information, check out her website, theoriginalheathergraham.com, or find Heather on Facebook.

B.J. Daniels, is a *New York Times* and *USA TODAY* bestselling author. She wrote her first book after a career as an award-winning newspaper journalist and author of thirty-seven published short stories. She lives in Montana with her husband, Parker, and three springer spaniels. When not writing, she quilts, boats and plays tennis. Contact her at bjdaniels.com, on Facebook or on Twitter, @bjdanielsauthor.

New York Times **Bestselling Author**

HEATHER GRAHAM

A MATTER OF CIRCUMSTANCE

HARLEQUIN
BESTSELLING
AUTHOR
COLLECTION

**HARLEQUIN®
BESTSELLING
AUTHOR
COLLECTION**

Recycling programs
for this product may
not exist in your area.

ISBN-13: 978-1-335-41800-5

A Matter of Circumstance
First published 1986. This edition published in 2020.
Copyright © 1986 by Heather Graham Pozzessere

The New Deputy in Town
First published in 2007. This edition published in 2020.
Copyright © 2007 by Barbara Heinlein

This edition published by arrangement with Harlequin Books S.A.

For questions and comments about the quality of this book,
please contact us at CustomerService@Harlequin.com.

Harlequin Enterprises ULC
22 Adelaide St. West, 40th Floor
Toronto, Ontario M5H 4E3, Canada
www.Harlequin.com

Printed in U.S.A.

CONTENTS

Also by Heather Graham

Harlequin Intrigue

Undercover Connection
Out of the Darkness
Shadows in the Night
Law and Disorder
Tangled Threat

MIRA

The Seekers
The Summoning
A Lethal Legacy

Krewe of Hunters

Echoes of Evil
Pale as Death
Fade to Black
Dark Rites
Dying Breath
Darkest Journey
Deadly Fate
Haunted Destiny
The Hidden
The Forgotten
The Silenced

New York Confidential

A Dangerous Game
A Perfect Obsession
Flawless

Visit her Author Profile page at Harlequin.com or
theoriginalheathergraham.com for more titles!

A MATTER OF CIRCUMSTANCE

Heather Graham

Chapter 1

From one of the assorted ketches, catamarans, speedboats and yachts, a Jimmy Buffet tune was rising high on the air, tarnished by only a shade of static. The late afternoon was tempering the heat, and a breeze was flowing in from the water, cooling Sean Ramiro's sun-sizzled arms and chest. To all outward appearances he was as negligent and lackadaisical as the carefree Sunday loafers who laughed, teased, flirted and played around the docks. But when he raised his head for a moment, tilting back the brim of his Panama hat, a careful observer might have noted that he surveyed the scene with startlingly intense green eyes.

All seemed peaceful and pleasant. A lazy afternoon by the water. Girls in bikinis, guys in cutoffs, tourists with white cream on their noses, and old geezers in bright flowered shirts. Kids threw fish tails to the gulls that hovered nearby. Sean arched his shoulders back, grimacing at the feel of the wooden dock piling that grated through the thin material of his cotton shirt. He'd been sitting there a long time now.

Farther down the dock Sunday fisherman were cleaning their catches. A young sailor in tie-dyed cut-offs was hosing down his small Cigarette boat. A group of beer drinkers passed him, heading for the refreshment stand that was located where the rustic-looking wooden docks gave way to the cold reality of the concrete parking lot.

Sean heard a little titter of laughter and gazed sideways, annoyed to realize that he had become an object of fascination for two well-endowed teenagers in string bikinis. He tensed, swearing to himself. If something was going to happen after this long and futile day, it would surely happen now, while the kiddies were in the way.

He lowered his head, feigning a nap, hoping they would go away.

At his side, what looked like a credit-card-sized AM/FM receiver suddenly made a little buzzing sound. Sean picked it up and brought it to his ear.

"Hey, Latin lover!" Anderson teased. Sean looked up; he could see Harvey Anderson in the refreshment stand, chatting while he turned hot dogs on a grill. "You got a fan club going there, you know? I think you should be on grill duty. You're too pretty to blend into the woodwork."

Sean idly moved the radio in front of his mouth. "Anderson, it's not that I'm too pretty—you're just too damned ugly. You'd scare away the devil himself."

Todd Bridges, unseen, but not far away in the parking lot, broke in on the conversation. "Must be those
Irish eyes, Sean. Keep 'em lowered, eh?"

"Todd…"

"Hey, who said duty was a chore?" Harvey interrupted. "Will you look at that? I am in love! Thunder-
struck and all that junk. Now I really think you should
be grilling the hot dogs, Ramiro! Ah, I'd like just a
whiff of the air she breathes!"

Harvey was always falling in love with anything in a
bikini. But Sean idly turned his head, tilting the brim of
his hat just a shade. He arched a dark brow and was surprised to discover that his breath had caught in his chest.

This time Harvey was right on the mark.

She was coming in from the end of the dock. She
walked slowly and casually, and with the most sensual
grace Sean had ever witnessed. She wasn't wearing a
bikini, but a one-piece thing cut high on the thighs, and
man-oh-man, did those slim sexy thighs go on forever.

If someone were to have asked Sean Ramiro what he
first noticed about a woman, he would have given it a
little thought, then answered with honesty, "Her eyes."
Eyes were the mirror of the soul, as the saying went.
And so he looked first at her eyes.

He couldn't see their color, not from his position, not
with the way he was forced to squint into the sun. He
did see that they were sparkling like the sun, that they
were large and exquisite, that they were framed with
thick lashes…that they enchanted.

He didn't know why, but his eyes fell then to take in
the whole of her. Her easy, idle movement. Her walk…

He was—even on duty—spellbound by that walk.

The never-ending length of her golden tanned legs, the curve of her hips. He liked her waistline, too, smooth and sleek. Just like Harvey, he was instantly in love. Spaghetti straps held the yellow swimsuit in place. The top was straight cut, but she needed no help to display her cleavage. Her still-damp skintight bathing suit couldn't hide the fact that her breasts were firm, round, perfect. Sean realized that he felt a bit like a kid in a candy store, almost overwhelmed by the desire to reach out and touch.

"Will you look at those...eyes," Harvey breathed in awe.

"What is it?" Todd demanded from the parking lot.

"Boy, did you draw the wrong straw!" Harvey told him.

Sean looked back to her face.

It was a perfect oval. High boned. Classical. She could have posed for history's most famous artists, and not one of them could have found a flaw. Her mouth was generous, but elegantly defined. Sean could imagine her laughing; the sound would be as provocative as the curve of those lips. Her nose was long and straight, and her eyes—those wondrous eyes!—were framed by high brows that added to their captivating size and beauty. And her hair...

Her hair matched the coming of the sunset in glorious color. It wasn't blond, neither was it dark. It was a tawny color, like a lion's mane, with deeper highlights of shimmering red to match the streak of the sun against the sky.

"I am in love!" Harvey repeated.

"Oh, watch your hot dogs!" Todd grumbled from the parking lot.

Sean grimaced, jerking involuntarily as the radio suddenly gave out a burst of static. Then Todd's voice came back on the air.

"I just got a buzz from Captain Mallory. Someone pulled in faulty information. Blayne isn't here, and he isn't coming. He's got a reservation on a flight north at six."

For a moment Sean completely forgot the woman, as he closed his eyes in disgust. Damn that Blayne! The senator had received threats against his life, but he had lifted his naive nose to the police, who had bent over backward to protect him. Still, as public servants, it was their job to protect him.

They'd been tipped off today that Blayne, who had mysteriously disappeared, had ordered a catered lunch delivered to the docks this morning for a sailboat registered as the *Flash Point*. Meanwhile, another threat had been phoned in to the police. Of all the lousy details to draw, Sean had drawn this one. He'd had to spend the whole stinking day on the dock, waiting for Peter Blayne to make an appearance and to see that he got off the docks without mishap.

Now it seemed the fool had never been anywhere near the docks to begin with, nor intended to be. The boat had gone out earlier, but without the senator aboard.

Sean opened his eyes again. Not even his disgust at the wasted day could really have any effect on him—not when he was staring at *her*, and she was coming closer. A scuba mask and a pair of flippers dangled from one hand as she moved along, still at that lazy, no-hurry pace. Her face was tilted upward, and the smallest signs of a smile curved her lip, as if she was savoring that soft kiss of sun and breeze against her cheeks.

Just like some ancient goddess, Sean thought, and he could almost see her walking along at that slow confident pace, naked and assured, in some flower-strewn field, while a primitive drumbeat pulsed out the rhythm of her fluid motion and an ancient man bowed down before her.

"Hey!" Harvey's voice, quiet and tense, suddenly jolted Sean from his daydream.

"What?"

"It's back. The *Flash Point*. Way down the dock— she didn't berth where she should have!"

Sean stared down the dock. It was true. The *Flash Point* was in, and two kids—or young men—were securing her lines.

He stood, slowly, carefully, unaware that he grimaced as all the muscles in his six-foot-two frame complained. Absently he rubbed a shoulder and stared down at the ketch. Nice. It had three masts and probably slept a dozen in privacy and comfort.

It was Blayne's boat, and someone had gone out on it. But if Peter Blayne was really catching a six o'clock flight, they couldn't possibly have picked him up and brought him back on the ketch. It was six now.

Someone behind him began an excited conversation, half in Spanish, half in English. Two men cleaning fish were talking about a woman, trying to decide if it was "her" or not. Without thinking, Sean tuned in the words, then tuned them out, more concerned with the arrival of the *Flash Point* than he was with "that rat's old lady."

He supposed he should saunter down and ask a few questions. Pulling his open shirt across his chest to conceal the holster strapped underneath, he stared at his quarry, then started toward it. He rubbed his jaw and the dark stubble there, wondering if he didn't look more than a little like a bum. Good for sitting around on a dock idly, but a little scary, maybe, to the elite teenagers battening down the *Flash Point*.

He didn't realize how quickly he was moving until he suddenly plowed into somebody—and knocked them down. He started to bend down and offer a hand, then he noticed that he wasn't the only person racing toward the *Flash Point*.

From the end of the pier a slim, handsome young Latin with a grim look of purpose and something bunched in his arms was hurrying toward the ketch—or toward the end of the dock. Sean wasn't sure.

What he *was* sure about was the man's identity.

It was Garcia. Definitely. Julio Garcia, old Jorge's son. He had his father's flashing dark eyes and arresting, near-gaunt face.

Sean immediately felt tension riddle him. The police might have been wrong about Blayne's whereabouts, but if so, it seemed a strange coincidence that the people threatening him had received the same faulty information.

"You stupid ox!"

Momentarily startled, Sean stared in the direction of the feminine voice that had spat out the epithet. It was her. The sensually swaying woman with the never-ending legs and great eyes.

Eyes...

They were topaz. Not brown. Not green. Not hazel. They were the color of light, shimmering honey, sparkling now like liquid sunlight, like precious gems reflecting the last dying rays of the sun in a burst of rebellious glory.

And he'd just knocked her down flat, without a word of apology. He could reach out and touch her. He could...

He offered her a hand. She took it with delicate fingers, watching him warily.

If only Garcia wasn't just yards away...

"Hey!" The voice came from down the dock. Garcia was gripping the arm of one of the kids who had been working on the *Flash Point*. "I don't know what you're talking about!"

Even from this distance Sean could hear the kid's angry retort to whatever Garcia had said. Then the kid's voice lowered, and Garcia said something with a frightening vehemence.

Sean didn't know that he had dropped the woman's hand when she was halfway up until she thudded back to the wood with a furious oath. "You are the rudest person I have ever met!"

He barely heard her; he was too tense, watching Garcia.

"Don't you speak English? *Estúpido!*" the woman snapped.

Absently he offered a hand to her again.

"Don't touch me! Just move, please. Honest to God, I don't know what's wrong with people these days!"

Sean ignored her, anxious to reach Garcia. But even as he stepped past her, the kid with Garcia looked up and started yelling. "Hey, Mrs. Blayne! Can you do something with this guy? He insists that the senator is aboard and I keep telling him that he isn't!"

Blayne!

Sean swung around and stared at the beauty he'd just knocked over, then ignored. Mrs. Blayne? His wife? She couldn't be! Blayne was in his mid-forties or early fifties if he was a day; this woman was twenty-five, twenty-eight, tops!

She was impatiently dusting herself off after her fall on the sandy dock, but she smiled at the kid with a rueful shake of her head. "Tell him Peter had to be in Washington tonight. He isn't on the *Flash Point*—he probably isn't even in the state anymore."

The kid started speaking earnestly to Garcia. Sean was momentarily frozen, with two thoughts registering in his mind.

Blayne wasn't here; they had all been wrong, and it was probably for the best. Garcia hadn't identified himself during any of the threatening calls, but who else could be so violently angry with the senator except for some crackpot? And Garcia was definitely a crackpot.

The other thought, which interrupted his professional logic in a way that annoyed him, was about her. She was married to the man. And quite obviously for his money, since the age difference was definitely vast!

It was irritating, and somehow it hurt—for all that any feelings on his part were ridiculous. She was just a dream. The absolute, perfect dream you might see on the page of some magazine, then forget just as soon as the page was turned. Yet he wanted to shake her. To demand where her morals were—and her dignity and pride!—that she would marry an old guy like Blayne just for the sake of material possessions.

But even as he thought that, he smiled a little ruefully. Because the question that was really bothering him was, why him and not me? I'm thirty-three and as healthy as the "ox" you just called me. I'm the one who could show you what life was meant to be, just what you were built for, lady!

He reminded himself that he didn't like blondes. But any man, face-to-face with this particular blonde, would want her.

"Roberto, man, it is her! Julio, the old lady!"

Sean frowned, realizing then that the two fishermen were yelling to Garcia. He was halfway to the man himself, but paused.

The two fishermen jumped into a speedboat.

"Hey, wait—" he called to them. Where the hell was Harvey? Couldn't he tell something was happening? But how would he? Nothing illegal was going on. Two men had jumped into a speedboat, and Julio Garcia was talking to a kid. Nothing to get arrested for, but...

"Get out of the way! Get down!"

The heavily accented command came from Julio Garcia. Sean ducked, then fell flat as a whole barrage of bullets was suddenly spewed haphazardly in his direction. He tasted sand as he fell hard against the wood, reaching for his .38 caliber Smith and Wesson as a second barrage began.

Julio was fast; he kept firing as he raced down the dock. The shots rang out discordantly against the absolute and lazy peace of the afternoon, shocking everyone, causing chaos and so many screams that Sean didn't know where to look.

The woman!

He rolled just in time to see that the thing under Julio's arm had been potato sacking, and that Julio had looped it over her head, thrown her struggling but constrained figure over his shoulder and made a wild leap for the speedboat.

Sean didn't dare shoot; he would hit the woman.

He didn't think; he just reacted. He dove into the water, determined to reach the boat before it could jet out into open water and head for the endless nooks and crannies that the mangrove islands could provide.

Chapter 2

He wasn't accustomed to making mistakes. A homicide detective simply couldn't make mistakes and expect to live.

But as he dove into the murky water his gun was swept from his hand by a stinging collision with the wood and instantly disappeared into a growth of seaweed. Still submerged, Sean could hear the motor of the speedboat revving up, and he knew he didn't have a spare second left. It seemed necessary at any cost to reach that boat and then come up with a plan of action, minus his gun.

His fingers grasped the edge of the boat while it was already in motion. Water splashed into his face, blinding him, gagging him. He held on, feeling the tremendous force of the pressure against him.

Ass! he accused himself, but too late. To give up now

would be to risk the murderous blades of the propeller, so, thinking himself the greatest idiot ever to draw breath, he grated his teeth against the agony of his hold and tried to bring his body as close as possible to the side of the boat.

The motor was suddenly cut, and Sean remembered just in time to ditch his ID card and gun clip.

"¿Qué pasa? ¿Qué pasa?"

He heard the furious query, then a colorful spate of oaths in Spanish. Someone reached over the side of the boat to pull his half-drowned body over the edge.

He was dizzy; his head reeled as he lay soaked between two side-to-side seats. He gasped in a breath even as he heard the motor rev into motion again and felt the vibrations with his entire body.

The three men—Garcia and the two fishermen— were fighting away, screaming and gesticulating over the terrible hum of the motor, an occasional word of English slipping into the Spanish tirades.

"What happened? Who the hell is he?"

"I don't know. Why didn't you kill him?"

"We're not murderers!"

"We agreed if we had to—"

Something pounded viciously against his head, and Sean groaned despite himself. Twisting, he saw that the burlap sack containing the girl was stretched out over the seat so that her feet dangled right over his head, only the toes bared.

Of all things he noticed that her toenails were filed and manicured and glazed in a deep wine red. For some reason that irritated him. Maybe he realized he'd half killed himself over some mercenary socialite.

"Why did we take her?" one of the fishermen whined.

"She's twice as good as the old man! Hey, if he wants her back, he'll see that my father is set free!" Garcia proclaimed.

"So who the hell is this guy?" the second fisherman asked.

Sean, blinking furiously, more to clear his head than his eyes, pushed himself up to his elbows. If the stinking motor would just stop! He would need his wits to get out of this one. In the last few minutes the sun had decided to make a sharp fall. The boat was carrying no lights. Everything seemed to be a haze of darkness: the sea joining the sky, the men seated in the motorboat nothing more than macabre silhouettes. There weren't even any stars out. He was grateful that there didn't seem to be any other boats out, either.

He felt, though, that all the men were staring at him. Especially Garcia, who was seated next to the bundled, struggling figure in burlap.

Her toes crashed into his nose when he tried to elbow himself into a better position.

"*Me llamo* Miguel Ramiro," he began, yelling above the motor, but just as he started screeching, the motor was cut.

"*Cállate!*" Garcia snapped. Shut up.

Sean heard the water lapping against the side of the boat, then a woman's shout from nearby, and Garcia's quick answer. They came alongside a much bigger vessel, some kind of motorized, two-masted sailboat. A ladder was dropped down; Garcia motioned the two fishermen up first, then turned to stare down at Sean.

Despite the poor light Sean could see the dark, wary glitter in his eyes.

"Who are you?"

"Miguel Ramiro."

"And who is Miguel Ramiro?"

The woman—Mrs. Blayne—could blow the whole thing in a matter of seconds, but he had to come up with something. He damn well couldn't introduce himself as a cop. He inclined his head toward the burlap. "She is mine," he replied in Spanish.

Garcia arched a dark brow, then leveled the gun at Sean. "Then you take her up the ladder—and then explain yourself."

Sean struggled to his feet between the wooden seats. He bent over the burlap, trying to figure out just where to grab her. He obviously made a mistake, because his hand encountered something nicely rounded, and the bundle let out an outraged shriek and began twisting and squirming all over again.

"Stop it!" he snapped in English. A recognizable piece of anatomy swung toward him, and in sudden exasperation he gave it a firm swat. Her outraged cry reached him again, and he tried to murmur convincingly, "It is Miguel. I am with you, my darling."

Garcia's brow arched higher; Sean figured he couldn't press his luck too far and decided it didn't matter in the least right now which part of her anatomy he came in contact with. He reached down, gripped her body and tossed her over his shoulder, wincing as she came in contact with a sore spot, right where he had hit the deck to avoid the gunfire.

"Up the ladder," Garcia said.

Sean nodded and started up. His squirming burden almost sent him catapulting back down.

For Garcia's benefit he swore heatedly in Spanish, then added contritely in English, "My love, please! It is me, Miguel!"

Her reply was inarticulate, but Sean knew what she was saying: who the hell was Miguel?

Maybe he would be better off if she remained wrapped in burlap for a while. He probably wouldn't have to carry this thing off for too long. Harry and Todd had been on the docks. Search boats and helicopters would be out soon.

Yeah, but the coastline was a maze of islands and shoals and shallows and roots.... The mangroves, the islets, the Everglades.... They had sheltered many a criminal throughout the years.

He couldn't think about it that way. He just had to play the whole thing moment by moment.

Starting now.

He crawled over the starboard side of the sailboat to find four people already studying him in the light of a single bulb projecting from the enclosure over the hull. There was a short, graying woman, plump and showing traces of past beauty, and a younger woman, somewhere in her early twenties, with huge almond eyes and a wealth of ink-dark hair. Then the two fishermen. They must have seen him on the dock all day, just as he had seen them. Well, he would just have to make that work to his advantage. They were both in their late twenties or early thirties, jeaned and sneakered, and dark. One wore a mustache; the other was slimmer and as wary as Garcia himself.

Garcia came up the ladder right behind Sean. They all stared at one another for a moment, then the older woman burst into a torrent of questions. What was going on here? Who was this man? Who was struggling in the sack? Where was Peter Blayne? Had they all gone loco?

Then she burst into tears.

Garcia took both her shoulders and held her against his chest. "Mama, Mama! It will be all right! We were wrong, you see. The senator was not on his boat. But his wife was—we've got his wife! And if he wants her back, we must get Papa back first. It's better than the senator."

The woman looked dubiously at the sack that twisted over Sean's shoulder, then pointed a finger in his direction. "Who is he?"

"That," Garcia said, rubbing his chin and looking keenly at Sean, "is something we're still trying to figure out."

Sean sighed deeply and spoke in heavily accented English. "I told you, *amigo*—I am Miguel Ramiro. And I am in love with her."

Garcia started to laugh, and the fishermen laughed with him.

"And she is in love with you, too, *amigo*?" Garcia asked skeptically.

Sean gave them a sheepish look, then gritted his teeth, because the girl in the burlap was screeching something and twisting with greater fury. He smiled grimly and gave her a firm swat once again, which shut her up for several well-needed moments.

"Sí, sí!" Sean cried passionately. He irritably mut-

tered a few epithets in Spanish, then added, "But you know these *Americanas!* She's fond of the hot Latin blood in private, but when we are in public I am not good enough to clean her shoes!"

"She's a senator's wife and she's having an affair with you?" Garcia said.

"I told you—"

"I believe it, Julio," the younger woman suddenly interrupted him. Sean paused, gazing her way. She was looking him up and down with an obvious appreciation that was quite gratifying—he needed someone to believe him!

"Maria, I did not ask you."

But Maria put her hand on Julio Garcia's arm and gave him a sexy little smile, her almond eyes wide. "But I tell you, because I am a woman, too, yes?"

"Yes, you are all woman, little one," Julio said pleasantly to her, and she laughed delightedly.

"Latin men make the best lovers, yes, Julio?" She giggled. "I see it all well! She is married to some dull old man, but who can live like that? So she finds Miguel—"

"*Sí!* I was the gardener!" Sean said quickly.

"And he is *muy hombre!*" Maria laughed. "So she calls him in on the side, but pretends, Oh, no! Never!"

The fishermen started to laugh again, too. They were all grinning like the most amiable friends.

Except that Garcia was leveling his gun at Sean's chest.

"Juan!" Garcia said. "Start her up. We leave the motorboat right where it is. We go to the cove where we intended. Mama, Maria, you go below. Now!"

"But—" Maria began.

"Now!" Garcia snapped, and Maria, with one last sultry grin for Sean, obeyed.

Sean and Garcia stared at each other, both ignoring the grunts and oaths that came from the burlap bag.

Sean heard the crank as the anchor was pulled in and felt the motion as the sailboat began to move.

"Amigo," Garcia said softly, "do you know what is going on here?"

Sean shook his head vehemently and lied. "I only know that she is mine. You took her, and I followed."

Garcia shrugged and stared at him a while longer.

"I mean you no harm. I mean no man any harm. All I seek is freedom for my father."

Sean remained mute, thinking that this wasn't the time to explain to an impassioned man that spraying a populated dock with bullets and kidnapping a young woman were not sound means to reach the end he sought.

"I know nothing of your father. I am here for her."

"So stay with her. But if her husband does not produce my father..."

"Then what?"

"Then we shall see. Justice should be equal." He waved the gun.

"Your father is not dead," Sean said.

Garcia shrugged again, then smiled. "But you will be, and the woman, if you cause trouble."

Sean lowered his head. Where the hell was everyone? There didn't seem to be another boat in the water; he hadn't heard a single damned helicopter out searching....

Night had fallen. And the Atlantic was one hell of a big ocean!

"Put her down."

Sean braced himself, then lowered her to the deck.

"Get the hood off her," Garcia continued.

His captors had spoken Spanish to one another, and Sean had spoken Spanish to them, but he was certain that Julio Garcia's English was completely fluent. Once she started to talk he could well be in serious trouble, despite his story.

"The hood!" Garcia snapped.

Sean hunched down and moved to take the burlap from her—a difficult procedure, because she was struggling so wildly. At last it came free, and she stared at him—glared at him—with eyes so wild they might have been those of a lioness, and her hair in such a tangle it could have been a massive tawny mane. She was pale, and those fascinating tawny eyes of hers were as wide as saucers, but she'd lost absolutely none of her fight. She stared at him and recognized him as the long-haired, unshaven, rude Cubano who had knocked her down just before this mess had begun.

"You!" She hauled back and struck him hard on the chin.

His eyes narrowed, and he thought quickly. No self-respecting man in his invented position would accept such behavior.

He hauled off and slapped her back, bringing a startled gasp from her—and further fury. She tore at him, nails raking, fists flying. Grunting as her elbow caught his ribs and her nails his cheek, he managed to wrap his arms around her, bringing them both crashing down on the deck. Scrambling hastily, he straddled her, caught her wrists and pinned them.

That didn't calm her at all. She called him every name he'd ever heard and writhed beneath him.

Garcia, still holding his gun, suddenly caused her to go quiet with his laughter. "Miguel," he told Sean in Spanish. "You have yourself a tigress here. Maybe it is good you are along."

Sean saw that she was struggling to understand the words, but her knowledge of Spanish just wasn't good enough. Then she started to scream again. "What the hell is going on here? I warn you, I will prosecute you to the full degree of the law! You'll go to prison! Let me go this instant! What in God's—"

"Shut up!" Sean hissed at her. "I'm on your side!"

Garcia crouched down beside them. She surely realized that she was in trouble, but if she hadn't before, she must now, because Garcia leveled the gun at her temple.

"Mother of God, but you've got a mouth!" he said in English. "Don't threaten me. Think of your sins. If your husband doesn't get my father out of that prison, you will die." He grinned. "You and your lover will die together."

Her eyes reverted to Sean's again, registering shock. "He's not—"

Sean didn't really have any choice in the matter. His hands were occupied securing hers. He had to shut her up.

He leaned down and kissed her.

Her mouth had been open, and he came in contact with all the liquid warmth of her lips, exerting a certain pressure that he hoped would be a warning.

She struggled anyway.

He held his fingers so tightly around her wrists that she didn't dare cry out. Garcia, chuckling again, rose.

Sean tried to take that opportunity to warn her. He moved his lips just above hers and whispered, "Behave! Shut up and follow my lead. For God's sake, the man has a gun and is upset enough to use the damn thing! I'm—"

"Get off me!" she whispered vehemently in turn. "You...kidnapper!"

"I'm not with them! I'm—"

"Get off me!"

"Shut up, then!"

She clamped her lips together, staring at him with utter loathing. He sighed inwardly, wishing that he hadn't bothered to stick with her. The hell with her. Let them shoot her!

Then she was talking again, this time to Garcia. "Look, I still don't get this. If you'll just let me go now we'll forget all about it. I promise. You can't get any money through me. I just don't have any. And as for him—"

"Shush!" Sean interrupted, glaring at her. He wasn't about to be shot and thrown to the sharks for his above-and-beyond-the-call-of-duty attempt to save her.

She was going to try to interrupt him again. He tightened his hold on her, his eyes daring her to denounce him to Garcia. He tried to come up with his best and most abusive Spanish to keep Garcia entertained and drown her words.

She must have put on suntan oil sometime during the day, because one of her hands slipped from his grasp, and she used it to lash out at him. His patience was growing thin. He was even beginning to wish that he had decided to practice law, as his mother had suggested. So far he'd been half drowned, thoroughly abused and was surely bloody and bruised from her flying fists and nails. This couldn't go on much longer.

What had happened to terrified victims?

"Don't touch me! Let me go! Get your filthy paws off me! You son of a bitch! Who the hell—"

He had to do something before they both wound up shot and thrown back into the sea.

She just wasn't going to see reason. Sighing inwardly, Sean twisted her quickly to the side and brought the side of his hand down hard just at the base of her skull. With a little whimper she fell peacefully silent at last.

Mandy hadn't panicked at the sound of gunfire; it had come too suddenly. Nor had she really panicked when the burlap had been thrown over her. That, also, had been too sudden. She hadn't even really panicked when she found herself absurdly cast into battle with the rude, green-eyed, unshaven Latin hulk on deck.

But when she returned to awareness in a narrow bunk below deck she *did* panic, because what brought her to awareness was the terrible feel of rope chafing against her wrists.

She was tied to the headboard of the small bunk, tied so tightly that she couldn't begin to move her arms.

She almost screamed—almost—as a feeling of absolute helplessness overwhelmed her. Not only were her wrists tied, but her ankles, too. Someone had tossed a worn army blanket over her poorly clad figure, but it didn't cover her feet, and adding insult to injury, she could see the cheap, filthy rope that was attached to the same type of panel posts framing the foot of the bunk. Someone knew how to tie knots—good knots.

Oh, hell! Just like a Boy Scout! Did they have Boy Scouts in Cuba?

She closed her eyes and tried to swallow the awful scream that hovered in her throat; she tried to reason, but reasoning seemed to give her little help.

What the hell was going on?

Facts, facts... Peter always warned her to look to the facts. Okay, fact: she had gone out this morning with a few students to study coral markings. Pleasant day, easy day. Peter had seen that a lunch had been catered. They'd done some work; they'd partied and picnicked, and absolutely nothing had been wrong in the least. Mark Griffen had given an excellent dissertation on the shark's incredible survival from prehistory to the present, and Katie Langtree had found some exceptional examples of fossilized coral. Easy, fun, educational, pleasant...

Her only responsibility—her one big worry for the day!—had been to see that the *Flash Point* was returned in good shape: galley clean, equipment hosed. And even that had seemed like a breeze, because the kids had vowed to do all the work, and they were a dependable group. They also knew they would never use the yacht again if she wasn't returned shipshape.

So...facts! They'd come in, they'd docked. Mark had started rinsing the deck; Katie and Sue had been at work in the galley; Henry Fisher had been covering the furled sails. Everything in A-B-C order. She had stepped off the *Flash Point*, seen that the kids were hard at work at their tasks, then started lazily down the dock, looking forward to a cold canned soda from the refreshment stand.

Facts....

Next thing she knew, she was out of breath and flat on her back, with a tall dark man standing over her and not paying the least attention to her—even though he had just knocked her down in the rudest fashion. She briefly pictured his face; unshaven; his hair a little long and near ebony in color; his nose as straight as a hawk's; his skin sun-darkened to a glistening bronze. And against all that darkness his eyes had been the brightest, most shocking green. If she lived to be a hundred she would never forget the impact of those kelly green eyes against the bronze of his skin.

Facts!

She had said something to him, something about his rudeness. He had barely paid attention. She'd realized then that he must be Latin—Cuban, Colombian, Nicarauguan. Spanish speaking, as were so many of the area's residents.

English or Spanish speaking, no one had the right to be so rude!

Rude! How the hell could she be worrying about rudeness right now! Fact: she was tied hand and foot to a bunk, and some wacko was running around with a gun. He'd already shot up half the docks; she could only pray he hadn't killed someone.

And she had been the target! Why? Why on earth would anyone kidnap her? She didn't have any money to speak of. She did okay, but paying one's electricity bill on time was tremendously different from coming up with hundreds of thousands of dollars to meet a ransom demand!

No, no…kidnappers demanded ransom from others, not the victim. Peter had money. Not tons of it, but he was certainly one of the affluent. Because of their deep friendship, Peter would surely pay to keep her from being—Don't think of it!

Murdered…

"Oh, God!"

The little breath of a prayer escaped and she fell into sheer panic once again, whimpering and tugging furiously at the ropes. All she managed to do was tighten the knots and chafe her flesh until it was raw.

"Oh, God!" she repeated, panting and lying still. Her wriggling had brought the blanket up to her nose; she was going to sneeze.

Why?

The question came back to haunt her again. There was a lot of money in south Florida. Tons of really rich people lived here. Why not abduct a banker's daughter, or a plastic surgeon's wife? Why her? Peter would pay for her, yes, but Peter just wasn't worth that much!

And who the hell was the green-eyed Cuban? Or Colombian, or whatever he was?

Involuntarily she moistened her lips with the tip of her tongue and squirmed uncomfortably. Panic was zooming in again. The young, intense, dark-haired man had been the one to shoot up the dock and throw the burlap over her. Then everything had been a blur; her strongest memory was of a motor screeching through the night, stopping long enough for her to hear a furious volley of Spanish, then starting up again. And then someone had touched her, and naturally she had tried to escape. The dark-eyed man had first imprisoned her. But once she had been freed from the burlap it had been that same rude, green-eyed man who had imprisoned her a second time. Rude! He was much more than rude! He was brutal. He'd slapped her, subdued her, kissed her—and knocked her out. And the other man had been saying something about Peter being her husband and the scruffy Latin being her lover!

"Oh, God!"

It seemed to be absolutely all she could think of to whisper, but then, the Almighty was surely the only one who could banish her absolute confusion and growing terror.

Once again panic, a sizzling sensation inside of her that grew and swelled and overwhelmed, seemed to be taking charge. She struggled some more and realized sickly that, once again, all she achieved was a greater misery. The knots grew tighter, and the coarse hem of the blanket tickled her nose.

She blew at it, trying to force it beneath her chin. Tears welled in her eyes, and she decided firmly that she wasn't going to cry.

And then she wondered why not. There was a group of crazy Latins outside who were intending to murder her—or worse. She'd already been mauled and bruised, and she didn't understand any of it, and she just very well might wind up shot, so why the hell shouldn't she cry?

For one minute she suddenly lay very, very still, her memory going back…back.

If it had been three years ago she wouldn't have cared

in the least. They could have done anything, and she simply wouldn't have cared. She could remember standing over the coffins, Paul's and the baby's, and hurting so badly that she yearned to be dead, too, to be going with them, wherever that might be. She could even remember the thought; take me, God. Take me, too. There is nothing left for me, nothing at all....

She'd cried then. Cried until there were no more tears, cried until she'd been numb, the only thought in her mind that it was so unfair. But of course, no one on earth could explain why life cold be so horribly unfair, and in time, still baffled, she'd had to learn acceptance, because the only alternative was insanity.

Peter had been there for her.

Crushed and nearly broken himself, he had still been there for her. Peter, her parents, her brother. But despite her love for her own family, Peter had been the one who somehow gave her the greatest comfort. Perhaps because his loss had been as keen: his only son, his only grandchild.

Huge burning tears were forming behind her eyes. She blinked furiously, trying to think of Peter. He was so strong, so moral. He'd never wavered under fire; he always did what he thought was right. He always went by principle. She wasn't going to cry, and she wasn't going to break. Somehow, no matter what happened to her, she would rise above these people.

She tensed, aware that someone had come below. Twisting, she could see that she was in the stern of the old sailboat. Another bunk, identical to the one she lay on, was straight across from her, and two small closets at the end of the bunks stood at the stern. There was a slatted wooden door just past her head; her entire space of confinement couldn't have been much more than fifty square feet.

Two people were somewhere beyond that door. At least two people, laughing and talking in Spanish. She strained to make out the words, but they spoke too quickly.

Why the hell hadn't she paid more attention to Spanish in school? Why? Because the teacher had been a horrible nasty woman whom everyone in the entire school had thought was creepy. She'd had the most awful way of pointing her finger and saying, *"¡Repitan, por favor!"* in a sickeningly sweet voice, and no one had paid her the least attention.

Irrelevant! Totally irrelevant right now! She'd been hearing Spanish all her life; surely she could comprehend something of what was being said, she insisted to herself.

She did. At long last she did.

Cerveza.

Someone was asking someone else if he wanted a beer. Great! That bit of genius would surely help her vastly!

But then she stopped worrying about her comprehension or lack thereof. Foootsteps were approaching the door. Her muscles cramped with tension from head to toe, and panic sizzled through her once again.

She was helpless, absolutely helpless. Trussed like a pig on its way to the slaughterhouse. Totally, horribly vulnerable.

The door opened; she thought about closing her eyes, but too late.

One of the men ducked as he stepped through the door. He straightened too soon, cracked his head and swore beneath his breath. He turned to her and she found herself staring into his eyes.

Green eyes. Bright, startlingly…tense as they stared into hers.

He glanced over his shoulder quickly, then moved to kneel down beside her.

"Mrs. Blayne."

He said it in English, and she couldn't detect any hint of an accent.

"Mrs. Blayne, are you all right? Juan was assigned to watch me all night. I couldn't get back to you. Maybe he trusts me now. I'm not sure. This is important, please listen."

He was reaching toward her.

She couldn't help herself; she let out a small scream. Oh, God, what was going on? Who was he? How on earth could he be on her side when he seemed to be just like them?

The young man with the dark eyes suddenly appeared in the doorway, laughing, saying something about *amor*.

"Amor?" Mandy shook her head. Lover! "N—"

A hand clamped down over her mouth, stifling her words, stealing her breath. He twisted his head toward the man at the door and laughed, too, and when he spoke next there was an accent in his words.

"Amigo, you got a gag anywhere?"

The dark-eyed man chuckled and responded in Spanish, then turned away. Then the green-eyed stranger leaned his furious face so close to hers that she felt the whisper of his breath and the blaze of his body heat.

"Damn it! The next time I try to say something, you shut up and listen!"

There was no accent at all this time...

He straightened and slowly drew his hand away. Still terrified, and completely baffled, Mandy stared up at him in silence.

"Good," he murmured grimly. "Now—"

"Who the hell—" she began, then froze. He was leaning toward her again, tangling his fingers in the hair at her nape, bringing his mouth to hers....

The dark-eyed man was at the door again, she realized, staring at her. And at him. At the green-eyed stranger.

Who was kissing her again. Pressing his mouth to hers urgently, feverishly, heatedly. Stealing away any words she might have spoken.

Chapter 3

Cerveza...

He tasted of beer, and though she stiffened and tried to twist away, she was in that horrible position of helplessness, chin caught by his powerful hand, mouth overpowered by his.

But beyond the terror, beyond the fury, beyond that awful helplessness, the kiss wasn't that bad.

Wasn't that bad!

Oh, Lord, she was getting hysterical. This was insane; she was going insane already. So much for inner strength. Not that bad! It was wretched; it was humiliating!

And it could get much, much worse, she reminded herself, and that was her last thought, because suddenly all the little sensations seemed to overwhelm her, and she felt as if she was nothing but burning kinetic energy.

She felt the rasp of his bearded cheek and the warm texture of his lips, the moisture that seemed like lava, and the taut muscles of his chest, crushed hard against her breast. She felt the whisper of his breath and thought ridiculously that he smelled rather nice, and that the slight taste of beer wasn't so awful, either, and really, she could live through this, because what other choice did she have?

The man in the doorway chuckled again, saying something and addressing the green-eyed man as Miguel.

At last "Miguel" drew away from her, but those green eyes remained on hers, as bright as gems, sparkling out a warning so potent that it might have been written on the air.

He kept staring at her as he answered the other man. What he said she didn't know, she just kept staring back into those green eyes, wishing with all her heart that she was free, not trussed and tied here so ignominiously. Wishing that she could reach up, wrench out a thatch of that ebony hair and punch him through a wall!

And then she was afraid all over again. Deeply afraid. Because every man on the sailboat could come in at any time and do anything to her, and all she would be able to do in turn was fight until her wrists bled from the cruel chafing of the rope.

She averted her eyes from his at last and suddenly realized that it was day. Ugly old curtains were pulled over the tiny portholes, but light was filtering in nevertheless.

She'd slept here the night through, and of all the ridiculous things, while her life hung in the balance, she was suddenly and desperately the recipient of nature's call. They were still prattling away, so she burst out in interruption, "I have to go to the bathroom."

They both stopped speaking and stared at her.

"¡Baño!" she snapped. "I have to...go!"

Then they both stared at each other and started laughing again. Miguel said something; the other man, addressed as Julio, shrugged, then turned away.

She cringed as Miguel pushed aside her hips with his own so he could sit and lean over her. He gave a disgusted oath, granted her another sizzling glance and moved on to his objective: freeing one of her wrists.

She breathed a little more easily, closed her eyes and prayed for strength, and said carefully, "Who are you?"

He glanced back toward the door quickly, then whispered, "For God's sake, trust me! Go along with me!"

Julio was back; she couldn't say anything more. Actually, she could have, because she didn't trust Miguel in the least, but somehow she chose not to.

He kept working on her wrist. She gazed past his broad bare shoulder to Julio. "Señora Blayne," he told her, "we really do not wish to hurt you. If you can behave, you will be well. Miguel says he can handle you—"

She couldn't help but interrupt. "Oh, he does, does he?" she asked, flashing Miguel a glance of pure loathing.

"And for your sake, señora, I hope he speaks the truth."

Her right hand fell free. Miguel clutched it, inhaling with concern at the rope burns there. She tried to snatch it from him, but he held tight, warning her with his eyes once again.

She clenched her teeth against the tears that threatened. He started to free her other hand. When her left wrist was released he moved to her feet. Rubbing her wrists, she turned her head defiantly to stare at Julio.

"Why are you doing this? You're mistaken if you think that Peter Blayne is a wealthy man. He isn't. If you're asking a huge ransom for my return you won't get it."

"*Señora*, we do not want money. Money, bah, what is that? A man wants money, it is easy. He works for it."

A new fear settled over her; they didn't want money! Then...

Julio suddenly pounded his heart. "Freedom! You will be our ticket to freedom!"

"But..."

Her feet were free. Miguel was standing above her again, taking her hands.

"Let me go! I can stand by myself."

He looked as if he were going to argue with her, but he didn't. He released her, and she swung her long bare legs over the bunk and attempted to stand in a huff.

She keeled over instantly, right into his arms. And she felt those hated hands encircle her waist, holding her steady.

"Damn you!" She tried to slap him, but he ducked, and she cried out when he caught her wrists. They were so sore!

Julio laughed. "You and Miguel had better make up, *señora*. Oh, you needn't worry—or pretend. We will say nothing to the senator about your affair. He might not think an unfaithful wife worth much."

"I'm not—"

"You said you had to go to the head!" Miguel snapped, his English heavily accented again.

She was certain that this ordeal had cost her her mind.

He muttered something to Julio in Spanish, then reached for her arm and wrenched her to her feet. Julio moved out of the way, and Miguel led her roughly through the little door and three feet down a narrow hallway to another door.

"The head!" he snapped, shoving her in.

Face flaming, she slammed the door.

And then she didn't even have to go anymore. She pressed her palms to her temples, dizzy, nauseated— and scared. He'd said she should trust him. How the hell could she, and who was he, anyway?

She tried to take deep breaths, and at last she felt that at least she wasn't going to be sick. She noticed then that the facilities were quite clean, and managed to use them. The water that ran into the sink was sporadic, but clear and clean, and she splashed a lot of it over her face, thinking how good it was to rinse the salty sticki- ness away. She stared into the mirror over the sink and saw that her eyes were as wide as gold doubloons; her cheeks appeared far too pale beneath her tan.

Feeling dizzy again, she gripped the small sink. At last she opened her eyes and stared longingly out the circular porthole. The sailboat's outer rail hid any view of the water, but she could see the sky, and it was a beau- tiful blue, with just a few puffs of cottonlike clouds.

What a glorious day! Monday. She should have been at work by now, joining her colleagues at the site.

White-smocked and gloved, she should have been up to her wrists in dirt, seeking the treasures beneath it.

Where was help? The whole dock had been chaos. Surely the police had been called. Surely someone—everyone!—knew that she was missing by now. They would have known it as soon as she had been taken; there had been witnesses all over the place!

"Señora Blayne!"

Her name, snapped out in a feminine voice, was followed by a rough pounding at the door.

"What?" she yelled back.

"Open the door! I will give you a robe, and you can take a shower."

Mandy gazed instantly at the tiny shower cubicle; the longing to feel clean was a strong one. She didn't know how many hours they had been at sea. She had no idea of where she was, or what the chances were that she would ever get back to civilization alive. It just didn't make any sense to turn down a shower.

Mandy threw open the door to find a young woman standing before her, a very young woman, somewhere between eighteen and twenty-one.

What she lacked in age, though, she made up for in manner. She was beautiful in an exotic way, with flashing dark eyes and a voluptuous figure, well defined in tight jeans and a red sweater, and with a head of richly curling, near-black hair.

She was shorter than Mandy's five-feet-eight inches, which for some odd reason—she was clutching at straws!—made Mandy feel just a little bit better.

The Latin girl lifted her chin, eyeing Mandy regally,

then stuffed something made of dull gray terry into Mandy's hands.

"I am Maria. Here, take this. The bathing suit is not much covering, eh?" the girl said, and once again swept Mandy with a disdainful glare. She chuckled, displaying a fine set of small white teeth beneath her generous rose-tinted lips. "Not that you have much to cover!" She shook her head. "What Miguel sees in you...but then, maybe he has not had enough to distract him!"

Mandy was about to tell her that she really didn't give a damn what Miguel saw in anyone. All she wanted to do was get away from the whole stinking lot of them. She decided to keep silent, though she wasn't sure why, because she certainly didn't trust Miguel.

"Thanks for the robe," she said flatly, and closed the door, smiling bitterly as she heard the girl burst into an outraged spate of Spanish. Maria was no part of the power here, that much was obvious. She was nothing more than a young girl—uncertain, insecure, and perhaps idolizing the handsome well-built Miguel.

Mandy turned on the water; it came out cold, but she hadn't been expecting anything better. Stepping beneath the weak spray even as she peeled away her bathing suit, she started shivering vehemently—and not from the cold. Fear swept through her again as she wondered just what was going on. Who was Miguel? Who was Julio? And, for that matter, just who the hell was Maria? And if they were after "freedom" instead of money, just how did they think she could supply it?

She swallowed convulsively and found a fairly new bar of soap. She let the water run over it as she stood there behind the strangely new pink plastic curtain in a state of something akin to numbness. She didn't want to use anything of theirs, but she decided that the soap would be okay if she let the water rinse away layer after layer in a pool of suds.

And then suddenly she began to feel better—angrier, but better. She really did have to fight them; she couldn't allow herself to be so victimized. Fight them... and use any means that she had. Maria's very childlike insecurity was a weapon she must remember and use.

She would get to the bottom of this! She would find out exactly what they wanted—and see that they never got it! There would be a chance for escape somewhere along the line. There would have to be!

She closed her eyes and ducked her head beneath the trickling water to rinse her hair, shaking and shivering still, but now just a bit calmer, a bit more in control. It was amazing what a cold shower could do.

But just then—just when she had convinced herself that she could survive!—she heard her name spoken again, and spoken much too close!

"Mrs. Blayne..."

She let out a shriek of horror, aware that the husky, low-timbred, unaccented tone belonged to green-eyed Miguel.

"Damn you!" he swore next, and she shrieked again, because his arms were suddenly around her, wrapping her in the pink plastic curtain. She dragged in a breath to scream again, but that massive tanned hand of his was suddenly over her mouth, and to her absolute horror he was standing behind her, touching her, in the tiny confines of the shower stall.

He pulled her hard against him. All the naked length

of her back was against his chest and hips; he wore only
a pair of cutoffs, and she could feel with painful clarity
all the rippling muscle that composed his shoulders and
arms, all the short dark hair that ran riot over his chest.
She squirmed, near hysteria, but she managed only to
wedge her bare buttocks more intimately against him.

"Stop it, please, will you?" he begged her in a whisper,
dipping his mouth near her ear. "I'll explain if you'll just—"

His hold had loosened. With a burst of strength she
wriggled away from him and opened her mouth to inhale again for a frenzied scream, too frightened to realize that her scream could do nothing but bring her
other captors running.

"Damn it, you're worse than a greased pig!" he
rasped out, and then his hands were on her again, but
far worse. Because this time, in his attempt to restrain
her, his fingers closed over her breast before finding a
hold against her ribs again, and he'd already regained
a smothering hold over her mouth.

Still swearing beneath his breath, he manipulated
her around to face him, and that, too, was far worse,
because then her breasts were pressed against his chest
and her hips were horribly level with his, and she had
never been forced to realize so staggeringly that a man
was a man, and this one was made of iron. She almost
passed out, but the water, cold and beating against her
back, revived her, and she found herself tilting her head
to stare into those incredibly green eyes. She realized
a little belatedly that he was angry and aggravated, but
intense and serious and not—apparently—about to mo-
lest her. Not any more than he already had, that was!

"Listen! I'm not going to hurt you! I had to come

in here because I had to talk to you without the others hearing. Mrs. Blayne, please, promise me that you won't scream again and I'll move my hand."

Promise that she wouldn't scream....

She wasn't sure that she could. The screams just kept building inside of her. She was standing naked in a two-by-two cubicle, crushed against a near-naked stranger with the muscled build of a prizefighter. Screaming was instinctive!

"Please!" he urged her again.

She didn't know why she nodded at last. Perhaps because she didn't have any choice. And perhaps because she wanted to believe him, because she wanted to trust someone. Perhaps it was something in his eyes that promised pride and integrity and sincerity. Perhaps it was because she would pass out and pitch helplessly against him, if she didn't breathe soon....

Slowly he eased his hand from her mouth. His eyes slipped from hers for just a moment, traveling downward, then upward once again, locking with hers.

"Mrs. Blayne," he whispered, "I'm a cop. If you want to come out of this, play along with me. I'm all that can stand between you and—"

"A cop!" she gasped incredulously. A cop? The hell he was! Where was his badge? Where was his gun? Cops didn't help kidnappers. They didn't assault the victims!

"Mrs. Blayne, I'm with—"

"If you're a cop," she demanded, shaking, realizing all over again that she was naked with him in a tiny space, "where's your badge?"

"I dumped it. I lost my gun coming after—"

"Get out of here!" she snapped suddenly, aware that hysteria was rising in her again. "Cops don't crawl into the shower with kidnap victims! They don't—"

She hadn't realized how her voice was rising until his hand fell over her face again, shutting her up.

"*Shh!* Are you trying to get us both killed? If they even get a whiff of who I am, I'll become shark bait, lady. And I'll be damned if I think you're worth it!"

Her eyes widened. Could it possibly be true? His Spanish had been perfect; his English, when he spoke to her alone, had no accent whatsoever. Yet when he spoke to Julio, he sounded as if he was barely comfortable with the language. Like a chameleon, he could change in the wink of an eye....

"Eh? Miguel?"

They both froze as someone rapped on the door again and called out to Miguel. A barrage of Spanish followed. Miguel held still for a moment, then called something back, something that she didn't understand a single word of.

Footsteps moved away from the door. Mandy was crushed so tightly to his chest that she felt the expulsion of his breath and the rapid beating of his heart.

He stared down at her then with absolute dislike and fury. Still holding her to him, he reached around and turned off the water; it seemed that his striking eyes became razors that sliced right through her.

"Listen to me, lady. Listen good. I'm a cop—whether you believe it or not. Go along with me. I'm only going to warn you once, because, honey, I can bail out of this thing real easy by myself. I spent all night talking my heart out to convince them that I'm a refugee, too, that

I was your gardener, that you're married to a man twice your age, and therefore became involved with me hot and heavy. They didn't take you to kill you or rape you. Julio Garcia is a desperate man, but fairly ethical, for a kidnapper. I don't trust his companions all that far, however. Julio decided to keep me around because he thinks I can keep you under control. Blow that, and we could both be dead. Pull one more stunt against me and I swear I'll jump overboard and swim out of this thing. I don't mind sticking around to fulfill my job, but I'll be damned if I'll keep worrying about getting killed *because of* you instead of *for* you!"

She stared at him, shaken by his anger, shaken by the intensity of his words. Was he really a cop? Or was he one of *them*, just a little more educated, a far better actor? What a way to control a captive, to convince her that a cop was with her and on her side!

He shook her suddenly. "Do you understand?"

She lowered her eyes, then closed them quickly. All she saw when she looked down was his muscled and hairy male chest, slick and hard against her breasts. And of all things, she felt her nipples harden against him.

"Yes!" She gasped, trying to escape him, but he held her against him, and she shook in sudden horror and confusion. "Yes! No! I don't understand any of this. I—"

"Just go along with me now! Julio just said to get the hell out, lunch is ready. I don't have time to try to convince you any further."

He released her completely and stepped out of the shower stall, finding a towel to dry his slick shoulders and chest. He didn't look back at Mandy but stuffed the towel toward her, then found the gray terry robe and shoved that to her over his shoulder.

Quivering and confused, Mandy hurriedly accepted the towel, though she didn't bother to dry herself thoroughly, and fumbled into the robe. It was worn and fell to her feet, but it didn't make her feel especially secure. She wrapped it around herself as tightly as she could, then knotted the belt.

His back was still to her, but just inches away. Beneath his tan she noted a smattering of freckles across his shoulder and thought them curious, considering his coloring.

Oh, God! Who the hell was he really?

"Are you decent?" he asked her.

She started to laugh, but caught herself quickly, afraid that if she got started, she would never quit. "You didn't worry whether I was 'decent' or not when you charged into the shower!" she accused him.

"Shh! Damn you!" he said in a vehement whisper, whirling around, hands on hips, to face her.

Her lip started to tremble, but she didn't intend to let it. She tossed back her head and stared at him dubiously. "Do cops always run around in the pursuit of duty with no weapons, no ID and no shoes?"

He groaned impatiently. "I told you—"

"Oh, I know what you told me," she said. "I'm just not sure I believe a word of it."

He closed his eyes and sighed, then stared at her in exasperation. "Gamble, then. You're with me, or you're not. But if you're against me, remember, I'm gone."

"Gone? From where?" she demanded.

"From wherever we are. Near Cat Cay, I think. I'm

a hell of a good swimmer. A dive overboard, that's all it would take. They don't watch me like they're going to watch you."

"And why the hell should they trust you?"

"Because I know how to play this game, lady," he said grimly.

"Either that, or you're one of them."

He smiled with a certain malicious humor and advanced those few inches to her, rounding his fingers over her shoulders so that she almost screamed again from the pure electricity of that touch.

Never had she seen anything as intense, as compelling, as frightening—as dangerous!—as the kelly green blaze of his eyes. She couldn't speak; she couldn't have screamed even if it had been her most ardent desire. She could only stare at him in silence.

"Lady, place your bet quickly. We've got to go now, unless you want Julio in this head along with the two of us! If I were you, though, I'd change my tune—quickly. I'd admit to this ignoble affair and cling to me as if we'd been passionately involved for ages! Hey—" he cocked his head, daring her "—you might not like your other options. Julio is fairly ethical, but those other two have been talking about your *senos* all day."

"My—my what?" Mandy swallowed.

"Breasts, Mrs. Blayne. They're quite entranced with…them."

She started to jerk away, and he laughed without a trace of amusement. "Like I said, there's only so far I'll go for you if you won't cooperate. So have it your way. I'm a fugitive like the others, probably a murdering rapist. Take me—or leave me."

She swallowed again, lowering her eyes, desperately trying to decide whether to trust him or not. She didn't.... But what were her options?

He'd kissed her, struck her, abused her! But not done half of what he might have, she reminded herself.

He was already reaching for the door. She clutched his arm, and he turned back to her, arching a dark brow.

"If you're really a cop, why can't you overpower them? Why can't you arrest them?"

"Oh, God help me!" he breathed, looking heavenward. "Mrs. Blayne, should I really introduce myself as a police officer? And arrest them? Now that's a laugh. I'll say, 'Hey, let's go to jail.' I haven't got a weapon on me, but they'll just say, 'Sure, let's go, you want to put us in jail, fine.'"

Mandy flushed. "But you should be trying...."

"I *am* trying!" He swore heatedly. "I'm trying to keep you alive—and I'm trying to stay on top of you myself to keep these guys from deciding that, hey, they have you, so what the hell...if you catch my meaning, Mrs. Blayne. Although God knows you seem to be strange enough! Maybe you'd enjoy their attentions. Did you marry Peter Blayne for his money? Yeah, I could be way off. Maybe you'd enjoy the excitement."

"What?" Stunned, outraged, she shrieked the word.

She should have learned not to shriek by now. He slapped a hand over her mouth before she could blink and drew her against his hard length in a frightening manner, staring down at her with danger sparking from his eyes.

"Shut up!"

Shut up? She had no choice. So she blinked, realizing that this man—this cop?—thought she was the senator's wife, just as the others had assumed. He actually assumed that she'd married an older man for money. Oh, how dare he!

His hand moved from her mouth. She smiled very sweetly, narrowing her eyes. "No, Miguel. I married Peter Blayne because he's fabulous in bed, and I don't need any excitement! So lead on. Just keep your hands off me and I'll be as quiet as a mouse."

He grinned crookedly, and she was startled at the effect of his expression on her. He was a handsome man, really handsome. Dark, tall, broad, muscled, sexy and very physical. And fascinating, with those strange bright eyes. And when he looked at her in that dry, insinuating fashion she felt an involuntary sizzle sweep through her. One she instantly denied, vehemently denied. She was still in love with a memory, still convinced that only a deep and rich emotion could ever create such steaming awareness....

She closed her eyes, dizzy. What if he wasn't a cop? And what if he was?

It was insane. Was she cracking already? So weak that she was willing to cling to anyone—especially anyone male and muscled—because she was scared? She wasn't. She wasn't!

His scent was all around her, the roughness of his touch, that feel of steel in his arms. She wanted to trust him.

"Mrs. Blayne," he said softly, with a touch of amusement, "I won't touch you, but I suggest that you *do* touch me now and then. You were having a passionate affair with me, remember?"

"Why...why," she whispered, head lowered, "would

they believe that? Why would they believe that you would risk your life to be with me?"

He chuckled dryly. "Because Latins are a passionate people, Mrs. Blayne. They usually love deeply, hate deeply—and possess their women as loyally and heatedly as they do their pride."

She stared at him, searching his features, seeking an answer, and she prayed that she wasn't a victim more of his arresting features and eyes than she was of the circumstances.

"Are you Latin?" she asked him.

"Half," he answered curtly.

"Miguel!"

The call came from very near the door. Had they been overheard? Mandy started to shiver all over again. If he *was* here to help her and she caused him to be murdered, she would never forgive herself in a thousand years—even if he was an SOB.

Damn him! She wouldn't tell him that she wasn't Peter's wife, either!

"Let's go!" he hissed.

She nodded. He took her hand, and she didn't resist him, but just before he opened the door he twisted his handsome head ruefully toward her and mouthed out a quick query.

"I almost forgot. What's your name?"

"Blayne! You know—"

"Your first name, stupid!"

"Amanda!"

"Mandy?"

"Only to friends," she said pointedly.

He smiled. "And lovers, Mrs. Blayne? Mandy, let's go!"

Chapter 4

Lunch consisted of a salad and *arroz con pollo*, chicken and rice, served belligerently to Mandy and charmingly to Miguel by Maria and another woman, up on deck.

Mandy had tried her hardest to assimilate the layout of the craft during her quick walk through the hall to the steps leading topside. There hadn't been much to assimilate. The vessel was old, at least forty years, worn, but well-kept. There were another two sets of sleeping quarters past the head, then a shabby salon and a galley, and to the extreme aft, the captain's cabin.

The older woman had stared at Mandy with extreme disapproval as they moved through the galley. Mandy had ignored her, but she hadn't been able to ignore the smell of the food; the aroma was captivating, and she was forced to realize that she was starving.

The deck of the motorized two-masted sailboat was

lined with old wooden seats, and that was where Miguel led her. Mandy kept her mouth shut for several minutes while she perused her surroundings and her curious party of abductors.

There was Julio, called Garcia by the others; the young woman, Maria; the older woman; and two more men, one a heavyset fellow with a swirling mustache, the other gaunt and hungry-looking. Mean, Mandy thought, and far different from Julio Garcia, who, strangely, had the look of a poet.

They all laughed and chatted in rapid Spanish, drinking Michelob out of bottles and eating off paper plates as if they were simply out for a picnic at sea.

Including Miguel. He laughed and chatted along with the others, tensing only slightly beside her when some apparently ribald comment was made about her by either the man with the mustache—Juan, she thought his name was—or Roberto, the gaunt man with the lascivious eyes.

If Miguel was on her side, he certainly knew how to enjoy himself in the interim. He ate with a hearty appetite, complimenting the two women on their cooking. So far Mandy hadn't been able to pick up more than a word or two of the conversation, but mannerisms were universal, and it was easy to tell that Miguel was managing to fit right in. There was only one difference between him and the other men: they were carrying large guns in shoulder holsters.

Miguel had none. He was still barefoot, bare chested, clad in his wet cutoffs, assuring her that he could not be hiding a weapon anywhere on his person.

She turned her gaze to the ocean surrounding them,

wondering how far they had come, and in what direction. Miguel had told her that he thought they were near Cat Cay, which meant the Bahamas. She saw nothing around them right now but the sea and sky, and her heart sank in desolation. She might never be found, never be rescued! There might well be hundreds of uninhabited islands in this stretch of the ocean. She'd been taken away in a little speedboat, and now she was on an old sailboat. The police—if they could even look for her now that they were out of American waters!—wouldn't even know what they were looking for.

The police!

She twisted her head slightly and stared at Miguel, seated so casually beside her, idly holding his beer and laughing at one of Roberto's jokes. Was he really a cop? It was hard to believe at the moment! He was taller, stronger, tougher than the other men, muscled but trim, lean and mean-looking. If he was a cop, why the hell hadn't he done something?

She told herself that no amount of muscle could combat a bullet, that maybe he was doing his best just to keep them both alive. It was hard, though, even if she realized that half her problem was that she resented him heartily for assuming that she was Peter's wife and that, being younger, she had latched on to him for material reasons.

And maybe she also resented him out of sheer frustration. By God, he was physically beautiful. His stomach was taut, his legs long and hard, his shoulders those of an Atlas.

That dark hair; those flashing eyes, emerald in the sun; that handsome face, high boned with arching dark brows, teeth pearly white against the full sensual curve of his mouth.... Not even the thick shadow of beard detracted from his looks. He seemed like a bulwark of character and strength—and he wasn't doing a damn thing for her! Just chatting away in Spanish and drinking his *cerveza*!

Maria collected his empty plate, and he stretched his free arm around Mandy. She tried not to stiffen; it was a casual gesture, and she decided she would rather trust him than be left vulnerable to Roberto's naked ogling.

Maria took Mandy's plate less than graciously, eyeing her maliciously, and to Mandy's own surprise she returned that nasty glare and inched closer to Miguel.

"Mandy." He spoke softly and she jumped, turning to look up at him. "You want something to drink?"

The accent was back in his words.

"Ah, yes. A diet Pepsi, please."

He started to laugh. "What do you think this is? They've got beer, water, guava juice and Coca-Cola. 'Classic', I believe."

She recognized his dry humor and just barely held her temper in check. "A Coke!" she snapped.

He started to translate her request to Maria, but Maria snapped, "I heard her," then disappeared below.

Maria returned with the soda and sat staring pointedly at Mandy. The older woman said something to her, which she ignored; then Julio grated out something impatiently and the two women—along with Roberto, Mandy noticed gratefully—went below deck. Mandy sipped her Coke, thinking that a soda had never tasted so delicious before. She stared around again, tensing as she realized that there was a small island on the ho-

rizon, and that a pleasure boat was anchored just beyond its beach.

How far away was it? she wondered yearningly.
Three miles—or five? And did it really matter? If she
had to, she could manage a five-mile swim....

"So, Señora Blayne, you are resigned to our company, sí?"

She started, forced into an awareness that the oddly
genteel Julio Garcia was watching her.

"Resigned?" she queried regally, ignoring the pinch
of Miguel's fingers suddenly tightening around her
shoulders. "Not in the least. Perhaps," she added sarcastically, "You'd be so kind as to explain to me just
what you're after so that I may become...resigned!"

Julio gazed curiously at Miguel then returned his
dark soulful eyes to hers. "Miguel has not explained
it to you?"

"She gave me no chance, this one!" Miguel pulled
her closer against him, irritating her beyond belief by
playfully fluffing her hair. She stiffened against him,
but his hold was a powerful one for all its casual appearance, and she had no recourse except to smile grimly
at Julio Garcia.

"I haven't the faintest idea of what is going on."

Julio shrugged and grimaced. "Your husband betrayed me, Mrs. Blayne. He swore to have my father
freed. Empty promises."

My husband is dead, she thought with fleeting pain,
and he never betrayed anyone in his life.

"My fath—my husband," she amended quickly, "is
a senator, not a warden! What are you talking about?

"He is still in prison! Jorge Garcia—statesman, poet,

one of the finest, most courageous freedom fighters ever to live!—still rots in prison! Peter Blayne promised to have something done. He said to trust in the law! Well, I have tried his laws for years! Ever since the Mariel boatlift—"

"Wait a minute!" Mandy interrupted in a burst of passion. "Are you trying to tell me that your father was a prisoner—a criminal—in Cuba, but that we should let him roam free in the United States?"

"Idiota!" Julio shouted, then went on in an irate shouting spree.

"Julio, Julio! She does not understand!" Miguel said, trying to soothe him.

Mandy was more furious than ever. She couldn't believe that this whole thing was over another criminal! "Don't swear at me in Spanish! Say it in English. *No hablo español!* This is the United States of America—"

Suddenly that long-fingered sun-bronzed hand was over her mouth again, and brilliant green eyes were boring into hers. *"Quieta! Cerra la boca,* Amanda!" Miguel snapped. "You want English? Shut your mouth. You don't understand! Julio, I will take her forward and explain, eh?"

Julio exploded into rapid speech again, pulling his gun from his holster and waving it around. Mandy inhaled deeply in shock as Miguel dragged her to her feet, his hand still over her mouth, and half led, half dragged her to the few clear feet of space that surrounded the main mast.

"Damn you!" he grated out tensely, releasing her mouth at last, but only to grip her shoulders and stare down at her like the wrath of God while he spoke. "Are you trying to get us both killed?"

She tossed her hair back. "He's crazy! I won't—"

"Yes, he's crazy! And that's exactly why you'd better start paying a little heed. Don't you know this story? Doesn't your husband ever talk to you about his work?"

Her husband? Oh, Peter...

Yes, Peter talked to her. But she'd been so involved with her own work lately that she hadn't really seen him in a while. She shook her head stiffly. "I don't know anything about any of this! Except that if Peter has refused to let some murderer roam the streets, then—"

He took a deep breath, a bitter breath. "For your information, Mrs. Blayne—Mrs. Bigot!—not everyone who came in on the Mariel boatlift was a murderer!"

"I am not a bigot! But don't you dare try to tell me that Castro didn't empty his prisons on the U.S.!"

"Oh, great! So everyone who is Cuban—"

"I didn't say that!"

"But you meant it!"

"The hell I did!"

"What are you, the head of the DAR, Mrs. Blayne? Your impeccable bloodlines go back to the *Mayflower*, I take it!"

"As a matter of fact," Mandy lied coolly, "they do!" She suddenly felt as if she was going to burst into tears. She hadn't meant to offend him, but she'd be damned if she would be responsible for putting a criminal—be he Irish, German, Spanish or all-American—back on the streets.

Her lashes fell over her eyes; she didn't understand why this terrible antagonism had suddenly erupted between them. He was her lifeline, however tenuous. She was simply terrified, and trying not to be.

Frightened, but determined to be strong. And there were so many chinks in her armor!

He was still angry, but was holding his temper in check. He spoke flatly to her, still holding her shoulders, his voice very distant.

"Jorge Garcia was not a murderer, a rapist, or even a thief. He was a political prisoner, but the charges trumped up against him could have sent him before a firing squad. He was, once upon a time, a brilliant man. Rich and a philanthropist, a lawyer, a scientist. He still had a few friends in the Castro regime, but even so his enemies managed to have him labeled as dangerously insane. He was sent out on the Mariel boatlift and consequently wound up with dozens of other cases, waiting to be reviewed by the immigration board."

"You're trying to tell me that Julio's father is not just a good man but a great one?"

"From all I've heard, yes."

She shook her head, her temper growing. "So we're at fault! The Americans are at fault, and it's okay for Julio to attempt to assassinate Peter and kidnap me."

"I didn't say it was all right! Julio has obviously snapped. Yes, gone mad, in a way. Apparently he's been frustrated half to death. It doesn't make him right. It just explains his behavior. You can't do anything—your husband probably couldn't even have done anything, no matter how hard he tried, except speed up some paperwork."

"Then why are you yelling at me?"

"I'm not yelling!"

"You sure as hell are!"

He released her shoulders abruptly. "Excuse me, Madame DAR. It's my Latin temper, you know."

"You're stereotyping yourself—not me!" Mandy snapped.

"I'm not trying to do anything except get us both out of this. I'm a cop, not a lawmaker, and not a politician. I don't even know what I'm doing here myself! But, Mrs. Blayne, please, if you're at all interested in living, please don't get into moral fights with Julio Garcia!"

She stared at him, then tossed her head. From the corner of her eye she glimpsed the island she had seen before—and the massive pleasure craft anchored right before it.

"I, uh, won't argue with Garcia anymore," Mandy said absently.

"Good. I don't think he wants to harm anyone. I—"

He broke off, frowning, as excited shouts suddenly came from the aft deck.

"Let's see what's up," Miguel murmured, and he started back. Mandy didn't follow him. She stood dead still where she was, feeling the ocean breeze, feeling the sun on her face.

The boat wasn't far away. No more than three miles, she was certain. And she really was a good swimmer. Her captors were so excited about whatever was happening off their own craft that she could probably be halfway to that other vessel before anyone even noticed that she was gone.

She hesitated just a second longer, thinking of Miguel. She didn't want to worry about him, yet she did. She had the sneaking suspicion that his presence had saved her from sexual abuse by the leering Roberto, and she didn't want him harmed on her behalf.

But he had managed to make himself one of them. They wouldn't kill him. At least, she convinced herself in those moments that they wouldn't. And if he was a cop, he would know how to take care of himself. She had a chance to escape, she didn't dare risk losing it.

She moved at last, staring forward. They were all there now: the two women, Roberto, Juan, Julio—and Miguel.

"A bloodbath!" she thought she heard someone say. But she wasn't really listening—or thinking.

Quietly she moved portside, stepped to the rail and dove into the water.

It was a good clean dive. The gray robe bulked around her somewhat, but to obtain her water safety certification every three years she'd had to swim a mile in her clothes—shoes, too—so the robe shouldn't be that bad. And of course she could always ditch it. And arrive at a strange boat stark naked. What a thing to think of at a time like this! Swim...

She broke the surface and took a breath, stroking smoothly, aware that she would have to pace herself to make the distance. Stroke, breathe, stroke, breathe. The sun was high in the sky, warm; the water was almost as warm as that sun, and very blue here, where it was deep. It felt good to swim, to feel the salt against her face, to feel the promise of freedom....

She cocked her head, inhaling, stroking, and heard shouts distantly from behind her. She clenched her teeth in dismay, having hoped to gain more distance before they discovered her absence.

She paused for a second, treading the water, to see what was happening. She was shocked to see that they were all watching her—not angry, but pale as a troop of ghosts.

"Stop, Amanda! Stop!"

It was Miguel shouting, and as she turned to begin swimming again with stronger strokes, she swore inwardly. Damn him! He'd said he was on her side, but he was the one standing on the rail, ready to dive after her and recapture her.

The salt stung her eyes; she felt like crying as she heard the splash of his body entering the water. He was coming after her. She renewed her strokes, still hoping she could outdistance him. She was good, she reminded herself. She really was a good swimmer....

But so was he. And he was stronger. In a matter of seconds he was almost at her feet.

"Amanda! Get back!"

His hand slid around her ankle, a vise that jerked her under water, then into his arms. She choked and gagged and came up against his chest, gasping.

"Damn you! Damn you!" she shrieked, furious and ready to cry. She could have done it except for him. "I hope you rot in hell for all eternity. Liar! You son of a bitch. You—"

He still looked white and grim. He shook her. "Get back. *Now!*"

He gave her a strong shove back toward the boat. The terry robe seemed to be locked all around her now, hampering her movements. She couldn't seem to swim at all anymore; she couldn't untangle her arms.

And Juan and Julio had already climbed into a little

dinghy with no motor. They reached furiously, desperately, for the oars, then began coming toward her.

Miguel gave her another shove.

"I can't!"

He jerked at her robe; she tried to hold the sodden material while struggling to stay afloat.

"Take it off!"

She'd never heard such a fervent command. The robe was suddenly gone. "Swim!" he bellowed, shoving her.

She didn't have to swim; the dinghy was right behind her, and Julio and Juan were bending over, grasping her arms. Naked and humiliated she was lifted from the water and cast to the rotting floorboards of the tiny dinghy.

Instinctively she brought her knees to her chest and locked her arms around them, and only then did she realize that they weren't paying her the least attention—they were pulling Miguel into the dinghy after her. He landed half on top of her, dripping wet. There was nowhere to move, and when she tried to shrink closer within herself, he opened his eyes and stared at her with such grim fury that it was as if his eyes had become a glittering inferno that meant to consume her.

He was still gasping for breath, but he threw the robe over her as he shook his head in disgust. "Stupid woman!" he muttered.

Julio muttered a few words to Juan, gesticulating with a sharp intake of breath, and it was then that she realized the awful danger she had almost encountered. Surrounding the little dinghy was an assortment of at least five fins. Shark fins...

And the creatures were still swimming about, thrashing, nearly upsetting the tiny dinghy.

"Sit!" Miguel snapped, and the other two men instantly obeyed.

Mandy shivered miserably beside him as he fumbled for the oars and slowly, carefully, rowed the dinghy toward the sailboat.

Oh, God! She'd nearly swum into the middle of a school of sharks! She would rather be shot ten times over than die such a gruesome death. This man had actually dived after her, pitting himself against the same danger....

"Up, and carefully!" he told her tensely when they reached the boat. Julio and Juan went up the rope ladder first. Julio looked very gray, and she thought that he might be a kidnapper, but he hadn't wanted to see her die—not that way! "Up!"

Somehow she was touching the wet rope ladder. Clinging to it. She didn't feel as if she had any strength at all.

He was behind her, using the force of his body to protect hers against its own weakness. She closed her eyes, fighting dizziness.

She could still hear the sharks thrashing in the water. She turned back and froze in renewed fear. The water was red now. Blood red. The others had turned on one of their own kind and were ripping it apart with their huge jaws and razor teeth....

"Amanda, go."

One foot after the other. Again and again. Julio was there to drag her over the rail. She pulled the robe about her shivering body and lay on the deck, spent, exhausted, and still in shock.

She saw the sun above her, slowly sinking into the west. She felt the chill of a night breeze coming on. The sky was becoming pink and crimson and beautifully gold, and the moon, pale but full, had risen even before the sun could set.

Twenty-four hours…it had been a full day, she thought numbly. A full day since she had been taken, and suddenly none of it mattered except for those last few minutes. She had always thought that she would never really be afraid to die, but she was. And she would have died. In her furious quest for escape she would have stirred up the water to such an extent that the mindless beasts would have found her—except for him.

She was dimly aware that he had come aboard the boat, dimly aware that tense Spanish was being spoken in bursts all around her.

She opened her eyes. Maria, her huge almond eyes ablaze, was staring down at her. She spat on the deck, then began speaking again.

Puta. That was one word Mandy recognized. Maria was screaming because Miguel had almost died to save his Anglo whore. She was trash; she was not worth it.

Julio said something curtly; Maria started to speak again, but he slapped her.

Mandy knew she had acquired a serious enemy. She couldn't even care about that. She felt totally exhausted and numb, and she shivered with spasms she could not halt.

She opened her eyes once again in startled surprise

when someone leaned down to her, wrapping strong arms around her.

She met glowing orbs of green: Miguel's eyes. She was too entangled in the robe to fight him, nor did she even think that she should. She stared at him, unable to find the words for an apology, unable even to form a "thank you" on her trembling lips.

Spanish broke out all around her again, but she didn't worry about it. In absolute exhaustion she laid her head against his chest and closed her eyes again.

"I am taking her below," Miguel said determinedly, breaking into English.

"*Sí.* Do it then, *amigo*," Julio agreed.

"*Madre de Dios!*" Juan swore, but Julio interrupted him.

"She will do us no good dying of pneumonia!"

Miguel walked past them with Mandy in his arms. She opened her eyes just before they came to the steps.

Night had almost fallen. It seemed to come so quickly out here on the water. Only a few stretches of gold and crimson lay against the eternal sea and sky. And then, as if they had been a delusion, those colors faded to black.

They moved through the galley, through the salon, down the hall. He used his foot to kick open the door, then laid her on the narrow bunk, swathing her in the blanket, holding her, his eyes enigmatic, only the pulse in his throat displaying any emotion.

"I—I'm sorry—" Mandy began.

"I swear to you," he interrupted her, "I *am* a cop! If you trust me, I'll get you out of this!"

He had every right to be furious, she knew. He'd put his own life on the line—for her. She shivered all over again, knowing she would never have had the nerve to dive into the water if she had known about all those sharks.

Suddenly there was a rapping at the door. Miguel stood quickly and opened it.

The older, gray-haired woman was there, a wooden tray in her hand. She spoke Spanish softly and gazed down at Mandy with the closest thing to sympathy that she had yet seen.

The woman lifted the tray, offering it to Miguel.

"Gracias, gracias," he told her, then she asked him something, and he answered her, stepping aside to allow her to enter the room. She sat down by Mandy's side, touched her forehead and cheeks, offered a weak smile, then wagged a finger beneath Mandy's nose, giving her a motherly scolding. She touched Mandy's cheek once again, shivered and then left.

"What...?" Mandy began, struggling to sit.

Miguel stuffed a shot glass of amber liquid into her fingers. "Drink it—it's rum. It will stop the chill."

She couldn't drink it. "Miguel..."

"Señora Garcia," he told her, wrapping his fingers around a second shot glass and setting the tray on the opposite bunk, "is not at all happy that her son took you. They meant to take your husband. Drink that!"

"Miguel..."

"Mrs. Blayne, by tomorrow they plan to reach some remote and private island where they have a little cottage. Juan will then return to Miami with the ransom note. Obviously your husband won't have any real power to give the Garcias what they want, but negotiations will start. At that time they will also be one man short. They don't want to hurt you. If you would have just one bit of faith in me and give me a little time, I could manage to settle this thing without risking your life."

"Miguel…"

"Drink that!"

She brought the shot glass to her lips with still-trembling hands, then gasped at the potency of the liquor, choked and coughed. He sat beside her and patted her back, but with little mercy. He tilted the glass toward her lips again.

"All of it!"

On her next try she drained the glass. He took it from her hands as she wheezed for breath once again. He swallowed his own without a grimace, haphazardly returned both glasses to the tray, then turned back to her.

He touched her lip, her cheek. "Good," he said. "You've got a little color back."

She lowered her head, her fingers plucking at the blanket. "I'm sorry. I had to do it." She moistened her lips and stared at him again. "Thank you," she whispered stiffly. "You saved my life."

"Line of duty," he told her, his eyes narrowing peculiarly on her hand. He clutched it, looking at the raw marks that still surrounded her wrists. "Do they hurt?" he asked, staring into her eyes again.

She shook her head. It was only a little lie.

The door suddenly burst open to reveal Julio Garcia. He gave a curt order to Miguel. Miguel shook his head vehemently. Chills of fear crept over Mandy again; she knew that they were arguing about her. Her wrist was suddenly shoved up toward Julio's face. He hesitated, then said something back to Miguel. Miguel glanced her way curiously then nodded to Julio. Then Julio, too, was gone, snapping out the cabin light as he went.

Darkness fell all around them. Mandy knew that she was still shivering, that he was still staring at her in the darkness.

"What…what was that all about?" she asked faintly.

"He wanted me to tie you up again."

"You tied those knots?"

"Yes. I had to make them good."

She sniffed in the darkness. "They *were*."

He didn't reply at first. Then he merely said, "Move over."

"What?"

"Move over. I can tie you up, or sleep next to you."

Something rebelled inside her. She wanted to tell him to tie her up, that she would rather suffer through that again than have him sleep beside her.

But she didn't. She didn't ever want to experience that panicky feeling of being so helplessly bound again. She didn't want the rope chafing her flesh until it was raw. And she felt so horribly tired and exhausted.

She moved as close as she could to the paneling that rimmed the bunk, painfully aware of his length and heat as he crawled in beside her. He didn't say a word. In time her eyes adjusted to the darkness and she realized that he was lying there very stiffly, hair still damp from his dive into the water, his profile clean and fascinating as he stared upward into the night.

"Miguel?" she whispered softly.

"What?"

"I really am sorry. I felt that I had to try.… It isn't that I distrust you so much, it's just that the opportunity was there. Thank you. I mean it. And I'm terribly sorry about putting you in danger."

She felt him shrug. The narrow bunk was barely wide enough for one person; two would necessarily feel each other's slightest movement.

"It's okay," he returned in the darkness. And then he was silent again.

"I know you're angry—"

"I'm not angry." He rolled toward her and touched her cheek in the darkness, lightly, for the briefest moment. Then he jerked his hand away from her, as if remembering something.

"I know what it's like to run for freedom, Mrs. Blayne. To seek escape at any cost. Go to sleep. You'll need rest and awareness, should another opportunity come along."

She swallowed and nodded, but knew she would never sleep. Escape…freedom. They seemed like hollow empty echoes now. He knew what it was like. That was what he had said.

She wished fervently that he was not beside her. And yet she was fervently glad of him, too. Of the feel of heat and strength.

She might detest him for some of the things he had said and done, but he was on her side; she had to believe that. And even if she feared him just a little in the deepest recesses of her heart, she could not help but admire him and believe in him.

Only a fool—or a very brave man—would dive into water teeming with sharks to save a woman who had done nothing to deserve it of him.

Sleep was impossible. She lay there miserably for

hours and hours, not daring to move, not daring to get any closer to him.

Memories drifted in and out of her mind, good ones, bad ones, some from the distant past, some more recent. She couldn't tell if the man beside her slept, or if he continued to stare into the darkness, lost in the recesses of his own mind.

Somewhere in the night exhaustion and nerves overwhelmed her and she fell into a restless sleep. But even there the memories plagued her. Her son's tiny coffin seemed to float in space, and then the larger one, Paul's. Then the coffins began to change. Darkness and shadow became red, dripping red, blood red, and she could hear and see the terrible gnashing teeth of the sharks....

"Shh, shh! It's over! I'm beside you...you're all right!"

She stiffened, unaware that she had cried out, biting her lip.

"Mandy, go back to sleep. Easy..."

His hand was on her hair; his body was like a heat lamp next to hers. His voice was like the soothing whisper of an ocean breeze.

And maybe because she was still half-lost in a shadow land herself, she allowed herself to listen to that whisper, to be soothed by that strong masculine touch.

She sighed softly.

"You're all right," he whispered again. "It was just a dream."

The tension fell away from her body, and she slept. And this time no dreams came to plague her, just the pleasant sensation of being held safely in strong arms.

Chapter 5

In the morning she came awake with a curious sense of peace, followed by a haunting disillusionment.

The senses could play such tricks upon the mind! She'd awakened to so many brilliant mornings feeling the lapping of waves, the movement of the ocean beneath her, the coolness of the dawn, and salt-flavored air all around her. Awakened smiling, warm, secure, content, her husband's arm wrapped around her, the lazy tempo of a night's anchorage away from the bustle of the city like a blissful balm.

All the things that went with it came back to her: laughter from above; calls that the "sleepyheads" should awaken; the smell of sizzling bacon—and then whispers. Whispers because Peter would be telling Miranda that the kids should be up, and Miranda would be hushing him, lowering her voice still further, and reminding him that the "kids" were still newlyweds, and newly-weds didn't spring right up from bed; they liked to stay there a while.

And of course by then Mandy and Paul would both be awake, staring at each other, giggling and trying very hard to shush each other so that his concerned parents wouldn't hear them. Then they would shoot out of bed anyway, because Jonathan would have awakened by then, and they were both still so overawed at being parents that they sprang to attention the second he opened his tiny mouth and let out his earsplitting cry.

Then they would be grabbing for robes, because the older Blaynes would come bursting in, so overawed at being grandparents that they too sprang to instant attention.

And then the bacon would burn, and it would have to be started all over. But it wouldn't matter, because they would have all weekend to dive and snorkel and swim and fish and play, and the real world would be miles away. The *Flash Point* would be their fantasyland until they all returned to their responsibilities.

Mandy opened her eyes and felt a nearly overwhelming hopelessness sweep through her. Those times were gone, Miranda was gone, Jonathan was gone and Paul was gone. She blinked against the sudden agony of reality. She hadn't felt this way in ages; she'd learned to insulate herself, to remember the good times, to find other things in life. She could even laugh aboard the *Flash Point*, bring flowers to the cemetery and smile as she remembered her infant son's beautiful smile.

It was this boat; it was this stinking boat. It was so much the opposite of all that had been beautiful. She was a prisoner, not a beloved wife, not an adored daughter-in-law, doted upon by her husband's happy parents. This was a rotting hulk, not the graceful *Flash Point*. It was all a mockery. There wasn't a grain of truth in any of the sensations.

Except that, rotting hulk or not, this vessel rolled on the sea just like any ship. The sea, the sky, the salt air—they were never ending. No matter what came and went in life, they would remain the same. But the warmth…

Mandy rolled over quickly. Miguel had taken the sodden robe off her when he put her on the bunk. Now she was barely covered by the worn blanket he had bundled around her. She was still warm, still warm from his body heat, gone now, but haunting her as thoroughly as the dream.

Mandy pulled the blanket back to her chin, wondering at the anguished stream of emotions he could elicit from her. She felt drawn like the proverbial moth to the candle, but she felt a little ashamed, too. He'd dragged her around half-naked—completely naked actually—bound her, knocked her out, reviled her—and saved her life. She knew exactly what he thought of her; he had said it in so many words. He'd prejudged her as a mercenary bigot, and he deserved to pay for that. Yet in his absurd way he was going above and beyond the call of duty, and he was certainly the most extraordinary man she had ever met.

And that was the main reason she resented him, Mandy thought. In the past three years she had become very independent. She'd been friends with Peter; she hadn't leaned on him. They both had their own work, and work had kept them sane.

But last night…last night had taught her something that she hadn't wanted to learn. Paul was gone; love was gone. Oh, every minute hadn't been perfect. They'd fought; they'd yelled. Any two people did that. Neither one of them had been able to cook worth a whit; she'd wanted a puppy; he'd thought one child was enough. Little things, big things. That was life. You just couldn't zoom through agreeing on everything. But through all those things there had been love. She'd barely known two years of it, but it had been good and solid and real. She had known when she buried her heart and very nearly her existence with her husband and son that she could never settle for anything less—and also that she didn't ever want to know that kind of love again. The pain of loss was so unbearable, so like a set of knives that whittled and whittled away at the insides….

She closed her eyes, inhaling and exhaling.

No, she didn't want to love again. And she certainly wasn't in danger of falling in love with this stranger. But it was dismaying to learn that sensation remained; just like the endless sea and sky, the basic need remained. A need to be held, to feel strength when one was failing, security when all was darkness. To admire, to respect a man, to like the feel of rippling muscle beneath her fingers, the tangy scent of sea and man, the gentle touch of fingers against her cheek.

She gave herself a furious shake, hoping to clear her mind of fantasy. She had to learn to get through these days one by one. She needed some good common sense. If only she had paid attention yesterday she would have known that the sharks were in the water and she would have never made that ridiculous attempt to escape. She had to learn to be wary and alert—and to try to remember that this was a team effort.

She started suddenly, aware not of sound but of a presence at the door. It was open, and Miguel was standing there, watching her with a strange dark expression. She frowned, and the expression faded. He was once again the same enigmatic man she was coming to know.

"I was trying to let you sleep," he said, sauntering in. His hair was damp, and he smelled like soap, and though he was still clad in cutoffs, they were different ones, undoubtedly borrowed from one of the other men. He carried a towel-wrapped bundle, which he gave her, tossing it over the blanket to land in the vicinity of her middle.

"Clothes. They're Maria's. She wasn't very happy about lending them, but Señora Garcia told her that you couldn't run around naked."

Mandy couldn't keep a rueful smile from creeping across her lips as her lashes fell over her cheeks. "Thanks," she said softly. "And thank Señora Garcia. Is there any chance of coming up with a toothbrush?"

"Yes, as a matter of fact, there is. Check below the sink in the head, there's a nice supply. Seems Julio is a tooth fanatic. He told me his teeth were riddled with cavities when he first came to the States. He's been trying to preserve the rest ever since."

"What about you?" she murmured.

"What?"

She kept her lashes downcast, wondering why she was so curious about him. "When you left Cuba…"

"I wasn't born in Cuba."

"But you said—"

"Oh, I am Cuban. Half. I just wasn't born there."

"Here?" She gazed up at him.

He grinned at her, sudden amusement in his eyes. "Here? Was I born in a boat? No. I wasn't born in the water, or in the Bahamas, which is where I'm pretty sure we are."

"I meant—"

"I was born in Dublin, Mrs. Blayne."

"Dublin! Ireland?"

He quickly brought his finger to his lips. "Would you please shush! Are you that determined to hang me?"

"No! Really, I'm sorry!"

She sat up as she spoke, and the blanket dropped to her waist.

She reached for it again quickly, embarrassed, and dragged it back around her before looking at Miguel again.

That strange expression was back…dark, tense. And hungry. Suddenly she was aware of exactly what it meant. He might be a cop, but he was a man, too, a man who found her appealing. He might think very little of her as a human being, but as a woman he found her appealing. Sexually appealing.

And that fact was not something he realized with any great fondness.

She tossed her hair back, a little bit indignant, and a little bit shaken.

She suddenly felt like teasing him! It would provide revenge that seemed very sweet. After all, he thought she was a mercenary woman who had married an old man for his wealth and position. And he was thoroughly convinced that she was a complete bigot. He deserved any torture she could dish out, even if he had dived into the sharks.

"Oh!" she murmured, sweetly distressed, holding the blanket to her breasts but allowing it to fall from her back. Then she had to lower her head and smile discreetly, because she had drawn exactly the response she wanted from him. He had stiffened like a poker. His jaw had squared, and she had heard the grating of his teeth.

She cleared her throat. "Really!" she whispered softly. "I wouldn't want to hang you at all. I appreciate everything that you've done for me!"

"For you and your husband, right?" he asked her softly.

"Peter? Ah…yes, of course."

She lowered her eyes again, very aware that he was doing his best to keep his distance from her because she was—in his mind—a married woman. His own assumption! Poor baby! Compelled by a sense of duty to dive into sharks after her. Compelled to sleep beside her to keep her from being bound and tied.

A part of her appreciated that sense of duty. But she didn't at all appreciate his continual jumping to conclusions about her, nor any number of his macho techniques. She'd suffered at his hands; he could damn well suffer at hers. He had taken his own sweet time to inform her that he was a cop, and he'd grabbed her in the shower to do it.

She gave him another wide-eyed innocent stare. "Do you know what the island will be like? I mean, what will the, uh, sleeping arrangements be?"

"You're stuck with me again, Mrs. Blayne. They'd

set up a room for your husband. It will be yours—and mine—now."

"Oh."

"Don't worry, Mandy, love. I'll be as safe to be with as a teddy bear. Married women aren't my style. Especially—"

"Bigots?" she inquired sweetly. "A young bigot married to an old man for his money?"

"Your words."

"Ah, but Miguel! Doesn't that scare you to pieces? What if the story were close to the truth? Poor young me, married to poor old Peter! I mean, after all, think about the situation! You half attacked me at first, but then I discovered that you're my savior." Dragging the blanket with her, she came up to him, still smiling sweetly. "And here you are…young…muscled like a panther. I could just lose my mind!" she told him, lightly stroking his cheek with the tips of her nails.

He didn't move. Not a muscle. Not until he grinned slowly and snaked an arm around her so swiftly that she wasn't even aware of his intent until it was complete. She was pulled against him, while his fingers brushed tantalizingly over the small of her back and her buttocks.

"Mrs. Blayne—Mandy, darling!" he drawled in a soft and perfect parody. "Aren't you forgetting that your husband is a wonderful, wonderful lover?"

"Let me go!" she snapped. He'd meant to call her bluff! He did, pushing her from him. "Like I said, *Mrs.* Blayne, I'll be as safe as a teddy bear."

She recovered somewhat and smiled coolly again. "Good." But she was bluffing again. Touching him had been dangerous. Coming too near him would always be like tempting fire. She had realized it too late.

"Dublin!" she muttered beneath her breath. "Like hell! Cop—I wonder."

"I am a cop."

"*Miami Vice*, I take it." She sighed elaborately. "Humph. Where is Sonny Crockett when you need him?"

"Metro Miami. Investigator, homicide. Homicide gets kidnappings and death threats. And I'm sorry about not being Sonny Crockett. Luck of the draw, what can I tell you?"

"The truth is always nice."

"That is the truth."

"You're a half-Cuban detective who was born in Dublin?"

He laughed. "I think I fascinate you, Mrs. Blayne."

"Egos like yours always fascinate." The words were out quickly; she suddenly regretted them, along with her foolish actions. "I'm sorry," she said for what felt like the thousandth time. "Really, I am. I'm alive. I'm grateful." She couldn't help looking back up at him and shrugging. "And you're a teddy bear, if you say so."

"I am."

He was still grinning, aware that he intrigued her. And if he was bitter about what he considered her bigotry, he was also amused. It was a mixture of feelings she didn't particularly appreciate, but what did it matter? They had been cast into this situation together, she by no choice at all, and he simply because he had become a little overinvolved in his job. Besides, he could laugh at her all he wanted. She had one on him, too. She wasn't Senator Peter Blayne's wife.

His smile faded suddenly as he watched her, and he sounded tense when he spoke next. "You can, uh, take a shower and get dressed now if you want. Breakfast is on, and then we're going on to the island."

Mandy nodded wearily, reminded that she was still a captive. She whispered her next words. "Do you really know where we are?"

"Yes, I think I do."

He stiffened suddenly, and she realized that someone had come up behind him in the hall. His next words carried the heavy Spanish accent again. "Now, my love! In the shower. We eat, we go!"

The door closed. She wrapped herself in the still-damp robe, collected the clothing he had given her and slipped from the cabin to the head.

She was delighted to find a stack of new toothbrushes beneath the sink, so pleased that she issued a little cry of sublime happiness. Then she paused, shivering to discover that joy could be found in such a little thing under these strange circumstances. But, she told herself wryly, it seemed that as long as she was breathing and alive there could be elation in little things, and she might do well to seek it out.

She was uninterrupted in the shower this time, though she didn't close the curtain completely but kept a wary eye on the door, determined to be prepared if someone did burst in on her. That thought made her shiver and burn all over again, and she wondered once more at the contradictory range of emotions Miguel could elicit from her. She clenched her teeth as she rinsed her face, reminding herself again that he was just a cop doing his duty as he saw it and that his opinion of her was a harsh one.

This wouldn't last long! It couldn't! If they'd met at a cocktail party she would have coolly accepted his hostile notions, shrugged, then forgotten him. It was nothing more than the situation and her fear that were creating this horrible tendency to lean on him, to care what he thought. She didn't know anything about him. Not even his whole name. Not whether he was married or not, maybe a father of four or five. Maybe…

She turned the water off and dried herself quickly, then dug into the clothing that Maria had so grudgingly lent to her. Well, pooh to Maria—Mandy didn't like the clothes. The shirt was some kind of a ridiculous halter top in bright red that should have been worn in the early seventies. The cutoff jeans had been tie-dyed with a total lack of artistry and were too big, but at least they came with a ribbon belt. The whole effect was ridiculous, and Mandy thought wryly that Maria had planned it that way. For God's sake, what was the girl jealous of? Mandy wondered irritably. Then she decided she was glad she wasn't eighteen anymore; it was a hard age, when it seemed that women, especially, struggled to find security.

And then she wondered why she cared what she wore as long as she was wearing something, and why she cared one way or another about Maria's psyche, when the girl was doing everything in her limited power to be miserable.

Chin up, kiddo, she told herself. This whole thing boiled down to attitude. The sharks had stripped away her courage yesterday; she was going to dredge it back up for today. She was caught in a nightmare vortex, but even nightmares came to an end. This, like all things, would pass.

Thus determined, she swung open the door—only to have her head-high attitude quickly lowered a peg in confusion, because it wasn't Miguel waiting for her when she emerged, but Roberto. She didn't like the way he looked at her, and she didn't like the way he reached for her arm, sliding his hand along her ribs. She jerked away from him, saying that she was quite able to walk by herself, and hurried topside with him at her heels.

The first thing Mandy saw was the island—if one could call it that. It was really nothing more than a large growth of mangroves with a few handfuls of sand creating a spit of beach. Straining her eyes against the sun and the foliage, she could see some sort of ramshackle structure.

Roberto shoved her in the back. "Move."

She did so, quickly taking a place beside Miguel, who was already eating. The food smelled wonderful. It appeared that they were eating omelets. Even the coffee smelled rich and strong.

Maria, pouring more coffee for Julio, lowered her rich dark lashes and gave Mandy a narrow glance, sniffing delicately at her appearance. Julio barked out something to her, which brought on an immediate argument, with Maria stamping her foot and sullenly shouting and gesticulating. Julio gestured back, totally infuriated, and to her own irritation Mandy found herself inching closer to Miguel, barely aware of the arm that came around her shoulders, except that it gave her a sense of safety and security.

She didn't have the faintest idea what the argument was about, except that she was involved, and if Maria had been in control of the weapons Mandy would surely have been shot on the spot.

Señora Garcia stood up suddenly, clapping her hands over her ears and snapped out a single word. Julio and Maria both ceased their fighting instantly; Maria tossed her head in silence and stalked off below deck, while Julio slipped an arm around his mother's shoulder and spoke to her softly, apologetically.

Miguel took that opportunity to whisper to her, "Maria resents waiting on you. She thinks that you should be made to work. Julio says that you cannot be blamed for your husband's incompetence."

"Peter is not incompetent!" Mandy snapped indignantly.

He gave her a strange gaze, then looked away. "That's rather beside the point right now, isn't it? Here comes Maria. Take your food."

Maria, still sullen, was approaching Mandy, balancing a mug of coffee and a plate at the same time. Mandy accepted the coffee and set it down with a stiff, *"Gracias,"* then held up her hands to accept the plate.

Maria—purposely, Mandy was certain—let go of the plate just short of Mandy's hands.

The hot eggs spilled over her bare legs, burning. Mandy jumped to her feet to get the scorching food off her, while Maria jumped back, ostensibly in a startled fit of apology.

It was suddenly too much for Mandy to handle; she

took two furious steps forward and caught the startled Maria by the shoulders and shook her.

"You little brat! Grow up! I didn't ask to be here, you idiot! You hurt me again and I'll find a way to hurt you back!"

Maria instantly started screaming as if Mandy had been trying to throttle her. Miguel leaped between the two, wrenching Mandy hard against his chest. Julio was shouting again in disgust, and Mandy suddenly realized with a little swallow that he was the only one who hadn't pulled out his gun. Both Roberto and a nervous Juan had their weapons aimed right at her.

She was wide-eyed with fright for a second, then she tossed her arms into the air. "You want me to behave? I'll behave! But keep that spoiled brat away from me!"

She spun around with such vengeance that she took even Miguel by surprise, returned to her seat and sipped her coffee while she wiped off her legs, looking for damage.

There was absolute silence for a moment. Then Mandy heard Julio say in English, "Clean it up, Maria."

"Me! The American whore dropped it. Julio, she half strangled me. *Me*—your cousin!—and you take her side!"

Mandy glanced up just in time to see Maria's huge almond eyes filling with tears. "Oh, for God's sake!" she snapped, and stood, doing her best to scoop up the eggs that lay on the deck onto the fallen plate. She shoved them at Miguel with a viciousness that caused him to raise one brow, but he gave her an amused grin and a little thumbs-up sign, then turned to give the plate to Maria.

Maria looked as if she would not accept it. She opened her mouth and closed it again, then finally snatched the debris and flounced away to discard it below.

Mandy hadn't seen Señora Garcia moving, but suddenly the dignified lady was standing before her, holding another plate. Mandy hesitated; Miguel sat down beside her. "Take it," he advised softly.

She did, thanking Julio's mother with another *"Gracias."* Señora Garcia smiled grimly in return and started into a soft monologue that left Mandy staring at her, quite lost.

"The *señora* apologizes to you for Maria's behavior," Miguel told her. "The girl is her niece, and not her daughter. If she had raised her, she would not be so rude. She would be much more a lady."

Mandy didn't know what to say; she merely nodded. She liked Mrs. Garcia, but she didn't know what she thought of her as a mother. After all, she had raised Julio, and Julio was definitely a kidnapper.

"Eat," Miguel warned her. "We are going to the island."

Mandy was startled to discover that she could eat with such an appetite; she was hungry, and the food was excellent. She finished one cup of coffee, then Señora Garcia came back over and offered her more. She asked Miguel something, and Miguel laughed.

"What?" Mandy asked.

"She asked if you wouldn't prefer Cuban coffee. I told her no."

"Did you?" Mandy asked him a little coolly. "As a matter of fact, I like Cuban coffee."

"Now and then, eh? Patronizing the locals?"

"Oh, God!" she muttered. "You're as bad as the rest of them! *You're* the damn bigot!"

"Shut up!" he told her suddenly.

"I will not—"

His fingers closed around her arm and he bent down to whisper to her tensely. "Mandy darling, we do not sound like a sweet pair of illicit lovers sitting here arguing about coffee!"

She glanced at Julio quickly and saw that he was gazing at the two of them suspiciously. She lowered her head quickly, then made a point of arguing back in a whisper that could be overheard.

"I'm sorry, Miguel, really!" She ran a finger delicately down his chest. "I'm just so afraid of everything! And Peter will certainly find out about the two of us now...." She let her voice trail away.

Miguel's eyes were on her in amazement—an amazement he quickly hid as he slipped an arm around her shoulders again. "You could always tell him the truth. You could get a divorce."

"Oh, but Miguel! I just love the money! Think what it does for us! I love making love in the Jacuzzi. I love the silk sheets, the champagne we sip—just touching one another—in the sunken garden...."

She heard him swallow sharply and, despite everything, she had to lower her head with a little shiver. What was wrong with her? She should be ashamed, but all she could think was that there were certain triumphs to be gleaned in any situation!

When she raised her head again she discovered that

all the men were staring at her, and that she didn't like the look in their eyes at all.

She inched closer to Miguel again and heard him swallow sharply. This time she didn't take any great pleasure in the effect she had caused.

"Well," Julio said stiffly, rising. "Juan—supplies. Roberto—get the dinghy ready. Juan—you and I will take Señora Blayne first. You will come back for the others. Move quickly now. You'll need the day to get back." Juan rose, following orders like a trained puppy.

Mandy discovered then that she didn't want to leave Miguel's side; she was nervous, but also grateful that she would be with Juan and Julio, not Roberto. Small comfort, but all she had.

"Señora Blayne—come!" Julio had a hand extended to her; she hesitated, so Miguel prodded her slightly. She stood, but didn't take Julio's hand. He shrugged. "Starboard, Mrs. Blayne. The dinghy is ready. Mama, you come, too."

Mandy preceded him to the rope ladder and climbed over without looking back. Juan was there, ready to help her into the dinghy. She cringed at the feel of his hands on her waist, but he released her quickly, and once again she was grateful that he was not Roberto.

Señora Garcia followed her down; Juan helped her, too, with the greatest respect. Julio came next, then the dinghy moved away from the ship.

Mandy stared straight ahead, toward the island.

Sean couldn't believe his good fortune—just Roberto and Maria left aboard with him. If he could only assure himself that the two of them were occupied he could take a chance at the ship's old radio. He'd found it easily that first night, when he sat around with the three men drinking beer and telling them his woeful tale of being madly, passionately in love with a married woman, a rich American bitch, but oh, so sweet!

"Hey, Miguel, help me!" Roberto told him. He was pulling boxes of food from the galley cabinets to the deck.

"*Sí, sí,*" Sean said agreeably and ambled down to the galley.

Maria was there. She turned and leaned against the counter, giving him a broad, welcoming grin.

"Hello," she said in a soft, sultry voice.

He smiled, because she was such a pretty kid—with such a lot of growing up to do. Circumstances, though, hadn't been in her favor. Maria had grown up in a household of political protesters. Her father and mother had died; her uncle had been jailed in the old country and then the new.

Sean felt that he could understand her, and even Julio Garcia, in a way that Mrs. Peter Blayne never would. Julio didn't know that he was wrong; in his own way he had been at war all his life. Involved in a dying protest that knew no rules, all was fair. He was too young to remember the revolution when Castro had overthrown Batista. He only knew that suppression had given way to new suppression.

He wanted to be an American. He just didn't know how. Just like Maria. She wanted to be a woman. She wanted to be free and liberated. She didn't know how to go about fulfilling her wishes, either.

"Hi," he answered casually.

Julio had given her a little pistol, too. She had it tucked into the waistband of her very American designer blue jeans.

He was very tempted to reach for it. Maria would be incredibly easy to seduce and overpower.

But the timing was wrong. Julio and Juan had Amanda Blayne on the shore, and though Sean instinctively believed that Julio would never kill her on purpose, he just might panic and become dangerous because of his very nervousness. He hadn't quailed at all when he had riddled the dock with bullets.

Maria sauntered up to Sean and drew a bloodred nail over his naked chest. "You are stupid!" she told him huskily. "She is not for you. You will grow tired of her, yet you risk so much for her!"

He had to think about that one. *She is not for you....*

No, she wasn't. She was a married woman. And though he had acquired a reputation for his nightlife and the chain of broken hearts in his wake, he'd always stopped short when it came to married women.

He was supposed to be distant, professional. Yet she—far beyond the situation—was making him crazy. At the moment he wished with all his heart that he'd never lost his mind and gone diving after the speedboat. He wished he'd never thought of his story....

He wished that he'd never seen her face. Her perfect, beautiful, delicate Anglo face. Tawny eyes, tawny hair, tawny...flesh. Sun golden, sleek, curved, sensual. He wished he'd never seen her, touched her, known her, watched her, listened to her....

It made professionalism damn near impossible. He even hated the fact that he liked her. Liked her brand of determination, so wholehearted that she'd been ready to swim miles in the dusk for freedom. So heated that she refused to bow to anyone—not even with a trio of guns aimed at her.

He gave himself a shake, took both Maria's hands, smiled and placed them back by her sides. "*Chica*, I walk here by a slender thread already. You want your cousin to kill me for your honor?"

"Julio?" She sniffed indelicately. "If Julio were a real man we would not be in this fix. He would have taken the right man, not some *puta*."

"Maria! Bring the food!" Roberto ordered from above.

She grimaced, but decided not to disobey the order. It seemed that everyone knew Roberto had a streak of meanness in him.

Maria disappeared above deck. Sean reached beneath the cabinet and started gathering up supplies with one hand while he reached across to the radio with the other, keeping his eyes trained on the ladder and the hatch above it.

At first he could get nothing. He had to forget the supplies and give his entire attention to the ancient radio. Finally a voice came in—and to Sean's vast relief and amazement he realized that he'd reached the Coast Guard.

Quietly he tried to give his location and discovered with little surprise that search parties had been out since they disappeared. He warned the voice over the radio that he might have to cut out quickly. He advised the man as to the number of kidnappers and said that Juan would be coming back in to make their demands, then assured the man that the senator's wife was fine.

He was surprised by the silence that followed.

"Lieutenant Ramiro, the senator's wife has been dead over a year."

"What?" Sean shouted, then realized what he had done. He lowered his voice quickly. "She's here, with me. They nabbed her, and I came after her!"

"Oh, you've got a Mrs. Blayne all right, but she's not his wife. She's his son's widow. But he's tearing his heart out over her just the same. Just keep calm, lieutenant. It may take us some time to find you."

"I am calm," Sean retorted dryly. "I'm a ten-year vet with the force. Don't you come barging in. Garcia is as nervous as a cat."

"We'll tell the FBI. You keep a lookout. You're out of the U.S., but I'm sure they'll get complete cooperation from the Bahamian authorities. We'll advise the senator that his daughter-in-law is doing—"

Sean heard Roberto yelling at Maria as he approached the ladder. He flicked the radio off and turned back to stacking cans.

"That's enough!" Roberto snapped, holding his gun on Sean. Sean knew that Roberto didn't trust him. The man just wasn't the trusting sort. They were a strange alliance, Roberto and Julio. Julio the idealist; Roberto the thug.

Sean stood up, shrugging. Roberto waved the gun at him. "Go up. The boat is back."

Sean obediently went up to the deck. Juan was back with the dinghy, and Maria was handing the supplies over the rail to him.

"I'll help," Sean told her.

"*Gracias*, Miguel," she purred softly.

He took over her work, moving mechanically and grinning despite himself.

So she wasn't the senator's wife. He'd been torturing himself for nothing. She'd been intentionally driving him up a wall, but now...now it was his turn.

"Miguel! Come aboard!" Roberto ordered.

Juan was staying on the sailboat so he could return to Miami. He waved to Sean, who crawled down to the dinghy.

Sean looked at the island before him. It would still be dangerous getting out of this mess; Roberto was a danger all by himself.

And he was still a cop, and she was still one of the citizens he was sworn to protect. He just couldn't stop that damn grin.

Because she was going to pay.

Chapter 6

It might have been a paradise, one of those quaint little outer islands where only those with their own boats might venture, a little piece of heavenly unaltered nature.

The island was beautiful, Mandy thought wryly, feeling the pressure of Julio's hand on her back as he urged her along. There was a stretch of beach so miraculously white it might have been snow rather than sand; to the left of the beach was an outcrop of coral and rock, fantastically entwined with the mangrove roots. To the right a stretch of rock and mangroves jutted out into the sea, creating a natural harbor. It was too small a spit of land to hold a hotel, just a dot on the ocean, but it was one of the loveliest little islands Mandy had ever seen.

"Señora Blayne, *por favor!*"

Julio prodded her once again, and she realized that

she was stopping every few feet to look around. He was ushering her toward the structure she had seen between the trees, and she wondered why he should be so insistent. There was nowhere for her to go, and he certainly couldn't think that she intended to overpower him—especially since he was carrying a gun.

She shrugged wearily and continued walking. Señora Garcia had already entered the ramshackle place through a screen door; Mandy followed her, curiously surveying her surroundings.

It was an old frame house, with a kitchen being the first room, and something like a parlor behind it, and two doors at the rear of that parlor. Someone had cleaned the place, and Mandy could only assume that that someone had been Señora Garcia. Even clean, though, it was dismal. There was a double-sided fireplace between the kitchen and the parlor, a rickety old table in the kitchen, and an even more rickety sofa in the parlor. There were two mattresses on the floor lined up against the wall by the left rear door. And there were three pickle-barrel end tables, one by the sofa, one between the mattresses and one near the fireplace. There were no electrical wires—what had she been expecting?—and the only concession to contemporary standards seemed to be a battery-powered icebox next to the counter in the kitchen.

"Go through," Julio told her. His mother glanced at her unhappily and started to say something, but Julio interrupted her.

"She can be trouble! You have seen so!"

Mandy kept walking. Julio indicated the left door, and she opened it.

It was a bedroom, or at least it resembled a bedroom. There was a mattress on the floor. And there was another door at the rear.

"Is that a bathroom? Or am I allowed to ask?" Mandy asked bitterly.

Julio compressed his lips and nodded. Mandy found herself studying him curiously. He was a young man, handsome, with curling dark hair and a slim, sinewy build. But his dark eyes were full of such a feverish tension! She couldn't believe that he would really harm her; he seemed such a different type from Roberto.

A trickling of unease sped along her spine, and for all that she was usually ready to strangle Miguel, she suddenly wished desperately that he was with her.

"Yes, it is a bathroom. Old and faulty—and the water is brackish. Do not drink it. You understand?"

She nodded.

He smiled peculiarly, a little sadly. "This is it, Mrs. Blayne. Make yourself at home. I'm afraid it will take some time to reach your husband and have my demands met."

He turned to leave her.

"Wait a minute!" Mandy cried, not at all sure what she meant to do, but suddenly determined to make the young man with the nice mother go straight.

"Julio! Señor Garcia! Listen to me. You haven't harmed me. Not really. I feel that this is all a great misunderstanding. If you were to bring me back now— well, I wouldn't press charges. I guess you wouldn't get off scot-free, because you did fire bullets all over the docks. But I don't think you hit anyone, did you? Really, Julio, you don't want to be a criminal! You could go for an insanity plea—temporary insanity. Mental duress. Julio, they will straighten your father's situation out. It just takes time. You don't want him to be free while you're forced to be in jail, do you? You can't get away with this. Think about it. What good is it going to do when you do get hold of Peter? Julio, if we stop this whole thing right now, I'll do my best to help you. Peter will—"

"Mrs. Blayne," Julio interrupted laconically.

"Yes, Julio?"

"Shut up."

From sheer surprise, she did so. He gave her a rueful smile, turned and left her. When he closed the door she heard the sharp final sound of a bolt sliding home.

"Damn you!" Mandy muttered, threading her fingers through her hair in frustration. "Damn you, you idiot!"

Exasperated and desolate, she sank onto the mattress. For several moments she just sat there, pressing her temples between her palms. Then she lay back on the bed and stared around. There was nothing to see. Nothing but four walls and the door to her primitive bathroom. There was only one window in the room, and that had been boarded over. There was nothing but gloom.

She wished she could sleep. She wished that they had left her just a square inch of window to look through. Time hung so heavily! Each second seemed like an hour, and her imprisonment had only begun. All she could do was lie there in the gloom with her own thoughts—which were not particularly good company.

Every once in a while she heard voices from beyond the door. They were faint, and she couldn't make out a thing, because they were speaking in Spanish.

Where the hell was Miguel?

To her irritation, she was longing to see him. Longing desperately to see him, just because she couldn't stand the shadowed gloom and her own company anymore.

She tried to think about her work; she tried to think of all the little tedious things she had to do when she got back. She tried to think about the sea, serene and calm. She even tried to imagine sheep jumping over a fence so she could sleep and keep her mind from going a million frustrated miles an hour. Nothing worked. She had never imagined that simple confinement could be so frightening, so wearing. She thought that soon she would go mad; she would race for that bolted door and scream and cry and beat her head against it.

Just when she felt that she had reached that point, the door suddenly swung open. Mandy blinked against the sudden light, shielding her eyes.

For a moment she froze; it was Roberto. Roberto, giving her his lascivious white-toothed smile. She shivered inside, going as cold as ice. She was alone in this room with nothing but a white-sheeted mattress, no avenue of escape. No strength, no hope—and fully aware of the man's feelings regarding her.

No, no, Julio wouldn't allow it. Miguel wouldn't allow it. But where the hell *was* Miguel?

"Amanda?"

She took a deep breath and felt the blood move through her veins once again.

Miguel stepped past Roberto and stared at her, offering her his hand.

She didn't think anything then. She bolted from the

mattress, straight toward him, grasping that hand and pressing herself against the strength of his naked chest, her head lowered.

She felt his free hand on her hair, hesitant, then soothing. He wrapped an arm around her and led her through the tacky parlor, Roberto at their heels.

Julio sat at the kitchen table, playing cards with Maria. Señora Garcia was standing over a frying pan set on a Sterno stove on the counter. She was cooking hamburgers; it might have been the great American barbecue.

Miguel started to move away from Mandy; she inched toward him with a little gasp, drawing a snicker from Maria. Mandy stiffened, while Miguel accepted two plates of food from Señora Garcia. He shoved them at Mandy with a curious expression, then turned back to accept two cans of Old Milwaukee.

"Two hours, no more," Julio warned Miguel without looking up from his game.

"Dos horas," Miguel agreed, and Julio did look up then, but not at them. He stared at Roberto, who insisted on keeping his gun out and trained on Miguel.

"I'll spell you soon, amigo," he said.

Roberto leered at Mandy and shrugged to Julio. Mandy thought she saw Julio shudder slightly, and she wondered again how these two had come together, an idealist and a...vulture.

"Come on," Miguel urged her with his Spanish accent. *"Dos horas!"*

She had no idea what he was talking about, but she eagerly followed him outdoors.

It was late afternoon again. The sea stretched out

eternally before them, touched by the reflection of the dying sun, sparkling and rippling like something magical. Even the white beach seemed to shimmer with the colors of the coming evening, gold and pink, delicate mauve and diamond glitter.

Miguel walked beside her; Roberto followed at a distance. "This way," Miguel advised, walking toward the part of the beach where the rock and mangroves formed a secretive little haven, shadowed now in dusk.

She looked back. Roberto had paused. He was sitting on the beach, watching them, but giving them a certain distance. Mandy expelled a long sigh, which drew a sharp gaze from Miguel.

"He makes me nervous," she muttered.

If she'd expected reassurance, she didn't get it. "He doesn't thrill me, either," Miguel agreed. "But forget him for now. I spent hours arguing to get Julio to agree that you would go mad and be far more difficult to handle if you didn't get out a little."

He led her as far away from Roberto as possible, to the place where the roots met the rocks.

"Have a seat, Mrs. Blayne," he told her with a grin.

She sat on a stump, balancing both plates of hamburgers until he settled himself on the sand beside her. He opened both cans of beer, then handed her one as he took his own plate.

"Thanks," Mandy muttered, then lowered her head, because she was thinking about him, and she didn't want him to guess. She was on the stump; he was at her side, the breadth of his bare shoulders and back at her knee, his dark head angled toward her, his rich green eyes looking out to the sea.

She found herself liking everything about him; his height, his build, those eyes—even his scruffy jaw, strong beneath the beard. He was attractive—and she was attracted. She despised herself for it, because she considered herself sane and mature, and thought she knew enough about the human psyche to keep herself under control. She'd barely known him for forty-eight hours, yet she was desperately glad of his presence, ready to race to the sound of his voice, more than willing to trust herself to him.

Naturally. She sensed that he was all that stood between her and Roberto. But he was a cop—that was his job. There was no reason she should feel so…quiveringly grateful. Especially when she knew what he really thought of her!

"Eat," he told her, and she saw that he was looking at her then, rather than the sea. And that there was a peculiar glint of amusement in his eyes.

Mechanically and a little warily, she brought her hamburger to her mouth. It seemed to stick against the dryness of her throat, and she sipped the beer to force it down.

Miguel seemed to have no such problems. He ate his hamburger with a hearty appetite, then leaned back against her legs, very relaxed—like an idle beach bum—while he sipped his beer.

She stiffened, ready to jerk her legs away. She stopped herself only because she knew that Roberto watched them, not fifty feet away.

The water, stretching out before them, was magically beautiful, as were the white purity of the sand, the wild and primitive tangle of mangrove and coral, the eternal sky, the twilight....

And the two of them. He was touching her, relaxed and lazy, as if they were the only two people on earth, a man and a woman.

She set her half-eaten hamburger down and sipped the beer. She was so glad to be out of that room, away from her own thoughts.

Yet she was so nervous, so horribly aware of him: of his tanned flesh, so sleek over the rippling muscles of his back and shoulders; his hair, ebony with the coming of the night; his scent, as fresh and salty as the night air, and here, in this wild splendor, so masculine that she felt nearly consumed just by his presence....

It was all because she had to rely on him, she told herself furiously. Circumstance! At a cocktail party she would have walked away from him.

But here she couldn't walk away. Being with him was playing dangerous havoc with her emotions and her senses, and she knew it.

But what was she afraid of? He assumed that she was married to Peter, and he steered clear of married women; he had told her so with indisputable passion.

Maybe she should be glad, grateful to learn that her instincts and emotions still functioned. She worked, she laughed, she enjoyed people, but she hadn't really felt anything in so long. Maybe even the fear and the fury were good; she was reacting, and there had been times when she had felt that anything would be better than the horrible numbness. But this...

Even Peter had tried to introduce her to a string of young men. She'd never felt the least interest, just the numbness. And now she felt like a traitor, to Paul and—far worse—to herself. How could she possibly be attracted to a man who treated her so poorly?

He was there; he was a buffer. That was all, absolutely all. And she wasn't only attracted to him. She was also indignant and outraged by his methods. To top it all off, she still didn't even know if she should really believe him or not, because he was a fabulous actor, slipping from accent to accent with barely a thought.

"You really are absolutely beautiful, you know."

Mandy started, choking on her beer, staring involuntarily into the heavy-lidded sparkling green eyes that were now resting on her in the most sensual fashion. She swallowed warily. "Thank you," she muttered. Then she asked, "You really are a cop?"

He chuckled softly. "Yeah, I really am."

Mandy stared out to sea again while confusion overwhelmed her. His voice...the huskiness in his voice. What had happened to him suddenly? The cut-and-dried manner was gone—as was the hard and passionate man who had vowed he didn't touch married women, who despised her for marrying an old man.

"Uh..." She cleared her throat, searching for a safe topic of conversation. "What is Julio doing with Roberto? They don't seem a bit alike."

He shrugged. "They're not. Juan is with him because they're second cousins or something. I think Roberto is merely in it for the money."

"The money?"

"Mmm. The Garcias still have family in Spain, and a number of wealthy Colombian connections. If I've gotten things right, Roberto is a mercenary. He's been hired for his expertise. That's why I don't trust him. God, you're beautiful."

"Would you stop that!" Mandy snapped after a moment. He'd changed his tone so quickly that it had taken her time to catch up, and now she knew that she was nearly as red as the twilight.

"I can't seem to help myself," he said, swallowing the last of his beer, then crushing the can in one hand while he continued to stare at her.

She swallowed the last of her beer, compelled to return his stare, fascinated, horrified.

He took her can from her hand, brushing her fingers with his own, rising to his knees, a breath away from her.

"You hate married women. Especially me. I married old Peter Blayne for his wealth and possessions, remember?" she told him quickly. Too quickly. Breathlessly...

"I know," he told her softly, his arm moving around her. His face wasn't an inch from hers. She felt the power of his chest and shoulders, saw the smoldering green fire in his eyes. "I know all that. But don't you feel it? The sea and the breeze and the night, you—and me?"

"No! No!" Mandy told him hastily. "I don't feel anything. Just that you hate me. Remember?"

He shook his head. "I don't hate you, Mandy, though I keep thinking of all the reasons why I should. I think and think of all the reasons why I should stay completely away from you. I tell myself over and over again that you're married. That I'm a cop. That you're completely off limits. But, Mandy... I tell you, I can't help myself. No matter what I think, I see you. I see those golden eyes of yours, that tawny lion's mane. I see your body—oh, God! Do I see your body! Naked and gold and glistening, lithe and curved—"

"Stop it!" Mandy shrieked, trying to edge away as his knuckles brushed over her cheek. She lost her balance instead and toppled over into the sand.

He was right behind her, stretching over her, bracing his weight on his hands, his palms beside her head. He seemed to cover her, his legs entangled with hers.

"Get up—" she began in panic.

"Oh, Mandy! I can't!" he vowed passionately, and she felt all the sexual quality of him, the power in his thighs, the brush of his hairy chest against her skin, the ridiculously sweet pressure of his hips on hers.

"Roberto! Roberto is watching us!" she protested.

"And I must convince him that we are lovers," Miguel whispered softly, shifting, bringing himself halfway to her side, cupping her jaw in his hand to bring her face to his.

"Amanda, I can't bear this. Being with you, night and day. Sleeping beside you. I'd sell my soul for you. I can't care that you're a married woman, I can't think of anything. I have to have you!"

Heat like liquid fire exploded through her—right along with a raging sense of panic. He was way too much male. She didn't know what to do with him; she didn't know how to escape him. She felt lost and overwhelmed and desperate!

"Wait. Wait!"

"Hold me, Mandy. Just hold me!"

Hold him? His arms were vise clamps around her, his body an inferno of steel. She was quivering like a cornered rabbit, straining against him with all her might—futilely.

"Miguel…"

"Oh, Lord, I was in agony, listening to you! I envisioned the two of us in a Jacuzzi, sipping champagne, just barely touching, coming nearer and nearer, until you were mine."

He shifted, touching her. Lightly. Fingertips against her cheek, stroking her throat, running over her collarbone, so near the neckline of her halter top. Fingertips… dancing dangerously over the mounds of her breasts, fascinated with the naked flesh of her midriff. Gentle, tender, erotic in their motion, in their very being. And she was powerless. Shivering and aware and powerless, and so keenly touched by the vibrant heat of his body, his weight, the rough feel of his legs.

"Champagne…you and me. The warm waters rushing around us. Mandy, you've got the most beautiful breasts I've ever seen."

"Miguel, don't you—"

"God, you're glorious…splendid. Champagne and pizza. Completely naked…us…together."

"Damn you! I'll strangle you once we're free."

"Remember when you touched me? This morning? Oh, Mandy, I felt desire in that touch. I know that Peter Blayne's an old man. I know that you're young and sensual and I can't see any reason why we shouldn't—"

"There are a million reasons!"

He smiled, totally disbelieving her. And then his fingertips were moving again. Just gently stroking her ribs…then moving higher, brushing her breasts. Her nipples were hard, and he could feel it, and that was making him grin even more widely.

"I'll report you. If we live I'll report you to all your superiors. Every one of them! They'll fire you."

"You're just saying that, Mandy. I can feel you. I knew this morning that you wanted me."

"I do not!"

"I don't care about anything! Report me. I'd give my job—my life—for one night with you."

Oh, no! What had she done this morning? Threats weren't working; they didn't mean a thing to him!

"Please…" she whispered, but even that did nothing.

"You've cast a spell on me," he told her huskily. "I can't let you go. It's all that I can think about—you, me, tangled together, hot, sweating, straining."

"Miguel, you're a cop! I'm a married woman!"

Suddenly he was laughing, staring down at her and laughing. Then he rolled away from her and sat up, wrapping his arms around his knees and staring out at the sea once again.

"Mrs. Blayne, you're the most ridiculous liar I've ever met," he told her with curt amusement.

"What?" Stunned, she scrambled to her feet and stared down at him, her hands on her hips. She felt relieved, furious—and bereft.

He gazed up at her, still smiling. "Amanda Blayne, you're Peter Blayne's daughter-in-law, not his wife."

"How do you know?"

"Because I managed to get through to the Coast Guard on the radio."

"What?"

"I keep telling you—I'm a cop. Sworn to protect and

all that jazz. I'm sorry I haven't tried to stop a bullet for you yet, but I did get to the radio."

Her temper flared out of all proportion. She should be jumping up and down with joy that someone had been advised of the situation, but he'd just made such a fool of her! Without thought she suddenly leapt at him, pummeling his chest and shoulders.

"You bastard! You didn't bother to tell me! Instead you pulled this little act. I'll kill you! I'll wring your stupid neck!"

"Whoa!" he protested, stunned by her vehemence, falling backward into the sand at her assault. He collected himself quickly and caught her flailing fists, then rolled and cast a knee over her hips and stretched her arms over her head, where he held them while he leaned against her, panting.

"Don't touch me! I swear, I *will* report you! How dare you?"

"Roberto is looking!"

"I don't give a damn!"

"You'd better—unless you want Roberto in this position!"

"What diff—"

"A lot, Mrs. Blayne. I'm not going to rape you, but Roberto would give his eyeteeth to do just that!"

Mandy went dead still, clenching her teeth and staring up at him, trying to regain her breath.

"You son of—"

"Hey! You lied to me! I risked my neck to let you know that I was a police officer. You lied—"

"I did not! You assumed that I was Peter's wife! You judged me without a—"

"You could have corrected me!"

"And why should I have bothered?"

"Courtesy, Mrs. Blayne. Common courtesy. Especially in this situation!"

"Courtesy! Oh—"

"Shush!"

She grated her teeth together again. He was staring down at her with an emerald spark in his eyes. He was amused.

And she was far too aware of him all over again. His fingers, curled within hers. His thigh, cast over her hips. His warmth. Everything about him that was male, that called to something inside her despite herself. She was quivering from the effect of his touch....

"Let me go, please, Miguel," she whispered.

He stared at her a moment longer, his eyes growing dark, tension suddenly lining his face. He sighed and released her, but still lay at her side.

"You asked for it, you know," he told her.

"Men!" she snapped. "They say you're all alike, and I believe it! You came at me with all kinds of insinuations and I just played along because *you* were the one who deserved it!"

He laughed again, and she was aware once more that she liked his smile, liked it very much.

"The champagne in the Jacuzzi was a killer," he told her.

She stiffened. "I was acting for the benefit of our captors, and you know it."

He shrugged. "You're just such a good little actress!"

"Oh, stop, please." And don't stay so close, please don't stay so close! she added silently, cast into an agony of confusion. It was just the circumstances, she told herself.

She closed her eyes. "Thank God you got to the radio! When is help coming?"

"I don't know."

Her eyes flew open again, and she edged up on her elbows to frown at him. "What do you mean you don't know? You just told me—"

"I mean I don't know! I tried to tell them where we were, but I'm not positive. It only takes a day to reach Cat Cay—we were on that old scow for two nights. I think that they motored in circles, backtracking on purpose. I still think that we're somewhere near Cat Cay. But there must be hundreds of these little swamp islands around. It may take time. And this has to be handled carefully. The Coast Guard can't just zoom up. That's not the way you handle a hostage situation You could—"

"Get shot?"

He shrugged. "That's not going to happen, Mandy." Distracted, he called her by her given name, not by the acid "Mrs. Blayne."

She looked from his profile to the ocean, picking up a handful of sand, letting it fall through her fingers.

He stood up abruptly and reached a hand down to her. "Let's walk on the beach. Our two hours are almost up."

"How can you tell?" she asked him despondently.

"Because," he said softly, "I can read the sky. And Julio has come out to take Roberto's place as watchdog."

Mandy glanced over her shoulder. It was true; Julio was sitting where Roberto had been.

She looked back to the strong hand being offered to her. She hesitated a moment longer, then took it. He pulled her to her feet, cast an arm around her and started walking idly down the beach.

Mandy went along because she felt she had little choice. It did feel good to move; it felt wonderful to be outside, rather than in that dim stuffy room. It felt good to have his arm around her. To know that he was with her, even if she still wanted to strangle him. Yet at the same time she knew that she needed him. He was her security, her buffer against fear and madness. This would end; all things ended. But for now...the evening sky was beautiful; the breeze was delightful. He was at her side—far better than facing Roberto's leers alone.

They walked through the surf, and the cool water bathed her feet. If she closed her eyes she could pretend that she was just on an outing, away for the day, taken to a primitive paradise on the winged sails of the *Flash Point*.

She sniffed suddenly and managed to cast Miguel a wry smile. "I don't even know your last name."

He gazed at her, hesitated a minute, then said, "Ramiro."

"Miguel Ramiro," she said. Strangely, he hesitated once again.

"Not exactly."

"Not exactly?"

"Well, don't tell these guys. My name is Sean. Sean Michael Ramiro."

"What?" Mandy started laughing. Maybe it was hysteria. She stared at him incredulously.

"Sean Michael Ramiro?" She moved away from him,

almost doubled over with laughter, so incredible did she find it all. "Now I know you're a liar!"

"I told you I was born in Dublin!" he retorted.

"You said you were Cuban—"

"I said *half*-Cuban! My father was Cuban, my mother is Irish."

She was still laughing. "What a combination!"

"Oh, yeah! I forgot! You're Miss DAR! Daughter of the old *Mayflower*!"

She was still laughing so hard she couldn't even take offense.

"Sean?"

"Yeah. Want to make something of it?"

"No, no!" She held out a defensive hand, but too late. He splashed over to her, gripped her hands, slid a foot behind her ankle and sent her crashing into the surf, then dropped down beside her.

"I'm sorry! I'm sorry!" she shrieked when he made a move to dunk her.

But he didn't dunk her. He touched her cheek, his weight and warmth against her again, while the cool surf raced delicately around them both. She felt the power of his arms on either side of her, saw the tension in his eyes, and she might well have been spellbound.

His head lowered. His lips brushed hers.... Just brushed them. And then his eyes were on hers again. Like the sea around them, reflected by the sinking sun, touched by the coming moon. They quested and they sought...and she must have answered.

Because his lips met hers again, with a coercive hungry pressure. His kiss filled her with that same hunger, captured her with fascination. She tasted sea and salt and passion and heat, felt the sweep of his tongue over her teeth…deep into her mouth. Filling her, entering her with a spiraling heat that sent a searing wonder rippling through her. He wasn't really touching her, just his mouth. Just the tickle of that growth of beard against her flesh, the fire of his lips, the fever of his mouth…

"Hey! Your two hours are up! She goes back to her room!"

Startled, they broke apart at Julio's announcement, shaken from the moment.

Mandy stared at Sean Michael Ramiro in absolute horror. She didn't accept his hand, nor did she even notice Julio, standing on the beach.

She raced back toward the house, eager now for her prison, desperate to be alone.

Chapter 7

When darkness came to her shuttered prison, it came completely.

Mandy was absolutely convinced that she would go mad. She couldn't see her own hand in front of her face. She hadn't known that she was afraid of the dark, but then, she'd never seen darkness so complete.

For hours she lay on the mattress, still soaked from the surf, shivering, then going deathly still before shivering all over again. Sometimes it seemed that her mind was blank; sometimes it was as if a cacophony of thoughts and ideas raced within it.

And always it came back to two things. The darkness. Haunting, suffocating, ebony darkness. And Miguel. No, not Miguel. Sean Michael Ramiro.

Her feelings, his touch. The strident need she was

beginning to feel for him. The moral horror that she could be so vulnerable, so dependent...

And so hungry. To be held, touched, loved. To laugh, to play and enjoy the play.

She yearned for him now in a terrible aching way. She thought that she could endure the darkness, if only he was next to her. Here, in this hell within paradise, he had become her salvation, and more. It seemed ridiculously complex; the emotional and the physical; the desire, the need. It seemed so incredibly basic and primitive. She simply wanted to fit against him, as nature had intended, without thought, without words.

There was no way to escape her sense of disloyalty, no way to lie in this utter darkness and not think of Paul, not think of the baby. No way to do anything other than lie there in anguish and agony, suffering the ceaseless gnawing of a fear that came not just from circumstances now, but, like desire, from instinct.

She went still when the door opened at last. The streak of light that entered was painful, as blinding as the darkness. Mandy closed her eyes against it, casting her arm over her face.

The light was quickly gone. Her whole existence suddenly centered around her other senses.

Someone was in the room.

She could feel that presence so strongly! Logic warned her that it could be Julio or Maria or Señora Garcia. A trembling within warned that it could too easily be Roberto.

But her world now knew no logic. She didn't need to be afraid; it was Sean. She knew from the presence that filled the room; she knew from his salty scent, the sound of his breath.

He stood just within the doorway for several moments, his eyes adjusting to the darkness. Then, very slowly, he came toward the mattress. He reached it and fumbled along the edge, then smoothed his hand over the sheet.

She shifted, giving him room. He started suddenly, aware of her movement.

"You're awake?"

"I'm awake."

"My God, it's darker than a coal mine in here."

"I couldn't find the light switch," she said, trying to joke, but she had no idea what his reaction was, since she couldn't see his face.

He didn't answer as he stretched out beside her. She didn't dare touch him, but she knew his position. Hands laced behind his head, ankles crossed, feet probably dangling over the edge.

"You okay?" he whispered after a while.

"Of course. Why wouldn't I be?"

She imagined that he might have grinned. "I guess you're not afraid of the dark."

"Terrified. But what could I possibly do about it?"

"Ask for a lantern."

"Would I get one?"

"Probably." He hesitated. "I don't think Julio means to be cruel. He just doesn't know that it's as black as Hades in here. Not that it matters if you're sleeping, but you've been in here quite a while. I'll get a lantern tomorrow."

She didn't answer him. She wasn't sure what to say.

She was excruciatingly glad of his presence; he was like a lantern against the darkness.

She was also excruciatingly aware of him—and the last moments they had shared. She was frightened, not of him, but of herself, and so keyed up that she would never sleep, so miserable that she longed for nothing except oblivion.

The silence seemed to grow in the darkness and become a black cloud above them, filled with the portent of wind and rain. They did not touch, though they were no more than an inch apart. Then suddenly Mandy sneezed, and that sneeze ended the silence.

"Bless you," he muttered, turning toward her. His hand brushed her arm, and suddenly she knew that he was above her, that his dark brows were furrowed with concern, and that his handsome features had hardened into a scowl. "You're shivering like a leaf, and you feel like an ice cube!"

"Do I?" Mandy murmured.

"Yes, you do." He quickly stood, pulling at the mattress, fumbling and swearing when he stubbed his toe against it.

"Get up—can you?"

"Of course I can," she murmured, confused. "But why?"

"There's a top sheet on this thing, and you need to get under it. Take your clothes off."

"What?"

"Oh, come on! I can't see a damn thing in here. Besides, I've already seen you. Your clothes are still all wet from the beach, and you'll get pneumonia if you sleep in them. And then, should the time come when you need to move quickly, you won't be able to. Take your clothes off."

"I think I'd rather risk pneumonia!"

"Than me?"

How could a voice do so much? Reach out through the air and darkness like a velvet brush, teasing, warming.

"Umm."

"Still don't trust me?"

"Not in the least."

"Well, that's okay. I don't trust *you*, either."

"I'm not asking you to take your clothes off."

"Not yet. You'll get to it, though. Women are all alike."

She rolled off the mattress, laughing, perplexed. Somehow he had brought light and warmth into the room. And also that sense of security that was so very easy to rely on, so very easy to need—and so very dangerous. More dangerous, perhaps, than Julio and his accomplices.

"Laugh at me, will you, Mrs. Blayne?" he charged softly, and she knew that he was walking around to her. He hunched down in front of her and felt for her. She didn't know what he was looking for, but he found her breast.

"Hey! And you're asking me to take my clothes off?"

"Sorry, I thought it was your face."

"Umm. You'll get yours one day."

"Promises, promises. Off with 'em, lady."

"I don't think this is proper police procedure."

"Off!"

"Well, move, then!"

He did. Feeling like a stripper in broad daylight, Mandy shed her soggy cutoffs and top, then groped with a fair amount of panic for the sheet.

It was there, in his hands, ready to be wrapped around her. She sensed that he was laughing at her.

"I've already slept with the…real…you, you know."

"Oh, shut up!"

She was still shivering, but she did feel much better; she hadn't realized how chilling her wet clothing had been. But even now, with the dry sheet wrapped around her, she was cold.

"Lie down now," he said huskily.

"What wonderful relationships you must have, Mr. Ramiro! Take off your clothes. Lie down."

He laughed softly in the darkness, and once again she felt touched by the sound, brushed by velvet.

"When it works, do it. Lie down."

Gritting her teeth, she did so, cocooning herself in the sheet. Then she tensed as he crawled over to her. He didn't keep his distance this time; he brought his chest to her back and wrapped an arm around her waist, pulling her close to absorb his heat.

She must have been as stiff and unyielding as concrete, though she made no protest, because he chuckled softly again. "Ease up. I'm just trying to make you warm."

She didn't know that she had held her breath until she released it in a long sigh.

"I'm not the big bad wolf."

"Are you sure?"

"Positive. Why do I make you so nervous?"

"I'm not nervous."

"You are."

"Well, I have a right to be! Since I've met you, you've knocked me down, thrown me around...."

"What's a lover for?" he teased. "Mandy—Mrs. Blayne—I do apologize for my rougher methods."

"And your gentler ones?" she murmured without thought.

His arm tightened slightly around her midriff. "Meaning?"

"Nothing!" she said quickly. What had caused her to say such a thing?

And even as she asked herself the question, she knew the answer. The kiss. The real one, in the salty foam of the surf, interrupted by Julio's appearance.

In the darkness she felt his every breath, knew his every movement, no matter how slight. Knew him, living and breathing beside her.

Silence spread again, total in the darkness. And in that silence she thought it would be the easiest thing in the world to turn to him, to give in to temptation under cover of darkness.

She'd always known that she was young, that she would make love again one day. But one day had always meant some indeterminate future. It was something she hadn't dwelled upon, had not imagined easily. It would be awkward and difficult, and she would be nervous and afraid and, certainly, making comparisons. She had even begun to imagine how difficult it would be to remove her clothing, or watch a man disrobe, knowing his intent.

She wore no clothing now, but it was dark. And in the darkness she would not have to see a man's face.

Not have to know if she brought pleasure or ennui, nor bear visible witness that she found it not thrilling in the least, but actually distasteful....

But it *would* be thrilling. With him. For her. She knew from his eyes, from his laughter, from his words, from the hands that touched her so well, from the hard length of his body, taut and warm against hers.

It was easy to forget because of circumstance. Easy to imagine that the darkness could cover her, and she could hide from truth and light and thought. Easy...

She would never do it; not even the darkness could take away her memories. And it wasn't just Paul; it was Paul and the baby. If one of them had made it—just one of them—she wouldn't have felt as if she had been stripped of everything. Everything that mattered. She wouldn't have been so afraid of emotion, of reaching out. But she had learned that pleasure brought pain.

She hadn't known that she was crying; her tears were as silent as the night. Then suddenly she felt a thumb against her cheek, wiping away the moisture there.

"How long?" he asked her very softly.

And she knew exactly what he meant. "Three years ago."

"What happened?"

She had to breathe very deeply before she could whisper out her answer. "A drunk driver," she said flatly. "The baby was killed instantly. Paul lingered a few hours."

"And the driver?"

"He died, too. There wasn't even anybody left to hate."

He didn't say anything else to her; he just ran his

fingers gently, idly against her cheek, then over her hair. And he stayed there, beside her, his warmth all around her.

And in time she slept.

She awoke to find his glittering green eyes upon her.

The absolute darkness was gone; hazy light filtered in, like a gray fog. She could see him now, and herself, too well.

In the night she had turned to him. Turned and twisted and left half of her sheet behind. Their legs were completely entangled, her left one beneath his, her right one thrown across his thigh. She'd made a pillow of his arm—which he couldn't possibly move without tearing out a handful of her hair. Thus his patient and amused stare as she opened her eyes wider and wider with the realization of her position.

"Oh! Get off me, you—"

"Hey, you're the one on top of me, Mrs. Blayne."

And of course she was. Clenching her teeth and emitting a soft oath, Mandy moved her legs away from his and wrenched furiously at the sheet. It wouldn't give, not until he laughed and shifted his weight. Groaning, she wrapped it around herself and stared disgustedly at the ceiling, drawing another soft chuckle from him.

"Can't you go somewhere, do something—get out of here? You're never around when I—" She broke off abruptly.

Naturally he pounced on her words, leaning on one elbow to watch her closely. "When you what?"

"I have no idea. I was just talking."

"You were not. You were about to say 'when I need you!'"

"I do not need you." She paused, lowering her lashes. "You're just better than some of the alternatives around here."

"Wow! What an endorsement!"

"Will you please go do whatever it is you do when you're not around?"

"Ah, jealousy becomes you."

Mandy sighed with exaggerated patience. "I'm not jealous." Then she turned suddenly, holding the sheet tightly to her breasts, surprised that it really did seem nice to wake up and find him there, smiling at her—even if she had been definitely disturbed at first.

"I'm curious," she murmured, remembering what she had intended to say. "Here I am, entirely harmless, and they keep me under lock and key. And there you are—at least two hundred pounds of you—and they let you run around. Why?"

"Because I'm madly in love with you. I'm allowed to be here to keep a lid on you. I'm a kindred spirit, a refugee, too, or so they believe. I'm one of them—a gardener—pulled into the bedroom. And you, Mrs. Blayne, are the farthest thing from harmless that I've ever come across."

"What?"

"You half killed me the other night."

"*I* half killed *you*?"

"Umm. Scratching, flailing, slapping—you're about as harmless as a basketful of vipers."

"Oh, really? Funny, you don't look much worse for wear!"

"But I am. You might well have cost me months of normal sexual activity."

"What?" she shrieked, astounded at his accusation.

"You must have learned your kicks from Bruce Lee. Honestly, I felt mortally wounded. My mother would never forgive you. She's expecting grandchildren one of these days."

She saw the grin he couldn't keep hidden then. "Oh, will you please get out of here? Go join your fellow refugees!"

The humor instantly fled from his eyes. "A refugee, Mrs. Blayne," he said, "is one who seeks refuge. I was born in Dublin, but both my parents were American citizens. Therefore I never had any need to seek refuge."

He rolled away from her and rose, leaving her feeling a strange remorse; she had been teasing him, and she wasn't sure what she had said to make him draw away from her with such disgust.

His back was to her, his hands on his hips. "It isn't a dirty word, you know," he said.

"What?"

"Refugee, Mrs. Blayne. Little Miss Mayflower Princess. This country was established because people sought a better life. The Irish have come, the English, Italians, Germans and so on forever. That's part of the reason we're so unique, Mrs. Blayne. What do I do out there? I talk with them—in Spanish. I try to watch which way the wind is blowing, I try to read people. For your safety, Mrs. Blayne. If you had bothered to learn some Spanish—"

"Why should I have?" she snapped, simply because

she needed some defense; he was definitely attacking. "It's an English-speaking country!"

He swung around then, and to her surprise he was suddenly on his knees on the mattress, green fire in his eyes and radiating enough tension to make her shiver. "Yes, Mrs. Blayne, yes! It's definitely an English-speaking country. And you're right—those who seek its shelter should learn its language! But what kind of an isolationist are you? Nine out of ten Europeans learn at least two languages. They have to. They have to be able to talk to their neighbors. Haven't you ever wanted to learn for the simple joy of learning. Relating? Are you so smug, so satisfied with what you are, that you feel no need to give?"

"What the hell is this?" Mandy retorted. "A soapbox? I took another language, Mr. Ramiro—it just happens to have been German, not Spanish. And I'm not a linguistics whiz. I'm ever so sorry. And if you think that I'm a bigot, I'm sorry about that, too, but it's certainly your prerogative." Mandy was gaining steam as she continued her argument. Gripping the sheet, she rose to her knees to face him, as angry as he was. "You'd better face a few facts, Mr. Ramiro! We had a lot of real criminals dumped on us! As a police officer, you should know that! And I don't care if a murderer is German, French, English, Japanese or all-American mongrel— he shouldn't be walking the streets!"

"So what are you saying? The Cubans are all murderers?"

"I didn't say that and you damn well know it!"

His hands suddenly clamped down on her bare shoulders; she felt their leashed force and the blaze of emotion that seemed to leap from him to her. And then, just when she was certain that he would either shake her or scream at her again or both, he released her with an oath of disgust and scrambled back to his feet.

He strode straight toward the door without a backward look, opened it and slammed it behind himself.

"Oh, you stupid son of a bitch!" Mandy muttered after him. But then she realized that tears were stinging her eyes, and she didn't know why.

She hurried up, stumbling to grasp her clothing, racing for the bathroom. Brackish water, a little yellowed from rusting pipes, spewed from the spigot. She closed her eyes to ignore the color and splashed her face. Why did they keep getting into all this? Why didn't he understand…? And why the hell was she worrying about him when she was still a kidnap victim?

She sighed and realized that she wasn't really frightened. Not anymore. Julio seemed more like a misguided child than a menace. Except that he did know how to use a gun.

But she didn't believe that he would really hurt her. The only person she was afraid of—bone deep!—was Roberto, but she didn't have to worry about Roberto, because Julio seemed determined that no harm would come to her.

"This is insane!" she whispered aloud.

She had faith that this would end, and it was strange what that feeling did for her morale. Strange, but even her arguments with Sean made her feel stronger—impatient, but optimistic.

"Pain in the…"

Her cutoffs and top were still damp, but since she

had no other choice, she took a brackish and slightly yellow shower, then donned them again. When she had finished, she noticed that a delicious aroma was reaching her from beyond the door of her prison.

Sean had simply walked out. Why shouldn't she do the same?

She stalked over to the door and wrenched at the knob. It didn't give; since Sean had left, someone had come to bolt the door.

"Probably did it himself!" she muttered.

"Hey!" She slammed a fist against the wood. To her surprise, the door opened. Julio was standing there, clean shaven, attractively dressed in a clean cotton shirt and jeans.

He looked just like a nice kid—except that he was still carrying the gun tucked into his boy-next-door blue jeans.

"Good morning, Señora Blayne. We expect to hear something from your husband by tonight."

He smiled at her as if Western Union was simply sending the money to get her out of a rather sorry jam.

"Great," she muttered.

"Coffee?"

"Please," she accepted, with just a trace of irony. He indicated that she should precede him into the kitchen. His mother was there, smiling at Mandy with her usual sympathetic apology as soon as she saw her. Eggs and bacon were cooking in a skillet, and two kinds of coffee were brewing: the thick sweet Cuban blend and what was—according to the nearby can—Maxwell House.

Julio noticed the direction of her gaze. "Mama brewed it specially just for you."

Marvelous, she thought. Cater to your kidnap victim. Except that that wasn't really true, and she knew it. Señora Garcia was very upset that Mandy had been taken; she had made both kinds of coffee in a sincere effort to do anything in her power for Mandy.

She went up to accept the cup the woman offered her, telling her thank you. Señora Garcia smiled, and Mandy glanced out the kitchen window to the beach beyond.

Maria, Roberto and Sean—Miguel! She had to remember that, no matter how mad she got!—were all sitting around, paper plates discarded, laughing and chatting while they drank coffee.

Maria, it seemed, was growing quite fond of Sean. She kept placing her red polished fingertips on his bare bronzed arms as she spoke to him, her dark eyes beautiful with laughter.

And Sean...well, he was laughing back.

Oh, nuts to you! Mandy decided belligerently.

"Señora, por favor..."

She turned around. Señora Garcia had pulled out a chair for her at the table, where she had set down a plate filled with bacon and eggs. Mandy thanked her again and sat down.

Julio was sipping his coffee by her side. She picked up her fork because she was hungry, but after a few minutes she turned to her captor and spoke to him. "You know, don't you, that what you're doing is very wrong?"

He gazed at her sharply. Then he lifted his hands and let them fall. "My father is getting old, and he is very ill. Too many years in a dank prison. He will not live long. Using any means that I can manage, I will see to it that he knows freedom before he dies."

"But—"

"Señora Blayne," he interrupted very softly, "I was three years old when Batista was overthrown. He was certainly not a prize, but we went from one dictator to another. In the States the exiles pray for another revolution. In Cuba, those who have not been indoctrinated into the new regime work for the next revolution. When I was a child gunfire raged, people bled, and people died. The needs create the means, don't they? Spying is fine—when it is for your country. A spy must be hanged when he is from the other side. This is life. Violence is an ugly thing, but it can also be a way of life. Secrets, trial and error, violence, abduction. They are all means to an end. I will see my father free. It is that simple."

"Not here it isn't!" Amanda protested, frustrated. "Julio, this is a huge country! Peter Blayne doesn't run it, he just plays his part. The courts can be slow, justice slower, but they're the best shot we've got! Julio…"

"I cannot go back," he said flatly, rising. "If you want some time away from your room, now is it. The day is beautiful, the surf is warm. Come out to the beach."

She rose along with him, ready to take her plate to the counter. Señora Garcia took it from her hands, smiling.

Mandy stepped outside with Julio. The others fell silent as they passed by. Mandy caught Sean's eyes on her, but they were filled with the sun's reflection, and she couldn't read their expression.

She gazed at him just as blandly, then walked on toward the surf with Julio.

"What happens," she asked softly, "if Peter Blayne doesn't respond to you? I'm telling you right now, he

doesn't have the power to walk up to a federal peniten-
tiary and demand that your father be released."

Julio stared at her. "He'd best find that power."

"You'd kill me?"

He sat down on the sand, letting the water rush over
his bare toes. Mandy did the same. "I would have to
send him a piece of you next."

"A...piece of me?"

"A finger, Mrs. Blayne."

She thought that she would keel over into the water.
It wouldn't happen; the Coast Guard were on their way.
Sean...

Sean was laughing away with the charmingly voluptuous Maria up at the house.

She lowered her head, thinking that no matter what
he thought of her, Sean would never allow her to be...
dismembered.

"I would not wish to harm you," Julio added.

"Thanks," Mandy breathed bitterly. She turned
around, looking back to the house. Sean, with his
guarded gaze, was still watching her.

And so was Roberto, in that fashion that sent horrible chills down her spine. There was something about
his grim look that was like a rabid dog's. She felt that
she could almost hear his teeth gnashing, as if he would
devour her like a shark.

Shivering, she looked back to the water. To the sea.
It stretched out endlessly, as if they were alone in the
world. With nothing better to do and a yearning to
move, Mandy stood and started walking out into the
waves.

"Where are you going?" Julio demanded sharply.

She turned and stared back at him, laughing with real humor. "Where could I go, Señor Garcia? I'm going to swim, nothing more. I certainly don't expect to swim back to Miami, if that's what you're afraid of."

He had the grace to laugh sheepishly in return, and Mandy kept walking until the water came to her chest, then she began to swim.

The sharks were still fresh in her mind, so she didn't venture too far, but it felt so good to be moving. She swam against the current; she swam with the current. She floated on her back and felt the sun on her face.

When she got back to the beach, Julio was gone. He was sitting with the others nearer the house. They had switched from coffee to beer to cool them against the heat of the sun.

Mandy lay back in the sand for a while, resting, then headed for the water once again. She knew the physical exertion would help her to sleep, to keep from thinking.

When she came out again, she faltered. The others had gone into the house; only Roberto waited for her. Roberto, who liked to keep his gun out, smoothing it with his fingers while he stared at her. He stroked that gun like...like a man would stroke a woman.

Mandy kept her distance from him, tossing her hair back, squeezing the water from it. She realized from the direction of his eyes that the soaked shirt was tight and see-through against her breasts.

Sucking in her breath, she crossed her arms over her chest and strode past him, heading for the house. He didn't follow her—except with his eyes.

In the house she discovered that Maria was loudly playing a portable radio. The girl was sitting in the parlor, idly dangling one long leg over the arm of the sofa, listening to the music. She looked Mandy up and down and smirked at her. Mandy ignored her, aware that she was damp and that her hair looked like a mop. What did it matter?

In an annoying way, though, something did matter. Mandy was still itching to slap Maria. She didn't like having that scornful laughter directed her way, nor did she like the way the girl watched Sean. Exactly what Maria wanted was written all over her lovely face, expressed soundlessly in her sensual pouting lips.

Poor kid, the teenage years were rough. Poor kid hell!

Mandy returned Maria's stare with a shrug, then looked around the kitchen. Lunch was on the table. Julio and Sean were eating; Maria had apparently already finished.

Señora Garcia laid out a plate for her. It was fish, deliciously spiced. Mandy sat and ate; Sean and Julio both glanced at her, then resumed their conversation.

She grew irritated again that Sean Ramiro—policeman *extraordinaire*—still did nothing. Then she noticed that even while he was eating, Julio carried his gun, one hand in his lap, ready to make a grab for it.

When Julio finished eating he went up to his mother, encircling her waist with his arms to say something. Sean leaned across the table to her. "Want to go back outside?"

She would never understand what possessed her to snap back at him, but she did. "No, thanks. We bigots like to be alone!"

He sat back, lashes shielding his eyes, his mouth tightened in a grim line.

Mandy stood up and waltzed past Maria and her radio, surprised to hear a voice with a beautiful Bahamian accent announce that it was almost four o'clock.

Swimming had done one thing for her; it had caused time to pass. But, like an idiot, she had resigned herself to a locked room when she might have known freedom.

With a sigh she sank down on her mattress, then realized with a bit of a start that there was a kerosene lantern on the floor, and a book of matches.

Sean had kept his word.

With shaking fingers she lit the lantern. It occurred to her that she could probably light a fire and burn down the entire place. It also occurred to her that they might let her burn to death, and she wasn't desperate enough—yet—to risk that.

She frowned suddenly as a little pool of light fell around her. There was a book beside the lantern. She picked it up and read the title; it was on Caribbean fish. It might not be compelling, but it was certainly better than nothing. It had probably been the only thing that Sean could find in the place.

Smiling slightly, she began to leaf through it. Then she began to yawn, and to her amazement she found that she was drifting off. She blew out the lantern and let sleep come.

Later, probably much later, because it had become dark, she awakened with a start. Puzzled, she rose up on her elbows, keenly attuned to the darkness, frightened to the core, but not sure why.

And then she knew. There was no sound, no movement—but she knew. Someone was in the room.

And it wasn't Sean.

Someone was in the room and moving swiftly. She opened her mouth to scream, but a hand came down over it. A heavy sinewy weight fell against her, and she heard a terse whisper in Spanish.

Madness catapulted through her. She couldn't scream, so she tried to bite. She tried to kick and flail and fight, but that wiry arm remained around her, firm and unrelenting.

She could feel his breath. She could see again that image of gnashing teeth, of brutal hunger.

She tried everything, but she couldn't dislodge the hand over her mouth nor the weight bearing down on her.

She heard the sudden tearing of fabric and realized that his free hand was on her halter top. She felt his palm on her flesh, hot, urgent.

That was when she managed to twist her mouth free at last in a spurt of desperate energy. She gasped for breath, then screamed as loud as she could, and long.

His open palm crashed against her cheek, and the world seemed to spin. But it didn't matter, not at all. Because the door had burst open, bringing help.

She needed no light, no sound, no movement. She recognized the presence filling the doorway, filling the room.

Sean.

Chapter 8

One moment Roberto was above her; the next he was not.

Light streamed surreally into the room from the parlor beyond. Gasping for breath, Mandy clutched the torn halter top to her, scrambling to her feet.

The still ebony night was immediately shattered. She was suddenly surrounded by shadows and shouts, and between those bursts of staccato noise she heard the heavy sounds of fists landing against flesh.

There was a loud crash. Roberto and Sean had gone flying through the doorway together to land on the parlor floor, both grim, both bloodied—both still at it. Shaken, Mandy followed them. Julio was yelling; Maria was screaming; and Señora Garcia was watching the proceedings, white-faced.

Just then a gun went off. Mandy screamed again, but

no one heard her that time. Sean and Roberto had both ceased fighting at that shot, twisting to stare at Julio.

Mandy didn't understand what followed. Everyone was speaking in Spanish. Roberto was obviously swearing vehemently and trying to make some point. Every bit as vehemently, Sean was arguing his side. Señora Garcia tried to say something, and Maria started up again, staring at Mandy, then spitting in her direction.

Julio shouted out a command, which everyone ignored, so he shot another bullet into the ceiling—which finally brought the silence he desired.

With everyone quiet once again he started to talk to Roberto, and then to Sean. Finally he paused to stare at Mandy who was standing, wide-eyed and ashen, in the doorway. He cocked his head with interest, then shrugged and spoke to the two men again. Roberto protested; Julio swore.

And then, whatever the argument had been, it was decided. Sean and Roberto both stood and walked grimly out the front door. Señora Garcia crossed herself and stepped into the second bedroom, slamming the door. Julio followed the two men outside.

"What is going on!" Mandy finally screamed, clenching her fists at her side.

Maria, elegantly decked out in a long gauzy nightgown that nicely displayed her attributes, gave Mandy another of her scornful looks and spoke disdainfully. "You—you are the problem! You will get him killed!"

"What?" Mandy demanded, startled and alarmed.

"It is all your fault."

She'd had it with Maria, and no one else was around. Mandy strode to her in a sudden fury and grabbed a handful of dark glistening hair. "You tell me this instant what is going on!"

"Oww! Let go!" Maria screeched, trying to free her hair. "Julio says they are welcome to fight it out over you! And Roberto is a killer, you stupid *puta*! You will get Miguel killed!"

"Julio is not going to let them kill one another!" Mandy snapped.

"Roberto will break Miguel's neck! And all because of you!"

"He tried to rape me, you stupid little witch!"

"You should have enjoyed him—"

"Enjoyed? Rape? If you like him so much, sweetie, you're welcome to him! Now get out of my way!"

Mandy shoved Maria aside, wondering just how much of a killer Roberto was. Any man could look tough with a gun, and that seemed to be the source of Roberto's strength. She tried to assure herself that he was nothing but hot air, and that Sean could take care of himself.

But she was frightened. Very frightened. If something did happen to him, she wouldn't be able to live with herself.

If she lived at all, she thought grimly, because she would fight Roberto herself until she had no breath left in her body.

Mandy swung open the front door. The natural coolness of the ocean breeze touched her cheeks soothingly, but she felt no ease as she paused and stared into the star-studded night. She could see the three of them down near the surf.

Julio's gun was in his hand; Sean and Roberto were

wrestling on the sand, coming together, drawing apart, falling to roll on the beach together.

Mandy ran down to where Julio stood. He was watching the action with no apparent emotion.

"Why are you letting them do this!" she screamed at him. "You can make them stop."

"I cannot. No one can."

"You've got the gun—"

"Miguel says that you are his, only his. Robert says that you are no virgin to be returned untouched. If you've had one lover, he should have rights, too."

"You didn't kidnap me for that vulture's amusement, Julio! Come on, think! You're in charge of this thing, aren't you? Julio, you're wrong in what you're doing, but you're a man with morals and ideals. You—"

"I am not in this alone now! If Roberto loses, he loses!"

"And if he doesn't? Julio! I can't believe this of you!" She paused, swallowing, because there was a set expression on his handsome face. "Julio! I am a person, not the spoils of war! And you know that!"

"Roberto cannot shoot Miguel. They are evenly matched, no weapons. That is fair—and it's all that I can do."

"Fair…" Mandy paused in horror, because beyond Julio, the two men were on their feet once again, carefully circling each other.

Mandy caught her breath. There was a scratch on Sean's shoulder, and a smear of blood at the right corner of his mouth, but he looked all right otherwise. The shimmering fury of the fight was in his narrowed eyes; he appeared more than ready to keep up the battle.

Roberto was the one looking the worse for wear. He was wiry and strong, but he simply didn't have Sean's powerful shoulders or arms. Roberto had already accrued one black eye—which was puffing and turning an ugly green color right now—and his jaw was swollen, too. But he still had a look of blood lust about him, as if he was playing right now. As if he would win when he was ready.

Sean suddenly ducked his head and made a lunge for Roberto, throwing him to the ground. They rolled together, then split apart. Roberto didn't look so self-assured this time, but he smiled slowly at his opponent and reached into his pocket, drawing out a switchblade.

"Look out!" Mandy screamed.

Sean saw the blade. It made a rushing sound as Roberto brought it slicing through the night, and Sean ducked. Roberto struck nothing but air. The pattern was repeated. Sean was a second ahead of it every time.

Mandy spun on Julio. "You told me he had no weapons! You said that it would be fair. You said—"

"I cannot intercede! Don't you understand? He must beat Roberto, or Roberto will not respect him."

Mandy didn't think that Roberto would ever respect anyone. No matter how this ended, he would try to stab Sean—or anyone—in the back whenever it suited his purpose.

She started walking across the sand, but Julio caught her shoulders. "What are you doing?"

"Roberto has a knife. Miguel will have me!"

"Get back here! Do you want to wind up cut?"

"I'd rather be cut," Mandy retorted vehemently, "than handed over like a trophy!"

"No!" Julio said, but she wrenched herself away from him, ignoring his gun as if it didn't exist. She didn't believe that he would shoot her.

Sean saw her coming. "Get out of here, Mandy!"

Roberto laughed, thinking to take advantage of the distraction. He lunged; Sean escaped in the nick of time. Mandy instinctively reached down for a handful of sand to throw in Roberto's eyes.

She did throw the sand, but it didn't matter. In that split second Sean had kicked Roberto's wrist, sending the switchblade flying out into the night.

Then Sean was flying, too. He threw himself against Roberto, sending the man down on his back, with Sean on top of him. He rolled Roberto over, wrenched the man's arm behind his back, then straddled him.

Mandy gasped with relief and sank onto the sand herself. She watched as Julio walked over to the two men and spoke to them, clipping out orders in a soft but furious rush of Spanish.

Mandy's fingers dug into the sand. She realized suddenly that she was touching something metallic. Her eyes fell to her fingers, and she saw that she had the knife. Her fingers curled completely around it. While the men were occupied with one another she slipped it into the pocket of her cutoffs.

Sean got back to his feet then; Julio was still talking to Roberto in scathing tones as Sean walked over to Mandy. He threaded his fingers through his hair, grinning at her, and reached down to help her to her feet.

She accepted his assistance, staring at him. "Are you—are you okay?"

His grin deepened and he shrugged. "Yeah, Ma, you should see the other guy."

She lowered her head, smiling, then allowed him to pull her to her feet. He slipped an arm around her, and they returned to the house together.

Maria was waiting in the kitchen. When she saw Sean, she gave a little cry of ecstasy and raced toward him, ignoring Mandy. Maria leaned on his free shoulder, kissing the cut there between bursts of excited concern.

Amanda eyed her with tolerant patience, raising a brow to Sean and moving away.

He set Maria away from him, speaking softly but firmly. She touched his shoulder again. "I will take care of it—"

"There is no need, Maria. It is nothing. I…" He paused, pulling Mandy back to his side. "We are going to bed."

He started walking, leading Mandy with him. She glanced back to see Maria standing there, and despite everything she felt sorry for the girl.

She and Sean seemed to share an opinion of Maria: that she was still a child, a child trying to play in a grown-up's world, no matter how lovely her face or figure.

I could be jealous, Mandy thought, and it was a disturbing idea. It was…the circumstances, she told herself. But it was more, and she knew it. Their time together had been limited, but it had also been very intense. She felt that she knew him better than people she had known for years and years. He angered her; he intrigued her. He absolutely fascinated her.

The other bedroom door opened before they reached

their own. Señora Garcia, still ashen, came out. She spoke softly to Sean, and he replied in kind. She smiled at last, nodded, then returned to the bedroom she apparently shared with Maria.

Mandy glanced back once again. Julio and Roberto still had not come in. Maria remained where she had been, though, watching them. Watching them just as tragically as Scarlett O'Hara had watched Ashley Wilkes walk into a bedroom with his Melanie.

Then she couldn't see Maria, because Sean prodded her into the bedroom. He lit the lantern before shutting the door.

Mandy stood still, feeling a little rueful, a little shy— and more than a little confused.

Sean placed the lantern by the bed, then noticed her standing there. He frowned curiously. "What's with you?"

"Thank you."

"For what?"

"You saved my life."

He shrugged, casting himself back on the mattress, locking his fingers behind his head, then gazing at her with an amused grin. "I didn't save your life. He had no intention of killing you."

"But I'd have rather died," she said softly. "And— and he might have killed you."

"I should hope not!" Sean snorted.

She walked over to the mattress and sank down beside him on her knees, then lightly ran a finger over the red scratch on his shoulder. "Shouldn't you clean it?"

He gritted his teeth and caught her hand. "It's no big deal. Just leave it alone."

She snatched her hand away, reddening. But he didn't notice; he was suddenly sitting up, playing with her torn shirt, trying to find a way to make it stay completely where it belonged.

"It's all right. Just leave it!" she snapped.

He drew his hand away, scowling. "If you walk around like that tomorrow we'll be in trouble all over again. In fact, if you hadn't flounced around today, all this might not have happened!"

"What are you talking about?" Mandy demanded furiously.

"You—in the water! Making that stupid outfit look like something from a centerfold."

"It's not *my* stupid outfit! Nobody warned me to dress for a kidnapping. And Maria didn't exactly give me the best stuff she had!"

"You could have stayed out of the water!"

"Oh, yeah? I'd like to see you locked up for hours and hours on end without going completely mad!"

He didn't have a ready answer for that one. He closed his eyes and lay back down, sighing. "I am going mad, I think," he mumbled. He kept talking in a flat monotone. "If I'd stayed locked up with you, I would be mad. And I wouldn't know anything."

Mandy hesitated a second. "What do you know?"

"Not too much," he admitted. "Juan was supposed to be back by now, but he isn't."

"Is Julio worried?"

"Not yet. He will be by tomorrow night, though. But if we're lucky, by tomorrow night we may be able to spot the Coast Guard."

Mandy moistened her lips. "What happens if Juan never makes it back? What will Julio do then?"

"Nothing," he told her.

"Nothing?"

"Stop worrying, will you? Things will break soon." She didn't answer.

"For God's sake, lie down, will you please? Get some rest. If things do move, you'll want to be alert."

She lay down beside him, not touching him, but all too aware that he was there. He didn't speak.

"He threatened to chop off one of my fingers," Mandy murmured at last. "Julio did. To send to Peter."

There was a soft sigh from beside her. "That was a threat, nothing more."

"It sounded real."

"What good is a threat if it doesn't sound real?" He sat up, leaning over to blow out the lantern.

"But—"

"Mandy, quit it! Trust me. Everything is going to work out all right. Please, go to sleep."

He flopped back down on the mattress, and the ebony darkness surrounded them once again.

There had been exasperation in his voice, and the harsh sound of his temper rising. Cast once again into a vortex of confusion, Mandy lay still and concentrated on each breath she took.

It wasn't fair; he was blaming her for things that were beyond her control. She'd tried to thank him for risking his life, but even that had annoyed him.

"I didn't ask to be here!" she snapped suddenly, whirling to face him, though she couldn't see him at all.

"I didn't say you did."

"You have an attitude about this whole thing! In fact, you're one great mass of attitudes! I have to thank you, because I couldn't have dealt with that weasel myself. But it's not my fault he's such scum, and it's not my fault I've been given such ridiculous clothes to wear."

"I—"

"You just shut up for a minute! Don't you dare blame me for anything! I didn't make you come along—that was your choice."

Silence followed her last emphatic words. He didn't move, and she wondered what his reaction would be to her sudden show of temper.

"Sean?"

He chuckled softly, and the sound touched her like a caress in the night. "Are you quite through?" he asked.

"Quite!"

"Good. I'm not blaming you for anything—except for the sleep I'm missing right now."

"Sorry," she said stiffly.

"Lie down."

"You're at it again."

"I'm not." She couldn't see his grin, but she could feel it. "I didn't tell you to take your clothes off, I just said to lie down."

"You—"

"You—" His movement was swift, startling, as he gently shushed her with a hand over her mouth. "*Querida*, go to sleep!"

Meekly she sank back onto the mattress, his touch, his voice, reducing her to quivers.

Querida...

He'd said it so softly. *Querida*...darling, loved one...

sweetheart. It wasn't just the word; it was the way he had said it, in Spanish, as if there wasn't an English word that would do justice to his meaning.

He curled up beside her, his back to her. She tried breathing again, deeply, counting each breath. She was no longer irritated, or even hurt, but she was still confused, both by him and by her own feelings. And also by the yearnings she felt in the darkness.

She tried to sleep, but she felt as if she was in the center of a maelstrom. It was of her own making, but it was there nevertheless. She heard the beat of her heart, each breath she took. And each breath that he took. She imagined that despite the space he had left between them she could hear the beat of his heart.

She couldn't sleep; she couldn't even keep her eyes closed. She felt a restless energy that defied the night, and if she closed her eyes too long, she thought of Roberto. She remembered waking up, not being able to see, yet knowing he was the one above her. She remembered feeling his hands, knew again the horror of failing in her fight against him....

She took a deep breath, then exhaled. Sean wanted to sleep, but maybe she could sit with the lantern on the other side of the room. Maybe he wouldn't mind.

Sean. She felt awareness ripple through her again, and she couldn't begin to understand herself. She should have been thinking of the million reasons why she didn't want anything to do with him. She should have been burying herself in guilt—even in pain. But none of that mattered, not tonight.

She didn't even really want the light; she wanted *him*, awake. Whispering to her, talking to her, reassuring her.

She wanted to run her fingers over the sun-browned sleekness of his chest, press soft kisses against his skin, taste the salt of the sea on his flesh....

It was dark, but she knew that she burned crimson. How could she be thinking this way? Feeling this way?

She sat up abruptly, determined to reach carefully across him for the lantern and matches. She would take the light to a corner of the room and read her book. That might distract her from the thoughts that were playing such havoc with her mind.

But when she groped her way over him the rounded curve of her breast fell against his arm, and her bare midriff collided with his naked chest. The short crisp hairs there seemed to tease her mercilessly, just as the contact of their bodies, hot despite the coolness of the night, seemed to create a kinetic energy so startling that she drew in her breath.

He caught her arm, holding her where she lay. "Mrs. Blayne, just what are you doing?"

"I was...just... I was—"

"Mrs. Blayne, please don't touch me unless you mean it."

He said it jokingly, lightly, but she knew that he wasn't teasing.

"I won't..." she began, but the words froze on her lips. "Don't touch me unless you mean it," he had said. And she had meant it with all her heart and soul and being...this night.

The midnight blackness left no room for reason or thought, for a past or for a future. All she knew was that she wanted him. Wanted to touch him. To be touched. To go wherever touching might lead them.

She leaned over him, pressing her lips against the hollow of his shoulder, holding them there for a fervent moment, then pushing the tip of her tongue between them, tasting his flesh, closing her eyes at the sleek salt sensation, savoring the elusive liquid quivering that burst and streaked through her like dancing stars. Savoring his gasp, the catch of his breath, the shudder that racked him.

"Hey!" He clutched her shoulders harshly, wrenching her high above him. Even in the night she could see the glitter of his eyes. His muscles were taut, his whisper harsh.

"I said—" he swallowed sharply and continued through clenched teeth "—not to touch me unless—"

"I mean it," she interrupted him abruptly, her voice as harsh as his. She didn't want to talk about it; she didn't want to be warned. She wanted to be held. She wanted to make love. To feel the world spiraling around her, to arch and writhe and roll in sensual splendor and temptation.

Still he only held her.

She tried to whisper to him, but sound eluded her.

And then it didn't really matter, because he lowered her against him, slowly, until their bodies touched completely, her length on his, legs tangling, her breasts hard against his chest, their mouths not an inch apart.

Then touching.

Perhaps he was still distrustful; perhaps he had a reason to be so. He held her shoulders when he first kissed her, just touching her lips, then pulling away. Then he touched them once again, curiously, questingly. He tasted them next, his tongue an exotic paintbrush that swirled across them like sable. He traced the shape of her mouth, then pressed his lips against her shoulder.

And then it was as if he gave up all thought of reason. Of sanity. Of the past. Of the future.

His arms wrapped strongly around her; his lips were hard against hers, almost bruising in their sudden passion. His tongue made an intimate invasion, demanding total entrance, total surrender, bending the night magic of her body solely to his will, throwing her heart to the four winds of chance.

He held her in his arms and rolled with her, sweeping her beneath him, and the magic continued. His body against hers felt incredibly good, right, as if they had been made not just as man and woman, but as this man meant specifically for this woman, this woman meant just for this man. His body seemed to meld to hers, a fusion of heat, of fire. Like flint to stone they sparked, drew away, then sparked again…and ignited. It was a blaze she never wanted to put out….

He drove his fingers through her hair, holding her still to meet his kiss. He cupped and massaged her skull, cherished the richness of her hair. She stroked his nape and then his back, skimming lightly over his spine with her nails. And she thrilled to the pressure of his hips against hers, his desire evident.

He broke the kiss, easing away from her, longing with all his heart to see her. To see the color of her hair. To watch her as he touched her, stripped her… slowly, relishing each new bit of golden flesh revealed to his gaze.

Rolling closer to her, he ran his fingers over her cheek, then kissed her again with slow fascination and let his hands roam, exploring the roundness of her breast, soft and yet firm, the nipples taut beneath the thin cotton material. Just thinking of them, he felt an inner combustion. Now. He had to have her now....

But he forced himself to stay under control. He stroked her naked ribs before seeking out the tie of the halter top, gently undoing it, letting the material fall aside. Urgency claimed him again, hot and strident, as her naked breasts fell freely into his hands, taunted his palms. He lowered his head to her, drawing a pattern with his tongue in the deep valley between her breasts, then feeling the splendor of imagination obliterated in the magic of truth as he savored her with his lips, the gentle tender grazing of his teeth.

He felt dizzy with desire. He moved his hands against her, fingers slipping beneath the waistband of her cutoffs, dipping low upon her abdomen, then nearly yanking at the snap and zipper. She issued a soft little cry, and he kissed her to silence her, the motion of his hands edging the cutoffs lower and lower.

And then it was he who cried out, an oath of impatience, and he moved away from her, grasping the tattered hems of the cutoffs, easing them down the wickedly lovely length of her legs.

He wanted the light. He wanted to see her: the glorious fan of sunlight and wheaten hair; the shimmering desire in her eyes; her features taut with passion. The rise of her breasts; the dip of her belly. Her back; the curves of her buttocks. He wanted to see all of her.

He started to move off the mattress, and she realized his intent. Crying out softly, she rose to meet him, grasping his shoulders, burying her head against his neck and seductively pressing her breasts against him.

"No! Please."

"I was just going to light the lamp."

"No. No light. Let it be darkness. Let it be magic."

He should refuse. He should tell her that there could be magic in the light. He should not allow her to make love in the darkness.

Done in the darkness, in the ebony night, it would not be real. It would not exist in the morning's light.

"Please, Sean. Please."

Her whisper, her breath against his flesh, stirred the blaze of his near-desperate passion once again. He couldn't refuse her anything.

Kneeling, they moved together. Kneeling, he felt the exquisite femininity of her body, touched so thoroughly by his own. He kissed her, explored her and forced her back at last, pressing her down upon her stomach.

He couldn't see her; he had to know her. He pressed his mouth against the small of her back, against her spine. Lust burned raw inside of him. It was torture; it was delicious.

All along her spine he kissed her, moving his hands down over her buttocks, down her legs, knowing their shape. Down to her feet, and even there he played, kissing her toes, stroking the soles of her feet, massaging them. She arched; she moaned softly; she made little inarticulate sounds. Dear God, he wanted to see her! He smiled a little grimly, even a little maliciously, for the movements of her body cried to his, though she choked back her cries of arousal, of readiness.

He had no intention of being had so easily.

When his fingers left her feet they stroked, slowly, excruciatingly slowly, to her inner thighs, urging them apart, finding she had no strength for denial.

He rolled her over. She was as pliable as a kitten, as passionate as a tigress as she reached for him, whispering incoherently for him to stop, to come to her.

"Not yet," he whispered against her lips. He waited there, above her, as his fingers played between her legs, as she gasped and arched against him, holding him, pushing him away, trying to touch him in turn.

Her nails scratched lightly over his chest, explored his back, tried to dip beneath the waistband of his cutoffs and met with frustration. She tugged at the button and the zipper with trembling fingers and found frustration again. They would not give for her. And again for him it was agony…and it was ecstasy.

He kissed her, his tongue delving deeply into her mouth. And then he whispered of the wonder of her body, and what it was doing, whispered with his lips just half an inch from her mouth until she thought she would go mad.

"Sean!"

"What?"

"Take—take your clothes off."

"Aha! I told you that you would get to it eventually. All women are alike!"

"Sean…"

"Mandy, I'd strip for you anytime. In private, of course."

She half giggled, half sobbed.

And he thought that if he waited any longer he would explode, and they would have to pick up the pieces of what had once been a man. In seconds he had obliged her, tossing his cutoffs somewhere into the magical black arena surrounding them, returning to her with the full strength of his desire evident.

She touched him, and his impatience soared. He held her face with his hands, spread her thighs with his knees, kissed her deeply and entered her deeply.

The black magic of the night swirled around them. At first the tempo of their loving was slow, then frenetic. Kisses, caresses and the spiraling maelstrom of desire set them apart from the world. This was passion, born in the darkness, bred by fear and sensation, gratitude and natural hunger. And something more....

He had to be mad. He was lost within her. Lost in the welcoming embrace of her body, shuddering with sensation, volatile, ecstatic, as he had never been before. Touching her inside and out, knowing her, caressing her, reaching the pinnacle together, holding each other, drifting.

It was passion only, he told himself.

Strange. When he touched her damp brow, when she curled against him, when the curve of her breast so comfortably touched his chest and her slender leg was cast so trustingly over his...

It was passion.

Yet it felt ridiculously as if he were falling in love.

Chapter 9

When Sean awoke, it was barely dawn with just the palest filtering of pink light entering the room. He could make out Mandy's huddled form, curled so trustingly against him, lips slightly parted as she breathed, her lashes falling against her cheeks, her hair falling over her shoulders—and his own.

He eased away from her and carefully pulled the covers to her shoulders. He wanted to hold her, to glory in her all over again, but the shield of darkness was gone, and he knew innately that she had been his only because of that darkness.

Sean rose silently and donned his cutoffs. He needed to be alone. He crept quietly from the room, closing the door tightly behind him.

Julio, on a mat outside the door, was awake, watching him, the ever-present Magnum at his side.

"I'm just going down to the beach," Sean said.

Julio nodded and lay back down on the mat. Sean continued on out the kitchen door. No one was really awake yet. No one but him.

He was glad. There was no time here like the breaking of the dawn. No time when the heavens appeared more magenta, no time when the coming sun kissed the sand more gently. A breeze stirred the trees and the rippling water.

He walked over the soft dunes and neared the water, listening to the soft rush of the tide, gazing at the glittering droplets caught and dazzled by the coming sun. Again the irony of it all struck him. Here, in this incredible Eden, they were prisoners. It should have been a place of freedom. No crime should touch this shore, only laughter and tenderness and…passion.

They should have made love beneath the stars, not on a shabby mattress inside a primitive cabin in the dark. This was a place of exquisite loveliness; it should have remained unsoiled.

Sean sat down and wrapped his arms around his knees.

So many things in his life had been beautiful, he thought.

Havana had been beautiful. Once upon a time it had been a fantastic city, a playground for the rich and famous. There had been dancing and music, beautiful women, poets and musicians, artisans and scholars. The warm Caribbean breezes had touched the patios of homes and nightclubs; the palms had swayed; the air had been touched by perfume.

Once upon a time…

He had been only six the last time he had seen Havana, but as long as he lived he would never forget that night.

Revolution had been brewing for a long time. The old men at the cafés had talked about it; the young men had shouted about it. Batista had been a dictator, and it was very true that the poor had suffered beneath him. Yes, revolution had been brewing. His father simply had not seen it clearly enough.

As a six-year-old Sean had adored both his parents. They'd met in New York City, where his mother had been a model and his father had been selling superior Havana cigars. They had fiery tempers, but totally different cultural backgrounds. Love had always been the tie that bound the two of them. It had been imperative that they learn about each other's cultures to appreciate and understand each other. Consequently, Sean had been born in Dublin, beneath the benign eyes of his maternal grandparents.

And consequently they had been in Havana on the night the gunfire began.

He could remember it all so clearly. December, but a hot night. His father had been downstairs on the patio, talking with a few cronies. His mother had been in the kitchen, humming, fixing rum punches for their company. Sean had been sitting at the kitchen table, laboriously practicing his handwriting.

And then it had started, a rat-tat-tatting somewhere down the street, so soft that they had ignored it at first. But then there had been screams, and his father, such a handsome man with his flashing dark eyes and lean whipcord physique, had come dashing up the stairs.

He'd shouted that they must go, that they must get to the airport. Sean could remember his mother bursting into tears when it became clear that his father was not going to join them.

"You're an American, too! You're an American citizen! This is not your—"

"I am an American, but I am also Cuban. Siobhan, go, now, for my son's sake! I will meet you in the States. I will meet you!"

And so they ran. His father's friend, Xavier, got them through the streets. Streets littered here and there with bodies. With soldiers, with revolutionaries. With the injured, with the dying. Streets that seemed alive with screaming.

At one point, they'd been stopped—by a looter, of all things on such a night. His mother had been held while he, a child, had struggled ineffectually. That had been when he decided he would never be helpless again.

With the pure fury of a child he had escaped the man holding him and bitten the man attacking his mother, giving Xavier the chance to wrest the gun from the man. Xavier had killed him, and their mad dash for freedom had continued.

They'd reached the embassy—and they'd gotten out.

But he'd never seen his father again, nor Xavier. They'd settled in Miami, where his mother had spent the next ten years of her life waiting for news of his father. When it came, it was bad. He had been shot that night. He had died with the revolution.

Adjusting to life in Miami had been hard. Sean spoke Spanish fluently, but his English had an Irish accent, and all the kids had made fun of him. Nobody had cared much what you sounded like in New York, because New York had been full of all kinds of people. But not Miami—not then.

Cubans began entering the city in droves, escaping to freedom. The federal government helped them, which led to resentment. Sean's life became ever harder. No one could understand a Cuban boy named Sean who had an Irish mother.

Somewhere along the line—the third grade?—he'd created a new world for himself. He started telling his schoolmates that Ramiro was Castilian, that his mother had married his father in Madrid.

Then his mother found out about the story. She'd gone as white as paste and started to cry in a way that tore his insides all to pieces. "Sean! How could you? How could you deny your father?"

That had been the last time he had ever done so. He had gone to his mother, and they had cried together. When he went to bed that night all he could think about was his father, his laughter, his temper, his total devotion to his wife—and to his son. His love for the world at large and for his own heritage.

From that moment on he was proud of what he was. Irish, Cuban—and American. American all the way.

And naturally, as time passed, things evened out. In high school half his classmates were various forms of Anglo, half were various forms of Latino. He played football with a natural ability, and by his junior year that made him incredibly popular.

He went to college in Nebraska on a football scholarship. He liked Nebraska, but not as much as home. And though he earned a law degree, he didn't want to practice. He wanted to be a cop. He'd wanted to be one ever since that night in Havana, when he had learned that law and order were precious commodities.

Then, when he'd first come home, he'd fallen in love. Her name was Sandra Johnson, and she had been beautiful. Blond and blue-eyed and blue-blooded all the way. They'd met at a nightclub and fallen in love to a John Denver tune, slow dancing beneath the colored lights. All he'd really known about her was that she worked in her family's business as a receptionist. That seemed to be all he needed to know at the time. They met every night. They made love on what seemed like every beach in the state.

She was passionate, lovely, and everything he had ever desired.

But on a cool September night, when he was twenty-four and thought that he owned the world, he had received a blow that nearly destroyed him.

She met him that night, tremendously nervous, teary-eyed, anxious and excited. She blurted out instantly that she was pregnant, then awaited his reaction.

He was thrilled. A home and a family. He was ready for them both. A child, his father's grandchild, to hold and love and nurture—and to whom to give the world, just as his parents had given it to him. America, with all its merging fascinating cultures.

He'd held her tenderly, and they'd planned their life. They would look into the nice new town houses on Miller Road, and they would be married in St. Theresa's. His pay wasn't great, but it was sufficient.

Sandra had been starry-eyed then, as happy as a lark. They had to meet each other's parents, of course. Sean knew that his mother would love Sandra. And by this time in his life he could see no reason why the Johnsons wouldn't like him.

He arrived at their house neatly suited. He was somewhat stunned by the mansion on the water, but he hadn't come from poverty. His mother had done well modeling, and his father's investments had all been in the U.S. His mom had a wonderful old home in Miami Shores. And if anyone was "class," it was Siobhan Ramiro.

But not to the Johnsons.

When the maid led him into the elegant receiving room Sandra was nowhere in sight. Only her mother and father were there, greeting him politely but informing him that Sandra was gone.

Where? he had demanded, confused.

And then it had all come out. They were terribly sorry, but didn't he understand that they were "the" Lockwood Johnsons; they couldn't possibly allow their daughter to marry a—a refugee.

Lockwood Johnson went on to say coolly that the baby had already been aborted.

Well, he—a cop—had gotten arrested that night. His temper—Irish, Cuban or all-American—had soared to a point where he had seen nothing but red, and he'd charged Lockwood Johnson with all the fury he had learned on the football field.

Johnson had probably expected something along those lines. He'd whistled, and four bodyguards had come rushing in. Even then, it had taken them fifteen minutes to wrestle him down.

He could still remember Mrs. Johnson murmuring

something about the behavior of "riffraff," but all he really knew was that he had woken up in a jail cell.

All he could think at the time was that the Johnsons were the ones who deserved to be in jail. They'd murdered his child; they'd taken a piece of his heart.

Logically, he had known that they represented an extreme. His friends, his best friends, his co-workers, all came in mixed nationalities. Half the Cuban girls he knew had married Anglo men, and vice versa. Of course there were still cultural differences. Some people resented those who spoke Spanish; some thought it was good to know two languages. Things didn't change that quickly. But people were people, and friendships formed where they would, as did love—when it was allowed.

He had decided then that he wouldn't fall in love again. Especially not with a blonde.

So what the hell was he doing now? It was ridiculous; it was impossible. He should be staying as far away as he could from Mrs. Amanda—Anglo—Blayne.

He closed his eyes tightly then opened them to the lightening sky. He realized that he was clenching his fists so tightly that his nails were cutting into his palms.

He wasn't in love, he told himself dully. This whole thing was nothing more than circumstance. He had known her only a few days, and she'd turned to him only because she was frightened and lonely. She'd turned to him in the dark, hiding.

He straightened his shoulders. God! If they could just get off of this damned island!

He tried to bring himself under control, but anger filled him. He reminded himself that under no circumstances could he risk her life, yet he was ready to run headfirst into Roberto, just to end it all. Last night had been ecstasy; this morning was hell.

"Sean?"

He turned around and saw her standing there. All blonde and all beautiful. Thin and lithe and curved, and yet suddenly so Anglo that he wanted to scream. Her face was so perfect: tawny eyes alive above the high Anglo cheekbones. He couldn't read her expression; she seemed a little pale beneath her tan. She carried two cups of coffee and pressed one toward him.

He accepted, and found himself staring at her legs. Long legs, slimly muscled. He thought about the way they had wrapped around him, and he felt dizzy once again.

Good God, he wanted her. With all the heat and tempest and passion inside him, he wanted her. Right here, on the beach. He wanted Julio and Roberto and even Mama Garcia and Maria to drop dead, to fall into a hole. He wanted her naked beneath him on the white sand, far away from society. Far from a nightmare that he had forgotten, far from a place where an unborn child could be killed because of his heritage.

She laughed softly, just a little bit nervously. "Aren't you going to ask me to sit down?"

"No. Thanks for the coffee. Go away. What are you doing out here, anyway?" He scowled, staring back toward the water. He felt her stiffen and knew it was for the best. He didn't have any difficulty being friends with beautiful Anglos, or with dating them, or with going to bed with them, for that matter.

Just falling in love with them.

"I just walked out with the coffee. No one stopped me."

"Well, walk somewhere else."

She told him exactly what he should do with himself and turned on her heel.

Where the hell was the damned FBI? he wondered. One lousy little kidnapping and they hadn't appeared yet! They had a lot of nerve calling the cops yokels!

She walked away, not back to the house, but down the beach. He felt as if part of him had frozen over.

He turned slightly. Roberto was outside now, sitting near the door, training his damn Magnum on Amanda.

Sean looked back in her direction. She had finished her coffee and thrown herself into the surf.

For a long while he just sat there, watching her swim. Then she stood, wringing her hair out. Her ribs were bare, gleaming with water. The torn halter she had somehow mended was clinging to her breasts like a second skin. The cutoffs were doing little better at her hips.

Sean twisted slightly to see Roberto watching her, leering. Sean stood and marched down the beach. With no thought whatsoever, his temper soaring toward red again, he strode through the shallows to reach her, then grasped her shoulders, shaking her.

"Let me go, you animal!" she snapped. Her beautiful tawny eyes were red-rimmed. From the salt water? Or had she been crying?

He started to soften.

"I mean it! Get your filthy hands off me!"

He released her. Just like that.

"You liked my filthy hands well enough last night," he sneered.

"That was last night," she said coolly.

"Good. Because if you keep on the way you're going,

it's not going to be my filthy hands on you—it will be Roberto's. And if you think I'll battle it out for you again, lady, you'd better think again."

He turned around and walked away from her.

By the time he reached the house Señora Garcia and Maria were outside. Maria had on a cute-little-nothing bikini. Accomplice to a kidnapping or not, Maria knew how to dress. She headed down to the water.

And at that moment Sean felt like speaking Spanish. He noticed that Amanda had stretched out facedown on the sand, a good distance away from them all. He strode back into the surf. Maria was just a kid, but right now he felt like nothing so much as playing kids' games in the water with her.

It was the longest day Mandy had ever experienced in her life.

When she awoke she was glad of the solitude he had given her. Though she was bundled in the covers, she felt her nudity acutely. Her nudity, and her body. Muscles that had been unused for a long time were delightfully sore. She felt guilt and she felt shame, yet she felt like a cat at the same time, wonderfully stroked and petted and loved.

Tears came to her eyes because it had been so good. Because he had been so tender and gentle and so wonderfully savage at just the right moment. Because she couldn't remember lovemaking being such a vivid experience, and because that made her feel guilty all over again, because she had loved her husband so much.

Yet even then, amid the guilt and shame, she had been all too aware of the forbidden knowledge that he had the power to ease the past, if not erase it. He was so powerful and fascinating that she savored the thought of him, just as her body savored the memory of his. His scent was still with her, as were the memories of his arms, of the way he felt inside her.

They were captives on an island, forced together, she reminded herself. It was a nightmare, and please God, it would end, and they would go their separate ways, back to the lives they had led before this one. And yet...

She had to see him. To talk to him. To admit that she was afraid of the light, but that she wasn't denying anything. She needed to touch him again, to know that his arms were still there—for now, at least. She needed to tell him how much she cared about him, how much she appreciated him, how much...she was fascinated by him.

It was almost like falling in love.

And so she had dressed, only to find her halter still ripped. She had stepped out of the room holding the shirt in place. Señora Garcia had clucked disapprovingly, then given her a needle and thread, and she had mended the halter. Then Señora Garcia had given her coffee, and she had hurried out to the beach, anxious to see Sean again.

She had received only the most horrible slap in the face, and it had hurt so badly that she had found herself awash with pain and confusion. The only way to rid herself of them had been to dive into the water.

Then he had touched her again, and she had felt such waves of shimmering heat, of anger, wash over her that she had been stunned all over again.

What had she done but make love with him?

She spent the morning lying in the sun; he spent it playing with Maria. Damn him. Cradle robber. What the hell did she care? She had been an idiot, and that was that.

So why in God's name was it tearing her to pieces? She should be worrying about her physical well-being. Juan wasn't back yet. When was Julio going to start snipping off her fingers?

A feminine voice started to chide her in Spanish. Mandy rolled over to find Señora Garcia standing beside her with a plate of food. She shook her head; she wasn't hungry.

Señora Garcia sighed, unhappily plumped her full figure down on the sand and pressed the plate into Mandy's hands.

Mandy ate resignedly. Lunch was a thin steak with rice and black beans, deliciously cooked. She ate everything on the plate, while Señora Garcia smiled at her.

At one point the older woman disappeared, then returned with a Coca-Cola. Mandy thanked her again and enjoyed the soda. The next time Señora Garcia left her, she didn't return.

Bored, and increasingly anxious and upset despite her determination not to be, Mandy took off for the water again. She swam and swam—and suddenly bumped into another body. Hands righted her, and she found herself staring into Roberto's dark eyes.

He laughed and gave her a mocking sneer. She kicked away from him swimming strenuously in the opposite direction, only to collide with another body.

Sean.

He pulled her back against his chest, but he didn't

look at her. Instead he stared over her head at Roberto, who shrugged, then swam away.

Still Sean didn't release her shoulders. The water was cool, but she could feel his body heat like an inferno. She could feel his body, every part of it, pressed against her.

She was furious; she wanted to jerk away from him. At the same time she felt as if all his heat was seeping into her, turning her muscles to liquid. Making her wish ridiculously that they were longtime friends and lovers. That they could laugh like guilty children, that under the cover of water they could shed their cutoffs and fit together....

Roberto swam toward Maria. Señora Garcia had gone back into the house. Only Julio was on the shore, leaning against the house.

It might have been a scene from a resort brochure—except for the Magnum that Julio was holding.

Mandy wanted to break the silence, to tell Sean that she hated him, that she wanted him to get away from her—now! But his whisper touched her ear, soft, silky, sensual. So raspy and exciting that her mind might have been swept completely clear of all thought, except for... except for that all-encompassing excitement. It raced through her; it took control of her.

"Don't move," he implored raggedly. "Don't move at all."

His arms tightened around her as he started backing into deeper water. She was weightless; her feet didn't touch the sand. She just drifted along with him, his arms around her keeping her hips level with his.

And then they were in deeper water. So cool, when

they were so hot. She didn't move; she didn't try to speak. His hands moved slightly, cupping her breasts, his thumbs grazing her nipples. A sound caught in her throat as he pressed his lips against her neck.

Then he moved so deftly that she was filled all over again with a quaking desire that was so physical it overrode even the sensation of the sun. She felt his hand near her midriff, and then his fingers were sweeping beneath the waistband of her cutoffs before sliding the zipper down. The pressure of his palm against her abdomen made her breath come too quickly, made her heart race. She thought that she was mad, then she felt that she had reached the clouds, because his mind held the same thought as hers. That simple touch, body to body, had brought this. The need...the desire...despite all else... It seemed somehow illicit, and therefore all the more fascinating. She should have been shocked; she should have hated him; she should have turned him away—she should have been screaming bloody murder.

And instead she couldn't wait to feel him inside her.

Her cutoffs fell, but he caught them. Beneath the water she was nude. He wrapped one arm around her waist and let his free hand play over her buttocks. Then, swiftly, he lifted her until her legs locked around his hips.

She couldn't stare into his eyes, so she rested her head against his shoulder. She stifled the cry that rose to her lips when he thrust into her, pressing her teeth lightly into his flesh.

"Look at me!" he warned her harshly. "Laugh, as if we're talking."

"I—I can't!" she gasped.

He was filling her. She burned; she ached; she needed more.

"Mandy…do it. Oh, Mandy."

He jerked, forcing her head back, forcing her to lace her fingers behind his neck and stare into his eyes. His smile was so wicked that once again it was as if the fact that they could get caught made every motion more thrilling. The friction of the water, the wonder of him, the pulsing of tension rose in her swiftly. Wonderfully. Suddenly she knew that she was going to burst, and that she would scream with the joy of it all.

But she didn't. He caught her lips in a kiss, and her animal cry of awe and shuddering satiation was caught between them. He held her tight, moving hard against her one last time, a part of her. She went lax, incapable of movement in the aftermath. Thank God he held her. Thank God that he groaned softly, crushing her against him. She couldn't have stood; she might well have drowned in reality, rather than just drowning in his arms.

The water rippled around them and actually began to grow cold.

"You've got to get these back on," he told her huskily.

"I can't move."

"You have to."

"You got them off, you get them back on."

She was so drowsy; his answering chuckle was so husky. She wanted to forget everything. She wanted to remain against his shoulder and fall asleep.

"All right," he said agreeably.

And then he let her go and dove beneath the water. But what he did to her there had nothing to do with getting her pants back on, and everything to do with getting her excited again. She started to protest, swallowed water, then wrenched the cutoffs back from him and struggled back into them.

When she finished, he was still laughing. "Not fair!" she cried.

Suddenly he wasn't laughing anymore. He pulled her close to him, against his heart. His whisper touched her ear. "I'm sorry. Do you forgive me?"

"I guess I just did."

"No, that was sex, not forgiveness. Do you forgive me?"

She couldn't say anything. She didn't know if she did or didn't; she just knew that she didn't want him to let her go.

"Damn it, Julio is waving that stinking gun of his around. Come on. We've got to go in. Night must be coming."

It was. And with the night came a horrendous argument between Julio and Roberto.

Mandy didn't understand any of it; it was all in Spanish. She was in the kitchen when it began, eating a sausage sandwich for dinner. Señora Garcia decided that Mandy shouldn't be a part of it. She hurried Mandy into her room, made her wait, then returned with shampoo and soap. Mandy knew that though her suggestion that Mandy might want a shower seemed casual, the older woman was very upset.

It also frightened her that Sean had seemed upset by the argument. He hadn't protested at all when Señora Garcia led Mandy out. He had remained at the table, listening tensely.

Mandy ambled restlessly around the room for a while as the argument went on. Finally she decided that she would take a shower; it would kill time.

When she came back into the bedroom Sean was there, lying under the blanket on the mattress, eyes open, staring up at the ceiling. He turned to her quickly, though, and flashed her a smile in the lantern light.

"What—?" she began.

But he didn't let her finish. He sprang up and she saw that he was naked. He walked quickly to her, then began unwinding the towel from her body. And then he began to kiss her shoulders, breasts, ribs.

She caught his shoulders. "Sean, wait. What—what was that all about? What's going on?"

"Later," he murmured.

His hands were on her hips, his lips pressed to her belly. His breath was against her flesh, and her flesh was responding.

She dug her fingers into his hair. "Sean..."

He nudged her legs farther apart, and his mouth rubbed over her until she thought she would fall.

She forgot the question she had asked. She forgot everything. She gasped and hung on to his hair, because she had to remain standing.

She came near to weeping, so vital was the sensation. She twisted and whimpered and gave herself gloriously to him. And only then did he stand to collect her weak form, carry her to the mattress and find his own reward.

The wonderful heat of the night wrapped itself around Mandy so completely that the island might in truth have been their own. Yet finally, when they had lain quietly together for some time, Sean turned to her, smoothing back her still-damp hair.

"We have to do something—tomorrow morning."

Her heart pitched and thudded; reality cut her like a knife. "Why? What happened?"

"Juan hasn't returned. Roberto thinks that he's been caught. He wants to take the skiff out tomorrow and go back."

In the darkness Mandy frowned. "I don't understand."

Sean hesitated for a long time.

"He wants to take one of your fingers with him. He called Julio a coward with no convictions and told him that his father will die in prison."

"Oh, God!" Mandy gasped.

Sean's fingers grabbed painfully at her hair. "You are to do nothing! Do you understand? Stay in here when you find me gone. Don't move, and I mean it. I won't be able to follow through with my plan if I have to worry about you, too. I mean it! Now go to sleep."

"Go to sleep?"

"Yes!"

She would never sleep. And that night she didn't.

Chapter 10

Sean didn't sleep, either; he lay awake, forming his plan.

There were certain things he had learned, and certain things that he had been taught. Individual heroics were seldom a part of police work. Shoot-outs were not day-to-day occurrences; not even the narcotics department ran around with their guns constantly blazing.

The basics of the job were to do your damnedest to see that the victim wasn't hurt in a hostage situation. If this had been a normal kidnapping, if Amanda had been stashed somewhere in the city without a resident cop, he and his partner and the team set up to investigate would have worked with the FBI, since kidnapping was a federal offense. As it was, he hadn't done any of the normal things. No paperwork in triplicate. No hours in his cubicle on the fifth floor. No arguments with the FBI.

But then, this situation was one in a million. He'd gotten to swim in the surf with a beautiful blond bombshell. What a lark. He'd even made love to her. God, wouldn't the guys at the station be green with envy?

Yeah, oh, yeah. Except that, like some green idiot, he'd gone and gotten involved. It couldn't last; it couldn't be. He and Miss DAR just weren't cut out to make a go of things.

But face it, he had a chip on his shoulder. And she didn't deserve his anger. So until she was taken away from him, for more reasons than one, she was his, and they would touch one hair on her head only over his dead body.

No joke there, he warned himself. So far he'd played the lackey because every fool knew what one bullet from a .357 Magnum could do to the human body. If one entered his body, there wouldn't be a prayer in hell that he could ever do anything for her again. But now...

Damn the FBI! They should have been here by now.

Divide and conquer—the saying was as old as time, but as true. He had to surprise one of them, get the gun and, if necessary, shoot the other.

Despite it all, he didn't hate Julio Garcia. Julio was just a dreamer, out of sync with the times, believing that he could change the world. This wasn't the way to do it, but Julio was no desperado. Sean just didn't know how far he would go.

Still, Julio would be the one he had to disarm. It would be risky, but it had to be done. Roberto was a hard-core criminal. He would slice off Mandy's finger without a second thought. Given half an opportunity, he would have raped her until she was half-dead—with no thought whatsoever.

Sean didn't think that Señora Garcia would interfere. She seemed to know that her son was diving straight for jail. She would just wait stoically for him.

And Maria? Maria was the long shot. Given a chance, she might well be dangerous. But then, she wouldn't want any of her precious beauty destroyed, either.

"Sean?"

Mandy whispered his name softly with the coming of morning, touching his arm, well aware that he was awake.

He shook her hand off. The last thing he wanted now was her touch. He couldn't waver; he couldn't think of her. He touched a finger to her lips in the darkness. "No words, no movement, no sound! Do you hear me?"

"Hey, it's my finger they're after!"

"Shut up. I mean it! Do you want to get me killed?" he asked angrily.

He thought he saw her eyes flash, even in the darkness. "No! I'd rather kill you myself!"

He chuckled softly, squeezed her hand and groped for his cutoffs. Then he stood quickly before she could say anything else and headed for the door.

As he'd expected, both Julio and Roberto were sleeping on mats outside the door. Roberto stirred slightly, gazing at Sean with wary contempt. Then Julio roused himself, so Roberto went back to sleep.

It was curious that Julio followed Sean so quickly, but it was to his advantage, and Sean was glad. He didn't look back, just hunched his shoulders instinctively and walked out the kitchen door and toward the beach. He paused just before the surf.

"You're upset, my friend?" Julio inquired from behind.

Sean shrugged, needing to get him to come closer.

"She won't be hurt, not really. She'll survive. What is one little finger, eh? They must know that I mean business."

Sean kept looking out to sea. "One little finger? Julio, I ask you, what is one little finger to you? And think about this—what if they catch you? So far you haven't hurt her. Perhaps she'll testify in your defense. She likes you."

Julio made an ugly sound. "The Americana testify for me? No, I do not think so. Her husband will not let an innocent man go free. Why should she bother with a guilty one?"

"Don't maim her, Julio."

"What? Maim?" Julio asked with annoyance, moving closer. "Will I touch her eyes? Her hair? Her legs? The things you cherish? I will leave plenty to love. It will one day be a brand of her courage for her."

"She'll probably die out here!" Sean replied bitterly. "Your dirty knives will give her tetanus. She'll bleed to death."

"Men have survived far worse things."

Julio was there—right where Sean wanted him. He never got a chance to say anything more. Sean smashed his elbow into Julio's ribs with such force that the man doubled over, unable to do more than gasp for breath.

Sean couldn't afford to show him any mercy. He

brought his knee up into Julio's chin, sending him keeling over backward.

The Magnum fell into the sand without a shot being fired, nothing but harmless metal.

Sean scooped it up and tucked it into his pants, then reached down to Julio. "Sorry, *amigo*, but you're not touching her finger."

Julio, his mouth bloodied, still unable to stand without clutching his middle, grasped Sean's hand and stared at him heatedly. "Roberto was right!" he gasped. "I should have killed you at the very beginning."

"I think you've got a few broken ribs," Sean said flatly.

"I will scream. I will shout that Roberto should kill her."

"You don't want her dead, and you know it. Nor do you want to face a murder charge. Besides, I don't think you could shout that loud right now."

Julio winced, and Sean knew that his ribs were hurting him. "Let's go," he said. "To the door. You will call to Roberto to come outside. You will not sound alarmed, or I will put a bullet through your eyes. Got it?"

Morosely, Julio let himself be dragged back to the door of the shack.

"Do it!" Sean demanded, shaking him.

"All right! All right!" He hesitated just a second longer, then called, "Roberto! Roberto! *Ven aquí!*"

They waited, Sean using Julio as his shield. He listened, and he heard footsteps. The door opened, and though Julio had not sounded alarmed, Roberto was wary. He looked around the corner of the door—and instantly took a shot at Sean.

Sean ducked his head without a second to spare. He fired a quick shot back; he had no other choice.

He winced as he heard Roberto scream. That was followed by another scream, then another. Maria was up, along with Señora Garcia, and everyone was screaming.

Sean shoved Julio ahead of him once again and entered the cabin, searching for Roberto.

The man was on the ground, slumped against the wall, a trail of blood trickling down the wood. Sean saw that only his arm had been hit, but blood was spouting everywhere.

Roberto was keening with pain. Maria was standing by the back door, arms up, shaking and screaming hysterically. Señora Garcia just stood there, white-faced.

Sean inclined his head toward the wounded man. "Tend to him," he said briefly, then he carefully reached over Roberto to retrieve the other gun.

He barely noticed when Maria disappeared back into her room. He ordered Julio to sit beside his wounded friend.

"You've killed him," Julio said reproachfully.

"I have not. He'll live."

"What are you?" Julio demanded, narrowing his eyes. "You're no gardener."

Sean sighed. "I'm Lieutenant Ramiro, Homicide Division."

"Eh, Roberto, his name was real at least, eh?" Julio tried to joke to the still-suffering man. Señora Garcia was bending over him by then, trying to do something with the wound.

"Drop it—*cop!*"

His eyes shot immediately to Maria, who was holding a small Smith and Wesson with a pearl handle. He trained the Magnum on her in return. "Sweetie, you're not going to use that. Drop it."

Maria smiled and raised the muzzle just above his head, letting off a shot that splintered wood.

"Don't bet on that, lieutenant," she said calmly, adding a very explicit threat in Spanish.

He was just about to call her bluff and fire back when the other bedroom door suddenly flew open, and there was Amanda Blayne, in all her blond glory and rage. To Sean's astonishment she was wielding a switchblade, which she instantly pressed into the small of Maria's back.

"You drop it, brat. I've just about had it with you!"

As meekly as a lamb, Maria dropped her gun.

"Get it!" Sean warned Amanda, and she instantly did so. "You two—Julio, Maria—into the bedroom. *Señora*, can you help Roberto?"

Señora Garcia looked imploringly at Sean. "He needs treatment. He needs medicine," she begged in Spanish.

"I'm sorry. He should have thought of that before he shot at me."

When they had all been hustled into the bedroom that he had shared with Mandy—Mrs. Blayne, he had to start thinking of her that way again—he stood in the doorway and formally placed them all under arrest, reciting their rights. Although, if this was the Bahamas, they would have to go through it all over again, since he didn't have any jurisdiction here. Still, he wanted to play it safe.

Just as he was locking and bolting the door, Amanda

started speaking excitedly. "Sean! The boat—Julio's boat—it's returning!"

Sean raced back to her and stared out the window. He turned to look at her. "I thought I told you to stay in the bedroom and not make a sound?"

Her huge tawny eyes met his. "You needed me!"

"I had the situation under control."

"Hmph!" Amanda sniffed indelicately. "She wanted to shoot…a certain part of your anatomy off! I rather thought you might miss it."

"I thought you didn't understand Spanish?"

"I've picked up a few words here and there."

"All the good ones, huh?"

"Sean, the boat!"

"Ah, yes."

"Well?"

He shrugged. "It could be Juan. Or it could be Juan and the Bahamian authorities and the FBI." He stared at her thoughtfully for a minute. "One way or the other, Mrs. Blayne, you'll be able to go home. Aren't you glad?"

"Of course. Aren't you?"

"Absolutely. I've got tons of paperwork waiting for me." He watched her speculatively a second longer, then stared back out the window. "As I said, it could be Juan. Or it could be Juan and the authorities. We have to find out. I'm going out. He won't be surprised to see me on the beach. You stay here. If anyone puts their face out that door—though the bolt should hold—shoot. Don't ask questions—shoot. Got it?"

"Sean—"

"Got it?"

"Oh, yes, sir! Yes, sir, Lieutenant Ramiro!"

"Damn WASP!" he muttered, pulling open the kitchen door.

"Excuse me, lieutenant!"

"What?" he asked, pausing. He felt empty. Already a gulf was opening up between them.

"I'm Catholic."

He frowned, shaking his head in confusion. "Good for you, Mrs. Blayne. What in hell does that have to do with anything?"

She smiled bitterly. "You just called me a WASP. It stands for white Anglo-Saxon Protestant. You'll have to think of something else to call me."

"Oh, Lord!" he groaned softly and slipped through the door.

He sat on the beach and watched as the boat moved closer. He sat stiffly, the gun concealed in his lap, feeling a niggling apprehension. Actually, it had gone easily. Far better than he had ever expected. No one was dead. And among the ones who were not dead were himself and the victim, Mrs. Amanda Blayne. They hadn't even been scratched.

But he was worried now that this might just be Juan, or Juan with a few reinforcements. He felt excitement and anxiety—and, strangely, that same overwhelming emptiness.

He'd wanted it to be over, right? Sure, right. It had been a kidnapping; a woman had been in danger. The fantasy had never been real. Never. It had all occurred in the midst of a nightmare.

But now it was over, and he felt empty.

He kept his eyes trained on the boat. It was about to anchor, and he saw Juan on the deck.

And then—moving so quickly he almost missed him—he saw another man. A tall black man in a uniform.

He stood up without thinking, hailing the boat, rushing down to the shoreline. "Hey! It's all right! Come on in!"

The figure stopped trying to disappear and stood, then brought a megaphone to his mouth. "Lieutenant Ramiro?"

"Yeah, yeah! Come on in!"

"Where is Mrs. Blayne?"

"Inside! She's—she's fine!"

The old boat was suddenly teeming with people. Juan was cuffed and disappeared with someone. The dinghy was lowered, and five men boarded it. Two Bahamian officials, a man in a three-piece suit—and an older, dignified looking man with a sad gaunt face and salt-and-pepper hair. Sean recognized him from his pictures. Senator Peter Blayne.

Sean just stood there as the dinghy came in. He was barely aware that Amanda came out of the house, that she stood slightly behind him. He wasn't aware of anything but the breeze and the sand beneath his bare feet.

"Mandy! Mandy!" The older man didn't wait for the dinghy to reach the shore. He stepped out while it was still in shallow water, soaking his shoes and his pant legs. "Mandy!"

In seconds she was racing down to meet him, and then she was in his arms. It was almost painfully apparent that they meant the world to each other.

Sean suddenly found it difficult to breathe. The older man was speaking, barely coherently, saying how frightened he had been, and what a fool, and how he'd never, never risk her again.

Sean had been as irritated as hell when Blayne had turned up his nose at police protection, but as he watched the scene and the man's agony he felt as if he should insist that this mess wasn't Blayne's fault at all. And, as it happened, if he'd accepted protection, the Miami PD wouldn't have been at the dock when Amanda Blayne was taken by the kidnappers.

Blayne wouldn't want any assurances from him, though; Sean knew that. The older man was staring at his daughter-in-law as if he could devour her, and Mandy was lightly trying to tell him that it hadn't been so bad, that she was fine, that he certainly wasn't at fault, that she was so glad to see him.

Then Sean couldn't give the tender scene his undivided attention anymore; one of the men in the three-piece suits was approaching him.

"Ramiro? Farkel, FBI. What's the situation here?"

What was it about cops and the FBI? Farkel had only introduced himself, but Sean disliked him already. He was a thin reedy sort of man, with a narrow nose, brown eyes, brown hair and a colorless complexion. When he smiled it looked more like a grimace.

Sean indicated the shack. "Two men, two women. They're in the back left bedroom. One has a gunshot wound to his shoulder, he probably needs medical attention as soon as possible."

The FBI man frowned. "You had a gun battle here? You were probably out of line, Lieutenant. You should have waited for us to come in. You could have caused injury to a civilian."

Sean curled his lip stiffly. "Sorry, Farkel. You see, they were going to start hacking off her fingers this morning, and it just didn't sound real nice to me."

"A finger would have been better than her life," Farkel said stiffly.

"They're in the back, Mr. Farkel. And I believe they're your responsibility now. Hey, go gentle on the old lady. She wasn't too happy about having anything to do with this."

The FBI agent walked past him; his associate—a younger blond man—glanced apologetically at Sean, who grinned in return. Some of the federal guys were okay. In fact, he was willing to bet that this one shared his opinion of Farkel.

"Damn yokel cops," Farkel was muttering. "They all think they're TV heroes."

"What's his first name?" Sean asked the young guy curiously. The man chuckled. "Fred. His name is Fred Farkel."

"He looks like a Fred Farkel," Sean muttered.

The blonde extended a hand. "Bill Duffy, Lieutenant. Sorry, he's my superior, but I'll try to be the liaison on the case in the future."

Sean nodded. Then the two Bahamian policemen walked up and introduced themselves, questioning him about the situation, too. They didn't seem to be any fonder of Fred Farkel than anyone else, and Sean had a feeling the man had made a few attempts to usurp their authority as well.

It didn't matter; it was all over for him now. All over but the paperwork.

The taller Bahamian, a guy named Matt Haines, told Sean quietly that a cutter would be coming in to take them back to Miami. Sean thanked him, then he and Bill Duffy went inside to deal with the fugitives in the house.

He was able to glance back at Mandy at last. For a moment her eyes met his. And for just a moment he thought that he saw something in them. Something warm. Something caring. Something that went beyond circumstances.

Then it disappeared. Her father-in-law's arm was around her shoulder, and he was suddenly pulling her enthusiastically forward, determined to reach Sean.

The senator's hand was extended, his smile deep and warm and real, and Sean thought in that moment that he knew why the man was elected over and over again.

"Lieutenant Ramiro! If I had a hundred lifetimes, I could never thank you enough!"

Sean returned his handshake, trying to keep his eyes off Mandy. "Senator, my pleasure. I mean, I didn't do anything out of the ordinary. I mean—"

She was turning bright, bright red. He didn't seem to be able to say anything that came out right.

"Didn't do anything out of the ordinary!" Peter Blayne exclaimed. "Why, son, you were seen! Jumping off that dock, trying to board a moving motorboat. Sir, I call that above and beyond the call of duty. You're too modest."

"Oh, yes, he's modest! Terribly modest!" Mandy said—and she felt the same confusion she knew he was feeling, because they both knew, even if Peter didn't, that neither of them had been modest at all.

And this was her father-in-law! Paul's father! Oh, God, if he found out, what would he think?

She stiffened miserably. There were so many things that she wanted to say to Sean; but none of them could be said. Not here. Not now.

She stared into his eyes and felt as if her insides congealed as he stared back.

His eyes were bright, as green as emeralds, as hard as diamonds. She must have been insane to think that there had ever been anything gentle about him. Or tender. He wasn't the man she had known, not the man with whom she had made love. With whom she had lain, afraid, in the night. With whom she had triumphed in the end.

His stare reduced the warmth of the Caribbean day to winter's chill. He was once again the stranger who had ordered her away from him on the beach, the man who had loved her—then hated her.

She lifted her chin, feeling her eyes well with tears, willing herself not to shed them. She didn't know what went on inside this man, and she decided then that she didn't want to know, that she didn't give a damn.

Circumstances…were over. Peter was standing beside her. She must consider the past few days a dream, a fantasy, a nightmare.

She extended her hand to Sean then, as cool as the waves that washed the beach. "Lieutenant, I want to thank you, too."

With a wry smile he took her hand. He remembered how it had felt on his body. It seemed so slim and soft and elegant—and now so remote. "No problem, Mrs. Blayne," he drawled. "Anytime."

"Oh, you'll be seeing more of us!" Peter Blayne assured him. "I'll see to it!"

Sean smiled. That was life as a cop. People you arrested wanted to kill you. People you got out of a jam wanted to be your friend for life. Peter Blayne would forget his promise. People always did.

"Sure," he said agreeably.

"Sean—Lieutenant, what will happen now?" Mandy asked him stiffly.

Sean shrugged. "The feds will press a number of charges. I assume they'll want you to testify in court." He gave her a slightly malicious grin, then laughed. "Fred Farkel will answer all your questions now. It's his ball game, as they say."

Mandy nodded. A silence fell over the three of them that seemed to puzzle Peter Blayne. It didn't matter. Two cutters had appeared on the horizon.

Matt Haines came out of the house and walked toward them. "Lieutenant, Mrs. Blayne, we'll have to invite you for a brief stay in Nassau. I hope you won't mind. We just have to clear up a few things and arrange our extradition procedures. It will just be for tonight. I'm sorry. I know you're anxious to get home."

Then everyone was on the beach—Julio, in handcuffs, Roberto, Maria, Señora Garcia, the FBI men and the Bahamians. Julio stopped in front of Mandy and Peter.

"Señor Blayne, I never wished to hurt her. But now perhaps you will understand. I wish for my father's freedom, just as you wished for hers."

Peter Blayne smiled sadly. "Julio, I told you I was doing my best. Your father will be out in a matter of weeks. But now *you* will go to prison."

"That does not matter, if my father is free."

"C'mon, Garcia," Farkel said roughly.

They passed by. Mandy was glad to see that they would not be on the same boat. She felt sorry for Señora Garcia; she even felt sorry for Julio. But she didn't ever want to see Roberto again, not as long as she lived.

She had to sit next to Sean in the dinghy that took them out to the cutter. She had to feel his bare leg, feathered with the short dark hairs, next to her own. To feel his breath, inhale his scent.

She didn't look at him; she stared straight ahead.

The cutter provided some relief; she was given a small cabin where she could bathe, and a soft terry robe that was totally decent and comfortable.

Mandy showered forever, loathe to leave the clean water. And loathe to reappear on deck, although she knew that Peter was waiting anxiously for her. Naturally Peter would quiz her. And naturally Sean would be there. And…oh, God!

Eventually she went out on deck. To her vast surprise and relief Sean was nowhere in sight.

She was given a delicious rum drink and an equally good meal, and Peter sat next to her, as if he never wanted to leave her side. He told her that her parents had been wired about her safety, that he'd had a student feed her cat. He chattered like a magpie, totally out of character. Then he asked her at last, "Oh, Amanda! Are you really all right? My dear, you're all I have left!"

Guilt churned in her stomach. "I'm fine, Peter, honest."

"But how—"

She took a deep breath. "Sean—Lieutenant Ramiro—pretended to be your gardener."

"My gardener?"

She grimaced and lowered her lashes, staring at her drink. "His Spanish is perfect. He's, uh, half Cuban. He convinced them that he was your downtrodden gardener, and my...my lover, and that he could convince me to be a well-behaved hostage. Julio really isn't a murderer, although I think his associate—Roberto—might have been. Thanks to the lieutenant I, well, I was as safe as possible the entire time. And Señora Garcia really shouldn't be punished, Peter, if there's a way around it. She was against what happened, and she was good to me."

He patted her hand. "We'll see, dear. We'll see what can be done. I'm sure you'll be able to speak in her defense at the trial."

She nodded, and then she wondered where Sean was.

Peter's thoughts must have been running along the same lines. "Where is that young man?" he wondered aloud. "What an interesting fellow. I'd quite enjoy getting to know him. He seems fascinating, don't you think?"

"Uh...fascinating," Mandy agreed, swallowing.

She didn't see him again, though, not on the boat. They docked in Nassau harbor and were given rooms in a hotel at the end of Market Street. Mandy had barely entered her own before Peter returned to her with a suitcase of her clothing, packed for her as soon as he'd received permission to come with the authorities to take her home.

She barely had time to dress before she was taken to the Bahamian police station. The authorities were charming, though. They asked her a million questions, which she answered to the best of her abilities.

Then she was free—or she thought she was. The FBI man, Farkel, was there, warning her that once she returned to the States she would be called upon once again.

She had a pounding headache by then, and Farkel felt like the last straw. She thought she was about to explode and then he was interrupted by Sean.

He, too, had changed. He was wearing a lightweight three-piece gray suit, austere, but very handsome on him. He stepped out from one of the little cubicles and spoke not to her, but to Farkel. "Fred, lighten up, will you? You'd think that Mrs. Blayne was the criminal. She's had enough for today, don't you think?"

Farkel stiffened. "I was just—"

"Every dog has his day, Farkel. You'll get yours. She's free for tonight. Our plane leaves in the morning, and once she's on U.S. soil you get to give her the whole third degree."

"And tonight?" Mandy heard herself whisper.

Peter answered for her. "Tonight we're going out on the town! That nice young Bahamian officer suggested Paradise Island for dinner, a show, even gambling." He chuckled, encircling Mandy's shoulder, pulling her close to him. "Mandy, I think we owe Lieutenant Ramiro the best dinner we can find. You, me, the lieutenant—and Paradise Island."

No, paradise is lost! Mandy thought a little frantically. But what could she do? Her father-in-law was on one side of her; the man with whom she had betrayed his deceased son was on the other.

Sean bowed whimsically, watching her in a strange way. He didn't want to go, she thought. No, he wanted to, and he didn't want to. Again she wondered if he hated her...or cared about her?

"A night on the town sounds good, senator," he told Peter. "Mrs. Blayne?" He offered her his arm.

Farkel snorted derisively and turned away. "Damned if they don't all think they're Sonny Crockett these days."

"Damn!" Sean snapped his fingers. "I just wish I could afford his wardrobe, Farkel."

"Your suit's not so bad."

"Thanks—your partner lent it to me."

"Gentlemen..." Peter began, distressed.

But he needn't have bothered. Sean didn't wait for Mandy to take his arm; he took hers. And the cool Bahamian breeze touched her heated face as they moved out into the night....

Chapter 11

Mandy didn't know why Sean had decided to come to dinner with them. The place was lovely, the food was wonderful, but he seemed stiff and uncomfortable. She wondered if she looked as rigid as he did.

Only Peter seemed to be having a good time. He delighted in the story that the kidnappers had assumed that Mandy was his wife, telling Sean, "Good Lord! What flattery, that I should have such a child bride!"

Then he and Sean went on to discuss the situation with the elder Garcia.

Mandy concentrated on her shrimp cocktail. It was amazing. Last night she had been in absolute terror, wondering how Sean would ever stand up to two guns. Staring at her fingers, she shivered. She glanced up and found Sean's eyes on her. He smiled. She looked down again quickly, hoping that Peter hadn't caught the exchange.

"Oh, Mandy! I forgot to tell you! The team from Colorado called the school. You've been invited to be a part of the new dig."

"Really? How wonderful," she murmured.

"Dig?" Sean inquired.

"Yes," Peter said proudly. "Mandy is a paleontologist."

Sean arched one dark brow. "Dinosaurs?"

Despite herself, she grinned. "Their bones, actually, lieutenant."

"She teaches at the state college these days, but this sounds like the perfect time for a leave of absence. You could still manage some skiing out in Colorado."

"Yes, I suppose I could."

Skiing. She loved to ski. But at the moment the prospect meant nothing to her. She closed her eyes briefly. The dig, though, the dig would be good. The painstaking exploration, the wonder of discovery. The piecing together of ancient puzzles. It would be far away and remote, and she could forget all about Julio and Roberto—and Sean Ramiro.

Their main course came, pompano, broiled and garnished and savory, but Mandy couldn't taste it. She could only feel Sean's eyes on her from across the table. She wanted to scream. She wanted to demand to know what he was trying to do to her, here, in front of Paul's father.

"Do you have a family, lieutenant?" Peter asked Sean.

Sean grinned, swallowed a piece of fish, then replied.

"Well, sir, everyone has some kind of family. But am I married? No. No children. My father is deceased, my mother lives in Miami Shores, and I've got no brothers or sisters."

"Divorced?" Peter asked him, and Mandy was stunned. Peter was never this rude.

"No, sir. I've never been married."

"Never came close?"

"Oh, yeah. I came close. Once."

Peter's curiosity was quelled by the tone of that reply. No further questions in that direction would be answered.

They bypassed dessert and ordered liqueurs. Mandy found herself feeling amazed. Last night she had been wearing old dirty clothing and sleeping in a hovel. Tonight she was surrounded by opulence: plush velvet, twinkling chandeliers, marble and silver. How quickly the world could change.

As quickly as Sean Ramiro.

They left the restaurant and went into the casino. Peter chose a roulette table; Sean sat down to play blackjack. Nervous and wishing that the evening would end, Mandy restlessly decided to play the slots.

Her little buzzer went off instantly to announce a two hundred dollar jackpot, and two hundred silver coins came spilling out into the catch tray.

She just stared at the coins, then started. Sean wasn't playing blackjack anymore. He was leaning casually against her machine, staring at her mockingly, lashes low over his eyes, looking sensual and handsome despite his negligent stance.

He touched a trailing lock of her hair. "Everything you touch turns to gold, huh?"

She jerked away from his touch. "Silver dollars, Mr. Ramiro. And my hair is dirty blond."

"Oh, I don't think anything about you touches…dirt."

"I work in the dirt. I dig up bones, remember?"

"I wonder why that never cropped up in casual conversation."

"We've never had a casual conversation."

"That's right. We were always pretty intense, weren't we? Need some help with your money?"

"No thanks. I'll just play it back."

He moved closer to her, his dark head bending. "Mind if I watch."

"Yes, I do. What are you trying to do to me?"

"What are you talking about?"

"Peter is here!"

He arched a cynical brow at her. "Peter is here?" he repeated. "And now that Peter is here you have to pretend that you don't know me? Funny, I don't see the senator as a snob."

"He's not—I'm not. Just go away, will you, please? Look, it's over. I never understood you, you never understood me. You've got a chip on your shoulder the size of a cement block. And I've got a few—"

"Prejudices?"

"No! Damn you. Problems of my own!"

"And what are they, Mrs. Blayne?"

How dare he? she wondered furiously. Confusion joined the tempest in her heart, and she was afraid that she would burst into tears right there.

She didn't. She just inhaled deeply and spoke with

a voice as sharp as a razor. "No one, Ramiro, will ever need to tell me that life can be rough. I don't care what's happened to you, there is nothing—*nothing* in life like losing a child!"

She turned around in a whirl, leaving her coins in the machine, fleeing the room.

Peter would be upset, of course. He would wonder what had sent her flying out. But she couldn't even care about Peter just then; she had to leave.

Mandy had no problem getting a taxi to take her back over the bridge to Nassau and her hotel. Once she got there she knew she had to leave a message for Peter. She did so, then started forlornly for the elevator. She didn't know why she felt so lost, so miserable. It was as if the past and the present had collided to bring her agony just when she should have been eternally grateful that she had been rescued and given a future.

She should have sensed that something was wrong the moment she entered the room, but she didn't. She didn't even bother to turn on the light; moonlight was drifting in through the parted curtains anyway. She just closed and bolted the door, tossed her handbag on the dresser and fell back on the plush double bed.

It was then that she heard the rustle of movement and saw the silhouette moving in the darkness.

She tensed and opened her mouth to scream, but a hand clamped tightly over it.

"Shut up. It's just me."

"Just you!" Furiously she twisted away from him, sitting up, wishing she could see him clearly enough to belt him a good one. "You scared me half to death!

What are you doing in here? I'm getting so sick of your strong-arm tactics."

"Take your clothes off, Mandy."

"What?"

"Take your clothes off. It seems to be the only way we can communicate."

"Get out of here! I'll call the co—"

"Cops? Honey, you've got one already."

"Sean…"

"Mandy?"

His fingers slid into the hair at her nape, his palm cradling her skull. He held her there while he came ever closer, his lips meeting hers at last, hesitating for just a breath, then coming alive. For an instant, she clenched her teeth against him, but the warm pressure of his tongue dissolved her resistance, and with a little sigh she fell into his arms.

Circumstances changed. People did not. And darkness had come again.

In seconds he was stretched out beside her. They were both fully clothed, but she felt as if she was touching him, all of him.

But it was not passion that goaded him, not that night. He brushed her cheek, and she felt his eyes, emerald flames that defied the darkness.

"I'm sorry, Mandy."

She couldn't answer him. She shrugged.

"I can't forget what happened."

"No one has asked you to forget."

"Mandy…"

"You're strange, Sean. I thought I was, but you're stranger. We make love at night, and in the morning you behave as if I'm a bee with a particularly annoying buzz. One second you're as charming as a prince, and then the next—"

"I had a few raw deals. I took it out on you."

"I can't help the color of my hair, or who my ancestors were."

"Wait a minute! Wait a minute! Get off my case. You were the one who didn't want to touch me with a ten-foot pole the second other people appeared on the scene!"

"You don't—oh, never mind. You just—"

"Mandy!"

"What?"

"Did you smell this bed? Did you touch it? Feel it. So soft, so fresh."

She didn't know why she obeyed the command, but she did, inhaling deeply. And it was true, of course. The bedding smelled wonderful.

"It's so clean," she murmured.

He ran his knuckles tenderly over her hair. "And you're so clean."

"I beg your pardon. I was always clean."

"Well, I wasn't so great."

"Really? For shame, Lieutenant Ramiro." She couldn't stop herself from grinning in the darkness. "I'd never thought your confidence could be so low. I always thought you were at least okay."

"I was…okay?"

"Oh, definitely."

"Hmm. Well…"

"Well?"

"I'm great now. Want to try me? Clean as a whistle. I even shaved, and you didn't even notice."

"Oh, but I did. I think. You looked so great in that suit."

"Aha! I told you I was great!"

"Bragging will get you nowhere."

"Okay. Take your clothes off. We'll go back to brute force."

"Sean..."

He stopped her words with a kiss that seemed the most natural thing in the world. It always seemed to be like that; the taunts and the bitterness, but then somehow the laughter, and the irresistible urge to touch.

She would probably never know which was real, the laughter or the pain. But in the darkness, even darkness kissed by moonlight, it didn't seem to matter. When she was with him she always felt as if she had a driving thirst, as if his touch was water that cascaded over her, a fountain that sparkled and rippled, soothing and delighting, sweeping her away to new heights.

His hands moved over her, frustrated by her dress. He groaned softly. "Take your clothes off."

"Is that the only line you know?" she whispered.

"It's a damn good one," he assured her. And she laughed, laughed until his fingers rode along her bare legs to her bikini panties and teased her flesh through the silky fabric. Then her breath caught and she could laugh no more, and she was suddenly thinking that surely this would be the last time that she had to drink in all of him; the bronze flesh and muscle and sinew; the dark hair that dusted his legs and chest; the powerful line of his profile....

"You take *your* clothes off," she told him huskily. "On second thought..."

She started working on the tiny pearl buttons of his

vest. He took a deep breath, watching her, watching the tiny frown that furrowed her brow. He held his breath as she undid the vest and then his shirt, and then he expelled it with a heady groan as she brought her mouth against him, delicately touching him with the tip of her tongue. Then she grew bolder, grazing his skin with gentle teeth that sent streams of lavalike desire rippling through his body. She moved sinuously against him, her hands moving over his back, his chest, then to his shoulders to shove the annoying material from the form she was so eager to know.

There was nothing like this, she thought. Nothing like feeling his reactions to her kiss, her touch. He trembled beneath her, yet he was taut, and with each ragged breath he took she felt bolder, more feminine, more vibrantly aroused herself. He was right: he was clean; he was great; the fresh masculine scent of his body was an aphrodisiac in itself, and she wondered at the beauty of him as her head reeled. She slipped her fingers along the waistband of his pants, teasing his belly, finding his belt buckle and leisurely working it free.

Too leisurely, perhaps. His groan resounded like thunder, and he set her aside, destroying her illusion of power. He left her to feverishly shed the remainder of his clothing, then lay back beside her.

"What's this?" he whispered huskily.

"My dress."

"Get rid of it!"

She giggled breathlessly. "I thought you were going to do a striptease and then dance."

"I intend to dance, all right." He swore softly in Spanish, having a miserable time with the tiny hook at her nape. He paused, shrugged and snapped it, and she didn't care in the least. She was suddenly as anxious as he was to feel their bodies together.

As soon as her clothes were gone she stepped back to him, remembering their first time. She knelt down and let her hair fall over his feet as she massaged them, then dusted them with kisses. Her body was liquid as she moved against him, using the tip of her tongue at the backs of his knees and all along his thighs.

He held his breath again, as taut as wire. She waited, drawing out the moment, her hair spilling over him.

And then she took him with her touch, with her kiss.

She heard his words, sweet and reverent, in English and in Spanish, and they all meant the same thing. His fingers were tempered steel when they closed around her arms as he drew her to him, moving swiftly, stunning her with the electric force of his entry. The moment was so fulfilling that she cried out softly, only to have her words stolen once again by a kiss.

They moved together in the moonlight, until finally she lay panting in sweet splendor. She was so tired, so spent, yet each new touch awakened her anew, until she moaned softly, curling into his chest with the sweetest sigh.

He held her there for what seemed like forever.

She didn't know when the change came, only that he suddenly stiffened and then rose before padding naked to the window to stare out at the Bahamian night.

She was too drowsy to rouse herself, and she wondered bitterly why he had decided to do so at such a time.

"What's the matter?" she asked softly.

He whipped around, like a lethal predator, and moved back to the bed, perching at the foot of it.

"What are we going to do now?" he asked her harshly.

"Sleep," she responded.

"That's not what I mean, and you know it."

"Sean, don't…" She lifted an imploring hand to him, but he ignored it.

"I asked you a question."

"Sean, I'm so tired."

"Then wake up. What are we going to do?"

"We're—we're going to fly back to the U.S. in the morning!" she snapped at last. "I have to go back to work. I assume that you do, too."

"And?"

"And what?"

"What about us?"

She held her breath, wondering what he was so upset about. Was he afraid that she would think she had some kind of hold on him? What was it with him? She didn't understand him, and when he was like this he actually frightened her.

She cared too much. Way too much. And she had promised herself that she wouldn't risk caring that much ever again. Her career, her love of the past, would be her life. Nice safe dinosaurs that had been extinct for years and years and years.…

"You don't have a thing in the world to worry about, lieutenant," she whispered wearily. "I have no intention of becoming involved with you. You're as free as a lark."

"Oh?" he said coldly.

Chills raced along her spine; she wanted to touch him

and erase the tension from his face. But she had already reached out to him, and he had ignored her.

"So," he murmured, "it all came true in a way, didn't it? I might as well have been your gardener, dragged in when the odd occasion warranted it, huh?"

She was instantly furious with him—and with herself, for always falling prey to him so easily. "You stupid bastard!"

"Yeah, you're kind of right there, too, aren't you?"

He prowled over to the window once again. "I've got just one more question for you, Mrs. Blayne."

"Do ask, lieutenant."

"I'm curious as to what precautions you've been taking."

"Precautions?" Mandy echoed hollowly.

He turned so suddenly that she thought he was about to take the drapes with him. "I'll be blunt, Mrs. Blayne. I'm talking about birth control."

"Don't you dare stand there and yell at me! I wasn't planning on having an affair! I was kidnapped! I usually don't worry about birth control when maniacs are abducting me! There's an old saying that it takes two to tango, and I'm here to tell you that it's true!"

"That's irrelevant."

"The hell it is!"

"It's irrelevant," he repeated, bending over her so that his arms surrounded her like a cage. "Because any precautions I might have taken would have been evident. So we know that wasn't the case."

She felt that she really did hate him at that moment. He stood over her like some superior god, the epitome of masculine force, beautiful still, and more hateful for it.

She stiffened her spine, as heedless of her nudity as he was of his. "You have no problems whatsoever, lieutenant. I will never again have a child. Does that satisfy you?"

For an instant she thought that he was going to hurt her, he looked so fierce. He didn't. He pushed himself away from the bed in a fury, muttering something she didn't understand. She shivered because without his warmth the night had grown cold.

She closed her eyes tightly. "Sean," she said miserably, "get out of here. Please, go!"

Once more he came back to her. He took a strand of her hair, curling it around in his fingers. She'd never seen him quite like this, and it was all she could do to keep from tearing away from him, to keep from screaming out.

"Not again, Mrs. Blayne," he said softly. "Not again. Here's another expression for you—those who play sometimes pay. And if you're given a price, my love, you will pay it."

"What—?"

"You can expect to see me again. Quite frequently. For the next few months, at least."

A new wave of trembling swept over her, along with a rush of conflicting emotions. She understood him now; at least, she thought she did. She'd assumed at first that he had no desire to be saddled with a child from their affair; now she knew it was the opposite. And with that knowledge she experienced a blank and cold dread, terrifying, horrible. It was if she had gone back in time, gone back to the time when the young highway patrolman had stood on her doorstep, telling her that not only her husband but her infant had been killed in the collision, the baby mercifully quickly....

But for her there had been no mercy. There had been her breasts, filled with milk for a tiny life that could never draw from them again. There had been the emptiness in her arms, the rage, the despair....

"Get out of here," she repeated dully.

He reached for her cheek, but she pushed his hand away. "I'll be around, Mandy."

"No," she pleaded.

And then she knew that he had misunderstood her entirely, because he swore again, then said, "What is it, Amanda? You couldn't handle a child named Ramiro? Too ethnic for your ears?"

She pressed her palms over her eyes tightly. "Yes! Yes! That's it! I'm planning to move to Boca Raton, too. Away from Miami. Haven't you heard that saying? 'Will the last American out please remember to bring the flag?' Please! Get out of here."

But he didn't. Not then. He straddled her and pulled her hands away from her face, then stared into her eyes with a gaze that burned into her soul. "No!" he thundered harshly. "You can't run away. Not this time!"

And then, miraculously, he released her.

She closed her eyes. She heard him dress swiftly, and then she heard him leave even more swiftly.

For at least an hour after that she didn't move. Not a muscle. She just lay there, trying to breathe.

And praying that she wasn't pregnant.

In the morning she felt awful.

The flight back took less than an hour. Peter's car

met them, and they reached her home in another thirty minutes.

Peter was worried and solicitous. She could only be grateful that Sean hadn't been on their plane. He must have altered his arrangements.

Peter had arranged for the police and the FBI to come to her; she spent the afternoon with a pleasant blond man and a sergeant from the Miami PD. Things weren't really difficult; all she had to do was repeat what had happened over and over again. It was a cut-and-dried situation, but the culprits still had to be prosecuted.

A twinge of conscience touched her, and Mandy remembered to tell them that in her opinion Mrs. Garcia had been an unhappy bystander. She hesitated, then even spoke up for Julio, saying that she didn't believe he was malicious, just misguided. She was told that if she would say so at the trial, she might lessen their sentences.

"But kidnapping is a federal offense, Mrs. Blayne. No one can walk away from it," the FBI man told her.

"I know." She paused, shivering. "And Roberto should be locked up, with the key thrown away." She lowered her lashes. She had told them, of course, that he had attempted to rape her. She told them, too, about Sean's fight to save her from him.

She hadn't mentioned what had happened after that, though.

They left her, and she was alone with Peter. He wanted to stay with her; he wanted her to drink warm milk and go to bed and get better, since her shadowed eyes and pale cheeks had convinced him that she was sick.

He was supposed to be in Washington, and she knew

it. With a dozen assurances she finally got him to go home, convincing him that she was determined to get a good night's sleep and go back to work in the morning. "All I want is Koala," she told Peter lightly.

Koala was her cat, so named not because he was cute, but because he was so ugly. He'd come to her door one day and moved in without giving her much choice.

Peter hugged her, then turned to leave at last, a haggard-looking man. She loved him so much. "Peter."

"Yes?"

"Promise me that you'll get a good night's sleep, okay?"

He grimaced. "Promise."

She thought that now her day was over. She thought that she could sink into a warm bath and try to think about about the new dig. She wanted to do everything she could to create distance between herself and Sean, the things he had said to her—and the horrible things she had said to him.

But she couldn't forget him; all she could do was miss him.

She couldn't even get comfortable. She ran her bath, but before she could step into the water, the phone rang.

It was her mother, sobbing over the phone, and once again Mandy was cast into the depths of guilt, aware that any decent daughter would have called her own parents by then. She talked to her mother for half an hour, then to her father for another twenty minutes.

They both wanted to fly in immediately, but her father was just recovering from bypass surgery, and Mandy didn't think he should be traveling yet. She managed to persuade them to wait a few weeks, telling them that she was absolutely fine and planning on a trip to Colorado anyway. She talked about the dig with forced enthusiasm, and at last they seemed to believe that it would be all right to wait to see her until the end of the month.

Hanging up from her parents brought no relief. The phone rang again instantly, and this time it was a reporter. She spoke politely to him, but then the doorbell rang. Another reporter. She spoke politely to him, too.

But when a third reporter reached her over the phone she was ready to scream. She had a pounding headache; all she wanted to do was hide.

She got through the third interview, then hurried through her small house, pulling all the drapes shut. She finally got into the freshly filled bathtub, where she strenuously ignored the phone every time it rang.

She sat in the tub for a long time, feeling the heat ease some of her tension away. Again she tried to think about work, to plan for the trip.

The water began to cool, and suddenly she jumped out of it as if she had been scalded. It had suddenly reminded her...of Sean. Of a day in the surf when she had surfaced to face Roberto, when she had backed away from him, when Sean had been there—and their minds had functioned as one.

She grabbed a towel and wrapped it around herself, shaking. She closed her eyes.

She couldn't stop thinking about him. Everything, every little thing, was a reminder.

After a few seconds she groped blindly in the medicine chest for one of the tranquilizers the doctor had given her just after the accident. She swallowed it quickly.

She paused for a minute, breathing deeply. Then she walked into the living room and resolutely did the one thing that would convince her that she had been right not to try. That it was better, much better, to have him hate her than...than anything else.

She picked up the picture on the mantle. The picture of a happy family. Herself, Paul and the baby.

As she stared at the tears welled in her eyes, and the immediate past dimmed slowly away.

Chapter 12

Sean was back in his cubicle on the fifth floor, sipping his coffee and reviewing his file on the McKinley murder case, when Harvey Anderson sauntered in, leaning against the divider, the daily paper in one hand, his styrofoam cup of coffee in the other.

There was such a grin on his face that Sean sat back, crossing his arms over his chest and arching a wary brow.

"Whew!" Harvey whistled. "Nice, man, nice! Damned if you don't get all the luck."

"All right, Harvey, what luck? So far the situation looks like hell to me. I'm gone for a week, and what did you guys do? You let the paperwork on my desk grow like the stinking yellow pages.

"Hey…!" Harvey lifted his shoulders innocently. "We missed you—what can I say?"

"Thanks. Thanks a lot."

The grin left Harvey's face. He indicated the top file on Sean's desk. "We just got the report back from ballistics. The murder weapon was a Smith and Wesson, fifteen shots. One bullet fired, the one that killed him."

"The same gun found in the house?"

Harvey nodded. "Looks like the wife to me, beyond doubt."

"We can't use 'looks like' with the D.A.'s office, Harvey. You know that. I think it was his wife, too. We're going to need a motive—especially since she's still claiming that it was a break-in. And we can't get anyone except her stepchildren to say that there might have been trouble in the marriage. Let's work on it from that angle."

"His money was motive enough," Harvey snorted.

"Yeah, well…"

"Viable proof in court, yeah, yeah. We'll get it. I've got a hunch on this one." He grinned once again, "They can't all be neat and clean and wrapped up in a bundle for the feds, with glowing praise and the word 'hero' in all the papers."

Sean's eyes narrowed. "Okay, Harvey, out with it."

"Out with what?" His face was all innocence beneath his shaggy brown hair. "What's with you? When did you stop reading the paper?"

"I overslept. Hand it over."

"Man, you get all the luck. A week in the Bahamas and the blonde to boot."

"The paper, Harvey!"

Sean snatched it from him. It was true. His name and

the word 'hero' were splattered all over the front page—along with a picture of Amanda Blayne in her doorway.

It shouldn't have been a flattering picture; it was a grainy black-and-white snapshot, and she was in the process of trying to close the door. Even so, she looked beautiful. Distressed, her hair tumbling about her face. Even in black-and-white, you could almost see the color, feel it…smell its fragrance.

Sean glanced over the article and gritted his teeth. The article was mainly about him; she couldn't have commended him more highly.

"Damn her," he muttered, the world suddenly turning a shade of red. What was she trying to do? Buy him off?

He slammed the paper down on the desk.

"Hey! What's with you?" Harvey protested. "If she were gushing all over me, I'd be halfway to heaven. And the big boys down at city hall are thrilled. What with so much corruption going on in the police force these days, they're thrilled to have gotten some favorable publicity for a change."

Sean just shook his head. "If the PR is good for the department, great. I just don't like being all over the paper, that's all."

Harvey didn't leave. He sat down on the edge of Sean's desk. "What was she like, huh?"

"Polite," Sean said curtly. Then he softened. Harvey wasn't actually his partner; Todd Bridges was. But homicide worked in teams, usually on several cases at a time, and the three of them, along with Harvey's partner, Jill Santini, had worked together many times.

They were friends, and Harvey's tone had been more curious than anything else.

"She's a...nice lady. Lots of spunk, lots of spirit. Hey, you can be the liaison between the PD and the FBI. You'll probably get to meet her that way."

"Naw, Sean. You're the man on this one."

"We're a team, right? You take it."

"Really?"

"Really."

"Wow!"

Harvey walked away, leaving his newspaper behind. Sean stared at it for a moment longer, threw it down, then picked it back up. He drummed his fingers on his desk, then picked up the phone and dialed information. He glanced at his watch. It was just after seven.

The hell with it. He dialed her number.

A soft, sleepy, too-sultry voice said, "Hello?"

"What the hell did you think you were doing?"

"I beg your pardon? Oh—Sean."

"Yeah, Sean."

"I don't know what you're talking about."

"Don't you get the paper?"

"I don't read it until I'm awake. Why?" she asked, suddenly defensive. "What did I do? Insult you?"

"No, no, you were glowing."

"Then what's your problem?"

"Too glowing, Mrs. Blayne. It isn't going to change the way I feel about anything."

She was silent, then she laughed bitterly. "Actually, I don't begin to understand how you do feel about anything. If anything I said offended you, I'm sorry. It wasn't intended. Excuse me. If you're done yelling, I have a class in an hour."

She didn't give him a chance to say anything else. She hung up.

He was left staring at the phone.

Harvey came back into his cubicle, his jacket slung over his shoulder. "Ready?"

"For what?"

The other man sighed. "You called me last night—at midnight, I might add—to say you wanted to go over to forensics first thing this morning."

"Oh, yeah. Give me just a second, will you?"

Harvey nodded and disappeared.

Sean stared at the phone again. He picked it up, not at all sure what he really intended to do.

"Hello?" She sounded more alert this time.

"Want to go to a party Friday night?"

"Sean?" she inquired skeptically.

"Yeah, it's me."

"And you're calling to see if I want to go to a party?"

"Yeah, well, it might be a little dull. It's just a…ethnic sort of thing. You're, uh, welcome to invite Peter, too."

"He's out of the state," she answered, and then dead silence came over the wire. "I don't believe you," she said at last.

"Will you come?"

"I…"

"Please."

"You're crazy."

"Probably."

"I…"

"I'll pick you up at seven."

He hung up quickly. He didn't want to give her a chance to refuse him.

"Sean?" Harvey called. Todd was standing there, too, now.

Sean grabbed his jacket, grinning as he joined them. He hadn't slept a wink all night, but suddenly he felt as if he could work three shifts straight.

Todd commented dismally on the weather as they went down in the elevator.

Sean cut him off. "You all coming to the annual bash this Friday?"

"Wouldn't miss it," Todd said, perking up.

Sean grinned. "Good. Harvey, you'll get to meet her after all."

"The blonde? She's coming?"

"Uh, yeah, I think so."

Harvey grinned suddenly, rolling his eyes. "I think there's a whole lot more to this story than the papers know!"

"And it's going to stay that way," Sean declared warningly.

"Sure. Sure it will," Harvey vowed solemnly.

Harvey stared speculatively at Sean's back as they walked out to the parking lot. Sean had sounded serious, and Harvey was surprised.

He and Sean had gone through the academy together. He'd been around when...well, he'd been with Sean's lawyer when they pulled a few strings to get Sean out of jail. It just...didn't seem possible.

He wondered who was in for the worse time, the beautiful blonde, or Sean Ramiro.

* * *

Amanda was still partially in shock when she reached the campus. In shock because he had called her, yelling, when she had given him every compliment she could, though she had been ready to scream at the mere mention of his name. And in shock because he had called her back and asked her to a party—just like that.

And also because she hadn't said no.

After a few minutes she roused herself somewhat from her stupor; it was wonderful to be back. There was a giant coffee cake waiting in her office, along with a score of her students and half the faculty. Everybody wanted to hug her, to tell her how grateful they were that she was fine, and how happy they were to see her back.

It was nice to feel so loved, but in time the furor died down.

She had an introductory class that morning, and a second, more advanced class after that. Teaching was fun. She loved it as much as she loved the subject, and it was good to back at work. It was so…normal.

But when her classes were over her mind returned to Sean—and to her own idiocy. Why in God's name hadn't she just told him that he was crazy, that he was absolutely insane, and that no, she wouldn't go anywhere with him? She didn't want to get involved with anyone, and especially a man who was like Dr. Jekyll and Mr. Hyde!

She had barely sat down behind the desk in her office when Valerie Gonzales, one of the associate professors, came by. "How about lunch?" the other woman asked.

"I'm not really hungry," Mandy told her ruefully.

Valerie wrinkled her nose. "I'm not, either, but Ed

Taylor came in with a decaying alligator that he's determined to preserve, and the smell of formaldehyde is driving me nuts. Let's get out of here."

Mandy leaned back and grinned. "All you want is the inside scoop."

"That's right. Are you going to give it to me?"

"No."

Valerie shrugged. "I'll buy you a Mai Tai. That ought to do it."

"Think so, huh?"

They went to one of the nearby malls, where one of the restaurants specialized in appetizers. They ordered two apiece. Amanda refused the Mai Tai that Valerie had been sure would make her open up, but she decided that a glass of Burgundy was just what she needed.

And though she certainly didn't open up, she found herself admitting that she was going out that Friday with the "way-out cop," as Valerie referred to Sean. Mandy decided that she needed a little advice, and that Valerie might be able to help her. "Val, all he said was that it's some ethnic thing. What do you think I should wear? Is there some kind of Cuban holiday coming up?"

Valerie sipped her beer and pondered the question. "Not that I know of, so go for something casual. If they're celebrating, they might roast a pig."

"So…?"

"Well, you roast them whole, in a pit in the ground. It's an all-day event. By night it's ready to eat."

"Can you teach me some Spanish? I think I'm going to feel like a fish out of water."

Valerie laughed. "I know you know some Spanish.

I swear all the time and you always know what I'm saying."

"Yeah, well, I don't think that's party conversation."

"Okay." Valerie hesitated. *"Buenas noches."*

"Good evening? Good night?"

"Yeah, both. *Como está usted?* How are you? *Bien, gracias*—fine, thank you. Umm...*dónde está el baño?* That one is very important to every woman."

"Why?"

"It means, where is the bathroom." She chuckled softly. "Then there's *te amo.*"

"Which means?"

"I love you."

"Valerie!"

"Aren't you in love with him? Just a little bit?"

"No. I'm not in love with anyone."

"Then it's just sex."

"Of course it's not just sex."

"Wow! Then you have made love, huh?"

"Valerie, stuff some more food into your mouth, will you, please?"

"Sure, but I can't teach you much Spanish that way!"

Friday seemed to roll around very slowly. Mandy fluctuated between longing to see him so badly that she hurt and dreading it so thoroughly that she almost called to cancel.

He didn't call her. She even began to wonder whether he had been serious. He hadn't asked for her address, but then, she was certain he could get it easily enough.

At some point she realized that although he might be crazy, she was the one suffering a terrible illness. She didn't want an involvement, yet she was involved. And that made her dilemma all the worse. She knew that she shouldn't see him. Seeing him would only bring more arguments, more disaster. She still couldn't tell whether he liked her or hated her—or if he was using her.

But none of it mattered. She had to see him. And not even the memory of her tragic past could intrude on that basic desire.

The week was a slow one on campus, too. They were almost at spring break. She made her arrangements to leave for the dig in Colorado on the Monday when the vacation began. She wouldn't really be able to get too involved in the work—she wouldn't have the time—but it would be fascinating just to be a part of it.

As much as she was looking forward with dread and fascination to seeing Sean again, she was glad that she could hop aboard a plane and leave—run away—the Monday after.

Friday night did come, as things inevitably did. He had said seven; at five she was in the shower, shampooing her hair, taking a long luxurious bath. She couldn't help reminding herself that he had usually seen her at her grubbiest, and she wanted to be perfect—as perfect as she could be.

If he was really coming for her...

She had never experienced anything in her life like the emotions and physical agitation that came to her unbidden that night, growing worse and worse as seven o'clock approached. She was anxious and scared and nervous—and her fingers shook so badly that her first application of mascara was applied to her cheeks rather than her eyelashes. Her stomach felt as if fifty jugglers were tossing eight balls apiece inside it. Her palms were damp; her body felt on fire. And to her eternal shame, she seemed incapable of remembering what he looked like dressed, recalling instead every nuance of his naked body. She was trying to pour herself a glass of wine when the doorbell rang.

She dropped the glass and stupidly watched it shatter all over the tile floor. She swept it up in a mad rush, raced to the door—then stopped herself, smoothing back her hair before throwing open the door.

At her first sight of him all the nervous heat and energy and anticipation churned through her anew. He was tan and clean shaven, his hair still damp from the shower. He was wearing a light suit, tailored to fit his physique, enhancing the breadth of his shoulders and the trimness of his waistline. The most noticeable thing about him, as always, was his eyes. So green, so shocking, against the strong planes of his face. The look of character in them gave him his rugged appeal, raised him above such an undistinguished word as "handsome."

Then she realized with dismay that he was in a suit—and she was in jeans. "Oh," she said softly.

"Does that mean come in?" he asked.

"Yes, yes, of course. Come in." She backed away from the door awkwardly. He followed her. For several seconds he stared at nothing but her, then he looked around her house.

There wasn't much on the first floor, just a living room that led to the kitchen on the left, the sun porch in the rear and the staircase to the right. It was pretty, though, she thought. The carpeting was deep cream, the furniture French provincial. The screen that separated the dining area from the rest of the room was Oriental.

"Nice," he said. He meant "rich."

She shrugged. "Thank you. Uh, would you like a drink? I think I need to change."

He acted as if he was just noticing her clothing. Then he frowned. "Where did you think I was taking you?"

"A friend of mine suggested…never mind. Why don't you help yourself. The kitchen is all yours. I'll be right down."

She fled up the stairs, tripping on the last one, and hoped he hadn't noticed. She changed into a kelly green cocktail dress, almost ripping it in her haste to reclothe herself. It seemed very illicit, suddenly, just to be in the same house with him, half-clad. Especially half-clad, and trembling, and thinking that she would just as easily, just as gladly, crawl into a bed, onto a floor—anywhere—with him as she ever had.

Unwilling to consider such thoughts for long, she raced hurriedly and breathlessly back down the stairs.

He was sipping wine and had poured a glass for her. He handed it to her, watching her. She thanked him, then they fell silent.

"How, was, uh, getting back to work?" she asked at last.

"Fine. How about you?"

"Fine."

Silence again.

"I've got great students," she offered.

He nodded. Eventually he said, "We should get going."

"Yes."

She was somewhat surprised to discover that his car was a lemon-yellow Ferrari. He smiled at her look, leaning over her shoulder as he opened the door to whisper tauntingly, "No, I'm not on the take. My father was a cigar king once upon a time, and he left a trust fund, which I managed to invest rather decently."

"Did I say anything?"

"Your eyes did."

She didn't even know where they were going; he drove in silence. When they got onto the Dolphin Expressway, and then onto I-95, she finally asked him.

"Miami Shores," he said simply then lapsed back into silence again.

She decided to break it. "I've been taking a few Spanish lessons."

His eyes met hers briefly in the mirror. "Oh? Why?"

"I thought I should be able to say a few things tonight."

He smiled. "That's nice."

There was something about that smile she didn't like.

He flicked on the radio. Mandy gave up, closed her eyes and leaned back in the seat. It was better than watching his hands on the steering wheel and remembering other places where they had been.

Eventually they turned off the highway and drove through a series of side streets until they pulled into a circular drive fronting a beautiful old Deco residence. Mandy wanted to ask him whose house it was, but he didn't give her a chance. He helped her out, then hurried to the door so quickly that she nearly tripped as she followed him.

He didn't ring the bell; he just walked in. And then Mandy understood that smile.

It was a party all right. It was even ethnic. Half the people there were dressed in green, and on a beautiful rich oak bar at the back of the living room was a massive glass keg of green beer.

"St. Patrick's Day!" she gasped.

"It is the seventeenth," Sean murmured.

"You rat!" It was all she could think of.

"Sean! You made it! Come in, dear, and introduce me to Mrs. Blayne!"

She didn't need to be introduced to his mother; Mrs. Ramiro had apparently given her son the emerald green of her eyes. She was a tiny creature, no more than five-two, slim and graceful, with marvelous silver hair and a smile that could melt a glacier.

Mrs. Ramiro was charming. She had a soft brogue and an equally soft voice, and she was entirely entrancing. "I'm Siobhan, Mrs. Blayne. You come with me!" She winked and tucked Mandy's arm into her own. Then she walked her guest around, introducing her to various people—who seemed to come in all nationalities. Spanish was spoken by some of them, but it was always broken off politely when Mandy appeared, and she was impressed with the sincere interest shown by those who met her.

At last Mrs. Ramiro brought her to the bar, where she was given a green beer.

"You look shell-shocked, child. What's the matter?" Siobhan asked her.

Mandy found herself being perfectly honest. "I thought I was going to have roast pig," she admitted finally, and Siobhan laughed. "I spent all week practicing my Spanish."

"Well, I daresay you'll get to use it. A number of my guests are Cuban and Colombian."

"On St. Patrick's Day," Mandy murmured.

"Oh, everyone's Irish on St. Patrick's Day." Siobhan laughed. "Aren't you, just a smidgen?"

Over the rim of her glass, Mandy saw Sean coming toward them, and she said very clearly for his benefit, "Oh, honestly, I don't know, Siobhan. As far as I know I'm just an American mongrel. No one ever seemed to be able to trace my family."

Siobhan laughed softly again. "I'll warrant there's some Irish in you somewhere!"

Sean smiled down at his mother, helping himself to the green beer. "Maybe there is, Mother. I tried to call her WASP once, and she told me that she was Catholic. Could mean a good Irish priest was nestled in the family somewhere."

"You called her what? Sean!"

"Dreadful of me, wasn't it?"

"Certainly. I don't know how you stood him for all that time, Amanda!" Siobhan shook her head. "I must get back to my other guests. Please, Amanda, have a wonderful time. I'm so glad to meet you. And I promise," she added, her eyes sparkling, "we'll roast you a pig next time!"

Mandy was left to face Sean again. She sipped her beer, staring steadily at him. "You really are a rat."

"Why?"

"You knew what I assumed."

"I'm sorry about the lack of a pig. Well, actually, we do have a pig. Cabbage and bacon."

"Umm."

He set his beer down on the bar and swept hers from her hand, then looped his arms around her and brought her against him. She stiffened, but he seemed not to notice. "There's music out on the patio. People are dancing. Dance with me, Mandy."

She didn't really have a chance to refuse. He simply led her out to the back, where a trio was playing and people were indeed dancing beneath soft colored lights.

The music was slow, and she found herself in his arms. Dancing with him came as easily as making love.

"Why did you come with me tonight?" he asked her at length.

Her face was against his shoulder; her hand was clasped in his. She could feel all the rhythms of his body, and the softness of his dark hair brushing her forehead as he bent his head.

"I—I don't know."

"Are you glad you did?"

"I don't know."

"Do you hate me?"

"I...no."

"You smell great."

"Thank you."

"You feel great."

"Thank you."

"Do you know what I'm thinking?"

"Do I want to know?"

"I don't know." He waited a moment, then continued. "I was thinking that I wish a leprechaun would suddenly whisk all these people away so I could ravish you this very second."

She wondered how just his words could affect her so deeply, but they could. She was glad that she was clinging to him; she needed the balance.

She closed her eyes before she spoke. "I didn't mean what I said, you know," she told him, then hesitated. "About Latins. You know. The, uh, last American remembering the flag."

His arms tightened around her as they swayed.

"You'd marry a Ramiro?"

"That wasn't the question. You never mentioned marriage."

"I suppose I didn't. But if I had—hypothetically, of course—what would your hypothetical answer have been?"

"I—I don't think that I—"

His interruption was a whisper that swept her ear like velvet. "But you can handle an affair?"

She didn't answer him.

"You'll sleep with me, but that's it, huh?"

Suddenly she wasn't leaning on his shoulder any longer; she was being held away from him, and his eyes were searching hers.

And she was desperately wondering why she was here. Dr. Jekyll always turned into Mr. Hyde.

He started to say something, but before he could a slim dark-haired young man tapped his shoulder apologetically, smiled with rueful fascination at Mandy, then cleared his throat as he remembered his mission. "Sean, we've got an emergency call. And you promised to introduce me."

"Harvey Anderson, Amanda Blayne. What's the call?" he inquired, annoyed.

"Mrs. McKinley's being treated at Jackson. Suicide attempt. Sorry, Mrs. Blayne. They want us. Pronto."

Sean's shoulders fell as he stared at Amanda. She knew that he was really aggravated, he had wanted the discussion to go further.

So had she. He never understood her, and it was largely her fault. Still, maybe this was for the best.

"I've got to go," he said. "Mom will see that you get home. I'm sorry."

"It's all right."

"I'll call you."

She nodded, knowing that he wouldn't reach her. She was going to change her flight and leave for Colorado in the morning.

He looked as if he was going to say something else, as if he longed to. As if he longed to touch her one more time.

But he didn't. He just closed his eyes briefly, shook his head and left her.

And perhaps it *was* for the best. Because although Mandy insisted again and again that she could call a cab, Siobhan Ramiro was determined to drive her home. She kept up a pleasant stream of chatter from the north of the city to the south and, surprisingly enough, agreed to come in for coffee before driving home.

Mandy soon discovered why.

As Siobhan sipped her coffee she dropped all pretense of casual interest and stared at Mandy with her clear green eyes. "I think my son is in love with you."

Mandy couldn't pull her eyes away from that green

stare. Nor could she give anything but a bitter, honest answer. "Sometimes I think he hates me."

Siobhan lowered her eyes, smiling slightly. "No, he just doesn't always handle himself very well. You see…" She hesitated briefly, then shrugged and continued. "I came here to tell you something. I hope I can trust you. I'm not supposed to know this. A friend of his told me about it, because I was beside myself, worrying about him. There was a spell a few years ago when he had a different woman every week. He almost seemed to— to delight in starting an affair. And ending it. And they were all…blond."

Siobhan sat back in her chair with a sigh. "He grew out of it quickly, though he never became really involved again. Cruelty really isn't a part of his nature. I should have known all along. You see, there was this particular girl…well, he'd been madly in love with her. He wanted to marry her. He was going to meet her parents, she was going to come and meet me. All of a sudden it was off. I found out later that she had been pregnant—and that her parents had forced her into an overseas boarding school after a quick abortion."

"Why?" Mandy gasped, stunned by the story.

Siobhan smiled with a trace of her son's bitterness. "They were very rich. And totally bigoted. The name Ramiro just didn't fit in with their idea of their daughter's future."

"Oh," Mandy said weakly.

Siobhan rose. "Well, that's it. I—I hope I've helped. I noticed the sparks flying at the bar tonight, and knowing him, well, I thought maybe you deserved an explanation."

Mandy bit her lip, rising to escort her visitor to the door. "Siobhan," she said impulsively, "It *has* helped. And I hope you believe that I would never feel that way. Sean... Sean thinks that I do, though. I've got a few problems that he doesn't understand."

"I know," Siobhan said softly. "I know about your husband and your child. And I'm so sorry. But you've got a long life ahead of you. Neither of them would have wished you to spend it in misery."

"I'm afraid," Mandy told her.

"To care again? We all are."

"Siobhan," Mandy said again impulsively, "I'm going away for a while. To work."

"And more than that, to think?"

"Yes."

"Well, whatever you decide, I wish you the best."

"Thank you."

Siobhan kissed her cheek, smiled encouragingly, then hurried down the walk to her car.

Mandy watched the taillights until they disappeared in the night, then thoughtfully closed her door.

Chapter 13

The dig was a recent one; the site had only been discovered about a year before. A camper had found a piece of bone sticking out of the ground in a field near the mountains. Curious, he had asked another friend to look at it, and luckily, the professionals had been called in before anything could be destroyed.

Mandy's time had just about expired, and she wasn't sure if she was sad—or grateful. There was a yearning in her to go home. She had desperately wanted to get away to think, but she hadn't really thought at all. By day she had chiseled and wrapped and plastered; by night she had lain alone and wished that she was not alone. What frightened her was that, though Sean hadn't actually said so, she knew that he wanted a wholehearted commitment, and she cringed like a child from that thought.

But then, she had thought she couldn't possibly make love with him, and that had occurred easily, beautifully. Maybe all things would follow suit. Maybe all she had to do was take the plunge.

As the afternoon fell she was sitting in her little spot in front of the phalanges of a Tyrannosaurus rex, carefully dusting the last of the sand from them with a sable brush so that they could be prepared for removal.

There was gigantic oak behind her, and a pile of rocks before her, so although the site was filled with workers, she was virtually alone. The find had been magnificent: a dozen of these particular beasts, and then any number of other creatures they had fed upon. She was glad to be alone, yet when she did try to think she panicked and wished that she was in the middle of a crowd.

A shadow suddenly fell across her work. Instinctively she looked up.

She was so surprised that the breath was swept cleanly from her.

Sean was standing there, in a standard three-piece suit. Tall and dark and handsome, a stray lock of hair falling over his forehead, his eyes as green as the spring fields. He stood there silently, then smiled slowly.

"Hello, Mandy."

She eased back at last, just staring for several moments. She lowered her head, thinking that this wasn't exactly how she had wanted to see him. She was in overalls and a dusty lab coat, and half the dirt that had been on the bones was smudging her face.

She shook her head, frowning, before she managed to speak. "What—what are you doing here?"

"I have a paper that needs your signature."

She frowned again. She'd heard from the FBI sporadically throughout the week, and no one had mentioned anything that required her signature.

"You're here on business?"

He hesitated a second too long. "Yes."

She smiled, looking back to the bones, delighted to see him, but wishing she'd had just a little more time.

He reached into his coat pocket for an envelope, then crouched down across from her. "This is it. You said you wanted to testify for Señora Garcia. This is a document compiled from your conversations with the FBI and the Miami PD. I need to get it back to the D.A.'s office. They've set a trial date for late September."

"Oh," Mandy murmured.

She read the document over. It had been accurately compiled and said exactly what she thought. She started to scrawl her name on it. "Is Señora Garcia in jail?"

"No. She's out on bond." He hesitated, then shrugged. "Julio's father is out, too. Peter had been pulling strings for him."

"What about Julio?"

Sean shook his head. "He's in jail. It's probably for the best. He'll definitely get time, and this will count toward it."

Mandy nodded. "Roberto?" she asked.

Sean's mouth twitched grimly. "I don't know what the courts will decide. But he's been connected to everything—drugs, robberies, murder. If they manage the case correctly, he'll end up with a dozen life sentences."

She lowered her head, shivering a bit. She still

couldn't help but feel that Roberto deserved whatever he got.

"I, uh, got a telegram from Peter."

She raised her head quickly, frowning. "You did? Why?"

He smiled and reached into his pocket again, then passed her the paper. There were only two words on it, other than the address and the signature: MARRY HER.

Her hand started to shake; she clasped it with the other one and pursed her lips. Finally she said, "I guess he knew something was going on."

"So it seems."

"And you were wrong. He doesn't mind."

"I'm sure he minds." He paused, then asked, "Do you mind what I do?"

She stared at him, then shrugged. "Police work isn't the safest profession."

"But I'm in homicide. I deal with people who are dead—and harmless."

"But the people who made them dead aren't harmless."

He sighed softly. "Mandy, narcotics is a little scary. Not homicide. The last time I pulled a gun before I was on those docks—except on a shooting range—was four years ago. You watch too many cop shows."

She grinned. "Actually, I don't watch any."

"Oh."

"Aren't you forgetting something?"

"What?"

She tilted her head back, determined that, no matter what followed, she would not be punished for anyone else's sins. "I'm a blonde. Daughter of the American Revolution all the way. Rich bitch."

"Yeah, I know. I'm willing to overlook that."

"Are you? And what made you decide that I might not be a bigot?"

He lowered his head. Lowered his head, and lifted his shoulders and hands a little helplessly. "Mandy—"

"Oh!" she cried suddenly.

"What?"

"You're on his hip!"

"What?"

"Move back! Move back quickly. You're on my bone!"

"Oh." Red-faced, Sean scrambled to his feet, quickly moving away. Mandy hurried back to the slightly protruding bone, checking it quickly for damage.

She sighed with relief.

"Er, uh, what is he?"

"Tyrannosaurus rex," she answered absently.

"The big bad guy? The one in all the Japanese horror films?"

"Uh-huh. Except that he wasn't really so bad. See, look."

She stood, skirting the area to show him the complete layout of the skeleton. "Look at his arms—there. See how tiny they were in comparison to his bulk? He couldn't really grab and rip and tear. He could barely get things to his mouth. We think now that he was a scavenger—a carnivore, but one who went in *after* the kill had already been made."

She glanced up and blushed, surprised by the softness in his eyes as he stared at her. "You like your work, don't you?"

"Yes, very much."

"I like it, too. You could teach—me."

She didn't know what to say. As the breeze lifted her hair and wafted it around her face, she knew she should say something but, at that moment, she couldn't.

And then the moment was gone, because Dr. Theo Winter, who was in charge, came around the oak tree with a group of workers behind him, ready to start the plastering process. Mandy introduced Sean, but Dr. Winter was understandably unimpressed with anything but the cache of bones. All he wanted was for Sean to get off the site.

It was a good thing Dr. Winter hadn't seen Sean standing on the protruding skeleton, she thought wryly.

"I guess I'd better go," he told her, surprising her. She wasn't sure whether she was relieved or disappointed.

One of the assistants was asking a question, and she knew she had no right to be standing there talking while everyone else was working. But she didn't seem to be able to move any more than she could talk.

Sean solved that dilemma. He saluted her with a rueful grin, then walked away. She simply stood there, feeling the breeze in her hair, watching him leave.

Why hadn't he asked her to dinner or something? she wondered over and over again as the day wore on. But it wasn't a question that took much pondering on her part. It was going to be all or nothing. They weren't going to date. They weren't going to go for dinner or cocktails, or to the movies, or for a picnic in the park.

They were either going to get married or not—and

only if she did marry him would she get to go to dinner and the movies and for walks on the beach. Maybe after the way they had begun it would be impossible to date.

She was beginning to understand him now; maybe he even understood her. She didn't think he was insensitive to her reasons for holding back; he just felt that they could be overcome—and should be.

Mandy thought she might hear from him the next day, but she didn't. He didn't contact her hotel, and he didn't appear on the site. She wondered if he had returned to Miami already and was startled to find herself annoyed at the thought. So much for hot pursuit!

On her last night there was a dinner party for her, which she made it through by rote. She realized that she had actually been doing all of her living by rote—until she met Sean.

There were a million good reasons why she should marry him, two that were extremely important. One, she loved him. Two, if the test she had bought at the drugstore worked, she was expecting his child.

The only thing that stood against her was the panic she felt at the prospect of loving so deeply again.

And the problem, which Sean didn't understand, was that it wasn't just an emotional reaction. It was physical. Her hands would sweat, her heart would beat too loudly. Confusion overwhelmed her at the thought.

Thought… Once upon a time she had assumed that she would simply never have another child, because the horror of loss was so deep. Of course, if not for circumstances, she would have been responsible enough never to let such a thing happen.

And now…now she knew that nothing would keep her from having this child.

Her thoughts would not leave her alone, not even for an instant. Not even while she said her goodbyes, lingered over breakfast to thank everyone—and nearly missed her plane because she seemed so incapable of doing anything right. She groaned while she raced through the airport terminal and decided that she was either going to marry Sean—he *was* serious, wasn't he?—or move to an isolated village in Alaska.

She settled into the sparsely populated first-class section of her plane and picked up a magazine. She had been staring at the picture of an elegant dining-room set for several seconds before she realized that it looked odd because it was upside down. She sighed, then froze.

Because Sean was on the plane, blocking those trying to board behind him, staring down at her in dismay.

"You're in first class?"

"What?"

"Oh, damn!"

He moved on by to let the others pass. Mandy just stared at the seat ahead of her. In a few minutes the passengers were all boarded and belted. The stewardess made her speech on safety, and then they were airborne.

At last Mandy kicked off her shoes and curled her feet beneath her, determined to get comfortable for the duration of the trip, despite the fact that her heart refused to slow its frantic beat. She didn't know if she wanted to laugh or cry. He really meant to force the issue.

The stewardess offered her champagne; she took it,

intending to sip it. Instead, she swallowed the contents with a toss of her head.

The stewardess, of course, came right back, thinly concealing a shocked expression—and offered her more champagne.

"There's really nothing to be afraid of," the attractive young blonde told her. "Honestly. Captain Hodges has been flying for twenty years. He's wonderful. You won't feel a bump the entire way."

Mandy shook her head, smiling. "I'm not afraid of flying. I love to fly."

"Oh." Confused, the woman smiled, then quickly walked away.

Mandy stared out the window. They were already high above the clouds. It seemed that they were standing still above a sea of pure white cotton. If only she could concentrate. If only she could think about anything besides the fact that Sean was on the plane.

Her stomach lurched. What was the matter with her? He really did care. He had to care, or he would never have gone so far.

She took a deep breath, shivering. Did she really want to spend the rest of her life alone? Life was full of risks, and, yes, loving was a risk. But what was life except for a lonely expanse of years without the loving?

And now that Sean had touched her life, it seem absurdly bleak without him.

But could she love again? Worry about him, day after day? Pray that he came home each night? And what about children? Could she hold a child again, always knowing how quickly that life could be snuffed out?

"Move your feet."

Mandy started at the sound of his voice, then gasped, spilled her champagne and stared up at him guiltily.

"C'mon, move your feet!"

She did so, and he slid in beside her.

"What are doing up here? You're supposed to be in economy class!" she demanded.

"I bribed the stewardess."

"Stewardesses don't take bribes."

"Everyone takes bribes."

As if on cue, the stewardess walked by, watching them with a curiously knowing eye.

"What did you tell her?" Mandy asked suddenly.

He shrugged.

"Sean?"

"Nothing major." He smiled. "I just said that you were a deranged criminal whom I was trailing from Miami. I said I didn't want to put cuffs on you and frighten the other passengers—I just wanted to keep an eye on you." He smiled pleasantly, reached for a magazine, and gazed idly around the first-class cabin. "Nice."

"Sean, you didn't—"

"I did."

"I'll kill you!" Mandy snapped angrily just as the stewardess walked by again. The woman's eyes, cornflower blue and already big, seemed to grow as wide as saucers.

"Now, now, calm down, Mrs. Blayne," he said in a professional soothing voice. He winked at the stewardess, giving her a thumbs-up sign of assurance.

"Sean Ramiro—"

"Maybe you can plea bargain, Mrs. Blayne. Just stay calm, and I'll be at your side."

"I'm not a criminal!"

"Tsk, tsk, Mrs. Blayne. I'm afraid the State believes that lacing your great-uncle's coffee with that arsenic was a criminal offense."

The stewardess, barely a row ahead of them, stiffened and swallowed, and almost poured champagne on a businessman's lap.

"Sean, I *will* kill you!"

"Please, Mrs. Blayne. I really don't want to have to use the handcuffs."

"Oh, Lord!" Mandy groaned, sinking back into her seat and giving up. "There's definitely Irish blood in you—I've never heard so much blarney in my life!"

"Behave," he said wickedly, "and I'll get us more champagne. I do like this," he observed casually. "First class. It's a pity the department is so cheap."

"You really got the department to send you out to Denver?"

"Of course. I had to talk to you about the trial."

Mandy groaned again and turned to face the window. She didn't see the clouds anymore; only the reflection of his face. And for all his dry humor, she thought she saw pain mirrored there.

Her heart began to beat faster. It was the strangest thing, the most awful emotion. There he was, and there it was, all the laughter, all the love. All she had to do was reach for it, but she was unable to, taking two steps backward for every step forward.

She closed her eyes, then jumped when she heard him call the stewardess back.

"Could we get some more champagne, please?" He

lowered his voice to a whisper. "I can control her much more easily if I keep her a bit sloshed, you know?"

"Oh, yes, of course!"

"Ohh!" Mandy groaned. "Couldn't you just have paid the difference for a first-class ticket?"

He started to answer her, then paused, thanking the stewardess gravely as she poured Mandy more champagne and offered a glass to Sean.

"Cheers!" he said, clinking his glass against hers.

She pursed her lips stubbornly, refusing to respond.

"Come on, where's the Mandy I used to know?"

A twitch tugged at her lips. "Damned if I know. Last I heard, you were taking a criminal back to Miami."

He started to smile wryly at her, but the stewardess returned with their lunch trays. And then, to Mandy's surprise, he didn't pay any attention to her at all. He was watching the stewardess.

The pretty woman seemed exceptionally nervous, which Mandy thought was Sean's fault, since he had convinced her that Mandy was a criminal.

The stewardess almost dropped the trays, but recovered her poise. Sean continued to watch her as she moved down the aisle, then sat back in his seat, perplexed.

"What's wrong?"

"Hmm?"

"What's wrong?"

She didn't like the way he looked. She really did love to fly, but suddenly she thought of all sorts of disasters. Someone had forgotten a little pin or something, and their jumbo jet was about to fall apart in midair.

Except that the flight wasn't even bumpy. It was so incredibly smooth that it felt as if they were standing still.

She gripped his arm tensely. "Sean," she whispered, "do you think there's something wrong with the plane?"

He stared at her. "The plane? Something wrong?" He shook his head. "I've never felt a smoother flight."

"Then what—?"

"Are you going to eat that steak?"

"What?"

"Eat, will you?"

He didn't pay any attention to his own food. He ate it, but he was giving all his attention to the stewardess.

The woman still seemed a little shaky when she returned. She had poise, though. She smiled; she chattered. It was just that her manner was slightly different, and not only with the two of them.

Mandy tried to quiz Sean again as soon as they trays were removed, but he interrupted her first word, murmuring, "Excuse me for a minute, please."

"Sean!"

But he was already gone. He disappeared into the little kitchen area—right behind the stewardess. And he seemed to stay there a long, long time.

When he emerged, he returned to his seat beside her like a sleepwalker, totally remote.

"Sean…"

"I don't believe it," he murmured distractedly.

"You don't believe what?"

"Shh. You didn't finish your champagne. Drink it."

Drink it. As if she would need it.

"Sean!" She slammed a fist against his shoulder.

"Shh!"

"You said there wasn't anything wrong with the plane."

"There isn't. I swear it."

The stewardess came hurriedly toward them once again, then bent to speak softly in Sean's ear. "We need you now, lieutenant."

He nodded and stood, ready to follow her again. She paused suddenly, looking back at Mandy with dismay.

"Will she be all right?"

"What? Oh, yes, of course. As long as you don't have any arsenic on board."

They disappeared together toward the cockpit. Mandy was ready to scream.

It seemed an eternity before he returned, though it was only about twenty minutes.

"Sean, what the hell is going on?"

"Hey!" someone complained loudly from behind them. "I take this flight constantly. What's going on? They should have announced landing by now. And we should be over land—not water!"

"Damn you, Sean Ramiro!" Mandy whispered, alarmed. "What's going on?"

He turned to her at last. "I didn't want to alarm you—"

"You didn't want to alarm me?"

"Shh! There's nothing wrong with the plane. Honest. In fact, there's really nothing wrong at all. We're just taking a little side trip."

"Side trip?"

"Er, yes."

Just then the pilot came over the loudspeaker. He sounded marvelously, wonderfully calm. He started by explaining that obviously their seasoned passengers would realize that they were not flying their usual route. He assured them that nothing was wrong. It was just that they had a "gentleman" aboard who was insisting that they fly on to José Marti airport—in Havana.

Mandy gasped and stared at Sean. "We're being hijacked to Cuba!"

"Yes, I know," he said uncomfortably. "I tried to talk him out of it."

The pilot then turned the microphone over to the "gentleman" in question, who told the passengers in broken English that he didn't want to hurt anybody, certainly not Captain Hodges, but that he had been away from his homeland now for eight years and was determined to go back.

"I don't believe this!" Mandy breathed. She stared at Sean again. "Can't you do something?"

"I'm afraid not. He's got a Bowie knife at the captain's back and a hand grenade to boot."

"How'd he ever get on the plane?"

"How the hell should I know?"

Their conversation ended at that point, because the stewardess began calmly putting them through a crash-landing procedure just in case they had difficulty landing. There was no panic on plane, possibly because the pilot came on again, assuring them that they had been cleared to land at José Marti.

"I really don't believe this!" Mandy whispered nervously as she prepared for landing.

"I am sorry, Mandy. Really."

"You're sorry?"

"Yeah. I'm trying to convince you that we're a great

people, and all you get to meet are the kidnappers and the hijackers."

She gripped his hand tightly. "That's not true. I got to meet one really great cop."

The plane jolted as the landing gear came down.

"Hey, you're admitting it at last. I told you I was really great."

The wheels touched the ground and the brakes came on with a little screech. Mandy prayed that the runway was long enough for the jet.

It was.

In seconds the plane came to a complete stop. And then, seconds later, it began filling with the Cuban military.

Mandy quickly lost Sean. The stewardess came back for him, desperate for a translator.

It seemed to Mandy that she sat there by herself forever. Nothing happened to her; nothing happened to anyone, but it seemed like absolute chaos. There were just too many people on the plane, and at some point, the air conditioning went out.

The heat was sweltering, and just when she thought she couldn't take it anymore an announcement was made that buses would be coming to take the passengers to the terminal, where they were welcome to exchange their money and buy food and souvenirs.

Mandy craned her neck to find Sean, but she couldn't see him. Unhappily, she started to leave along with the others.

She was stopped at the steps by a trim officer with a Clark Gable mustache. She couldn't understand him, and he couldn't understand her. All she could tell was that he was insisting she stay behind, and a case of the jitters assailed her again. Why her? Oh, God! Maybe *they* though she was a murderess, too!

But she merely found herself escorted back to the center of the plane, where Sean was in earnest conversation with several more mustachioed officers. The talking went on and on, with everyone gesticulating.

Finally the man who looked to be the ranking officer shrugged, and the others laughed, then stared at her, smirking.

Sean turned to her then and gripped her arm. "Quick!" he whispered into her ear. "Let's go. There will be a car at the foot of the steps. Get right into it, and act as if you love me to death!"

"What?"

"Shh! Just do it!"

"I—"

"Mandy! Please!"

He didn't give her any choice. He shoved her down the aisle, then hurried her down the stairs.

The car was there, just as he had said, a black stretch limo. She climbed into the back with Sean, and was surprised when the official with the Clark Gable mustache followed.

At last they reached an impressive building with emblems all over beautiful wrought-iron gates. She managed to whisper to Sean, "Where the hell are we, and what the hell is going on?"

"The Swiss embassy," he whispered back. "The pilot is around here somewhere, too. He has to make special arrangements for fuel to get home."

The car stopped. The Cuban official was greeted by a tall blond man, but though this might have been the Swiss embassy, they were still speaking Spanish, and she was lost.

"Sean, I don't care about the pilot. What are *we* doing here?"

"They're, uh, trying to keep me here," he said.

"What?"

He took both her hands earnestly. "Just help me, Mandy. Go along with me. They know who I am."

"Who are you?"

"Oh, it all goes way back. You wouldn't want me to be stuck here forever, would you?"

She gazed at him warily. "Go on."

"Marry me. If I marry an American citizen—"

"You are an American citizen."

"Ah, but I told you, they know me! My father was involved in some things that—"

"Uh-uh! This guy is acting like your long-lost friend."

"Actually, he is. I was in school with him until the night I fled the country."

"I thought you were born in Ireland."

"I was. It's a long story." He put his hands on her shoulders and pulled her anxiously to him. "Well? They've given me a chance. The Swiss will give us a license and a minister. Mandy! Come on! You've got to get me out of this one."

She stared at him for a long, long time. At the sun above them, at the flowers, at the sky, at the beautiful mountains in the distance.

This wasn't how she had expected things to go at all. The other passengers were busy buying trinkets as mementos of their incredible day, while she was here with Sean, listening to the most outrageous cock-and-bull story she had ever heard in her life.

She lowered her head, smiling slowly, and just a little painfully. After all these years, he had come back to his Cuban heritage, and it was his Irish blarney that was showing!

Her past flashed before her eyes. And she knew that although it would always be there, the time had come to gently close the door on it.

"If I don't do this, they'll keep you here, huh?"

"They could put me in prison."

"Oh."

"Well?"

"I don't suppose I could let that happen to you, could I?"

"It would be terribly mean, considering all I've done for you."

She was silent. He gazed at his watch impatiently. "Mandy! We have to do this before they make the fuel arrangements!"

She shrugged. "Then let's do it."

The Swiss were charming. Papers were secured, and they were ushered into a little chapel that adjoined the building. The ceremony was in French, and amazingly quick, because everyone was rushing.

Mandy smiled through it all, wondering how Sean had ever convinced the Cuban military authorities to let him get away with this nonsense.

But when her "I do" was followed by a very passionate kiss, she assumed it would be something they could talk about for ages.

They were whisked very quickly back to the airport. The fuel had been secured, and all the passengers had reboarded with the rum, cigars, and so forth.

They were in the air before Sean turned to her sheepishly at last. "I have a confession to make. I asked Captain Rotello for special permission to marry you. I lied, though I really did go to school with him. And he did know about my father. Our dads had been friends."

"Oh," Mandy said simply.

"Well, do you hate me?"

She looked at him regally, a superior smile playing on her lips. She saw the tension and passion in his wonderful green eyes.

"Actually, no, I have a confession to make myself."

"Oh, really?"

"I knew you were lying all along. I may not speak Spanish, but I'm not a fool."

"Oh," he said blankly.

"I did intend to learn the language, of course. Completely. I mean, I'll be damned if I'll have you and our son talking about me when I don't understand a single word you're saying!"

"Our son?"

"Or daughter."

"We're—we're having one?"

"In December. Maybe November."

He swallowed then, a little stiffly. "You married me…because you're pregnant?"

"I swear I'll hit you! I married you because I love you! Not because of your ridiculous story, and not because I'm pregnant. Come to think of it, you did threaten me about that! But—"

He smiled, his arm coming around her as he interrupted her. "You love me, huh?"

"Yes, and you know it."

"Yeah, well, it just sounds real nice to hear the words now and then. You'd better start practicing, because I'd like to hear them more frequently from now on."

"Hey, what's good for the goose—"

"I love you, Mrs. Ramiro. Desperately. Passionately. I love you, I love you, I love you—"

Unfortunately, the stewardess made an appearance just then.

"She loves me! She married me!" Sean told the woman.

"But I thought she was—you just married a murderess?"

"Oh, well, that—"

"Lieutenant Ramiro, what a line you gave me! Get back where you're supposed to be—in economy!"

But she wasn't serious. After all, it had been a most unusual flight. She merely arranged for more champagne.

Mandy laughed with him while they sipped champagne, then sobered slightly. "Is this real?"

"It's real."

"Sean... I may need help sometimes."

"We all need help sometimes."

"I do love you. So much. I guess I did, even on the island. I wanted to be rescued, but I didn't want to go back. Not to a life without you."

"Mandy..."

His champagne glass clinked down on his tray. His arms swept around her, his fingers curling into her hair.

And when his lips touched hers she was hungry for him, so hungry that it was easy to become swept up in his embrace and to forget that they were on a populated plane.

He broke away from her, groaning softly, excitingly, against her cheek. "Mrs. Ramiro, watch your hands."

"No one can see me."

"Well, they might see me! Oh, God, I can't wait till we get off this plane. Your place or mine?"

"Mine. I think we should sell yours."

"I think we should sell *yours*." He smiled. "Oh, hell! I don't care where we go—as long as we get there!"

It took them another two hours to get anywhere; in the end he went to her house, because it was closer to the airport. And though Mandy would have thought that such a feat was impossible, he managed to disrobe them both while climbing the stairs, strewing fabric down the length of the steps, then landing them on her bed in what was surely record time.

She was so happy. So amazed that she was his wife, that they were making love on the evening of their marriage. That they were both totally, completely committed.

It was fast; it was feverish—it had to be at first.

But the night stretched before them. Time for her to warn him that she owned one of the ugliest cats in the world, time for him to warn her that his partners could be a pain in the neck. Time to discuss things that hurt; time to talk about the past, and time to put it to rest.

And then time to make love all over again.

"Te amo," Mandy told him carefully, practicing the Spanish she had learned.

He smiled, tenderness blazing in his eyes, and she murmured the strange words again, "*Te amo*—here," she said, meeting his eyes, then kissing his chest. "And *te amo*—here."

With each repetition she moved against him, finding more and more deliciously erogenous zones.

"And *te amo*—here."

He gripped her hair, breathless, ablaze. He groaned, and at last swept her beneath him, pausing just an instant to whisper, "Mrs. Ramiro. I have never, never heard Spanish more eloquently spoken."

"*Querido!*" she whispered, and contentedly locked her arms about him.

He found life in her arms. And he gave her a new life, all she would ever ask in the world.

"*Querida!* My love, my love."

He kissed her abdomen and smiled as she arched to him.

She knew that she could love again.

Love a child, love a husband.

Even if he was rather manipulating and most certainly strange—and, oh, passionate!—and...

"Sean..."

She simply couldn't ponder it any longer.

It was the...circumstances.

Epilogue

Sean hesitated momentarily after he opened the door, wondering what Mandy's reaction would be to the visitor he was bringing home.

"Amanda?"

He stepped into the entryway of the big old frame house they had bought and stared through the living room to the office. As he had expected, she was at her desk, her reading glasses at the tip of her nose as she pored over term papers.

Katie—a toddling and mischievous two now—was playing sedately with her locking plastic blocks, probably trying to recreate a dinosaur like the one her mother had made her the night before, Sean thought wryly.

"Mandy?" he called again.

She looked up, saw him, threw her glasses down and

scooped Katie into her arms before coming to meet him excitedly, her words rushing out.

"Sean, believe it or not, I had the best time in the world today! I went into the market on Flagler because they have the best ham in the world. I have to admit I always resented going there before, because everyone spoke Spanish, but mine has gotten so good, and I got into this wonderful conversation with the clerk and I started to teach her English! I—oh!"

Her spiel came to an abrupt halt when she saw that her husband was not alone, and she stared at her visitor in dead surprise.

Sean slipped an arm around her. "Julio stepped into my office just when I was getting off for the day. He was just paroled, and he was anxious to see you."

"Oh," Mandy murmured.

Julio Garcia, gaunt-looking in a too-big suit, smiled hesitantly and offered his hand.

She took it, balancing her daughter in her other arm.

"I had to come," he told her softly. "The government has released me. But that is nothing. I must ask you to forgive me. I must hope that you understand and can believe that I did not ever wish to harm you. That—that I know now how wrong I was." His eyes were totally in earnest.

Mandy smiled at last, feeling the assurance of her husband's arm around her shoulders. "I forgive you, Julio. How…how are your parents?"

He gave her a smile that seemed to light up the room. "They are well. Even my father is well. The United States gave him a doctor who is good. And Mama, Mama is Mama."

Mandy nodded, then asked curiously, "And Maria?"

Julio laughed. "Mama married Maria off to a man with a will like iron. She is like you—one babe in her arms, one to come."

Mandy didn't ask about Juan or Roberto. Sean had assured her at the trial that Roberto faced so many charges that even if he lived to be an old, old man, he would probably never leave prison again.

Juan, too, would not come up for parole. He had been involved in a narcotics case before the kidnapping, and the judge hadn't shown him one bit of leniency.

"I am very happy for you, Mrs. Ramiro," Julio said. "Congratulations. Your daughter is beautiful."

Mandy discovered that she was able to laugh proudly. "Yes, she is. Thank you."

Katie was staring at Julio with her knuckles shoved into her mouth, but she really was beautiful. She had Sean's green eyes and a headful of ebony curls.

"You wish a son now, yes?" Julio asked.

It was Sean, lightly massaging his wife's nape, who answered. "Not necessarily. I'm awfully fond of girls. A son, a daughter, it doesn't matter. Mandy and I were both only children, and we both wished that we'd had a brother or a sister, so…"

He shrugged, and Mandy flushed, because though they'd both been quite happy about it, this baby was as completely unplanned as Katie had been.

"Well…" Julio cleared his throat and shifted his weight from foot to foot. "I must go now, I did not wish to impose. I just wanted you to know that I appreciate how you told them at the trial that you did not think I was cruel, but needed help. And that I wished so much for your forgiveness. I have a good job already, too. I am a mechanic. One day I will own my own garage."

"I'm sure you will," Mandy said softly.

"Goodbye, then, *señora*. I wish you and your husband and your lovely family all the best."

Sean walked him to the door. Mandy watched them, hugging Katie to her.

When Sean returned she was still smiling, so he arched one of his dark brows curiously. "Okay, out with it. What are you thinking?"

She laughed, managing to hug him and Katie at the same time. "I was just thinking that I really do forgive him with all my heart. Without him, I'd have never met this weird cop who stuck by me through thick and thin—and then married me, to boot."

"Hey, duty called. And you were such a marvelous blond bombshell."

"Yeah?"

"Yeah."

He grinned, then kissed her warmly and deeply until Kate let out an outraged squawk that Mommy and Daddy were crushing her.

They laughed together again, and their eyes touched, full of promises.

* * * * *

Also available from B.J. Daniels

Harlequin Intrigue

Cardwell Ranch: Montana Legacy

Steel Resolve
Iron Will
Ambush Before Sunrise
Double Action Deputy

Whitehorse, Montana: The McGraw Kidnapping

Dark Horse
Dead Ringer
Rough Rider

HQN

Montana Justice

Restless Hearts
Heartbreaker

Sterling's Montana

Stroke of Luck
Luck of the Draw
Just His Luck

The Montana Cahills

Renegade's Pride
Outlaw's Honor
Hero's Return
Rancher's Dream

Visit her Author Profile page at Harlequin.com
or bjdaniels.com for more titles!

THE NEW DEPUTY
IN TOWN

B.J. Daniels

This book is dedicated to Chris and Jessica Kerr,
the cutest couple I know and the sweetest.
It's a joy to know the two of you.

Chapter 1

Her hand trembled as she opened the closet to find the baseball bat where she'd hidden it in the very back corner. After last time, she'd considered getting rid of the bat. Instead, she'd wiped off the splattering of blood as best she could and kept it.

She wasn't stupid. She watched *CSI* and all the other forensics television shows. She knew about blood splatters, about DNA, about trace evidence.

But she also knew it wouldn't be good to change anything. Ritual, she knew, was important. It should always be a Saturday night. She should always wear the same blue dress she'd worn the first time. She should always use the old baseball bat she'd found.

"I thought you were going out with friends?" called a voice from the living room. She could hear the TV.

One of those reality shows was on. "It's getting kind of late though to be going now, isn't it?"

She bit down on her irritation. She was sick of being told what to do. Sick of other people's expectations for her. She put the bat on the bed and reached for her blue dress. There was one little blood spot along the hem that she'd had trouble getting out. She frowned, worried that even one spot might be enough to change things. To ruin the routine. To jinx her.

She worried at the spot for a moment. Maybe she shouldn't go into town tonight. But it was Saturday. There would be a band at one of the bars. There would be men who would get drunk and want to dance with her.

She thought of the smell of them, the feel of their sweaty hands on the blue dress, the sound of their breathing as they pressed themselves against her.

She put on the dress and picked up the bat. A woman on TV was gagging loudly as if unable to swallow something revolting.

She went out the back door, letting it slam. It was Saturday night. She was wearing her blue dress. She had the bat. And wouldn't some man be surprised tonight.

Chapter 2

Sunday morning Laney Cavanaugh looked down at the book in her lap, then out at the country. She was having trouble keeping her mind on what was being touted *the* summer beach-book read. Maybe it required a beach.

This part of northeastern Montana couldn't be farther from the shore. She could see from horizon to horizon, the rolling landscape awash with tall golden grass that undulated in the morning breeze. Etched against the horizon to the east was the dark outline of an old windmill. To the southwest was the faint smudge of the Little Rockies and the Bear Paw Mountains. In between was prairie, miles and miles of it.

"Boring, huh?" her sister said as she came out of the house, the screen door slamming behind her. "No wonder Mother hated it here." Laci plopped down in the chair next to Laney's with a huge sigh.

Laney didn't hate it here. Coming here had always given her a sense of peace. She liked the quiet, the only sound crickets chirping in the grass or the closer buzz of a bee in the flower bed along the porch. At night sometimes the wind blew or rain fell in a monotonous drone that lulled her to sleep.

Today though, she felt restless. The July air seemed to be holding its breath, waiting for something. She felt that same sense of anticipation inside her like the flutter of butterfly wings. Something was about to happen.

She didn't share these thoughts with Laci, who would have made fun of her. "You are *so* dramatic," her younger sister often said. "You should have been an actor or a writer or well, anything but an accountant."

"I'm going to bake some cookies," Laci said, shoving herself out of the chair. Her sister had never been able to sit still for long. It was only nine in the morning. Laci had already made them both breakfast including a blueberry coffee cake, a spinach-and-bacon quiche and smoothies. But then Laci wasn't happy unless she was cooking.

"I've never understood why Gramps keeps this place," Laci said as the screen slammed behind her.

Laney understood. This house was all they had left of their daughter Geneva. She and Laci had been born here. That was before their father had been killed in a car accident between here and the small Montana town of Whitehorse to the north.

The first settlement of Whitehorse had been nearer the Missouri River. But when the railroad came through, the town migrated five miles north, taking the name with it.

The original settlement of Whitehorse was now little more than a ghost town except for a handful of ranches and a few of the original remaining buildings. It was locally referred to as Old Town.

Old Town Whitehorse had once been the home of horse thieves who'd been either hanged or forced out by the early settlers. Laney's family had been one of the first to settle here, just miles from where the Missouri River wound a deep cut through the land.

This house and the early memories of their daughter were all Gramps and Gramma Pearl had. Titus kept the place up as if he believed that one day Geneva would return.

Laney and Laci visited each summer for the promised two weeks. Laney felt guilty that it wasn't more, but both she and Laci had their own lives, Laci in Seattle and Laney in Mesa, Arizona. The house sat empty the rest of the time. Waiting for someone who was never going to return.

Laney tried to go back to her book, but her mind kept wandering. She found herself looking down the long dirt road. If anyone had been coming, she would have been able to see the dust cloud miles away.

Nothing moved. Huge cumulus clouds bobbed along in an ocean of blue as the sun rose higher and the day began to get hot. A cloud floated over, casting a dark, cool shadow over her. Laney shivered, sensing a change in the air.

An instant later she was startled by the unexpected thunder of hooves as her cousin Maddie came riding around the end of the house. Maddie leaped off her horse in a cloud of dust, her face flushed with excitement under her western straw hat.

"I heard you were here," Maddie said as she bounded over the railing just as she'd done since she was a child. "Mother's coming by later, but I couldn't wait so I rode over," she said as she gave Laney a hug.

"Got in last night." Laney smiled in spite of herself as she looked at her cousin. Now nineteen, Maddie hadn't changed that much from the gangly freckle-faced girl she'd been. She was tall and slim to the point of being skinny, with a mop of thick reddish-blond hair and light blue eyes. She wore a western shirt, jeans and boots.

"Where's Laci?" Maddie asked excitedly. "Cooking, I'll bet. Oh, what is that heavenly smell?"

From inside the house came the warm rich scent of chocolate-chip cookies baking even though it was way too hot to bake. As if that had ever stopped Laci.

"Who wants a warm cookie?" her sister called on cue from inside the house.

"Guess who!" Maddie called back laughing, then looked at Laney, her expression sobering. "I wish you lived here. I hate these short visits. They are never enough." She gave Laney another hug, hanging on longer this time.

Laney sensed a small shudder in her cousin's thin frame. She pulled back, taking Maddie's arms to look at her, and felt her flinch. Shoving back Maddie's shirtsleeve, Laney saw dark bruises, each spread evenly apart as if someone had grasped her too roughly.

"What is this?" What she wanted to say was "who did this to you?"

"You know me," Maddie replied quickly, drawing

her sleeve down over the bruises. "I've always been such a klutz. It's nothing."

It was something; Laney could feel it as Maddie flashed her a reassuring smile that didn't quite ring true and hurried into the kitchen.

The new Deputy Sheriff, Nick Rogers, had been covering the weekend shifts until Sheriff Carter Jackson returned from Florida. So he wasn't surprised when he got called out on another assault Sunday morning.

There'd been two assaults since he'd taken the job. The victims were men who'd been attacked outside one of the bars on a Saturday night when the place was packed and there was a live band. Which probably explained why no one heard a disturbance in the parking lot.

He found Curtis McAlheney at the bar nursing a beer. Nick slid up onto the stool next to him and ordered a cup of coffee since it was only nine-thirty in the morning.

Curtis had a split lip, a black eye, a broken nose and was stooped over as if his ribs were bothering him.

"Broken or cracked?" Nick asked.

"Cracked, but they hurt like hell," Curtis said.

"You see your assailant?"

Curtis looked over at him. Thirty-something, he had thinning brown hair that stuck out the bottom of his John Deere cap. His eyes were small and brown, and his belly hung over his jeans into a T-shirt that proclaimed he was God's gift to women.

"Assailant?" Curtis repeated. "Didn't see no *assailant*—just some bastard with a baseball bat."

"You see his face?"

Curtis shook his head regretfully. "It was dark. He hit me from behind, knocked me down then beat me up good. He was big, I can tell you that much."

Nick nodded. This was pretty much the same description he'd gotten from the other men. Nick suspected the assailant was anything but big. A big man armed with a baseball bat would have done a lot more damage. "He rob you?"

Curtis looked sheepish. "I imagine he planned to. I think he came to his senses and took off before I got up and took that bat away from him and showed him what for."

Right. The motive in all the cases didn't appear to be robbery since nothing was taken but each man's pride. The assailant had just attacked, beaten up the men and taken off.

"Before you left the bar, did you get into a disagreement with anyone?"

"Naw. I just had a few beers, danced a little."

Same story Nick was getting from the others, although he suspected each had had more than a few beers.

"Well, if you think of anything else," Nick said finishing his coffee.

"Has to be some bastard not from around here, ain't that right, Shirley?" Curtis said to the bartender.

The bartender, a fifty-something stick of a woman, nodded. "No one around here would do something like that for no good reason."

Nick suspected whoever the assailant was, he had a reason, one good enough for him anyway. Tossing money on the bar for his coffee and a tip, Nick left as his cell phone began to vibrate.

"Trouble down in Old Town Whitehorse," the dispatcher said. "Alice Miller says someone stole her chickens."

As Maddie rode off, Laci put her feet up on the porch railing and sighed. "We need to have a party for her."

Laney looked up from her book, although she hadn't been reading. She'd been thinking about her cousin.

Laci took a cookie from the plate she'd brought out earlier. They'd had cookies and lemonade on the porch and talked about old times, although Laney hadn't been able to shake her worry for her cousin.

"An engagement party," Laci said between bites.

"I'm not sure that's a good idea," Laney said. "Didn't Maddie seem...different to you?"

Her sister shot her a look. "She's lost a bunch of weight since last summer. Don't all soon-to-be brides do that though?"

Maybe. "She's too skinny, but that's not what I'm talking about. She doesn't seem..."

"Happy?" Laci started laughing. "Maddie could be the poster child for happy."

"I felt like she was trying a little too hard," Laney said. She'd seen her cousin when they'd gotten into town last night. Only Maddie hadn't seen them. Laney had called to her cousin, who was leaving the back way just as they were coming in the front. But their cousin obviously hadn't heard them over the din of the bar as she left. "Like last night when we saw her leaving the bar. She wasn't with her fiancé."

Her sister groaned. "Maddie's fine. I'm sure she

wasn't doing anything more than dancing with a few ranch hands just like we were. She left the bar alone, didn't she?"

Laney nodded.

"See. Maddie's just stretching her wings a little."

Maybe, but Laney wasn't convinced.

"Now help me with the engagement-party menu," Laci said excitedly. "I want it to be something the town of Whitehorse has never seen. What do you think we should have to eat?"

"Don't you think you should at least talk to Maddie about this first? Maybe she doesn't want an engagement party."

Laci laughed as she rose from her chair. "Who doesn't want an engagement party? I'm going to start going through some of Gramma's old recipes. I think I'll do all desserts. What do you think?"

But she didn't wait to hear what Laney thought. The screen door slammed. Laney stared out at the horizon, trying to put her finger on what was bothering her about Maddie. Maybe it was the way her cousin had talked about her fiancé, Bo Evans, as if she would die without him. Or the way she played with her engagement ring. Or the way she brushed off her original plans to attend college, even giving up a scholarship.

All of that Laney could chalk up to love.

All except the bruises on Maddie's arm.

And Laney's own feeling that something wasn't right with her cousin.

She closed her book, glancing up the lane. That sense of nagging expectation washed over her again as if at any minute she would see someone coming down the road toward the house with bad news.

"Let's take some cookies to the hospital for the nurses," Laney said as she brought the plate and lemonade glasses into the kitchen to find her sister deep in an old cookbook. "I want to go visit Gramma."

Laci looked up. "Do you mind going without me? I hate seeing Gram like that and I really need to get to work on this party. I'm thinking it should be next Saturday. I'm sure we can use the community center."

Laney knew how hard it was for her sister to see their grandmother Pearl after her stroke. Gramma's eyes were open, but she was unresponsive. It was questionable if she could even understand what they said to her. Or if she recognized her granddaughters at all.

Gramma Pearl had been in the hospital with pneumonia when she'd suddenly had a stroke. Gramps said she'd been upset about some things that had been going on in Old Town Whitehorse.

"I think we both should go see Gramma," Laney said. "As it is, Gramps won't be happy with us since we didn't attend his church service this morning at the center. Maybe we can bribe him with some of your cookies because you know he'll be with Gramma."

Laci nodded although with obvious reluctance. "As long as you keep him from talking about Mother. I can't bear it. He really believes Geneva will just come home one day as if nothing happened. Why can't he accept that she's gone and won't ever be back? For all we know she's dead."

"He has to believe he'll see her again," Laney said although she agreed with her sister. Wherever Geneva Cavanaugh Cherry was, this was the last place she'd ever return.

Deputy Sheriff Nick Rogers had never been to Old Town Whitehorse before. He would have missed it entirely, if he hadn't slowed down to let a dog cross in front of his patrol car and seen the sign barely sticking up out of the weeds beside the road.

Whitehorse. Population 50.

He truly doubted that, given the age of the sign.

Nick had driven five miles through rolling grassland and open sky. He'd heard this land called the Big Open. He could well understand why.

And after all that way, he'd arrived in Old Town Whitehorse. Well, what was left of the original Whitehorse. There were a few buildings. No store. No gas station. No bar. Just what appeared to be a community center, an ancient abandoned gas station and a few houses still standing.

He could make out the trees and roofs of a few farms or ranches not far from town, but this whole place felt more like a ghost town than anything else.

One big old house in particular reminded him of a haunted house he and his friends used to throw rocks at when he was a kid. He stared at the two-story house. It sat apart from the others. The paint had peeled and it appeared kids had broken out most of the upstairs windows. The lower ones were boarded up. The mailbox out front had fallen over, but he made out the word *Cherry* as he drove past.

He rolled his window down and breathed in the smell of fresh-cut hay. He couldn't help but laugh at himself.

He'd been looking for a place to escape. Literally. And he'd found it in Montana. No one would ever look for him here—let alone find him. At least if he hoped to stay alive.

If Whitehorse wasn't the end of the earth, then Old Town definitely was. He'd heard someone joke the first night he'd gotten into town that "Whitehorse isn't the end of the earth, but you can see the fires of hell on a clear night."

Nick had been to hell. Maybe that was why he'd felt at home here right off.

Alice Miller lived in a big white ranch house west of town. As he pulled into the yard, two blue heelers with spooky white eyes came out to bite at his tires.

The house was sheltered by rows of trees that had to stand over fifteen feet tall. Past the house and trees, the country ran south through open prairie to what appeared to be a thin line of green. The Missouri Breaks.

He could understand why Old West outlaws had made this isolated, underpopulated country their hideouts. It had worked for Kid Curry and Butch Cassidy and the Sundance Kid. At least for a while.

Nick was counting on it working for him.

At least for a while.

He eyed the barking dogs. He had a healthy respect for ranch dogs since arriving in Montana and waited until an elderly woman in a housedress and apron opened the front door and called off the dogs before he got out.

Alice Miller was petite with serious blue eyes and bobbed gray hair. She led him around the back of the house to a chicken coop.

"There you are," she said as if that should clear things up for him.

He looked into the empty coop. Yep, things were clear as mud. "How many chickens did you have?"

"A dozen layers, four roosters and three old stewing hens."

"Nineteen chickens and they were all gone this morning," he said.

She nodded and waited as if she expected him to produce them like a magician pulling a rabbit out of his hat.

"That's a lot of chickens to disappear," he remarked. When he'd found this job, he'd been amazed at the kind of calls a deputy sheriff in Whitehorse, Montana, had to deal with. Dog at large, owner warned. Drunken disturbance at rodeo, citizen given ride home. Missing resident, found two doors down.

As a big-city cop, he'd dealt with every crime imaginable. At least he thought he had. But he'd never been called out to investigate nineteen missing chickens.

He was out of his league and he knew it.

"What do you think happened to them?" he asked Mrs. Miller.

She cocked her head and looked up at him as if he might be pulling her leg. "Clearly someone stole them."

"How do you know a coyote or something didn't come in and eat them all?"

"You see any feathers?"

Actually, he did. There were feathers all over the chicken coop.

"You see any blood, any bones?" she asked with growing impatience. "Where are you from anyway?"

"Houston."

"Where's your Texas accent?" she asked.

"I wasn't born there. My father was in the military. We traveled all over." It was the story he'd come up with. It made things simpler. And safer.

Mrs. Miller let out a little huff sound and put her hands on her hips. "Aren't you going to look for fingerprints? Tracks? Something?"

Fingerprints? She couldn't be serious. As for tracks, it had rained the night before. There were lots of tracks, all appearing to have been made by her dogs.

"I got wash to do," she said and headed for the side yard.

He circled the chicken coop, feeling like a fool. He'd never tracked anything in his life. This was nothing like chasing a convenience-store robber down an alley and over a couple of fences.

To his surprise, he found some tracks that looked out of place. He squatted down next to one of the prints. The sun had already baked the surface of the yard. The print was that of a boot. A small one. A kid's.

Nick walked around to where Mrs. Miller was hanging sheets and towels on a clothesline.

"Who all lives here?" he asked.

"Me and my husband. He's out cutting hay. Why?"

"You have any grandchildren, any children who have been over to visit in the last day or so?"

"No. What does that have to do with my chickens?"

"No neighbors with kids?" he asked.

Alice Miller wrinkled her brow. "There is that boy, his aunt and uncle are renting the farm next door."

Nick pulled out his notebook and pencil. "What do these chickens look like?" He glanced up when she didn't answer and saw her expression. "Okay, would you be able to recognize them if you saw them again?"

"Just find my chickens," she said and went back to hanging up her wash.

Nick followed the boy's tracks, wondering how the kid had pulled it off. Nineteen chickens were a lot. Wouldn't they have caused a ruckus that could be heard up at the house?

He could envision Mrs. Miller with a shotgun coming out in her flannel nightgown, blood in her eye. So why hadn't that happened?

He glanced up at the sound of a dog growling and realized he'd reached the farm closest to the Millers'.

"Hello!" he called and eyed the dog. It wasn't a blue heeler, but some kind of mutt, large and hairy. "Hello!" He feared the dog would key on the fear in his voice and attack. Easy, Cujo.

"The chickens aren't hurt," said a young voice from the back steps of the house. The kid was twelve tops, lanky with sandy-blond hair and big ears.

"That's good," Nick said. "Could you call off your dog?"

"Prince, no," the boy said. The dog eyed Nick for a moment, then ambled over to the kid and sat down.

"I'm Deputy Sheriff Nick Rogers." He'd taken the *Rogers* from an old western he'd seen on television the night he'd left town. "What's your name?"

"Chaz. It's actually Charles, but that's what everyone calls me," the boy said. "My aunt and uncle are in town if you're going to arrest me. I'm not sure when they'll be back."

"Where are Mrs. Miller's chickens?"

He pointed toward a shed at the back of the property. "I was going to return them. Really."

"Why'd you take them in the first place?" Nick asked, glancing toward the house. "You need the food?"

"No," Chaz said indignantly as they walked back to the shed. A ruckus was coming from inside. "I got plenty to eat and I didn't take anyone's chickens."

Right. That was why Nick had just followed the kid's boot prints to his house straight from the chicken coop.

At the shed, Chaz opened the door a crack so Nick could see that all nineteen chickens were there. The chickens looked a little funny to him, their feathers kind of glued to them, but what did he know about chickens other than buying cut-up fryers in plastic wrap at the grocery?

"We need to get the chickens back to Mrs. Miller," Nick said.

"I know. I was thinking about how to get them to her," the boy said.

"Why not take them back the same way you stole them?"

"I told you, I didn't steal them."

"Right."

Just then one of the chickens made a beeline for the door, slipping through to take off at a run across the yard.

Before Nick could react, Prince darted after the chicken. "No!" Nick called to the dog. Too late. In an instant, Prince had the chicken clutched in his jaws and was prancing back toward them looking like the cat that ate the canary.

To Nick's astonishment, the dog dropped the slobber-coated bird at Chaz's feet, the chicken jerking to its feet unhurt. The boy grabbed the bird and tossed it back in the shed.

"See the problem?" Chaz said. "I took one back when Prince brought it home. I didn't know he was going back last night to get them all."

Nick stared at the dog. "Are you trying to tell me that Prince stole the chickens?"

Chaz nodded. "I told him not to, but Prince likes to collect things." The boy shrugged. "It's his only bad habit. Other than that, he's a really good dog."

Prince was leaning against the boy's leg, looking up at him. Chaz patted the dog's big head. The dog's tongue lolled. He could have been smiling.

Nick swore, pulled off his hat and raked a hand through his hair. "I've got to tell you. I don't know much about transporting chickens. I'd consider any idea you might have on how to get them back in Mrs. Miller's chicken coop."

"I've been thinking on it," Chaz said. "I might have an idea."

Two hours later, all nineteen chickens were safely back in Mrs. Miller's chicken coop. Nick left Chaz on the Millers' porch eating fresh-baked apple pie and sipping a large glass of milk, Prince at his feet. Chaz had promised to keep a closer eye on his dog.

Nick was feeling good. He'd solved his first mystery in Montana. With a little help from a kid and a dog.

Back at his office, he was hoping the rest of his shift would be as uneventful when he looked up and saw a young reddish-blonde woman get out of her car. As she started toward his office, another car raced up, tires screeching as the driver came to a stop and rolled down his window.

The woman turned. Clearly, the two knew each other. Nick watched from his window, not liking the change in the woman's demeanor when she saw the young man behind the wheel. Nick had covered enough domestic-violence cases to recognize one on the street.

The woman said something to the man, who appeared to be about her age, no more than twenty, then she turned and started walking toward the sheriff's department again.

The man threw open his door and went after her, grabbing her arm and swinging her around to face him.

Nick shot out of his chair, hitting the door at a run. As he exited the courthouse building, he heard the raised voices.

"Let go of her," Nick said in his calm cop voice.

"This isn't any of your business," the young man said. He had brown hair, brown eyes, classic good looks.

"Let go of her," Nick repeated.

The young man did, but with obvious reluctance and definitely an attitude. "I'm not breaking any law."

"Domestic abuse is against the law," Nick said.

"Domestic abuse?" The young man scoffed at that. "My girlfri—fiancée and I were just having a little private disagreement."

The young woman was rubbing her arm where the man had grabbed her. "He's right. It's nothing."

"Why don't you step inside and we can talk about it," Nick said to the woman.

She shook her head, eyes wide. "It's nothing, really."

"You were headed for my office. There must be something you wanted."

"I wasn't. That is, I was going up to the treasury department upstairs. I got turned around." She was lying and Nick could see that she was afraid.

"What's your name?" he asked the young man.

"Bo Evans." He said it as if it should mean something. It didn't to Nick.

"You live around here?"

"Old Town Whitehorse." Bo was giving him an are-you-stupid look. "You're not from around here, huh?"

"What's your name?" Nick asked the woman.

She hesitated. "Maddie Cavanaugh."

She was edging toward her car. "I have to get to work," she said.

"Where do you work?" Nick asked.

Maddie Cavanaugh looked around as if searching for an answer. "In Old Town Whitehorse. I just help Geraldine Shaw out."

Nick nodded and turned to Bo Evans. "Disagreements are one thing, but you were scaring your fiancée. Keep your hands off her when you're angry, okay?"

Bo Evans shook his head as if in disbelief. "I wouldn't hurt Maddie. I love her. We're getting married. What is wrong with you, man?"

Nick watched them leave in separate cars, worried about the young woman. Whatever she'd been planning to tell someone at the sheriff's office, her fiancé had done a good job of changing her mind.

Chapter 3

Laney Cavanaugh saw him as she came out of the hospital. He stood across the street talking to her grandfather Titus.

She wasn't sure what it was about the man that caught her attention let alone held it as she crossed the street. He wore jeans and boots, a tan short-sleeved shirt and a cowboy hat. Nothing unusual about that in Whitehorse, Montana.

He had one boot sole resting on the bumper of Titus's pickup truck and was leaning forward, listening intently. She tried to imagine what her grandfather might be saying that would require that kind of attention as she crossed the street.

It wasn't until she was almost to the pair that the sun glinted off the man's silver star and she realized that the tan shirt was actually part of a uniform.

"Laney, I want you to meet the town's new deputy sheriff, Nick Rogers," Titus said. "This is my granddaughter Laney Cavanaugh."

She smiled and extended her hand, which quickly disappeared into the lawman's large sun-browned one. His handshake was firm, his skin warm and dry. His dark-eyed gaze made the already hot day sizzle. She sensed that odd expectation in the air that she'd felt earlier as if she wasn't the only one holding her breath.

"I was just telling Nick that you and your sister are staying out at my daughter's place," Titus said. "Nick's new to the area. I'm sure it's all a bit strange after Houston."

"I'm adjusting," he said, never taking his eyes off Laney. He had the kind of face that she'd thought only existed in the movies. Rugged and yet as handsome as any she'd ever seen, with dark hair and eyes. But it was the way he stood, his head cocked to one side, an air of confidence about him, that drew her like a moth to a flame.

"I told Nick we'd have to get him back down our way for dinner sometime," Titus said.

"He should come to the party," Laci said, coming up behind them. She'd hung back to give their grandmother's nurses the chocolate-chip cookies. Laney could feel her sister's gaze on her, hear the humor in her voice. "Shouldn't he, Laney?"

"Of course," Laney said because what else could she say under the circumstances? She looked down, surprised to see he was still holding her hand.

"What kind of party is this?" he asked as he let go, as if as reluctant to break the connection as she'd been.

His gaze, however, came right back to her after he shook her sister's hand.

"It's our cousin's engagement party," Laci said.

He smiled. "Thank you, but I really couldn't intrude."

"It's no intrusion," Laci said, grinning curiously from Laney to Nick. "The entire town is invited and half the county. That's the way things are done around here. Haven't you seen the baby shower and anniversary notices in the local newspaper inviting the whole county? Welcome to small-town America."

"A lot different from the big city," Nick said. "But still I don't think I—"

"It's for our cousin Maddie Cavanaugh and her fiancé, Bo Evans," Laci interrupted. "It would be a good time to meet more of the locals. Everyone will be there."

Laney saw the change in Nick's expression. "Maybe I *will* reconsider," he said. "When is this party?"

"Saturday afternoon," Laci said. "Wear your dancing boots. Gramps will be playing his fiddle as part of the Whitehorse Country Band."

Nick met Laney's gaze. "Save me a dance?"

She nodded, feeling sixteen again and just as foolish because she was beginning to think this engagement party for Maddie wasn't such a bad idea after all.

Arlene Evans looked across the table at her handsome son and smiled. She'd suggested dinner at the Hi-Line Café because she had something important to announce.

"I'm going to have the steak sandwich," Bo said,

closing his menu. He glanced toward the street and drummed his fingers on the table as if bored.

Arlene tamped down her annoyance. "Have whatever you want," she said, feeling magnanimous. Bo was the light of her life. *Her son.* The one who would carry on the family name. It was especially important to have a son when you lived on a farm. Sons stayed and worked the place and, although Bo had shown little interest in farming, she knew he would once he was married.

Daughters, on the other hand, well, they were supposed to get married and leave.

She let her gaze shift from her son to her youngest daughter, Charlotte. Charlotte was staring at a lank of her long straight blond hair, looking for split ends. Arlene applauded Charlotte's interest in her looks at seventeen. At least one of her daughters understood the importance of looking her best from her hair to her prettily painted acrylic nails.

Arlene glanced at her other daughter and scowled. Violet, her *unmarried* daughter, was her burden to bear. Not pretty, not overly bright, certainly not ambitious, Violet was thirty-four with few prospects. No matter what Violet wore, she looked…well, frumpy.

Her hair was a dull brown and her complexion muddy, and her nails! Arlene had done everything possible to break Violet of biting her nails and it had done no good.

Arlene feared her daughter would never marry and leave home as was natural. And how would that reflect on Arlene? She couldn't bear such a blight on her as a mother.

"I'll have a cheeseburger with fries and a chocolate milk shake," Violet said tentatively.

"Are you sure you don't want a nice salad, dear? All that fried food. It isn't a problem for the rest of us, but with you watching your weight…"

Violet closed her menu. "Why don't you order for me, Mother?"

Arlene thought she detected an edge to her daughter's voice, but that would be so unlike Violet that she dismissed it.

"So what's this about?" Bo asked impatiently. "You said you had something you wanted to tell us?"

Arlene refused to be rushed. Fortunately, the waitress came to take their orders just then. A steak sandwich and jojos for Bo, the grilled chicken salad for Violet, a side salad with vinegar and oil for Charlotte and a strawberry milk shake, the fish basket with fries for Arlene.

"So did anything interesting happen last night?" she asked Violet after the waitress had gone.

Violet looked at her brother. "Well," she said dragging out the word, "I did see Maddie at the bar last night. She was dancing with *Curtis McAlheney*."

"So?" Bo snapped. "It's not like we're married yet. She can dance with anyone she wants."

"Curtis McAlheney?" Violet let out that irritating loud laugh of hers. "He's old enough to be her father!"

"Please! Could we just have one meal together without you two arguing?" Arlene glared at Violet, took a breath and let it out slowly, upset to hear about Maddie.

She wondered if Maddie had been drinking. She wouldn't have been surprised, given that Charlotte had gotten served when the bars were really busy even though she was only seventeen. Or maybe the girls had fake IDs. That would be just like Maddie.

"You weren't with Maddie, Bo?" Arlene asked, surprised and a little concerned. She'd thought that he was meeting Maddie when he'd left the house before his sisters last night.

"I went to Havre with some friends," he said, obviously not happy to hear that Maddie had been at the bar—and dancing with Curtis McAlheney even though Curtis was no prize. "It's not like Maddie and I are attached at the hip, you know."

"You're right," Arlene quickly agreed. "It's good to have friends and do things with them even after you're married."

"*If* he gets married," Violet said under her breath.

"What is that supposed to mean?" both Arlene and Bo demanded. Charlotte hummed quietly to herself, apparently oblivious to the rest of them.

Violet only gave her brother one of her that's-for-me-to-know-and-you-to-find-out looks.

Arlene wanted to slap her. Instead, she decided it was time to make her announcement. "I have great news. I've started a home business."

Both Bo and Violet were noticeably surprised. Charlotte glanced up, but went back to her split ends; she would never need a dating service.

"What kind of business?" Violet asked as if worried she might have to work it.

"On the Internet," Arlene said excitedly. She'd done her best to find Violet a man, throwing her together with every eligible man she could find in several counties.

Now it was time to expand her territory. "It's an Internet dating service for rural singles."

Violet gasped.

Bo began to laugh, shaking his head as his gaze went to Violet then his mother. "This is going to be good."

On Saturday, Nick told himself he had no business going to a party in Old Town Whitehorse or anywhere else. His plan had been to keep a low profile while in Montana. That meant doing his job, staying to himself, having as little contact with the locals as was necessary.

It wasn't as if it had slipped his mind why he was here or what was at stake if he screwed up. He had to keep his head down. Dancing with a pretty young local woman with emerald-green eyes wasn't just risky business. It could get him killed.

And yet, dancing with Laney Cavanaugh was all he could think about as he checked his messages at his office before getting ready to head to Old Town.

He told himself he was just doing his job by going to the party. That he wouldn't have accepted the party invitation if it hadn't been for Maddie Cavanaugh and Bo Evans's engagement. He hadn't been able to forget the fear he'd seen in Maddie's eyes that day outside his office. Nor could he shake the instant dislike he'd felt for Bo Evans. The kid was trouble. Nick had seen enough young men like Bo to spot his kind a mile away.

And what would just one dance hurt?

Nick looked up at the sound of a man clearing his throat.

"I—I—I was attacked."

The man standing in his doorway was average

height, average build, average in most every way. He looked vaguely familiar.

"I'm the reporter for the *Milk River Examiner*. I tried to do a story on you when you came to town," the man said as if seeing Nick attempting to place him.

"Right."

"Glen Whitaker," the man said. He'd looked sheepish when Nick had first looked up, but now he appeared a little aggravated at not being remembered. Or maybe it was because Nick had declined to be interviewed.

"You say you were attacked?" Nick asked. The man didn't appear to be in pain. Nor did his clothing suggest an attack. He wore dark slacks, a white shirt, loafers. He obviously was a transplant from somewhere else. His hair was slicked back in an old-fashioned cut although he appeared to be in his thirties. Hard to tell age with a man like that.

"The attack happened a month ago, right before you were hired," Glen Whitaker said, glancing around as if he wanted to make sure no one was listening. There wasn't anyone in the office and the dispatcher's desk was far enough away she couldn't have heard. Nor did she seem even interested in what the reporter was doing here.

"Sit down," Nick said as Glen drew up a chair, pulling it close to the deputy's desk. "You say it happened before I was hired. Did you report it?"

"No." Glen looked nervous. "I wasn't sure."

"You weren't sure you were attacked?" Nick was beginning to wonder about this guy.

"You see, I was told that I'd been down at Old Town.

It's a near ghost town south of here by the Missouri Breaks."

Nick nodded. "I've been there."

"Anyway, about a month ago I woke up beside the road, my car smashed into a fence post, miles from everything. I couldn't remember anything. I later found out that I was in Old Town Whitehorse. I had two large bumps on my head that I thought must have caused the memory loss."

"Were you drinking?" Nick had to ask.

"I don't drink. Several people saw me leave the Whitehorse Community Center and can attest to the fact that I hadn't had a thing to drink. That was the night before. I woke up beside the road the next morning feeling like I'd been run over." Glen leaned in closer. "When I got home I found bruises all over my body as if I'd been beaten."

Nick had been thinking the man was a nutcase. But his story was a little too much like the others Nick had been hearing. Also, the attack had been on a Saturday night.

"Would you say the bruises indicated you might have been kicked? Or beaten with a weapon of some sort?" Nick asked.

Glen Whitaker sat back, relief drowning his features. "You believe me then?"

"There have been some other reports of this sort of thing."

"I was afraid to come in." Glen looked away as if too upset to go on. "I was afraid you'd think I was crazy."

Nick pulled out a report. "When exactly did this happen?"

Glen stood abruptly. "I don't want to file a complaint."

"Why not?"

"I don't want this all over town. That's why I came to you. You don't know anyone. I just needed to tell someone."

"But don't you want your attack on record?"

The reporter wagged his head. "And have it end up in the newspaper? No way." He started backing toward the door.

"Okay," Nick said putting the form away. "I won't make out a report. But tell me when it happened. There appears to be a series of these attacks. Yours might have been the first."

"Saturday, four weeks ago, when that Bailey woman went missing. I can't remember the exact date."

Nick had heard about the Bailey woman, that she'd been discovered down in the Breaks and everything that had happened because of it.

"You have any idea who's responsible for these attacks?" Glen asked.

"Not yet, but your information might prove critical to the investigation." Nick checked his calendar. "From what I can tell, yours was the first attack."

"No kidding." Clearly, he was glad he wasn't the only one. "I'm afraid I wouldn't be much help. I still can't remember anything about those lost twenty-four hours." He paused. "There was one thing though." He looked sheepish again. "It's probably nothing."

Nick smiled to himself. He'd been a cop long enough to know that whenever anyone said "it's probably nothing," it was usually something.

"I smelled something on my clothes afterward," he said, flushing a little. "I think it might have been perfume."

Nick could see how uncomfortable this admission made the reporter. "Do you have a woman friend?"

Glen shook his head. "I like women, don't get me wrong."

"Of course. But you can't recall being around a woman that day."

"I can't recall anything, that's the problem."

"Okay, this perfume. You recognize the scent?"

Another shake of his head.

"What was it like?"

"Some flower I think."

That narrowed it down. "A flower you'd recall if you smelled it again?"

"It was an old flower, you know the kind—" he hesitated "—that older women wear."

Nick nodded. "Okay, that could help." He couldn't imagine how, since Glen Whitaker had no idea who he'd come in contact with before he'd woken up beside a road in the middle of nowhere. Apparently an older woman.

"Okay," Glen echoed. "I just thought you ought to know."

"I'm glad you came in," Nick said.

Glen hesitated at the door. "My editor still wants a story on you."

"Thanks," Nick said, "but I'll pass. I'm shy and the story of my life would put your readers to sleep."

Glen shook his head. "We print stories like that all the time."

"Yeah," Nick agreed with a laugh, "I've read your paper."

As Glen left looking like a whipped puppy, Nick checked. Sure enough, there'd been an assault every Saturday night for apparently the last four weeks.

But this Saturday everyone would be in Old Town Whitehorse at Maddie Cavanaugh's engagement party. At least this afternoon.

As he stood to leave for the party, Nick thought of Maddie. That young woman was in some kind of trouble. But he didn't know what to do about it if she wasn't willing to tell him.

He considered confiding in Maddie's cousin Laney, telling her his concerns, and quickly nixed the idea. He didn't know Laney Cavanaugh, although he felt as if he did. Crazy.

Still he couldn't shake the thought of inviting her to town for dinner one night and seeing what he could find out about the cousin and her fiancé. Maybe he'd ask Laney at the party. Maybe while they were dancing.

Just a man doing his job.

As he started to leave his office, he glanced back at his desk. Time for a reality check, he thought as he walked back and unlocked the bottom drawer of his desk. The cell phone he'd bought when he'd left California was right where he'd put it. He only turned it on to check for messages once a day.

He hadn't checked it yet today. Hell, he'd forgotten for a while there what he was doing in Montana. He picked up the phone and turned it on. No messages.

Nick breathed a sigh of relief although he knew it was just a matter of time before he got the call. One that would tell him it was time to return to California. Or a call that would tell him his cover was blown and to run.

He turned off the cell phone and put it back in the bottom drawer, locked the drawer and stood for a moment, hesitating. Just checking the phone had been a reminder how foolish it would be for him to get too involved, either in his work or with anyone while in Montana.

That was why he should just back off. If Maddie Cavanaugh really was in trouble, then let her come to him. And as for Laney Cavanaugh… He shook his head, reminding himself that his life here was one big fat lie. The closer he got to Laney Cavanaugh, the greater his chance of being found out. And if that happened, he was as good as dead.

During the week, news of the engagement party for Maddie Cavanaugh and Bo Evans spread like wildfire through the county. Few people were apt to turn down a party, especially one being thrown by a Cavanaugh. Some just wanted to come to critique Laci Cavanaugh's cuisine. There was a rumor going round that she was planning to start her own catering business and was trying out recipes at the party.

Only two of the people who heard about the party were upset.

Arlene Evans was insulted that she hadn't been asked to at least bring some of the food for the party. After all, she had taken the most blue ribbons at the Phillips County Fair and the Whitehorse Fourth of July picnic.

And in case no one had noticed, Bo was her son.

"The mother of the groom isn't allowed to throw

the engagement party," Alice Miller told her one afternoon at the Whitehorse Sewing Circle. "Actually, you shouldn't even be allowed to work on your daughter-in-law's wedding quilt, but since we're shorthanded with Lila Bailey and Pearl Cavanaugh gone…"

That had distracted Arlene. "I still can't believe that Lila Bailey would just up and run off like she did." She waited a moment for the other women in the circle to jump in. Arlene lowered her voice. "I always wondered about the paternity of her oldest daughter, Eve. She didn't look anything like the rest of them."

"Arlene," Geraldine Shaw said impatiently and totally out of character. Pearl was the one who usually chastised Arlene for talking about anything interesting. "You missed a stitch. Perhaps you should tend to your quilting."

Geraldine's rebuff was so unexpected that Arlene was at a loss for words.

Down the road from Whitehorse, Maddie Cavanaugh took the news of the engagement party even harder.

"No, that's not possible. Laci can't, I mean, she didn't say anything about—"

"It's wonderful that your cousin is doing this for you," her mother said, cutting her off. "You should be thankful."

Since Sarah Cavanaugh had married into the family, she'd been trying to gain her rightful place. While she lived in a nice enough house to the east of Old Town Whitehorse, she had always been overshadowed by Titus and Pearl Cavanaugh, who were like royalty in this part of the county.

Sarah had felt slighted even though she'd tried to be part of this community and the Cavanaugh family. This party for her daughter though would finally put her part of the family in the limelight. It was only right that she and Maddie would get some attention. It angered her that Maddie didn't want the party—and she said as much to her.

"It just seems…premature," Maddie said.

"Premature? You've been engaged for over a month."

"Bo and I haven't even set a date."

"Well, then I suggest you do. You can announce it at the party," Sarah said.

"I wish Laci had asked me about this," Maddie said. "Saturday? I had plans that night."

"The party's in the afternoon. But even if it runs into evening, you can just change your plans," Sarah said gruffly, frowning at her daughter, who had once been so malleable.

Sarah blamed it on the fact that Maddie had been spending way too much time away from her fiancé. Sarah had hoped Bo would be able to handle Maddie. But she'd heard her daughter had been seen at the bars, dancing with older men. If she hadn't known how much Maddie loved Bo and needed him, Sarah Cavanaugh would have been worried.

Chapter 4

All week, Laci had been baking, forcing anyone who came by to try her treats. From candy to cookies to tarts and turnovers, and individual cobblers and cheesecakes, she'd worked to come up with the perfect dessert menu with growing expectation of Saturday's event.

Laney had her own expectations as the day finally arrived. She hadn't seen Deputy Nick Rogers, wasn't even sure he would show for the party, but she was still anxious anyway—and upset with herself for being so excited about seeing him again. She'd seen the man only once, had barely said two words to him. This was so unlike her to be excited about a man she'd just met. Unlike her younger sister, she *always* looked before she leaped. But this time, she just wanted to jump—and that should have scared her.

Maddie had stopped by the day after Laci had started inviting everyone to the engagement party.

"I wish you'd mentioned a party to me," Maddie had said. "Not that I don't love the idea."

Laney had seen that Maddie was anything but delighted with the party idea.

"Don't thank me," Laci had said, giving her cousin a hug. "I just wanted to do something special for you. Because you're special."

Maddie's blue eyes had filled with tears. She'd bit her lip and said nothing more.

But Laney had seen her expression. Maddie wasn't just displeased about the party, she seemed…worried. Since that day, Maddie hadn't been by, which was strange in itself.

When Laney had called to make sure she was all right, Maddie had told her she'd taken a job helping Geraldine Shaw clean out her attic.

"I like this kind of work. I think it might be like accounting," her cousin had said. "Something that actually makes sense, you know?"

"Maddie, is anything wrong?" Laney had asked. "Because if you need someone to talk to—"

"Wrong? Of course not. Everything is wonderful. I'm marrying Bo." Laney had heard the catch in her cousin's voice. "I can't imagine life without him."

"You don't have to," Laney had said.

"No, I don't. Bo is perfect for me." Another catch in her voice.

"Still, every bride-to-be gets cold feet," Laney said.

"Not me." She'd hesitated. "We've had our problems,

just like any other couple. But once we're married things will be different."

Her cousin didn't really believe that marriage solved the problems, did she? "Maddie—"

"I'm fine. Really. There is nothing to worry about."

But Laney had worried.

Now she heard a car and glanced at her watch. Aunt Sarah had called and offered to take some of the desserts for the party to the community center in her van.

Sarah had also helped with the decorations and volunteered to taste treats as was needed over the week.

"Because of your darned sister, I've gained ten pounds," Sarah said as she came into the house.

"I had to refuse to taste another thing," Laney said. "Laci was giving me a toothache. Is Maddie ready for the party?"

Sarah nodded, her face beaming. "This is so exciting. A party for my baby. Thank you for doing this. I can't tell you what it means to us."

"It's all Laci's doing," Laney said, but she could see what it meant to Sarah. She wasn't so sure about Maddie. She considered broaching her concerns about Maddie to her aunt but Laci came out of the kitchen with a container full of bite-size chocolate-covered cherry cheesecakes, and Sarah began oohing and aahing over them. They *were* beautiful. And much too pretty to eat.

After Sarah left with the back of her van full, Laney checked her watch again.

"Shouldn't we be getting over to the community center?" she asked her sister.

Laci was nervously staring through the oven glass. "Just a few more minutes on the caramel puffs. They're best if served warm. I have the macaroons resting at room temperature."

Laney shook her head. "Lace, there is no way we're going to be able to eat all of this."

A knock at the door surprised them both. Laney thought it might be Sarah back for something. "I'll get it. You watch your puffs."

Geraldine Shaw was standing on the porch. She wasn't dressed for the party. She looked harried and upset as Laney opened the door.

"Where's Maddie?" Geraldine asked abruptly.

"I don't know."

"She was gone when I returned from the post office and my mother's diamond bracelet is missing," Geraldine said, looking past Laney. "Are you sure she isn't here?"

"Yes. She might be at home or at the community center, but I'm sure if the bracelet is missing, Maddie had nothing to do with it."

"I showed her the bracelet when we were cleaning out some things. When I left, I told her to be sure and put it back in the box." Geraldine sounded near tears. "It's *gone*."

"I'm sure it's just misplaced," Laney said with concern. "Why don't I call Maddie and see if—"

But Geraldine was already off the porch steps, huffing as she climbed into her car and tore off in a cloud of dust.

A shriek came from the kitchen. Laney went racing in to find her sister hysterical.

"My caramel puffs fell. This is an omen. The party is going to be a disaster."

Laney calmed down her sister and sent her to get ready. She didn't have the heart to tell Laci that there were worse problems with the party than some fallen caramel puffs. Not that Laci would appreciate the gravity of the missing bracelet. Not when gravity had ruined her caramel puffs.

When Nick drove into Old Town Whitehorse, he was amazed at how many vehicles were parked around the community center. Laci Cavanaugh was right about one thing: the entire county had turned out for the engagement party.

He parked and walked down the road to the center, reminding himself he was on a case—even if not technically on duty. He planned to leave in time to watch the bars tonight in Whitehorse. It was Saturday and if the assailant was true to form, he'd be attacking some poor cowboy before the night was over.

As Nick slipped into the crowded building, the band broke into a country ballad. His best friend would have gotten a real kick out of this.

Just the thought of Danny O'Shay cut like a blade into his heart. Danny couldn't see this because Danny was dead. And Nick was the reason.

"Deputy Nick Rogers," said a female voice dripping with sugar. "I don't think we've met."

A tall, thin middle-aged woman with a braying laugh reached for his hand and shook it vigorously. "I'm Arlene Evans. This party is for my son and his fiancée."

Bo's mother. While her son was a nice-looking young man, Arlene Evans was one of those raw-boned ranch women.

"And this is my daughter Violet," Arlene said as she grabbed the woman's arm next to her and literally dragged her over. "Violet, say hello to Deputy Rogers."

Violet Evans gave a meek nod.

"Hello, it's nice to meet you," Nick said. With Violet it was hard to tell her age. She was as plain as any woman he'd ever seen. She had her mother's raw-boned look but on a larger frame.

"Deputy Sheriff Rogers is new in town and single," Arlene said and winked at Nick. "The Whitehorse grapevine."

Violet stared at the floor, but Nick noticed a flush creep up her neck and several veins pop up prominently. The woman was more than embarrassed.

"If you'll excuse me, I need to speak with Titus," Nick said as the band took a break. As he escaped, he heard Arlene chastising her daughter about not saying something interesting to make Nick stay. This was the woman who'd raised Bo Evans, he reminded himself. It could explain a lot.

"I see you made it," Titus said and looked past him to the crowd. Titus Cavanaugh was a large, white-headed man with a powerful voice and a strong handshake. "My granddaughters are here somewhere. Quite the turnout. I hope you've tried some of Laci's desserts. She really did go all out, but then that's Laci. She was born with a spoon in her hand." He laughed at his small joke.

Nick wanted to ask about Laci and Laney's parents. He hadn't heard anything about them. But he didn't get the chance.

Across the room, he spotted Maddie Cavanaugh. She was dressed in a pale blue dress the same color as her eyes. Even from here he could see that her face was drawn, her freckles seeming to jump out. She looked upset.

He saw that she was listening to something Arlene Evans, her future mother-in-law, was saying. Arlene had a firm grip on Maddie's arm and seemed to be trying to lead her out the back door.

"Here's one of my granddaughters!" Titus announced.

Nick turned to come face-to-face with Laney Cavanaugh. She was dressed in a peach-colored dress that fell like water over her curves. Her face had a glow to it that had nothing to do with makeup, and those eyes, those amazing emerald eyes...

Past Laney, he saw Arlene Evans drag Maddie outside.

Nick cursed under his breath. "Excuse me a minute. I'll be right back," he said to Laney and made his way through the crowd after Arlene and Maddie.

Well, that went well. Laney tried to hide her disappointment. She'd been looking forward to seeing Nick Rogers all week. In fact, when she'd spotted him talking to her grandfather, she'd made her way through the crowd, too impatient to wait for him to find her.

Or maybe worried he wouldn't.

Laney wasn't used to behaving like this. She turned away, fighting the urge to flee. Instead, she went over to the dessert table to see if she could help her sister.

"It's a success," Laci announced and sighed. "My first catered party. I can tell you now. I'm opening my own catering business, Cavanaugh Catering, right here."

"Here?" Laney stared at her sister. Not because this surprised her. The way Laci loved to cook, it was the perfect career choice. "Here in Old Town?"

"Not just Old Town and Whitehorse, silly. I was thinking that it's crazy that nobody lives in Mother's house. I could run my catering business from the house. That way I would be close to Gramma and Gramps. But I would cater the whole county."

Laney didn't know what to say. Laci had always been the one who couldn't wait to get out of here after their two-week summer visit each year. "What about Seattle?"

"It will always be there," Laci said with a laugh.

Laney eyed her sister. "This seems kind of sudden."

"Not really. I've given it a lot of thought. I've already told Gramma."

Gramma hadn't been responding to anything since her stroke.

"It was the weirdest thing," Laci confided. "She looked right at me. I swear she squeezed my hand. It was like there was something she wanted to tell me, needed to tell me, then she closed her eyes..."

"She's happy for you," Laney said quickly, not knowing if that was true or not. Gramma Pearl had always encouraged them to do what made them happy. Laney wasn't sure what their grandmother would think about Laci staying here though. But she was positive what Gramps would say. Titus would be thrilled.

"I thought I'd tell Gramps after the party," Laci said. "Oh no, we're almost out of those chocolate-covered cherry cheesecakes. I should have made more."

Or kept Violet Evans away from them, Laney thought

as she watched Violet devour the last of the little cakes and then move down the buffet table toward the macaroons, stuffing a handful into the big pockets of her jumper when she thought no one was looking.

But Laney was distracted by the sight of Geraldine Shaw heading for the dessert table. Had she found her diamond bracelet? Laney could only hope so. She glanced around for Maddie, but didn't see her anywhere.

By the time Nick stepped out through the back door of the community center, whatever Arlene had dragged Maddie out there for was over.

The two were standing a short ways from the back door. Maddie had her arms folded over her chest, her eyes on the ground. She'd been crying. Arlene was standing over her, glowering down at her.

"Is there a problem?" Nick asked pointedly.

Arlene turned in surprise, her expression instantly changing as she stepped back from Maddie. "Why, Deputy, you're missing the dance. My daughter Violet—"

"I was hoping to dance with the bride-to-be," Nick said, looking at Maddie. He could hear the music coming from the center, but he was more interested in what Arlene had been saying to Maddie. Whatever it had been, he was betting it hadn't been good. Arlene had been giving Maddie hell—and at her engagement party. That didn't bode well for their future relationship.

Arlene's look soured as she glanced from Nick to Maddie and back.

"I wanted to wish her well on her engagement," he added. "If you'll give us a moment," he said pointedly to Arlene.

"Of course," the older woman said, sending a warning glance at Maddie before she went back inside.

"Are you all right?" he asked.

Maddie looked up, her blue eyes filled with tears. She made a swipe at them. "I'm fine."

"I don't think so."

"Please," Maddie said, looking nervously toward the door. "Don't. You'll only make things worse."

"Is that possible?" he asked.

Maddie dried her eyes.

"Let me help you," Nick said.

"What's going on out here?" asked a strident male voice.

Nick recognized it without turning. Bo Evans. His mother's doing no doubt. She'd sent him out here. "I meant what I said," Nick whispered to Maddie. "I can help if you'll let me."

She gave him an indecipherable nod and, putting a smile on her face, stepped around him.

Nick watched as Bo pulled Maddie to him none too gently and the two disappeared back inside. Nick swore and went to find Laney Cavanaugh.

But as he entered the center, he heard a bloodcurdling scream and saw the crowd converge to a spot in front of the dessert table.

Nick pushed his way through to find Geraldine Shaw on the floor. She was gasping for breath, her face bright red, her eyes bulging. "Everyone get back!" he yelled as he knelt down next to her. "Can you hear me?" He could see the panic in her face. She tried to lift her arm from the floor and he saw what was left of a macaroon clutched in her fist.

Nick felt the woman's panic. He'd been here before. But like before, there was no time to do anything. The poison was too fast acting. Geraldine Shaw went into convulsions and he caught the familiar odor of bitter almond just before she died.

Chapter 5

"Internal asphyxia," the state coroner said as he came out of the autopsy room. "She literally died due to lack of oxygen."

"And the macaroon she had in her hand?" Nick asked.

"Laced with enough cyanide to kill a horse. But her age and health were obviously factors in how quickly the poison acted."

Nick cursed under his breath. He'd known Geraldine Shaw was poisoned with cyanide. He'd just hoped he was wrong. "What about the other macaroons?"

The coroner shook his head. "We also checked the other desserts that you brought us. None had poison in them."

"So it was just the one cookie?"

"Apparently so."

Nick shook his head. How could the killer be sure that the one poisoned cookie went to the right victim? Or was it random? He raked a hand through his hair, worried that this had nothing to do with Geraldine Shaw and a whole hell of a lot to do with him.

But there was no way Keller could have found him because no one knew he was here, right? Nick hadn't trusted anyone after what had happened in L.A. It was just a coincidence that Geraldine Shaw had been poisoned with cyanide—the same poison that had been used to kill his friend Danny.

Cyanide was a common poison and yet he still wondered if his cover was blown. If this was Keller's way of letting him know that he'd found him.

Nick felt that old panic rise in him. He couldn't bear the idea of being responsible for another innocent person's life.

He'd leave town. He could be gone from this place in a matter of minutes. He'd traveled light getting here. He could travel even lighter leaving.

He tamped down his fear. Keller was desperate. He was through playing games. He would just kill Nick and get it over with. Why kill some poor woman instead? It made no sense.

Nick tried to relax. With the sheriff in Florida, Nick was tempted to call in a state investigator to help with the case, but he feared that would only attract more attention to the case—and him, something he couldn't do.

Busy with the murder Saturday afternoon, Nick hadn't done surveillance at the bars as he'd planned and there'd been another attack. Same M.O. as the others. The assailant had used a baseball bat.

"Do you know who baked the cookies?" the coroner asked.

Nick nodded. Laci Cavanaugh. He thought of her sister, Laney. Hell, he hadn't even gotten to dance with her. Which, all things considered, was probably a blessing in disguise. He couldn't let it slip his mind that Keller would be frantically looking for him. Nick's days here were numbered. As soon as he got the call, he'd be gone as quickly as he'd appeared in Montana.

"Unfortunately, the cookie was smashed in Geraldine Shaw's hand so we have no way of knowing how the cyanide got into the cookie."

Which meant anyone at the party could have doctored the macaroon.

Nick thanked the coroner and headed for Old Town Whitehorse and the Cavanaughs.

"Poisoned?" Laney Cavanaugh couldn't believe what she was hearing. She'd been sitting on the porch when she'd seen dust in the distance. Her first reaction to seeing the patrol car coming up the road had been a flutter of excitement. Her heart had kicked up a beat at just the sight of Nick as he'd climbed out.

She stood now, going to stand at the porch railing, looking out at the country, but seeing nothing through her fear. "I thought Geraldine had a heart attack?"

"I'm going to need to talk to your sister," he said, joining her at the railing.

"You don't really believe that Laci poisoned that woman!" she said, trying to keep the tremor out of her voice.

"Frankly, all I know is that Geraldine Shaw was poisoned by a macaroon that your sister baked."

"What was her motive?" Laney demanded, turning to look at him.

"You tell me."

Laney was reminded of Geraldine's visit just before the party. "We barely know Geraldine Shaw." Unfortunately though, Geraldine had accused their cousin of taking her diamond bracelet. Not that it had anything to do with this.

She saw him glance to where Laci's car was usually parked, the space empty.

"Laci went into town."

"When will she be back?"

"I'm not sure. I hope you're looking into other suspects."

"Such as?" he asked. He had the darkest eyes.

Laney shook her head. She didn't have a clue who might have a grudge against poor Geraldine Shaw, let alone who would want to kill her. She shuddered at even the thought of one of Laci's cookies containing *poison*.

"Where were you when Geraldine Shaw collapsed?"

She thought for a moment. "I had gone over to see if Laci needed any help."

"So you were behind the tables or in front of them?"

"I was standing at the end."

"And what was Laci doing?"

Laney tried to picture it in her mind. "She was refilling the dishes with the desserts and fretting because she wished she'd made more of some things than others."

"Such as?"

"The bite-size chocolate-covered cherry cheesecakes

and—" She stopped and looked at him. "The maca-roons. There was only one left on the plate. Earlier I'd seen Violet Evans stuffing her face and her pockets. Laci was about to refill the plate when someone picked it up."

"You don't remember who?"

She shook her head. "Violet was standing there with her mother. I saw Charlotte join them. Laci was reach-ing for the plate to refill it when someone took the last macaroon."

"Geraldine Shaw," he said. "Did you hear anyone offer her the cookie?"

Laney shook her head. "The band had started up again and everyone was talking."

"So the poisoned macaroon could have been meant for someone farther down the table even past Arlene. You remember who was standing next to her?"

"Sorry."

He nodded. "Please have your sister give me a call when she gets back." The deputy sheriff put his hat back on, then hesitated. "I'm sorry we didn't get that dance," he said, then gave her a quick nod and left before she could say, "Me, too."

Laney watched his vehicle disappear down the dirt road, dust billowing up behind it, before she hurried into the house to get her car keys.

Arlene Evans was furious. It was so like Geraldine Shaw to have a heart attack at Bo's engagement party of all places. If the woman wasn't feeling well she should have excused herself. Geraldine had spoiled everything in more ways than one.

To make matters worse, Arlene's Rural Montana Meet-a-Mate Internet dating service wasn't taking off. Everyone she'd talked to didn't want their photo and personal information out there for just anyone to see.

"I can't believe this," she muttered as she stared at her computer. Nothing was going right. Bo and Maddie had gotten into a fight right after the ambulance had pulled away with Geraldine—and Bo had taken off angry.

Not that Arlene could blame him. She just wanted to know if they were broken up for good. She always thought Bo could do better. Case in point: This morning Violet had announced she'd seen Maddie at the bar again last night dancing with anyone and everyone. Surely there was a better match for Bo.

Arlene glanced at her camera sitting next to her computer. She'd gotten some good shots of the guests before Geraldine had taken her swan dive under the dessert table. As she hooked the digital camera up to the computer and started going through the photographs looking for a possible match for her son, she got an idea.

She knew everyone in the county, knew more personal things about them than anyone else. And now she had photographs of a lot of the rural singles. They were just shy about her new business. Once they started getting called for dates, they'd thank her.

Arlene began to scan in the photographs, getting more excited as she went. She'd get money from the suitors. She wouldn't make as much this way, but she had to get her business going, and she had to find Violet a husband and Bo a better woman to marry.

She scanned in the photo of Violet at the party.

Why had her daughter worn that horrible jumper? It just made her look bigger and fatter. Oh well, at least she'd changed before she'd gone into town last night with her sister.

Arlene cropped the photo and put it up, adding as glowing information as she could about her oldest daughter.

Then she flipped through the other candid photos she'd taken and stopped on one in particular. Deputy Sheriff Nick Rogers. She didn't know a lot about him, but she could always wing it.

She put his photo up on the dating site. Like the others, he'd thank her when she found him the woman of his dreams.

Maddie Cavanaugh still lived with her parents in a farmhouse outside of Old Town Whitehorse. Nick found it at the end of a dusty road in the middle of nowhere.

He noticed as he pulled into the yard that Maddie's car, the one he'd seen her driving the day she'd stopped by the sheriff's department, wasn't parked in the yard.

No one seemed to be home today. He started to turn around when the screen door opened. The woman in the doorway was fifty-something, blonde and blue-eyed.

He climbed out of his patrol car and walked toward the porch. The sun beat down, baking the earth beneath his feet. "I'm Deputy Sheriff Nick Rogers. I was looking for Maddie Cavanaugh."

"Maddie? I'm sorry but she's not here." The woman introduced herself as Maddie's mother, Sarah Cavanaugh.

"Do you know where she is?" he asked, still worried about her. The murder of Geraldine Shaw had side-tracked him. But if anything, he was more concerned about Maddie Cavanaugh after that little scene he'd witnessed between her and Arlene Evans, her future mother-in-law.

"She stayed with a friend in Whitehorse last night. Wasn't that just dreadful about Geraldine collapsing like that? No one knew she had a bad heart. Why, she wasn't that much older than me."

He didn't tell her that Geraldine's heart had been fine before she'd been poisoned. "Can you give me the name of this friend Maddie stayed with?"

"Why, you know I didn't even ask. She has lots of friends and stays at different places when she goes into town," Sarah said, frowning. "Why do you need to see my daughter?"

"I'm questioning anyone who was close to Geraldine," he said.

"Oh. Well, I wouldn't say Maddie was close to her. I mean, Maddie helped her out from time to time. Geraldine paid her some measly amount. Geraldine was tight-fisted and not close to anyone in Old Town. She stayed to herself mostly. I think she quilted with the women from the Whitehorse Sewing Circle…."

"You don't?"

"Me?" She seemed surprised by the question. "My mother did and her mother before her, but I found it all rather boring. I had too much to do raising my daughter and taking care of my home to spend a bunch of time sitting around with old women talking about the weather. My aunt Pearl, well, that's another story."

Nick could see that the house behind him was immaculate. He imagined Sarah Cavanaugh spent her days keeping it that way.

"Well, I appreciate your time. I'll try to catch Maddie later," he said.

"All right." There was a vagueness about Sarah Cavanaugh, like someone who'd spent too much time alone. He wondered what other farm and ranch women did during the day. Like Arlene Evans.

Laney drove over to Geraldine Shaw's house. When she'd called Maddie earlier, her cousin had said that was where she was headed.

The women of the community always gathered to do whatever was needed in a time of crisis. Had her grandmother been able, she would have been at Geraldine's as well. Geraldine's husband, Ollie, had been dead for a little less than a year now. The widow had lived alone and as far as Laney knew, had no living relatives. There would be animals to feed, a refrigerator to be cleaned out, watering to be done. And a will to be read.

Maddie's car was parked in the yard along with a variety of other rigs. As Laney let herself in, she saw Maddie sitting in a corner, the rest of the local women scattered around the room.

At the center stood a man in a dark suit. He looked uncomfortable in a room filled with women. His suit and demeanor alone made him stand out in Old Town Whitehorse as either an insurance salesman or a lawyer.

Laney sat down next to her cousin. Maddie took her hand and squeezed it, eyes welling in gratitude.

"As Mrs. Shaw's attorney, I can tell you that before her death she made provisions for the disposal of her possessions as well as her house and property," the man said.

Laney looked down at Maddie's hand gripping hers. There were new bruises on her cousin's wrist. Laney winced at the sight of them. She was glad at least that Maddie wasn't wearing the missing diamond bracelet. She hadn't had a chance to speak to her cousin about Geraldine's visit yesterday. In the chaos after Geraldine's collapse, Maddie had disappeared and now certainly wasn't the time to try to talk to her.

"Since Mrs. Shaw had no living relatives," the attorney continued, "she has left her house and property to the Whitehorse Sewing Circle to be used as they see fit."

There was a murmur of surprise among the women.

"That is very generous," Alice Miller said to the nods of the other women.

The attorney cleared his throat. "As for her personal belongings, some jewelry and what money Mrs. Shaw had accumulated, those are to go to a Ms. Madeline Renée Cavanaugh."

Maddie burst into tears.

As Nick was leaving Sarah Cavanaugh's house in the country, he got a call from one of the deputies that the man who'd been attacked behind the bar last night in Whitehorse had come in finally to file a report.

Someone had found Harvey T. Brown out behind the bar and called the sheriff's department. Brown, a known bar brawler who hated to ever lose a fight, hadn't wanted to make a statement because of his embarrassment at being beaten.

"Take Mr. Brown's statement and tell him I'll get

back to him later," Nick told the dispatcher. He was starting to see a disturbing pattern. All of the attacks had been on a Saturday night. All except one behind a crowded Whitehorse bar. The oddball one was reporter Glen Whitaker's, but then Glen said he couldn't remember the attack. If his was part of the pattern, then it would have been the first. Glen, Nick recalled, had been the only one to mention perfume.

"Ask Mr. Brown if he remembered anything, like a sound or a smell," Nick said.

"Also, Laci Cavanaugh called. She said she'll be at home if you need to reach her."

He found Laci in the kitchen. Laney wasn't anywhere in sight and her rental car was gone. He should have been relieved. It had been difficult earlier keeping his visit professional when what he'd really wanted to do was invite her to dinner.

"Can we talk while I cook?" Laci asked, visibly nervous. "I do better when I cook."

"What are you making?" he asked as he watched her drop a stick of butter into a skillet on the stove and begin to chop cloves of garlic.

"Shrimp scampi. I would love to bake something for dessert, but after what happened—"

"Your sister told you that Geraldine Shaw was poisoned."

She nodded. "I can't believe it."

"How well did you know Geraldine?"

"I didn't. I mean I've seen her around. My grandmother knew her because she was part of the Whitehorse Sewing Circle. I don't think I've ever said two words to the woman."

"What about your grandmother? Did she get along with Geraldine?"

Laci laughed as she swept the chopped garlic into the melted butter, the scent wafting through the kitchen and making his stomach growl. "Gramma gets along with everyone. She's one of those people who never has a bad word to say about anyone." Laci rolled her eyes. "I'm serious. She hates gossip and won't even allow Arlene Evans to talk about other people when she's around."

Laci stopped, her eyes tearing up. "You know my grandmother had a stroke and is in the hospital."

"I'm sorry. Can you think of anyone who had a motive for killing Mrs. Shaw?"

She shook her head.

"So tell me where you were when Geraldine Shaw collapsed."

Laci said she'd been behind the serving table setting out the desserts. "The desserts were going fast. I was worried I hadn't made enough."

"The macaroons?" he asked.

"When I looked there was only one left on the plate." She shook her head as if surprised by that. "I reached for the empty plate to refill it when I heard someone gasping. When I looked up, Geraldine was on the floor and people were screaming."

"Why did you make macaroons?"

Laci frowned. "They're Bo Evans's favorite."

"Who told you that?"

"His mother. Or maybe it was his sister Charlotte. Or was it Violet?" Laci shrugged. "It could have even been

Maddie. I really can't remember. But you have to believe I would never put anything bad in what I cooked. What would that do to my catering business?"

He smiled to himself at her logic, hating to point out that if she put the poison in the macaroons, she wouldn't have to worry about her catering business. She'd be working in the prison cafeteria wearing a hairnet and making macaroni-and-cheese rather than shrimp scampi.

Laci turned to him suddenly, her eyes wide with alarm. "What is *this* going to do to my catering business? I mean I haven't really started it, but when someone drops dead from one of my macaroons at the first party I cater…"

She turned back to the stove, slid several dozen fresh, deveined shrimp into the skillet with the butter and garlic, then began to chop some scallions with a cleaver, seeming to lose herself in her cooking again.

He watched her, fascinated. He could see that she loved cooking and believed her that she would never use her food to kill anyone.

"Tell me about the macaroons," he said.

"They're an old family recipe," she said. "My mother used to make them when Laney and I were little. It's the only thing I remember her making for us."

He heard the sadness in her voice. "Is your mother…?"

"Dead?" She shrugged. "One day we woke up and she was just gone. No one has seen her since." She slid the chopped scallions into the skillet, turned off the burner and looked at her watch.

"Expecting someone for lunch?" he asked.

"My sister and cousin. They should be here any minute." She must have heard his stomach growl. "You're joining us, aren't you? I always make extra."

Laney didn't get a chance to talk to Maddie until everyone left Geraldine's house.

"Geraldine was poisoned?" Maddie cried. "That's not possible."

Laney tried to calm her cousin. "Maddie, talk to me. I know something is going on with you."

Maddie was shaking her head from side to side and crying hysterically.

"Geraldine stopped by the house looking for you before the party. She was very upset. She thought you might know where her diamond bracelet was."

Maddie's tears slowed into jerky sobs. She looked up, fear in her eyes.

"Where is Geraldine's bracelet, Maddie?" Laney asked, her heart in her throat.

"I don't know. I put it back in the box before I left for the party. I swear I did."

Laney felt sick. "Who else might have come into the house after you left?"

"How should I know?" Maddie cried. "You know no one here locks their doors. Anyone could have stopped by and seen the jewelry box. I left it on the table with the rest of the things Geraldine had brought out for me to get ready."

"Ready for what?"

"To sell. Geraldine was going to sell some of the jewelry to a woman at an antique store in Billings."

"She was selling her jewelry?" Laney asked, her heart pounding. "Did she say why?"

Maddie shook her head.

Laney looked around the empty house, disgusted with herself for what she was about to do. But now both her sister and her cousin were in trouble. "Do you know where Geraldine kept her important papers?"

Nick helped with the salad while Laci whipped up her favorite salad dressing. He couldn't help the excitement he felt at the thought of seeing Laney again. He tried to put his finger on what it was about Laney Cavanaugh and smiled to himself.

She made him think of a summer breeze billowing white curtains, fresh-baked apple pie cooling on a kitchen windowsill, hot dogs roasting over a grill in the backyard on the Fourth of July. It made no sense and yet it felt as if it were the only thing that made any sense in his crazy world.

He'd grown up in L.A., a rough street kid who'd straightened up in time to become a cop like the rest of his family. His old man had been a cop. So had three of his uncles and a couple of his cousins.

His father was Irish, his mother Italian. A terrible combination since they were both pigheaded and opinionated. His father was large and loud. Nick never thought he'd miss them, but he did.

He thought about Laney and how she wouldn't be intimidated by any of them, not his great-aunt Elvira or even his uncle Cosmos. Cosmos would love Montana. Nick doubted he'd ever been out of California since he'd migrated from New York back in the forties.

Nick heard a car, then another one, pull up outside. He warned himself not to do anything stupid as he watched Laci taste the salad dressing, closing her eyes, savoring it before announcing it was ready.

"You really do love to cook, don't you?" he said.

Her face softened. "It's all I've ever wanted to do. All my favorite memories are tied to cooking, the smells, the tastes, the feel of something as simple as stirring." She grinned. "You think I'm nuts, huh?"

"No, I like to cook. My Italian grandmother taught me to make a mean rigatoni."

"So you're Italian?" Laney Cavanaugh said from the doorway. "That explains your dark looks, but not the name Rogers."

He felt his pulse take off at just the sight of her. She was wearing white capri pants and a pale yellow sleeveless top, her skin tanned and sleek. Her blond hair was pulled back in a ponytail, her eyes that wonderful deep sea-green.

"I have no idea where the Rogers came from," he said, feeling tongue-tied. For a moment talking to Laci, he'd forgotten his cover story and had offered more than he'd meant to.

Laney was eyeing him as if she'd seen that moment when he'd let down his guard. "Are you through grilling my sister?" she asked, coming into the room.

"A little cooking humor?" Laci asked with a nervous laugh. "I told him I wouldn't poison anyone with anything I cooked and he believes me."

Laney lifted a brow. "Is that true?" she asked him pointedly.

"I've just begun my investigation. I'll let you know if I survive lunch."

* * *

Nick smiled, revealing two small dimples Laney hadn't noticed before. She was so distracted that it took her a moment to register what he was saying.

"You're staying for lunch?"

"Your sister invited me and after watching her cook, I just couldn't say no."

She was going to have to sit through an entire meal with him? The last thing she wanted was the deputy sheriff at the table and she had a feeling her cousin didn't either as Maddie came into the room, stopping short at the sight of Nick.

"The deputy is joining us for lunch," Laney said to Maddie and stepped around the breakfast counter to join her sister at the stove.

"How you are doing, Maddie?" she heard Nick ask her cousin, but didn't hear Maddie's reply.

"What were you thinking, asking him to lunch?" Laney demanded in a hushed whisper to her sister.

"It was the polite thing to do," Laci whispered back. "Anyway, he's cute and you like him. I thought you'd be happy."

Laney groaned. She wanted to remind her sister that Nick was investigating a murder. But Laci being Laci knew she was innocent so wasn't in the least concerned.

Laney wished she shared her confidence in the judicial system. Unfortunately, Laney had seen enough true-life crime stories to know that innocent people went to prison all the time for crimes they didn't commit.

And after what she'd discovered in Geraldine Shaw's financial records, she was even more worried. Geraldine had been withdrawing rather large amounts of cash for months.

Given how frugally the woman had lived otherwise, the withdrawals sent up a red flag that it didn't take an accountant to question.

When Deputy Sheriff Nick Rogers found out about the unexplained monthly withdrawals, Laney knew he was going to think the same thing she did.

Someone had been blackmailing Geraldine Shaw—and the money had been about to run out.

Chapter 6

Nick could feel the tension at the table all during lunch. Maddie picked at her food, seeming to make a point of not looking in his direction. Her eyes were red from crying and he noticed that her hand holding her fork was shaking.

He had to wonder what had her so upset. He planned to ask her the moment he got her alone.

"This is an amazing meal," he said to Laci. "I can't remember one I've enjoyed more. What is the herb in the salad dressing? I can't quite place it."

She grinned, obviously pleased. "Chervil. It's the secret ingredient. You weren't kidding, you really do like to cook."

"I wouldn't lie about a thing like that."

"But you would other things?" Laney asked.

He glanced over at her. She hadn't said two words during lunch. Until now. "It's a figure of speech."

"Really?" she said sarcastically. Like a mother hen with Laci and Maddie, she was obviously angry with him for suspecting her sister and cousin. He found that and her all the more appealing.

Laci chattered about everything under the sun as they finished their meals, none of it requiring a comment from her sister or cousin. He concentrated on his meal, reminding himself why he was in Montana and just what he had to lose if he messed up. Getting involved with Laney would be the worst thing he could do.

"So do you like to cook, Laney?" he asked when Laci went into the kitchen to get the fresh fruit she'd prepared for dessert.

Laney's head jerked up as if she'd been miles away. "I can't even boil water."

"Now who's lying," Laci said as she returned with the fruit. "You have to excuse my sister. She's the *analytical* one." She grinned at Laney.

He looked from Laci to Laney, sensing an inside joke.

"I'm an accountant," Laney said with a sigh. "My sister has always given me a hard time because I look before I leap."

"What about you, Maddie?" Nick asked.

Maddie's eyes widened in alarm. "What about me?"

"Do you like to cook?"

She flushed and looked around as if trying to find a safe place to land. "Arlene is trying to teach me. She says I'm impossible."

"I'll teach you," Laci jumped in. "It's easy and fun. You'll see."

Nick doubted anything would be easy and fun with Arlene.

Maddie went back to moving her food around her plate.

He had to get Maddie alone to talk to her. Getting her to confide in him he feared would be much harder.

"I need to ask you a few questions," Nick said to Maddie after lunch. He saw the young woman glance at Laney. "It's just preliminary questions."

"I suppose it would be all right," Maddie said.

He gave her a reassuring smile. "Why don't we step outside to my patrol car."

Maddie hesitated, then followed him out. Once inside, he started the engine and saw her jump.

"Just turning on the air-conditioning," he said. "I want you to be comfortable." She was anything but. The slightest movement from him and she looked as if she might fly off the seat.

"Why don't you tell me about your relationship with Mrs. Shaw," he said.

"I didn't have a relationship with her."

"You worked for her. You knew her. Were you friends? Or just employee-employer?"

"The last. I just helped her out once in a while. I barely knew her."

Nick raised a brow. "I talked to her attorney this morning. I understand she left you everything but her house and property. It's not a lot but you're the only single person named in her will."

Maddie looked shocked that he knew this. "How did you…"

"You must have meant something to her for her to

leave you all her personal possessions and what money she had."

"I don't know why she did that," Maddie said, sounding near tears. "I had no idea."

Nick believed that she hadn't been expecting the inheritance. He just couldn't figure out why Geraldine Shaw had put Maddie Cavanaugh in her will. But he suspected Maddie did know why and that was what had her so upset.

Laney stood at the window, peering out through the curtains, worry making her ill.

"What is wrong with you?" Laci demanded as she dragged Laney away from the window.

"I probably shouldn't have let him talk to Maddie without an attorney present."

"For heaven's sake, why? It's not like she poisoned Geraldine," Laci said.

"I didn't tell you this, but Geraldine stopped by before the party. She was very upset. She couldn't find a diamond bracelet that she'd shown Maddie earlier."

Laci was shaking her head. "Maddie didn't take it."

"I hope not. What makes it more complicated is that Geraldine named Maddie in the will, leaving her all her personal belongings, including her jewelry."

"Well, see, then it doesn't matter. Maddie would get the bracelet anyway."

Laney stared at her little sister. Oh, to be Laci and live life in rose-colored glasses. "If the deputy finds out about the missing diamond bracelet, he might consider that a motive for murdering Geraldine. You know, to keep it from coming out that she'd taken the bracelet.

After all, Maddie didn't know Geraldine was leaving her anything." At least Laney hoped Maddie's reaction at the Shaw house had been an indication of that rather than guilt. "And when you consider how oddly Maddie has been acting lately..."

"There's an explanation for all of this," Laci said, looking worried. "I'm going to have to bake something. Chocolate. Chocolate pudding cake." She headed for the kitchen. "Maybe the deputy would like some."

Laney could only shake her head as she heard her sister searching for the recipe. She stepped back to the window as Maddie climbed out of the deputy's patrol car. Her cousin looked scared to death.

Laney's two-week summer vacation in Montana was up in a few days but she knew she couldn't leave until she'd cleared her sister—and cousin.

As Nick left, he mulled everything over in his mind. Geraldine had been a penny-pincher. She'd been paying Maddie Cavanaugh only a couple dollars an hour to help her sort through her things.

So why had Maddie taken the job? Even babysitters made more than two dollars an hour. At least where he was from. Nick reminded himself to ask Maddie when he saw her again.

Arlene Evans seemed glad to see him. "I wanted to talk to you about Geraldine Shaw," Nick said as he sat down gingerly on the plastic-covered chair she offered him.

Arlene perched primly on the matching plastic-covered couch, her hands in her lap, a virtuous look on her face. He could hear the throb of the stereo coming from down the hall. At least one of her offspring apparently was home.

"Geraldine Shaw?" Arlene asked as if surprised he would ask about her.

"Did you know her long?"

"All my life."

"What was she like?"

Arlene took a deep breath and let it out slowly. "Cheap. The woman wouldn't spend a penny if she could get away with it."

"Maybe she didn't have it to spend," he said. "I heard her husband Ollie died last summer and didn't have any life insurance."

Arlene scoffed. "He left her well-off enough. Ollie was just like her, had the first dime he ever made. Tight-fisted, he was." She leaned toward him conspiratorially. "Geraldine came from old money back East. She and Ollie *had* money. Hoarders, that's what they were. Didn't trust banks either." She nodded knowingly.

"Are you saying they buried their money in the back-yard?"

She smiled. "Maybe. Or hid it in that house. Never invited anyone over. Stayed to themselves. Who knows what's hidden over there?"

He could see Arlene going over there at night digging up the floorboards looking for the loot. Was there loot? Nick doubted it. Just a rumor that someone, probably Arlene, had started. And just such a rumor could have gotten Geraldine Shaw killed.

"I know for a fact that Mrs. Shaw died almost broke," Nick said.

Arlene smiled. "She just wanted everyone to think

that was the case. Don't let anyone kid you, Geraldine Shaw didn't look all that bright, but she was a smart one."

"If she was so smart then how is it she managed to eat the only poisoned macaroon at the party?" It gave him an immense amount of pleasure to see Arlene Evans at a loss for words. Her mouth opened and closed like a guppy's, but nothing was coming out for a full thirty seconds.

"Poisoned?"

He nodded. "I was wondering if you had any idea who might have wanted her dead?"

"Who?" She sucked in a breath, then expelled it in a rush. "I'll tell you who." She glanced down the hallway toward what he assumed were her son's and daughters' rooms in the direction where the music boomed behind a closed door.

"Yes?" he asked.

Arlene looked a little guilty before she said, "Maddie Cavanaugh. I hate to say it about my son's fiancée, but I overheard Maddie and Geraldine arguing outside the community center right before the party."

"About what?"

"A missing diamond bracelet. Geraldine was convinced that Maddie had taken it. Maddie, of course, swore she hadn't." Arlene made a face. "I tried to get the truth out of her later."

When he'd caught the two of them behind the center.

"I told her I wouldn't have a thief in my family. I threatened to tell Bo."

"Did you?" he asked.

Arlene glanced back down the hall. "I couldn't keep

something like that from him. He's my *son*. You probably heard they had a huge fight later. Bo hasn't said whether or not they'd broken up for good, but he's been in his room ever since except for meals."

"He doesn't have a job?"

She looked indignant. "He helps his father run this place when his father needs him."

Nick nodded. The kid seldom helped out. A mama's boy. "Can you tell me where you were when Geraldine collapsed?" Nick asked.

Arlene frowned. "I was outside with you."

"I believe you'd returned to the center. Someone saw you at the dessert table with your daughters."

"Then why did you ask me?" Arlene snapped. "I can't remember. It was all so traumatic. My son's engagement party of all places for her to die." She shook her head as though she couldn't believe Geraldine's gall.

"Do you have any idea what Geraldine might have eaten just before she collapsed?"

"How should I know what she ate?"

"Someone saw your daughters pass down the last macaroon possibly to you," he said.

"Me?" She shook her head.

"Don't you like macaroons?"

"I love them, but I was waiting for Laci to refill the plate. I didn't want that old stale one. I was glad when Geraldine took it." She sniffed as if there were a bad smell in the air. "Frankly, Laci has a lot to learn about baking. Macaroons should be moist, not wet, slightly rounded and never have almond flavoring in them."

"What makes you think the cookie had almond flavoring in it?"

She smiled pitying. "You're new here. You don't know that I am considered the best cook in the county." She motioned to a glassed-in cabinet that he hadn't noticed. It was full of blue ribbons.

"I *know* my cooking," she said with a nod. "Anyway, I smelled almond flavoring as Geraldine took it."

"Your daughter seemed to like the macaroons," he said.

"You're mistaken. Charlotte wouldn't touch a macaroon and Bo's allergic to coconut."

"Your other daughter. Violet."

"Oh, her." She did an eye roll. "Violet will eat anything. I've tried to teach her to cook...." She lifted a brow as if to say it was hopeless.

"You're also teaching your son's fiancée to cook, I understand. Maddie?"

Another eye roll. "Not everyone is capable of cooking. There is a talent to it."

"Your daughter Charlotte, is she a good cook?"

"Charlotte?" She let out a laugh. "She won't need to learn to cook. She'll do fine on her looks alone because she'll marry well."

Nick tried not to show his distaste for Arlene's theories.

"What are *you* looking for in a wife?" Arlene asked.

He chuckled uncomfortably. "I'm *not* looking."

"You're a handsome man. Too old for Charlotte, but there is always Violet or other single women in the area you might be interested in. I can sign you up for my Internet Meet-a-Mate business. It only takes a minute—"

"No thanks." He got to his feet, wanting to clear out

as soon as possible. "What kind of poisons do you keep in the place?"

It was his lucky day. He'd caught Arlene Evans speechless twice in a row. Unfortunately nothing lasted long.

"How can you even ask something like that?" Arlene snapped. "Of course I don't have any poisons in this house, Deputy."

"Of course," he said as he moved to the door to leave.

"If you change your mind about the Meet-a-Mate," Arlene called from her porch, "you just let me know. First month free!"

He drove off as if heading for a fire and decided to run by Geraldine Shaw's house. The attorney had told him that the women from the community had been in the house earlier that day to take care of a few things.

There was safety in numbers so he didn't think he'd find the floorboards dug up where someone had been searching for hidden loot.

But he did worry about what he wouldn't find. A missing diamond bracelet. The attorney had gathered up the rest of Geraldine's jewelry. It was to be turned over to Maddie Cavanaugh once the estate was settled. There was no diamond bracelet.

What disturbed Nick was the fact that as far as he knew, the only person who'd spent much time in the house with Geraldine Shaw was Maddie Cavanaugh. So who else could have taken the bracelet? Unless it had just been misplaced.

He parked his pickup in the back and entered through the rear. He'd been dumbfounded to find out that no one in Whitehorse or most of rural Montana locked their doors.

The house had an old smell that went with the furnishings. It was cool and dark inside and resembled some museums he'd been in. He went from room to room trying to get a feel for Geraldine Shaw. The drapes were old but clean, the sheets on her bed threadbare, her clothing matronly and dated, the cupboard filled mostly with home-canned items from her garden.

Arlene had been right about one thing. Geraldine Shaw lived frugally. But because she had to? Or because she was a skinflint as Arlene and probably the rest of the town believed?

He heard the creak of a footfall on the front steps and slipped back into the shadows as the front door groaned open. He'd thought there might be visitors—but not until dark.

The door closed, then the sound of tentative footsteps grew closer. Nick would have expected Maddie to show up here. Or Arlene Evans.

So he was more than a little surprised when the intruder turned out to be the last person he'd expected.

He stepped out, startling Laney Cavanaugh. She slapped a hand over her heart, both surprised and guilty-looking.

"Hello," he said, unable to hide his grin. Laney made the cutest criminal.

"What are you doing here?" she demanded.

"Funny, but that was what I was just about to ask you."

She reddened, glancing around as if there would be something in the room that could save her.

"You're not interfering in my investigation, are you, Miss Cavanaugh?"

She straightened to her full height, her expression resolute. "You are *investigating* people I care about."

He nodded. "Your cousin Maddie is hiding something." He could see she wanted to argue that, but didn't even try. "Why don't you tell me what you're doing here."

"I was by earlier with the rest of the community women to see what I could do to help," she said. "I left my sweater here."

She picked up a pale blue sweater from the arm of a rocker by the window.

Was it her sweater? Or was she just fast on her feet under pressure? He couldn't tell. She was that cool.

But given the way she'd entered the house, he'd say she was fast on her feet. Not that he didn't like that about her.

"That color goes well with your eyes," he said, smiling as he stepped closer and caught a whiff of perfume.

Laney, the times he'd been around her, smelled like fresh air and sunshine. The perfume, he realized, was coming from the blue sweater she had over her arm. How had Glen Whitaker described it? Old flowers.

"What is that scent?" he asked, thinking this wasn't the first time he'd smelled it. Arlene Evans's house had a faint hint of it. In fact, he would have sworn he'd seen Violet Evans a couple of days ago in a blue sweater just like this one.

Laney frowned. "What scent?"

"The perfume on your sweater."

Some of the cool left those emerald eyes of hers. She raised the sweater to her nose and sniffed. "Lavender."

Chapter 7

Laney didn't like the look in Nick's eyes. It was as if he knew something she didn't. Worse, she was awful at this deceptive stuff. Or maybe she just didn't like withholding evidence. Especially from Nick.

"I have a confession," she blurted. "Geraldine Shaw stopped by the house right before the party. She'd misplaced a diamond bracelet. She thought Maddie had it and was upset."

He nodded. "So where is this bracelet?"

"That's just it. No one knows."

"You asked Maddie?"

She'd tried to get Maddie to open up to her after her interrogation in Nick's patrol car in front of the house. But Maddie, clearly upset, had said she needed to find Bo and had left in a rush.

"Maddie swears she left it in the jewelry box with

the other items Geraldine had planned to sell and I be-lieve her," Laney said with more force than she really felt. Something was going on with Maddie. Laney had sensed it from the moment she'd seen her cousin. With each passing day, Laney was becoming more concerned that Maddie was in serious trouble.

"Can you describe this diamond bracelet?" Nick asked.

"I can do better than that." Laney handed him the snapshots Geraldine had had Maddie take and send cop-ies to the antique jeweler.

"The rest of the jewelry is accounted for?"

She nodded.

He took the photo of the diamond bracelet and put it in his pocket. "Any more confessions?"

She met his dark eyes, tempted to confess that she'd wanted to kiss him from the moment she'd met him. "I think that about covers it. Except I was mistaken. This isn't my sweater." She hooked the blue sweater back over the arm of the rocker and turned to give him her best sheepish smile.

He seemed about to say something, then must have thought better of it. "No more investigating on your own, right?"

She didn't answer as she left. She didn't want to have to lie to him on top of everything else.

After Laney left, Nick stood listening to her drive away. Clearly she hadn't come here for her sweater. But what? What would she have been looking for? The miss-ing diamond bracelet? Or… He spied a drawer that was slightly cocked as if closed too quickly.

Stepping to it, he saw the dust was disturbed on the cabinet as if someone had put a hand down on it. The handprint could have been Laney Cavanaugh's. It was that small, the fingers long and slim.

He pulled open the drawer, not surprised to find it contained Mrs. Shaw's personal financial records. Laney Cavanaugh was an accountant. He wondered what she might have found interesting in Geraldine's records.

As he started to leave, he had a thought. In the kitchen he found a clean trash bag under the sink. He put the sweater smelling of lavender in the bag and closed the top. If he was right, Glen Whitaker would recognize the scent.

He was anxious to get back to his office, to get the photo of the diamond bracelet on the wire. He was counting on whoever stole the bracelet to have pawned it as quickly as possible thinking that was safer than hanging on to it—especially after Geraldine Shaw dropped dead.

But as he drove by the community center, he noticed that the door was cracked open. Since he'd asked Titus to keep the place locked until the investigation was over, the door shouldn't have been open. There was no car parked out front, but he'd noticed a trail behind the center that led down to more parking at the bottom of the hill.

He slowed to a stop, parked at the edge of the road and walked back. As he neared, he heard a thud, as if someone had bumped against something inside the center. *Someone* was definitely in there.

He climbed the steps and eased the door open, peering into the cool darkness. From what he could see, everything was just as it had been the day of the murder sans the food.

He pushed the door open farther and stepped in.

Laney Cavanaugh stood at the end of the table where the desserts had been during the engagement party. She had her hands on her hips, her head tilted to one side. He could hear her muttering to herself.

He smiled, shaking his head. She hadn't exactly taken his warning about staying out of his investigation, now had she?

He thought about arresting her. He also thought about kissing her. The latter had the most appeal.

"And we meet again."

She jumped, spinning around, guilt written all over her face. "I was just—"

"Looking for your sweater? No, that's right, you found it at Geraldine Shaw's. But then it turned out not to be yours after all. I hope you at least found what you were looking for here. And please don't insult my intelligence with another story about a missing item of clothing."

She met his gaze. "Fine. I'm trying to find out who killed Geraldine Shaw so I can clear my sister."

He liked honesty. Hell, he liked this woman and found himself liking her more all the time. "I thought we'd already had this discussion. I'm the one who's going to find out who killed Geraldine Shaw. You were the one who was going to stay out of it. At least that's the way I remember it."

"I can't stay out of it. You don't know these people. I do. I know this town. I know its history."

He shook his head, afraid he knew what was coming. "You need my help."

He smiled at that, tempting though it was. "I'm an officer of the law." He didn't add that he'd had more experience than he wanted to admit with murder. And an even closer brush with cyanide poisoning.

She said nothing, but still had that determined look in her eyes.

"You realize there's a law against impeding an investigation."

Determination brought her chin up. "You can arrest me if you don't like it."

What he liked was the idea of taking her back to town, but not to jail.

"I can help," she said, hesitated, then added, "I found Geraldine Shaw's financial records."

Yeah, so he'd discovered. He raised a brow though, curious what she'd made of what she'd found.

"She'd been withdrawing a thousand dollars a month in cash out of her savings account for the last year."

Which probably explained why Geraldine's savings account had less than a hundred dollars in it now.

"Blackmail?" he asked.

Laney shrugged then grinned. "You're the officer of the law here."

He shook his head at her, unable not to grin. "Arlene Evans thinks Geraldine hid thousands of dollars in her house."

"That's a rumor that's been going around for years." She shook her head. "They weren't poor, but they weren't rich either. Like most of the people who live in and around here, they lived off the land and made a living. No one around here gets rich. Or lives extravagantly."

"So what would anyone have to blackmail her about?" he asked.

"Your guess is as good as mine."

He took off his hat and scratched his head. "I'm sorry, where does your knowledge of these people and this community come in again?"

She glared at him. "I do have several theories about the murder if you're interested. It's one reason I stopped by here."

He put his hat back on, pushed back the brim and crossed his arms as he leaned against the wall. "I can't wait to hear them."

Laney ignored his sarcasm. She could put up with a lot to save her sister. And her cousin, because like him, she feared Maddie was somehow involved in all this.

But putting up with Nick Rogers also meant ignoring the way her heart took off at a gallop when he was around. He seemed to fill any space he was in, changed the air pressure and the temperature. Made her body feel hypersensitive as if just his nearness was a caress across her bare skin.

What Nick Rogers did was remind her that she was a woman and it had been a long while since any man had done that.

"If the poison wasn't in the macaroons—which it wasn't since Laci baked them—then it had to have been added between the time she baked them and they ended up on this table," she said, corralling her thoughts.

He nodded. "Who took them from the house to the center?"

"Aunt Sarah, Maddie's mom, brought some of the baked goods, Laci and I brought the rest." Before he could ask, she added, "I personally loaded the macaroons." She met his gaze. "In case you're wondering, I didn't poison them."

"So you carried the macaroons in and left them on the back counter behind the tables. Laci put them on the table and Laci was the only one who had access to the rest, right?"

She hated to admit it. "Yes."

"So if Laci didn't put the poison in the cookie, then it had to be administered while the macaroons were on the table, right?" His dark eyes reminded her of this part of Montana, vast.

She shook her head. "Too sloppy. The killer couldn't chance being seen adding the poison to the cookie. So if you were the killer, what would you do?"

He shrugged. "Enlighten me."

"Bring your own macaroon with the poison already in it."

"Your sister's right about you. She said you had a very analytical mind."

She heard his words, not just the ones he spoke, but the ones he didn't as his gaze washed over her. She felt heat flush her skin as she turned her back on him to study the counter behind the table. She hated that her behavior probably only made her look guilty.

Better him think that, she reasoned, than what she really had on her mind.

Nick studied her backside, liking the set of her shoulders, the determined tilt of her head, the way her jeans fit her. The fact that she was hiding something from him only intrigued him as much as the woman herself. Since lunch she had changed to jeans and a sleeveless blouse, both dark blue. He suspected this was her investigating outfit.

"Nice theory," he said as he debated what to do about Laney Cavanaugh. She was definitely too smart for her own good. The killer was bound to find out that she was doing some investigating on her own. From what she'd said, she wasn't going to give up until she found out the truth.

And that was the problem. This was way too dangerous for her to be nosing around in. Worse, she could go too far—and find not only the killer—but also uncover things about Nick Rogers and what he was really doing here.

The problem was that warning her to stay out of his investigation was a waste of breath. She was right. She knew the locals, she knew the area, and maybe even harder to accept, he needed her.

He also needed to keep an eye on her. For his own protection if not hers. Mostly, keeping an eye on Laney Cavanaugh was exactly what he wanted to do.

"So the killer baked one macaroon with almond extract and poison in it?" he asked, having a few theories of his own, but curious to see what she'd come up with.

She turned around to look at him. Her eyes were that clear cool-water mix of greens. "Almond extract?"

He nodded. "Arlene Evans said she smelled it in the cookie."

"Laci would never have changed the recipe that way.

She's a purist about old family recipes. Our macaroons don't have almond extract in them."

He loved the way she not only defended her sister, but also the family recipe. "How did the killer know Laci was making macaroons?"

"Someone told her they were Bo's favorite," she said.

"But I talked to Arlene. Bo is allergic to coconut."

"The intended victim would have had to have liked macaroons."

He smiled and nodded. "Apparently Geraldine liked macaroons. And Arlene—although she says she prefers her own recipe. And Violet apparently was a big fan of the cookies."

"The macaroon would have to be identical to the others," she said more to herself than to him.

"Where did she get what your sister said was an old family recipe, then?"

"The Whitehorse Sewing Circle's cookbook. My grandmother donated the recipe to raise money for the center."

He nodded. Of course she had. "You're right. You know these people, this place. I'm out of my league."

She smiled. "I really doubt that."

He saw Laney consider him, the steel of her gaze and spine not quite as severe. "You don't think Laci poisoned Geraldine."

He shook his head.

She seemed to relax a little more, softening as she did. He felt a pull stronger than gravity toward her and fought it as a drowning man fought water.

"Have dinner with me." The words were out before he could call them back.

"Thanks but I don't think that would be a good idea."

"Why not?"

She studied him openly. "Wouldn't it look bad if you were fraternizing with a suspect? I am a suspect, right?"

"I can't see you poisoning anyone."

"Really? Didn't I hear somewhere that poison is a woman's weapon?"

She was definitely a woman.

"If you were the killer, you wouldn't leave anything to chance," he said.

"True," she agreed.

"This killer couldn't be sure her intended victim got the cookie," he pointed out.

"Unless she gave the victim the cookie and Geraldine was the intended victim."

"Good point. Except neither of us believes Geraldine was the intended victim."

She smiled again. "How do you know that?"

"Because the only person who benefited from Geraldine Shaw's death was Maddie."

"And the Whitehorse Sewing Circle."

"I got the impression from talking to the lawyer that the women of the sewing circle had no idea Geraldine was leaving them anything," he said.

She nodded. "I was there. Everyone was shocked."

"So that leaves Maddie," he said quietly. "It would appear she killed Geraldine to cover up the thief of the diamond bracelet."

Laney shook her head. "The bracelet went missing the day of the party. Maddie didn't have time to bake a poison macaroon."

"Unless she'd been planning to rip off Geraldine all

along," he pointed out. "Maddie was the only one who knew about the jewelry, knew Geraldine would be sending it to Billings to that antique dealer soon, so she had to act fast. Her party was the perfect place."

"Why not just conk Geraldine on the head and take the jewelry then? Wouldn't that be much easier? She could say the woman fell. And no one knew about the jewelry except Geraldine and Maddie. No one would know what was missing."

He smiled at Laney. He liked her mind. "Good points. Also, Arlene says Maddie can't cook. Plus Maddie was outside with me. Bo came and got her. She didn't have time to slip Geraldine a cookie."

"So you were just playing devil's advocate?" Laney demanded. Anger flashed in all that emerald-green.

"Just seeing if there were any holes in my logic."

She glared at him. "You could have told me up front that you didn't believe Laci *or* Maddie were guilty."

"I didn't say Maddie wasn't guilty. I just don't think she killed Geraldine Shaw."

"You think she took that diamond bracelet?"

"Maybe. If not, she knows who did," he said. "As for the murder, I think the killer decided to take advantage of the party." And if that made Laci Cavanaugh look guilty in the process, so much the better.

"Any ideas who could have baked the counterfeit cookie?" he asked.

"Anyone who might have a Whitehorse Sewing Circle cookbook."

"Do you recall how many copies were printed?"

"Two hundred."

"That leaves it wide open." He let out a low whistle. "Remind me to get one before I leave."

"Are you planning to leave?" she asked, her gaze intent on him suddenly.

"Before I leave Old Town today," he said, catching himself. "They are still for sale, aren't they?"

She shook her head. "But I could probably get you a copy sometime."

Was it just his imagination that she seemed to be eyeing him with suspicion? Probably.

But then again, the woman was sharp. He'd have to watch himself around her.

"So what now?" she asked.

He glanced at his watch. "Better decide where to go for dinner. Since you know the area…"

She shook her head, but she was smiling. "Have you been to the Tin Cup?"

After Nick made Laney promise she wouldn't do any more snooping around in the case without him, he watched her drive off in the direction of home before he returned to Whitehorse. His first stop was his office to fax the photograph of the missing diamond bracelet to pawn shops and cop departments in a two-hundred-mile area.

Next he dropped by the *Milk River Examiner* office. Glen Whitaker looked up from his desk as Nick came in carrying the trash bag with the sweater inside.

"I have something I was hoping you might be able to help me with," Nick said. "There's a scent on this sweater and I wondered…" He opened the bag and held it for the reporter to take a whiff.

"That's it!" Glen cried, then lowered his voice. There was no one else in the office, but Glen must have known from experience that walls sometimes had big ears. "That's the smell that was on my clothing after I was attacked. What is it?"

"Lavender."

Glen wrinkled his nose. "That smell makes me a little sick."

Nick wondered just what had happened to Glen before he'd regained consciousness beside that road.

"Why would I smell lavender after my attack?" Glen asked.

"I'm working on that," Nick said and, closing the bag with the sweater, headed for the sheriff's department.

Harvey T. Brown had filed an assault report. The deputy who'd handled the complaint had written down that Brown remembered smelling something sweet, like maybe flowers or perfume, or "those things people put in their cars to cover up odors." He'd also glimpsed a baseball bat just before he'd been hit.

Nick drove the bagged sweater out to Brown's place north of town. Harvey T. Brown was a large man with a beer belly and a bald spot.

"That could be the smell," Brown said from his recliner. He recoiled at the scent much as Glen Whitaker had, lying back in his chair. "Was there some of that kind of flower that smelled like that growing outside the bar?"

Nick had to shake his head. "I think there's a good possibility the person wielding the baseball bat was a woman."

"No way," Brown said, shooting to his feet. He

marched into the kitchen, opened the fridge and took out a can of beer. "You tell anyone in this town that I was beat up by a woman and so help me I will—"

"Take it easy," Nick told him. "It's just a theory."

"It better not be one I ever hear again," Brown said, sitting back down in his recliner and popping the top on his beer. He chugged most of the can, belched and glared at Nick. "I was beat up by some big burly guy. I didn't smell nothing. Got it?"

"Got it."

"I like this place," Nick said later when he and Laney were sitting in the dining room at the country club overlooking the golf course. Mostly he liked the company he was with.

"Surprised Whitehorse has a golf course?" she asked, smiling across the table at him. "There's two in the area. Another one out at Sleeping Buffalo." She was wearing a pale green dress that brought out the tropical-green of her eyes. The dress seemed to float over her curves as gently as a caress. She smelled good, too. Something fruity that went with the summer evening.

Nick knew he would never forget that scent. Or this night. No matter what happened in the future.

During dinner they talked about their childhoods, Laney's growing up in Old Town Whitehorse, Nick's edited story of growing up in a large Italian family. They had the place pretty much to themselves since it was a weekday.

The food was wonderful, the view breathtaking as the sun set in a glow of colors and night shadows drifted over the place like a warm breeze.

"I'm serious about you being careful," he said as the evening drew to an end. She'd insisted on driving in from Old Town, saying she had to visit her grandmother in the hospital anyway and it would save him the trip out and back.

As the restaurant emptied out completely, he reached across the table and put his hand over hers, something he'd wanted to do all evening.

"I'm always careful." Her gaze met his. "Well, almost always." She was flirting with him, he was pretty sure of it.

He was treading on thin ice. But what worried him was that she didn't seem in the least bit afraid. Not of flirting with him. Or looking for a killer. Both were much more dangerous than she imagined.

He drew his hand back. "There's a killer out there and until we find out why Geraldine is dead—"

She shook her head. "Don't you think what we have to find out is who the killer really wanted dead since neither of us believes the intended victim was Geraldine Shaw?"

He smiled. "But neither of us has any evidence to substantiate that."

"I was there, remember? I didn't see her take a bite of the macaroon or collapse, but when I got through the crowd to her, I remember hearing someone crying, 'no, oh no.'"

He could argue that "no, oh no" wasn't conclusive evidence of anything but shock or surprise when Geraldine had collapsed.

"The other odd thing was that I couldn't see one of Geraldine's arms with everyone crowded around her,"

Laney said. "But I could see that she was struggling as if someone had hold of her wrist. When you moved everyone back, I saw that her fingers holding the cookie were white they were gripped so tightly and there were several red marks on her palm where it appeared someone had tried to pry her fingers open."

"The killer was probably trying to get the evidence to destroy it," he said.

"Maybe," she agreed. "Or maybe the killer was upset and trying to get the cookie back because she'd just killed the wrong person."

"She?"

Laney nodded. "The voice I heard was definitely a woman's. And wouldn't a man have been able to pry Geraldine's fingers open?"

He chuckled and took a sip of his drink. Brains and beauty, a deadly combination. He hoped the fact that the killer had used cyanide was just a terrible coincidence, because otherwise this Nancy Drew sitting across the table from him might just stumble on the truth not only about the killer, but him as well. That should have frightened him more than it did. Hell, the truth was, he wanted to tell her everything. He hated lying to her.

He took a sip of his drink, dropping his gaze, as he tried to talk some sense into himself. Telling anyone was like signing his own death warrant. What the hell was he thinking?

"You like women to think you're shy, don't you?" she said, studying him.

He looked up at her, meeting her gaze, and grinned. "Oh, that's real. At least with you."

She cocked a brow at him.

"You're a scary woman."

"You do look frightened."

He laughed. She didn't know how close to the truth she'd come.

Chapter 8

Nick couldn't help thinking about Laney. For a lot of reasons. Her grandfather Titus dropped off a copy of the Whitehorse Sewing Circle cookbook first thing the next morning.

Nick found her grandmother's recipe and read through it, then called Laney. "Would you have to be a pretty good cook to make your grandmother's macaroons?" he asked. "They don't look that easy."

"They aren't."

"Then our killer is a better than average cook, whose victim likes coconut, right?" He heard her smile even over the phone. "Any suggestions who to talk to?"

"Pretty near every woman in Old Town Whitehorse," she said with a laugh. "Haven't you heard? They're the best cooks in the county. At least according to Arlene Evans and she has the blue ribbons to prove it."

"Yes, she mentioned that. And she was closest to the poisoned macaroon when Geraldine ate it." He fiddled for a moment with a pen on his desk. "I had a good time last night at dinner."

"Me, too." Her voice was soft and low. He imagined her still in her pj's. Silk, the color of her eyes. The image of emerald-green silk draped over that body—

"Would you mind telling me what you're wearing right now?"

"What?" She laughed. "You aren't serious."

He needed a good dose of reality. "Yes, I am."

Silence, then a small embarrassed laugh. "Well, I have on a pair of old jeans and one of my grandfather's flannel shirts and a ratty pair of tennis shoes I found at the back of the closet. All of the above are covered in paint."

"What color paint?"

She laughed again. "White. I'm painting the picket fence out front." She lowered her voice. "So what does my attire do for you?"

He sat up, tossing down the pen. "It makes me realize that I have to see you again."

Another smile in her voice as she said, "Good."

"Great. Oh, and, no investigating without me, right?"

"Right. Just painting."

"Good girl." He hung up still smiling. He caught his reflection in the window. "Wipe that stupid smile off your face," he told himself. "You look like a fool. Worse, you're acting like one."

He forced himself to turn his thoughts to the murder of Geraldine Shaw. The plan had been amateurish at best. A plan born of passion—not precision. Passion

meant anger and anger was a detriment to the killer—
and an advantage for the lawman. So who was angry
with Geraldine Shaw?

Apparently no one.

What did that leave him? An angry killer who had
failed at poisoning his intended victim? *Her* intended
victim, he corrected, remembering what Laney had
said. Going with Laney's theory, the killer would also
need at least a passing knowledge of poison—and cooking. And a motive.

The call came as he was leaving his office.

"Deputy Rogers? This is Clyde Banner. I own the
Pawn and Go in Great Falls. I think I have the diamond
bracelet you're looking for. I just took a digital photo of
it and e-mailed it to your office."

Nick sat down and called up the Internet. There was
an e-mail from Pawn and Go. He clicked on it. A photo
came up. Geraldine Shaw's bracelet.

"That's it," he told Clyde. "Can you tell me who
pawned it?"

"Well, that's what's kind of curious about the pawn
slip. The guy who came in said his name was Nick
Rogers."

Cute. Someone playing games with him.

"You weren't suspicious?" Nick asked.

"I'm always suspicious, but unless it comes up on
a hot sheet…"

"What did this Nick Rogers look like?" he asked.

"Young. Nineteen, twenty. Brown hair, brown eyes.
Good-looking kid. Clean cut. He looked legit enough.
Hell, he was driving a nice car."

"How nice?" Nick asked and listened as Clyde Banner described Bo Evans's car to a T. "I might need you to ID the kid."

"No problem. I'll put the bracelet in the safe. I assume you'll have someone pick it up?"

"Thanks." Nick hung up and sat for a moment before he dialed Laney's number. "I need to talk to your cousin. Want to ride along?"

"I'll be ready when you get here," she said, obviously hearing something in his voice that warned her it wasn't good news.

Maddie was surprised to see them. Her car was in the yard. Her mother's was gone. From the look on her face, she wished she hadn't answered the door. She stood in the doorway, looking from one to the other, looking scared.

"Mind if we come in?" Nick asked.

"I was just going to town to—"

"This won't take long," he said.

Maddie looked to her cousin. Laney nodded and they stepped into the cool, clean house.

The place smelled of lemon cleaner. There was no dust on the end table next to the couch, no magazines or newspapers cluttering up the coffee table. Nick was surprised there wasn't any plastic on the furniture.

He took a seat on the couch. Laney hugged her cousin and sat on one of the chairs. Maddie stood as if lost. She ran her hands along the sides of her jeans, clearly nervous.

"Can I get you something to drink?" she asked, flashing them a nervous smile. "You both look so serious."

"Sit down, Maddie," Nick said.

She dropped into a chair, her blue eyes wide with fear. "Has something happened?"

"The photographs you took of Geraldine Shaw's jewelry? Who did you show them to?" Nick asked.

Maddie swallowed, her eyes swimming in tears. "Nobody."

"You didn't show them to your fiancé?"

One tear broke loose and cascaded down her freckled cheek. "I..."

"Maddie, I found Geraldine's diamond bracelet. It was pawned at a shop in Great Falls. The clerk described Bo Evans as the person who pawned it."

She began to cry, shaking her head from side to side.

"Did you give him the bracelet?"

Her eyes widened in alarm. "No," she cried. "I swear. I told him about the bracelet, but I never dreamed he'd..." Her words were lost in tears.

Laney handed her cousin a tissue.

"You and Bo had a fight after his mother told him that Geraldine Shaw thought you'd taken the diamond bracelet," Nick said.

Maddie looked up at him, tears cascading down her face, but no sound coming out of her now.

"Didn't he mention then that he'd taken the bracelet?" Nick asked. "Surely, he wouldn't let his mother think you were a thief and not defend you."

Maddie began to sob openly in answer. Just as Nick had suspected, Bo hadn't cleared things up for his mother or his fiancée.

"Bo's going to be arrested," Nick told her. "You might want to rethink your engagement to him."

"No, you can't arrest him," Maddie cried through

her tears. "Can't you just give him a warning? Arlene will blame me."

"Arlene? Why would she blame you?" Laney demanded.

"She just will."

Nick studied the young woman. "Arlene's the one who put those bruises on your arms, isn't she?"

Maddie looked down, plucking at her sleeves to hide them. "I'm just a klutz."

"Maddie, stop covering for that family," Laney said, going to her cousin and kneeling down in front of her.

"She's right," Nick said. "If this is the way they treat you now, trust me, it will only get worse once you're married to Bo."

"But I love Bo," Maddie wailed. "I can't live without him. No one will love me like Bo does."

Laney handed her cousin more tissues and put her arm around her. "Come stay with me and Laci. We won't let anyone hurt you anymore."

Maddie sounded like a wounded animal, her cries heartbreaking, as Nick left Laney to take care of her cousin.

At the Evans house, Nick could hear music blaring as he knocked on the screen door. Arlene's truck was gone, but Bo's souped-up ride was sitting out front.

Nick banged on the doorframe. "Bo," he called loudly. No response. He banged again.

Violet appeared from the semidarkness inside, giving him a start. She must have been sitting in the darkened living room, the drapes drawn. He hadn't heard the creak of plastic as she'd gotten up. Nor had she made a sound as she'd approached.

"Mother's not here," she said meekly. Her face was paler than he remembered and there were dark circles under her eyes. "She's at the doctor's."

"She's not feeling well?"

She shook her head.

"Your brother around?"

Violet seemed to hesitate as if tempted to lie. It surprised him she might lie for her brother. Nick had gotten the impression she wasn't close to her siblings.

"Could you tell him I'm here?" Nick said, opening the screen door and stepping in.

"I'm not sure he's home." Violet was forced to take a step back.

"Why don't I try his room," Nick said. He moved past her across the living room and down the hall, following the sound of a heavy-metal band with no talent for songwriting. The monotonous beat made his teeth ache.

He pounded on Bo's bedroom door.

"Go away!"

Nick opened the door. Bo looked up from where he was sprawled on his rumpled bed. Apparently Arlene hadn't felt well enough to make her son's bed this morning.

"What do you want?" he yelled over the racket coming from the stereo.

Nick stepped over to the stereo and shut if off.

"What do you think you're doing?" Bo demanded.

"Reading you your rights."

"What?" He sat up.

The room had a funky smell. The kid was a slob and it took all Nick's control not to tell him so.

"You have the right to remain—"

"Whoa. Don't you have to tell me why you're arresting me first?" Bo demanded, only the slight squeak in his voice giving away his concern.

"Guess," Nick said as he pulled out his cuffs.

"I don't know anything about that bracelet."

"Did I say anything about a bracelet, Bo?"

"Maddie. She gave it to me. She's the one who made me do it."

"Your mother might believe that story, but it isn't going to fly with me," Nick said. "And if it were true, wouldn't a fiancé try to cover for the woman he loved? You're despicable. Now get on your feet."

He saw Bo look toward the door as if gauging his chances of escaping.

"*Please,* try to resist arrest," Nick said. "There is nothing I would like better than to kick your ass."

Bo Evans scowled as he stood and held out his hands. "You're going to regret this. My mother will have your job," he said, but his voice broke.

Nick shoved Bo toward the door. Violet watched as Nick took her brother away, her gaze unreadable.

As he shoved Bo into the back of the patrol car, Charlotte Evans drove up. She glanced at her brother in cuffs in the backseat, then at Nick. With apparent disinterest, she got out and started toward the house.

"Charlotte, do you know where I can find your mother?" Nick asked her.

"At the hospital," she said, sounding surprised. "Didn't Bo tell you? Mother took a nasty spill down the basement stairs last night. She broke her arm and has a concussion."

* * *

It rained that Saturday, the day of Geraldine Shaw's funeral. Laney stood on the hillside overlooking Old Town. Only a few black umbrellas huddled around the grave site as Titus stood with Bible in hand and said a few kind words over Geraldine's grave.

The low turnout could have been because of the gray rainy day. But Laney knew it had more to do with the fact that most everyone didn't know Geraldine well.

"Dust to dust…" Laney's grandfather's words were lost to her as she noticed Deputy Nick Rogers standing back in the darkness of the trees some distance away. He seemed to be watching the people around the grave.

All of the women of the Whitehorse Sewing Circle were there either out of respect or because Geraldine had left them her house and property. It wouldn't amount to a lot of money in this part of Montana, but the sentiment was definitely there.

Even Arlene Evans had shown up wearing a cast on her broken arm like a badge of honor. Her bruised face had healed to purple and yellow. She'd told everyone in the county how the top step on the basement stairs had been loose and with Bo in jail for a crime he didn't commit and her husband too busy with farming to fix it, she'd fallen.

Most everyone knew Arlene had fallen before Bo had been arrested. But Arlene had ridden the story like a dying horse.

Flanking her on each side were her two daughters. Violet in a black cape reminiscent of Dracula. Charlotte in a little black dress and heels with a knitted shawl draped around her as if on a fashion runway. Arlene wore a hat with a short black veil that hid most of the damage to her face. She sniffed loudly every few minutes. Laney suspected the sniffing had more to do with her son's arrest than Geraldine Shaw's funeral service.

Laney noticed that Arlene had made a point of not standing anywhere near Maddie. Instead Maddie stood at the edge of the grave next to her cousins. She cried softly, her head down, her reddish-blond hair wet from the rain. Laney had tried to get her to stay under the large umbrella she'd brought, but Maddie wouldn't hear of it.

She stood in the rain as if it would wash away her pain.

"I can't live without Bo," she'd cried whenever Laci or Laney had tried to talk to her about his arrest and the engagement. "You don't understand. I'll never find anyone who loves me as much as Bo."

Laney had argued that if Bo loved her, he wouldn't have taken Geraldine Shaw's diamond bracelet and pawned it, letting Maddie take the rap.

"He wanted the money for our wedding," Maddie had cried.

"If he needed money, he should have gotten a job," Laney had said.

Maddie had burst into tears and run from the room.

"You could have been a little more diplomatic," Laci had said to her and gone to Maddie.

Laney wanted to shake some sense into her cousin, but she feared that love was truly blind, deaf and painfully stupid.

The thought sent her gaze in the direction of Deputy Sheriff Nick Rogers. She hadn't seen him in days.

Maybe more troubling was the fact that he hadn't even tried to kiss her the night they'd gone to dinner.

He'd walked her out to her car and they'd stood under a canopy of stars, a breeze stirring the leaves on a nearby tree, the summer evening rich with warmth.

She'd given him every opportunity and yet he'd hung back as if, as he'd said, he was afraid. Afraid of what? she wondered as she studied him. He didn't seem like a man who scared easily.

Her grandfather closed his Bible, his words dying off.

"If anyone would like to say a few words…" Titus looked around the small group. "Then—"

"I want to say something," Maddie blurted out. She swallowed, her eyes wet from the rain and tears, her face red and swollen from all the crying she'd been doing. "I didn't know Geraldine, not hardly at all. But she was nice to me. I'm sorry she's dead." With that she began to cry harder.

Titus signaled that the funeral service was over and everyone dispersed like dark seeds blown to the wind.

Laney watched them go. All except Nick. He seemed to be waiting for her. She walked to where he stood, his western hat catching most of the rain, that and the heavy boughs of the ponderosa pine he stood under.

"Hello," she said, feeling strangely shy.

"Hello." He smiled at her. "I thought I should warn you, I think Arlene is going to get Bo sprung from jail."

Laney groaned.

"Maddie still determined to marry him?"

She nodded. "How can she not see what kind of man he is?"

Nick shook his head. "People see what they want."

His dark eyes were intent on her. "I've missed you." The admission seemed to come hard for him. "Any chance I could take you to town for an early dinner and a show?"

"What's playing?" she asked.

"Whatever the Villa is showing this week. Does it matter?"

It didn't.

Nick had never lived in a town that had only one theater. Not only that, the old-time theater screened only one show, and even that for only a few nights a week. But he loved the Villa. It was big and classic and reminded him of when he was a kid and his uncle Cosmos used to take him to matinees in a huge neighborhood theater with a balcony.

Those kinds of theaters were gone. Whitehorse's was one of the few left in Montana.

"It would be like a real date. I'd pick you up and take you home. I'd even buy you popcorn," he said, warming to the idea, hoping she would say yes.

"Buttered popcorn?" she asked.

He grinned. "You are a woman after my own heart."

"I guess it's a date then."

He felt as if the sun had come out as he walked through the rain with her to her car. They agreed on a time and he stood in the downpour and watched her drive away, wishing things were different.

But the truth was he could be leaving any day.

Not to mention the fact that he was lying about who he was, where he was from, what he was doing here. Guilt pricked at his conscience. With each passing day, he hated that he was living a lie. It was why he'd made a point of avoiding Laney.

He didn't want to lie to her anymore.

But he also couldn't tell her the truth.

Just the thought turned the day gray and rainy again as he walked to his patrol car. He couldn't tell her. He couldn't tell anyone. He was on borrowed time. Any day he could get the call. Any day might be the last he ever saw Laney Cavanaugh. Or the day he came face-to-face again with Keller—and a bullet.

Chapter 9

The rain had stopped as he'd started out of town. Nick couldn't believe how many accidents there'd been in the last few weeks in Old Town Whitehorse.

Arlene Evans had fallen down her stairs. Alice Miller had wrecked her car on the way out of town. Muriel Brown's house had caught fire. If her dog hadn't started barking, she might have died in her sleep. Fortunately, the fire had started in a trash can on her back porch and she'd been able to put it out before it had done any real damage.

There'd been too many near accidents for the size of the near ghost town. If he and Laney were right about Geraldine Shaw not being the intended victim, then maybe the killer was playing havoc with the town. Nick had the bad feeling it wasn't over. That the killer wouldn't be done until Old Town Whitehorse had another dead body on its hands.

He spotted Chaz and his dog, Prince, walking up the road near the Evans place. He drove down, turning around in the Evans yard, and rolled down his window as Prince came bounding over. The dog licked his hand, tongue lolling.

"Stolen any chickens lately?" Nick asked Prince.

"No, sir," Chaz answered for the dog. "I've been keeping a close eye on him. Just like you said."

Nick had seen the boy walking the dog most every day he'd been down here. New to the area, Chaz probably didn't have many friends. For one thing, there weren't a lot of kids his age around. The residents were older; the next generation had left. The few who had come back here were young, their children still in diapers.

Chaz put a protective hand on his dog's head as Charlotte Evans came roaring down the road to swing into her yard. She got out of her car, spotted Chaz and Prince and made a beeline for the dog. She was still dressed in her funeral outfit, black high heels and a skinny little black dress, but she'd ditched the shawl.

"What's your dog's name?" she asked with more enthusiasm than Nick had ever seen in her.

"Prince," Chaz said shyly.

"Prince," Charlotte repeated and smiled. "I like that. Can I pet him?"

Chaz nodded. Nick saw that the boy was taken with Charlotte. Not that he could blame him. A boy his age would see Charlotte as an attractive older woman.

"How's your mother doing?" Nick asked Charlotte.

"Fine. Violet had to take her back to the hospital. She has some kind of infection." She dismissed her mother and turned her attention to the dog. "Prince seems real nice," she said as the dog licked her hand and leaned against her leg. "We can't have a dog. Bo is allergic. He's allergic to *everything*."

Especially work, Nick thought.

"Would you like a glass of iced tea?" Charlotte asked Chaz. "Prince can have some water on the porch."

"Sure," Chaz said as he and Prince left Nick without a backward glance. As Nick pulled away, he saw both Chaz and Prince go into the house. So much for Bo's allergies.

Nick wasn't surprised when he returned to his office to find a call from the town judge.

"Arlene makes a good argument," the judge said when Nick returned his call. "She needs her boy at home right now. She can't drive and her husband is busy in the fields."

Nick realized he'd never seen her husband. He was beginning to wonder if Floyd Evans even existed.

"What I'm getting at," the judge continued, "is that this is Bo's first offense. I'm inclined to let him go home. He's promised to make restitution."

"You realize that the woman he stole the diamond bracelet from is dead and that Bo's fiancée inherited the bracelet," Nick pointed out. "I really doubt he'll make restitution to his fiancée."

"That's neither here nor there. I think the boy has learned his lesson," the judge said. "I've known Floyd and Arlene Evans all my life. Arlene's pretty much had to raise those kids by herself. You probably don't know it, but Bo used to be quite the athlete. He took the school to state both his junior and senior years."

Nick started to argue that the judge wouldn't be doing that family any favors releasing Bo.

"Arlene needs her son at home to help her," the judge said, cutting him off. "Since this is Bo's first offense, I'm going to give him fifty hours of community service."

Nick heard in the judge's voice that it wouldn't do any good to argue further. Bo was a local boy. Nick wasn't. Bo was a good-looking kid who'd ride those two years of fame in high school as long as he could.

"I'll see that he gets home," Nick said.

"No need. His fiancée is here to pick him up," the judge said.

Maddie. Apparently Laney hadn't had any more luck convincing her that Bo wasn't the love of her life than Nick had.

"How is the investigation going?" Laney asked as she dredged a French fry through a lake of ketchup.

Nick looked up from his bacon cheeseburger. "Slow."

They'd picked up burgers, fries and shakes at the Dairy Queen and taken them to a picnic table in Trafton Park near the Milk River. The leaves of the huge cottonwoods rustled overhead.

"I did some asking around about cyanide," she said between bites. "I guess they use it in mining."

"One use," he agreed. "Unfortunately, cyanide is used in everything from photography to metal cleaning. If you grind up enough chokecherry seeds, the cyanide in them will probably kill you. Cyanide is too common to probably ever track down the source."

Laney couldn't help but be disappointed. She didn't want this hanging over her sister's head. Or her cousin's. They had to find out who had killed Geraldine Shaw and why.

"Don't worry, I'm not going to quit looking for the killer," he said as if reading her expression.

She smiled at him, wanting to reach across the table and cup his strong jaw. She knew the skin would feel warm and dry, a little rough with just the hint of his beard. She shivered.

"If you're cold we could—"

"No, I'm fine." She concentrated on her burger for a few moments. "You must find Montana very different from Texas, especially our area of the state."

He smiled as he met her gaze. He had the darkest eyes. "I like it here. I like the open country and the people. Everyone is so friendly."

She eyed him suspiciously. "You don't think we're all backwoodsy local yokels?"

He laughed and shook his head. "I find you all charming and unique. Especially you." He grinned at her. "I like that it feels as if nothing has changed around here in the last hundred years."

She laughed. "It hasn't. And you're saying that's a good thing?"

"Yeah. It is. There's history here that you can feel. You know what I mean?"

She did. It was one reason she loved coming here every summer. Everyone knew everyone else and their families. Generation after generation had stayed to work the land; they'd planted deep roots; they had shared memories. She loved that feeling of belonging.

"Can I ask about your mother and father?"

She met his gaze. "There isn't much to tell. They fell in love in high school, got married young. My father was Russ Cherry. You know that big old empty house in Whitehorse?"

"The one that looks haunted?"

She winced. "I wouldn't be surprised if it was haunted. That house saw a lot of tragedy. My grandfather Cherry killed himself and my grandmother Cherry in that house. The place has been empty ever since."

"I'm so sorry," Nick said. "Your father...?"

"He and my mother had been childhood sweethearts. They married young and moved into the house Laci and I stay in every summer. My grandfather Titus built it for them out on the ranch as a wedding present. They hadn't been married long when they had me, then Laci, right after that."

"I'm sorry, if this is too painful—"

"No, it's like someone else's story since Laci and I were so young when it all happened. My father had gone into town a few weeks after the funeral. He was coming home. They said he'd been drinking. He rolled his pickup and was killed. My mother never got over his death, I guess. One day she just disappeared and was never seen again."

Nick reached across the table and took her hand. "You lost so many people in such a short time."

"Laci and I had Gramps and Gramma. They raised us. We were lucky really because we couldn't have asked for a more idyllic childhood. I wish you could have met my grandmother before her stroke. She was the most vibrant woman. Strong, determined homestead woman."

"Like her granddaughter."

She smiled at that. "I hope to be like my grandmother someday. But those will be huge shoes to fill."

"I have no doubt you'll make her proud."

She could hear the rustle of trees, smell fresh-cut grass and feel the slow, reassuring warmth of Nick's hand.

Then he drew back as he always did. "How is your cousin?" he asked, changing the subject.

"I haven't been able to talk to her." Laney hated to admit it. "When I call, I'm told she's out."

"You don't believe it?"

She shook her head. "Maddie's upset with me and Laci because we tried to talk her into breaking her engagement. I wasn't very diplomatic, I'm afraid."

He smiled knowingly. "I probably didn't use the best tack either. She's nineteen. Legally she can marry anyone she wants."

Laney let out a sigh. "I think she's just afraid that she will never love anyone the way she does Bo. I can understand that."

"Who was he?" Nick asked.

She blinked in surprise. "I… I…" She looked away. "A boy I met my first year at college. I thought he hung the moon."

"What happened?"

"Life," she said with a rueful laugh. "We were too young to make a lifetime commitment. We both went our separate ways. I heard he got a job in a large corporation back East and married the boss's daughter. It would never have worked for the two of us. That wasn't the life I wanted, and this," she said with the wave of her hand, "wasn't even close to what he wanted." She met Nick's nearly black gaze. "What about you?"

"My heart's been broken so many times I've lost count," he said.

"I seriously doubt that."

"It's true. Women always think they want the strong, silent type until they realize that we're just dull."

She laughed, studying him as they finished eating in a companionable silence. Funny, but she was beginning to notice that he often didn't give her a straight answer. Almost as if he was afraid she'd get too close to the truth.

"We'd better get to the Villa," he said as he rose from the table. "I hope you left room for buttered popcorn." He collected the wrappers from their picnic and took them over to the large trash can.

Laney watched him go, thinking he was the sexiest man she'd ever met. And the most intriguing. But she couldn't ignore that underlying feeling that she would be smart not to get too close either.

There was more to Nick Rogers than he wanted her to know. And the more time she spent around him, the more convinced she was that he was hiding something from her.

On the ride home from the movie, Nick noticed that Laney seemed lost in thought.

"Did you enjoy the movie?" he asked, realizing he

couldn't even recall the plot. He'd spent the time too aware of the woman sitting next to him.

"Yes. I'm just worried about my cousin," she said.

He wasn't sure he believed that. Laney had been distant since the park earlier. He feared it was something he'd said. Or hadn't.

"I've been wondering myself whether Geraldine left Maddie something out of gratitude for helping her from time to time—or to keep Maddie quiet," he said.

"What?"

He saw her shocked, angry expression and wondered why he'd brought this up. To get her take on it? Or to keep her at arm's length?

"I'm just trying to understand their relationship and maybe what is going on with your cousin. Geraldine supposedly didn't have any enemies. Nor friends, from what I can tell. Maddie *was* one of the few people allowed in that house. I have to ask myself, why Maddie?"

"Because Maddie is sweet and nice and—"

"I didn't mean to upset you," Nick said, looking over at her, wondering if that was true.

She turned away from him as if to look out the side window into the darkness.

"Did you notice how much Geraldine was paying Maddie?" he asked.

"Two dollars an hour," she said, "which proves that Maddie was helping her out of the goodness of her heart—not some dark ulterior motive."

"Or Maddie was getting a lot more than two bucks an hour so she wasn't about to ask for more."

Laney glared over at him. "You've spent time around Maddie. Do you really believe she's a blackmailer?"

He had to admit Maddie was the furthest thing from his image of a blackmailer. "But Maddie is all messed up, even you have to admit that or she wouldn't still want to marry Bo Evans."

"You won't get any argument out of me in that regard, but she wasn't blackmailing Geraldine Shaw."

"Someone apparently was. Which brings up the question of what Geraldine had to hide."

"Nothing."

He shook his head. "Most people have something to hide no matter how small."

She cocked a brow at him. "Like you?"

The question surprised him. Even in the dim light from the dash, he could see that she was serious. He'd thought he'd been so careful, but obviously he'd made her suspicious somehow. He grinned. "We all have our little secrets. Even you, I'd bet."

He saw something fleeting in her eyes. Laney was an open book. Or was she? Maybe it was true. Maybe everyone really did have things they wanted to hide.

He quickly changed the subject back to Geraldine. "You said her husband died last year?"

"At the end of the summer. Laci and I had already left when it happened."

Nick frowned. "I didn't see his grave up on the hill. In fact, the only grave near Geraldine's was an unnamed child."

"Geraldine lost her daughter a month before the baby was born." Laney's voice was flat. She seemed resigned to talking about Geraldine's murder rather than what he had to hide although she obviously wasn't happy about it.

"She never had any other children?"

Laney shook her head. "My grandmother said Geraldine never wanted *any* children. The baby had been Ollie's idea. There is some sort of birth defect that ran in Geraldine's family. I guess she feared it would affect her baby—and she was right."

Nick took that in, kicking himself for bringing this subject up in the first place. No wonder Laney was leery of him. He would come on to her, then pull away as if he didn't know what he wanted. That was just it. He knew what he wanted. Her. And under other circumstances…

"As for Ollie, her husband," Laney continued, "he was back in Minnesota visiting relatives when he died. His last wish was to be buried back there."

Nick chewed that over for a moment. "Doesn't it seem funny to you that Geraldine wouldn't want to be buried beside him?"

She shrugged. "She had more ties to Old Town Whitehorse than Ollie. The house belonged to her grandparents, who homesteaded here. I guess she wanted to be where her roots were. All her relatives are buried up on the hill."

He drove down the long road that ended just past her house. He understood roots better than she might imagine.

"So your roots are in Texas?"

"No," he said too quickly, then shook his head. "I have no real roots."

"That's right, you said your family was in the military and you moved a lot."

He could feel her gaze on him, feel her trying to understand him. "You're lucky. Your roots are here. I envy you that, the kind of history you have here."

"We all make our own history," she said. "Few of the young people stay here anymore because there aren't enough decent-paying jobs. Life here is changing."

"That's too bad." He studied her face for a moment as they neared her house. "What about you? Do you think you will ever settle here?"

"My sister is determined to. At least that's what she says."

"What about you?"

"I do love it here and, being an accountant, I'm sure I could make a career here."

"But?"

She looked away, biting down on her lower lip before she said, "It would take the right man for me to stay."

Nick felt her words pierce his heart. That right man definitely wasn't Nick Rogers.

Laney knew he wasn't going to kiss her. As he walked her to her door, she heard his radio in the patrol car squawk. He trotted back to the car. She listened as the dispatcher told him there'd been another attack outside a bar back in Whitehorse.

"You'd better go," she called to him. "Thank you for dinner and the movie. It was nice."

As she started to open the front door, she heard his boots on the porch steps. An instant later, he spun her around and into his arms. And the next thing she knew, he was kissing her.

And then he was gone, leaving her standing on the porch, wondering if she'd only dreamed the kiss. But even she couldn't have dreamed such a kiss. Or such a man.

Nick Rogers left her dazed and wanting more. And while her analytical mind didn't like the odds, her heart was willing to bet it all on him.

Chapter 10

On a hunch the next morning, Nick e-mailed the department that handled births and deaths in Minnesota and inquired about an Oliver "Ollie" Raymond Shaw who had died last summer while on a visit from Montana.

They had no record of Ollie's death. Nor did Montana.

At the *Milk River Examiner,* Nick asked Glen Whitaker to see if Geraldine had run an obituary for her husband. Sure enough, the obit said Ollie had died in North Pond, Minnesota, almost a year ago to the day.

Glen made a copy of the obituary for him and asked, "Any leads on Geraldine's murder or that other case?"

Nick wished he could tell Glen that he'd found the person who'd beaten him up. He doubted Glen wanted to hear that Nick suspected it had been a woman with a baseball bat.

"Not yet," he said. "But you'll be the first to know when I do."

Back at his office, Nick contacted the state department of investigation in Minnesota only to be told there was no town by the name of North Pond. No funeral home by the name of the one Geraldine Shaw had said in the obit had handled the arrangements. No cemetery where Ollie Shaw was said to have been buried.

Oliver "Ollie" Raymond Shaw had been born in Minneapolis, but as far as Minnesota knew, Ollie hadn't died there. Nor in Montana.

Nick sat for a moment, taking it all in. He'd been around cops long before he'd became one. Maybe that was why he felt as if he'd been a cop for way too long. He'd seen too much. And yet as the pieces started falling together, the picture that started forming made him sick to his stomach. Sometimes he hated this job.

On impulse, he unlocked the bottom desk drawer and took out the cell phone as he'd done each day since he'd arrived in Montana. Only all the other times there'd been no message.

His heart began to pound, fear making his palms sweat as he turned on the phone and retrieved the message. He told himself he was prepared for the worst. A message telling him to get the hell out of Dodge because Keller had found him. But he'd always known that by the time he was sent that message, he'd probably already be dead.

Maybe that was why he'd feared the other message

as well. The voice on the other end of the line was flat, official. The message was short and sweet.

"The trial's been moved up. We'll need you here by the beginning of next week."

A blade of ice wedged itself in his heart. He had to go back to California. He recoiled at the thought, but if he didn't return, he'd have more than Keller to worry about. As if Keller wasn't enough to cause him sleepless nights.

Next week.

A part of him wanted to run. But there was no place he'd ever be safe. He'd known that when he'd come to Montana. Not even out here in the Big Open would he ever be free of his past.

In the meantime, he had a murder on his hands. He picked up his car keys and headed for Old Town Whitehorse. At the edge of town, he spotted Chaz pulling a large red wagon, his dog walking beside it.

Nick pulled over when he saw the expression on Chaz's face.

"I guess you heard Prince got in trouble again," Chaz said quickly as Nick got out. "But I'm returning everything he borrowed."

"Borrowed?" Nick asked, looking into the wagon. It held a variety of items, everything from a garden sprinkler to a TV remote.

"Prince took all of this stuff from people's houses?" Nick asked, picking up an old baseball bat.

"He's really smart. He knows how to open screen doors." The boy's shoulders slumped. "He's been going into people's houses and taking things."

Nick stared down at the bat in his hands. The bat

was weathered and cracked. In one crack there was a dark red crusted substance that unless he missed his guess was blood.

"Where did Prince get this?" Nick asked, trying to keep his voice even.

Chaz shrugged. "I don't know where he got any of the stuff. I'm going from house to house and letting people take back the things that belong to them. And apologize for Prince like my aunt told me to."

Nick nodded, trying to decide how best to handle this. "This bat looks familiar. Will you do me a favor? Keep track of who takes what so I can write up a report. Don't make a big deal out of it. I don't want any of the residents to press charges against you. You think you can remember who takes what?"

Chaz nodded quickly.

Nick placed the bat back into the wagon. "After you return everything, write it all down and I'll stop by and pick it up, okay?"

"Yes, sir. And there won't be any more problems with Prince. My aunt says I have to keep him on a chain in the yard at night from now on."

"That's probably a good idea," Nick agreed before climbing back into his patrol car and driving up the road to Maddie Cavanaugh's.

Laney stumbled across the website quite by accident. It was amateurishly done with lots of bells and whistles and bright colors.

She almost didn't click on the "Take a Tour" of prospective dates. But her curiosity got the better of her.

The first face that came up was no surprise. Violet.

It was an awful photo, cropped down from a regular photograph into a mug shot. Poor Violet. Laney was sure the woman hadn't agreed to this photo, let alone being on the site.

The next prospective date was a woman who lived in Whitehorse. Laney couldn't remember her name, but she recognized her face. What was interesting about the photo was that Arlene had left some of the background in this one.

With a start, Laney realized that the photograph had been taken at the engagement party that Laci had thrown for Maddie and Bo.

"What's going on?" Laci asked, coming into the room. "Did I hear you swear?"

Laney hadn't realized she'd even spoken. "You aren't going to believe this," she said to her sister as she quickly clicked to the next photo.

"I know that woman. She was at the party," Laci said as she pulled up a chair.

"I suspect they were all at the party," Laney said as she advanced through the photographs until hers came up. Her mouth fell open—just as it was in the candid snapshot that Arlene Evans had taken of her at the engagement party.

"No," Laci said beside her. "She didn't."

Arlene had caught Laney in the middle of saying something. It was the least flattering photograph Laney had ever seen of herself. But to make matters worse, Arlene had "coupled" Laney with Deputy Sheriff Nick Rogers as a "match." His photo was at least better than hers.

"I can't believe this," Laney said. "She put me up on

her website without my knowledge?" And surely Nick hadn't signed up on Meet-a-Mate, had he?

Laci reached over and advanced to the next photograph. "At least she got one of me that isn't too bad, and look—you can see some of the desserts I made in the background."

"Wait a minute," Laney said as she stared at the photograph of her sister. "Arlene didn't take this one." The photograph had been shot down the table so even though Arlene had cropped out the people at the dessert table, she hadn't been able to get them completely out of the photograph.

"You're right," Laci said. "That's Arlene's hand there. I recognize her ring and that must be her daughter Charlotte's hand complete with fake fingernails."

"But whose hand is that?" Laney shivered. "That must be Geraldine's reaching for the last macaroon." She looked over at her sister. "I've got to tell Nick about this. If there's more of these photographs, there could be one of the killer putting the poison macaroon on the plate."

Nick found Maddie out behind her mother's house working in the flower garden. She seemed lost in a world of her own, oblivious to everything but the dark soil she was digging in.

"Hello, Maddie."

She started, surprise and instant fear in her eyes. "I didn't hear you drive up."

He'd purposely parked down the road and walked. The times he'd called, her mother had always told him her daughter wasn't home. Maddie had taken to parking her car behind the house or in the garage, so even the times he'd stopped by, Sarah Cavanaugh had covered for Maddie.

Nick had known he was getting a runaround. He could have pushed it, but he hadn't. As worried as he'd been about Maddie, he hadn't had an official reason to force a conversation. Until now.

"Did you used to help Geraldine with her gardening?" he asked as he took a seat on a small bench beside a bed of petunias.

"Sometimes," Maddie said, looking nervous.

"I've never raised anything in a garden, but I'd like to try sometime."

She looked up at him. "Don't people have gardens in Houston?"

"Sure, the ones who live outside the city. I was a city kid though, all concrete and asphalt. My mother used to have this pot with cherry tomatoes in it that she kept in the window. That's about the closest I ever got to real dirt."

"That's sad," she said as she turned a clump of earth with her spade, loosening it, before digging up what must have been a weed because she tossed it into a pile she'd made behind her on the grass.

"What did Geraldine grow?" he asked.

"Why do you keep asking me about her?"

"I still have to find out who killed her," he said.

"But what she grew doesn't have anything to do with her being dead," Maddie said.

"Doesn't it?" he asked.

She stared down at her spade. "I don't know anything about it. I already told you that."

"Tell me this. A year ago this month, did you help her put in a new flower bed beside her house?"

She looked up in shock, her eyes wide.

"Who helped her with the body?" Nick asked.

"What?"

"Her husband's body. Geraldine wouldn't have been able to move the body by herself. I asked around. Ollie was a big man. She would have needed help. Your help, since you were her friend. Her only close friend."

Maddie was shaking her head, her eyes full of tears. "He had a heart attack. She couldn't afford to have him buried."

"You know better than that. You helped her cover up what she'd done. Why?"

Maddie was crying now, sobbing as if a dam had broken. "She was nice to me. She was teaching me to crochet and cook and to grow flowers. She said I was like a daughter to her. She let me make messes. She never yelled at me if I didn't get it right."

He stared at the girl. "Didn't your own mother do that?"

"Mother hated it when I made a mess. She would shoo me outside. I would go to Geraldine's and she would…" She cried as if there was no end to her tears, no longer able to speak.

"Who did you tell about Ollie?" Nick asked when she'd caught her breath.

She glanced toward the house and made a swipe at her tears.

"It's just you and me," Nick said. He'd been relieved to see that Sarah's car was gone when he'd driven by the house before he'd parked down the road. "Maddie, whoever you told about what happened was blackmailing Geraldine. Was it Bo you told?"

She shook her head frantically.

"Geraldine was running out of money. I think she told her blackmailer that she wasn't going to pay him anymore. Maybe she even threatened to turn herself in—and him with her—so he killed her."

"I didn't tell *anyone*. I swear it." She glanced toward the house again.

"But someone figured it out, figured out that Geraldine killed Ollie?" he asked.

She was crying again, stabbing the spade into the ground as she spoke. "Ollie was sick. He didn't know what he was doing. She didn't mean to kill him, just stop him from hurting me."

Nick's eyes widened. "Oh, my God, Maddie." He reached for her, drawing her to him as she sobbed in his arms. "It's all right. It's all right," he kept saying. But it was far from all right.

Everything was starting to make sense. The change Laney said she'd seen in her cousin after last summer. The way Maddie had let Bo and his family mistreat her. It all made a sick kind of sense. Anyone familiar with sexual-abuse victims would have recognized the symptoms sooner.

Maddie's sobs finally slowed, then shuddered to a stop.

"Geraldine killed him because he was hurting you," Nick said softly. "That's why you helped her bury his body." He pulled back to look in her eyes. "It wasn't your fault, Maddie. You have to know that."

She nodded, but he could see that she didn't really believe it.

"Who figured it out, Maddie? Who was blackmailing Geraldine?" Who had taken advantage of what had happened to this young woman and used it to extort money from the one person Maddie had loved and trusted?

Maddie looked toward the house again.

He felt her shudder and turned slowly, already knowing what he would see—Sarah Cavanaugh's face in the window.

"Your *mother?*"

Laney was excited when she heard Nick's voice on the phone. She'd even been thinking about calling him. Maybe inviting him to dinner. Getting Laci to cook something special and disappear for the evening.

"Laney, I need your help," Nick said.

"Of course you do," she joked, then belatedly registered that he didn't sound like himself. She dropped into a chair at the kitchen table. "What's wrong?"

"It's Maddie. Can we come right over?"

"Of course," she said. "But, Nick, what—" She realized he'd hung up. She stood holding the receiver, her heart pounding so hard her chest hurt. Maddie. A thousand thoughts chased around in her head. But he'd said *we.* Can *we* come over? He had to mean him and Maddie. So it couldn't be that bad, right?

Unfortunately, as she went to wait on the porch, Laney kept hearing the tone of Nick's voice. Something was terribly wrong. She stood at the railing watching the road as she'd done her first day here this summer, only this time, she *knew* it would be bad news.

Maddie looked a mess when she got out of the patrol car. Laney could see that she'd been crying. Her face was puffy and red, her eyes downcast.

Laney ran to her and threw her arms around her cousin. Bo Evans. That was what it had to be about. What had that man done now? It didn't matter. Whatever it was, they would deal with it. She would deal with it. As she held her cousin, she watched Nick get out of the car. He looked devastated.

"I'm getting you dirty. I was planting flowers," Maddie said as she pulled back to look down at her dirty gardening clothes and the soil on her hands. Tears welled in her eyes. "Can I get a shower?"

"Just a minute," Nick said. He went into the house, leaving them alone.

"What's wrong, Maddie?" Laney asked.

But her cousin only shook her head. "I just need a shower. And some clothes. I need some clothes."

"Of course." The monotone of her cousin's voice was enough to scare Laney. Something horrible had happened. But what?

Nick came out of the house and nodded to Maddie. She went inside, her movements like those of a sleepwalker as her shoes scuffed across the porch.

"What happened?" Laney demanded in a whisper the moment Maddie was out of earshot.

He raised a finger, stepped in the house and returned a few moments later. "I can hear the water running. I think she's in the shower. I removed anything she could hurt herself with from the bathrooms."

Laney felt her eyes widen, then tear as she swallowed back the lump in her throat. "Why would she hurt herself?"

"I think you'd better sit down."

He didn't have to tell her twice. She dropped into the chair on the porch, the day's heat making waves across the dark soil of the road, a faint breeze carrying the scent of hay and dust and inevitably the end of summer. The end of a lot of things.

Laney would never forget that moment or the way Nick drew his chair up next to hers and cupped her hands in his and softly said the words that shattered her heart.

Nick held Laney in his arms. He could feel her pain, her anger. He was having trouble dealing with his own. Sometimes he hated being a cop. He'd thought he'd escaped it up here in Montana. But human nature could be ugly and geography didn't change that.

At the sound of water shutting off inside the house, Laney hurriedly dried her eyes and pulled back from him.

"I need to see to my cousin," she said. "What about Aunt Sarah?"

"She's agreed to turn herself in."

"Does Uncle Roy know?" Laney asked.

Nick nodded. "He didn't take it well."

"No, I'm sure he didn't. Thank you. I knew something was wrong, but I had no idea."

"None of us did," Nick said. "She needs counseling."

Laney nodded. "Don't worry. I'll see that she gets whatever she needs."

"I knew you would." He rose. "I'll call you."

Laney nodded as she opened the screen door and stepped inside the house.

Nick moved through the afternoon heat to his car. He rolled down the windows as he drove slowly back toward Whitehorse. He felt sick to his stomach. He was just thankful that Maddie had Laney and Laci in her life.

Not far down the road, he saw Chaz coming down the road pulling his wagon along the edge of the barren pit. Prince trotted beside the boy, his tongue lolling. The day had gotten fierce and even now with the sun dipping toward the western horizon, the heat still beared down oppressively.

Nick slowed the car as he came alongside the boy. "How did it go?" he asked, glancing toward the wagon.

"No one claimed the bat," Chaz said, sounding apologetic. "I asked everyone. I don't know where Prince got it."

Possibly not from anyone's house. Someone could have thrown the bat away. The dog could have gotten it from anywhere.

"Did you make that list for me?" Nick asked.

"Yes, sir." He dug a stubby piece of pencil from his pocket, then a wadded-up scrap of paper. "Sorry, it's kind of messy. But I printed real neat so you could read it."

Nick smiled. "You did a great job." He glanced at the list, then put it on the seat next to him. "Would you mind if I took the bat to see if I can find its owner?"

Chaz shook his head, clearly relieved since everything else had been accounted for, and handed Nick the baseball bat.

"In the meantime—"

"I'm going to keep Prince at home," the boy said with a grin.

"Good thinking," Nick said. "You might stay close to home as well." He told himself that the dog had probably found the baseball bat in a ditch or a trash can. If, as Nick suspected, the stain on the bat was blood, then the owner wouldn't have kept the weapon in his house, he would have disposed of it.

But as Nick drove back to Whitehorse, he couldn't help worrying as he glanced back to see the silhouette of the boy and his dog before both disappeared from view.

Chapter 11

"**M**addie has agreed to get counseling," Laney said when Nick answered the phone Saturday. She couldn't believe how good it was to hear his voice. She hadn't seen him since he'd brought her the horrible news about Maddie. "Laci went with her to Billings."

"I'm glad. And Bo?"

"The deal Laci made with Maddie was that Bo wouldn't know where she was."

"Good," he said.

"So, you're staying for a while longer? Your grandfather told me you usually only stay a couple of weeks in the summer."

He sounded worried. Did he think she was staying because of him?

"Don't worry, I have to get back to work soon. But I can't leave until I'm sure that Maddie is all right." And until Geraldine's murderer was caught. Unless she already had been, Laney thought, thinking of her aunt Sarah.

Laney couldn't stand to think of what her aunt had done. "I can't believe Aunt Sarah didn't get Maddie help. And to use what she knew to bleed Geraldine dry…" She shook her head.

"Sarah was like everyone else. She apparently believed Geraldine was rich and wouldn't miss the money. At least that's her story," Nick said.

Laney sighed in disgust. "Do you think Geraldine knew that the person blackmailing her was Maddie's own mother?"

"I don't think she had any idea."

Laney braced herself and asked, "Did Aunt Sarah kill Geraldine?"

"She swears she didn't."

"You believe her?"

"There's no proof that she did. It will be up to the county attorney to decide what to charge her with. Sarah was smart enough not to put the money in her account, but she has admitted to blackmailing Geraldine."

"My uncle Roy is divorcing her," Laney said. "I've heard he's putting the place up for sale. He can't forgive Aunt Sarah and he's just so ashamed. I know how he feels, but a part of me is sorry for her. I think she thought marrying a Cavanaugh was a bigger deal than it was. Maddie told me that her mother felt she wasn't good enough for the rest of the family, that they looked down on her."

"Yeah, as a matter of fact I'm very familiar with *that* feeling in my own family," Nick quipped.

This was more like the Nick Rogers she'd come to know. Not the one who'd sounded so businesslike on the phone just moments before. She chewed at her lip for a moment. "I've missed you."

Silence.

Then a sigh. "I've missed you, too. Laney—"

"I was thinking you might come out for dinner tonight. I'm not as good a cook as my sister, but I try."

More silence. She could hear her pulse pounding in her ears, her heart a drum inside her chest. What was it about this man? Why did it matter so much? She didn't know. She just knew it did matter.

"I can't tonight, but thanks for the offer."

"Okay, how about tomorrow night then?" she asked, shocked by her own boldness.

She heard him shuffle his feet, move something on his desk, and grimaced. "Are you sure about this, Laney?"

Yes. No. "I'll be going back to Arizona Monday." She almost added that she had stumbled across something that might help solve Geraldine's murder, but she hated that she'd resorted to even telling him she was leaving to get him to come over for dinner. And she wasn't sure Arlene even had the photos in her camera anymore.

"What time?" he said, sounding resigned.

"How does seven sound?" she asked, more excited than she'd been in too long to remember.

"Seven. Fine. What can I bring?"

"Just your appetite," she said and wanted to bite her tongue.

A beat of silence when she knew they were both

thinking about a completely different kind of appetite that had nothing to do with food.

"I'll see you at seven."

She hung up before he would change his mind. She'd heard his fear. Had he been hurt in a relationship? Was that why he was so afraid of where this was going between the two of them?

Or was he just afraid of being alone with her?

Well, tomorrow night he wouldn't have a choice. It would just be the two of them, alone on a warm summer night. For the last time.

Nick mentally kicked himself for accepting Laney's invitation. He'd promised himself he'd keep his distance. Especially since he'd be leaving as well. Right after dinner. Right after he said goodbye to Laney.

It had felt like a death sentence. Hell, it could very well be one if Keller got word he'd returned to the state of California.

He was glad Laney was going back to Arizona. Mesa wasn't that far from L.A. Depending on how things went, maybe… He shoved that thought away. He couldn't let himself go down that road. Even if things went well in California, he wasn't sure she'd want to see him once she knew who he really was.

For so long it had only been about staying hidden, staying alive. Laney had made him forget all that. She'd made him hopeful. She'd made him want not only her, but also a life. He knew that even if Keller didn't kill him first, he wouldn't have a life after the trial.

He looked at the list in his hand. Chaz had written down all the items he'd returned—and to which houses.

Nick had overnighted the baseball bat to the crime lab in Missoula along with DNA samples from each of the men who'd been attacked. He'd seen enough weapons with dried blood on them. All he needed was verification that the blood was human. And if he could get a DNA match....

When the phone rang, he jumped.

"Deputy Sheriff Rogers," he answered, surprised how easily he'd been able to play this role. Maybe it had been the years he'd spent undercover, pretending he was someone he wasn't. Right now this role felt more real than his old life in California.

"This is Maximilian Roswell with the crime lab."

Nick held his breath.

"That bat you sent us? Just as you suspected, the substance on it is definitely human blood."

"Were you able to get a DNA sample from it?"

"As a matter of fact, it matched up with one of the other samples you sent us. A Curtis McAlheney's."

McAlheney's nose had bled, splattering all over he'd said. Nick let out the breath he'd been holding and got off the line as quickly as possible. He called Chaz's house, spoke with the boy's aunt. Chaz and Prince were just outside in the yard, she assured him.

"Please make sure they stay there," Nick said.

"Is that dog in trouble again?" the aunt asked, sounding more weary than upset.

"Not at all," Nick said. "That's a very smart dog. He might have just helped me solve one of my cases."

Nick hung up and picked up his keys. What worried him was that one of those residents had recognized the bat but hadn't claimed it, afraid of incriminating himself.

Nick couldn't have the assailant thinking Chaz still had that bat. The last thing he wanted to do was put the kid in danger, although Prince had already done that with his thieving.

At the hardware store, Nick bought a baseball bat like the one the dog had stolen and a small can of dark reddish-brown paint. He took it back to his apartment, roughed up the bat on his concrete back step, then taking a rag he added just enough of the paint until the bat looked like the old one he'd gotten from Chaz.

Tossing the bat into his patrol car, he headed for Whitehorse. As he drove, he went over the list in his head that Chaz had made him. There was one house in that neighborhood that apparently the dog hadn't taken anything from. At least, no one at that house had claimed any of the items.

And yet Nick knew for a fact that the dog had been in that house.

Laney was too restless to hang around home. The place felt empty without Laci there. Laney had gotten a call that morning from her sister. Laci thought Maddie seemed to be doing better. The counseling was helping.

"Just a minute," Laci had said. "Maddie wants to say hello."

Maddie wanted to know if Bo had called. He hadn't.

"I'm going over to the Evanses' now as a matter of fact," Laney had told her. "Is there a message you want me to give him?"

"No. That's okay."

Laney felt for her cousin. All she could do was hope that the counseling would make Maddie see what kind of man Bo Evans really was.

As Laney neared the Evanses' house, she saw the ambulance pulling away, lights flashing. She pulled to the side of the road to let it pass, then hurriedly drove down to the house to see what had happened.

Violet answered the door looking as if she'd just woken up. She wore a muumuu, the fabric faded and worn, and fuzzy pink bunny slippers.

"I saw the ambulance," Laney said.

Violet nodded. "Mother took too many of her pain pills."

"Is she all right?" Laney asked.

"They pumped her stomach, but they wanted to take her to the hospital for observation."

Laney stared at the woman. "They think she might have taken the pills on purpose?"

Bo came into the room from down the hall. He, too, looked as if he'd just gotten up although it was after eleven. He was wearing a wrinkled T-shirt and pajama bottoms, his feet bare.

"What are you telling her?" he demanded of his sister. "Mom didn't try to kill herself. It was an accident. Her broken arm's been bothering her. She just got confused about how many pills she'd taken."

He gave Violet a dirty look as he turned and went into the kitchen.

Violet looked after him, no love in her gaze.

Laney wondered where Charlotte was, then remembered she hadn't seen her car. The only one of the Evans offspring with a job, Charlotte must be at work. Charlotte was the shampoo girl at the Clip and Curl. She also was learning to do nails, Laney had heard.

"Well, I'm sorry to hear about your mother," Laney said. More sorry than she wanted to admit. She'd hoped to talk to Arlene. She'd especially wanted Arlene to take the Laney and Nick "match" photo off her website. But she also had hoped to get copies of the photographs from the party to show to Nick.

In the kitchen, Bo was banging pots and pans as if searching for something.

"Your mother was going to give me copies of the photographs she took at Maddie and Bo's party," she fibbed to Violet. "I would be happy to pay for them."

Violet looked at her as if she'd lost her mind. "Geraldine dropped dead at that party."

"Yes, I remember," Laney said. "I promised your mother twenty for the copies but I'll pay more if—"

Before Violet could answer, Bo came out. "How much more?" he demanded.

"Forty dollars," Laney said, wincing at the greed she saw shining in his eyes.

"I don't know why you'd want photographs from *that* party, the party from hell, but I can make you copies."

Laney stood in the living room, Violet waiting as well. Neither spoke. Laney could hear Bo in a back room mumbling to himself as a printer whirred. At one point, she thought about sitting down, eyed the plastic-covered furniture and decided to remain standing.

When Bo came out with a couple dozen photographs, she gave him two twenty-dollar bills from her purse.

He took them, stuffed it in his pocket and went back into the kitchen without a word.

Laney let herself out.

Nick passed the ambulance on the way to Old Town. He got on his radio and found out that Arlene Evans had overdosed on drugs and was being taken to the hospital. Turning around, he followed the ambulance back into Whitehorse.

Arlene was conscious, sitting up in bed, complaining to the nurse when he entered her room.

"How are you doing?" he asked her.

"I'm fine," she snapped. "I don't know why everyone is making such a fuss. I mixed up my pills. It could have happened to anyone."

"I was on my way out to your house when I saw the ambulance," Nick said. "I just wanted to check on you."

Arlene softened a little. "That was nice of you. But it doesn't make up for you arresting my son for something he didn't do."

Whatever. "Well, I can see that you're going to be fine." He started to turn from her bed to leave, when he caught a whiff of her perfume.

"What?" she demanded, no doubt seeing the look on his face.

"Your perfume. It's familiar."

"You like it?" she asked, smiling broadly. "It was my mother's. I get compliments on it all the time. It's my favorite. It reminds me of my mother. She loved lavender."

On the way out to the Evans house, Nick debated what he was about to do. It was a gamble. A risk he wasn't sure he should take. But it was Saturday afternoon. And he was determined to tie up some loose ends before he left.

He thought about Laney, about saying goodbye. He would do that tomorrow night. She wouldn't know it was goodbye though.

The thought that he would probably never see her again devastated him. He'd considered canceling dinner, knowing seeing her again would only make it that much harder to say goodbye. Selfishly he wanted that last evening with her.

Just as he had to take this gamble tonight, he thought, as he parked in front of the Evans house, and taking the baseball bat, climbed out, noting that all three Evans offspring appeared to be home since it was still early evening.

In the distance, Nick could make out a tractor in a field, the silhouette of a man hunched over the wheel, the tractor dragging something that stirred up dust as the driver inched across the horizon.

At his knock, Violet peered at Nick through the screen. In the background, he could hear loud music and Bo's souped-up car was parked out front.

"I was hoping your mother was home," Nick said, lying through his teeth.

"She's at the hospital," Violet said.

"I hope it's nothing serious."

"No." She glanced from Nick to the bat at his side.

"Mind if I come in?" he asked, raising his voice.

Without a word, she pushed open the screen door and motioned him inside. He noticed she was wearing what looked like the dresses his great-aunt wore. On Violet's feet were furry bunny slippers.

Past her on the plastic couch was Charlotte. She was wearing a crop top and short shorts. She had her legs tucked under herself and she was chewing on the end of a lock of her hair as she watched something on television.

"Did you want to see Bo?" Violet asked.

Nick noted that the music had stopped. "I thought one of you could help me. That new boy in the neighborhood has a dog that picks up things," he said over the sound of the television. Loud enough that Bo would be able to hear down the hall. "I thought this might belong to one of you." He held up the bat.

As expected, Bo's curiosity was peaked at what Nick was offering. He came out of his room and down the hall, looking disheveled and half-asleep.

"Where the hell did you get my old bat?" he demanded.

"This is *yours?*" Nick asked.

Bo held out a hand. Nick slapped the bat into Bo's palm. "Hell, yes, it's mine. I wondered what happened to it."

"Has it been missing long?" Nick asked.

"Long enough," Bo said. "How did some dog get it?"

Nick shrugged. "I wasn't even sure it was yours. The boy brought it around. I thought he showed it to you and you said it wasn't yours."

Bo shot a look at Violet. "Did some kid bring this bat by here and you told him it wasn't mine?"

"How was I to know it was your bat?" Violet demanded. "Charlotte said yours got broken."

Bo swung around to glare at his youngest sister.

"I said I thought it had." Charlotte shrugged. "It's old and icky, why do you want it anyway?"

Bo was shaking his head and swinging the bat, clearly angry.

"Well, you have it back now," Nick said and turned to leave, glancing at Charlotte. She had stopped chewing on her hair. She dragged her gaze away from the television. He saw the tension in her expression. Was she worried that he was going to tell Bo that she was the one who'd let the dog into the house? She swung her gaze back at the television.

"Tell your mother I stopped by," Nick said.

"You tell that kid to keep his damn dog away from my house!" Bo called as Nick walked out to his patrol car and climbed in. He was shaking inside. Partly from fear he'd just messed up big-time. And partly from the bad vibes he'd felt inside the house. Add to that the faint hint of lavender and it had the makings of a deadly potion.

There was only one live band in town Saturday night at one of the four bars.

Nick staked out the bar with the band, finding himself a place where he could watch the back of the building without being seen.

The night was cool and very dark, and he was counting on the person with the bat making an appearance. Unless the assailant realized Nick had returned the wrong bat. Or unless Nick had taken the bat to the wrong house.

There were too many variables. Too much chance that he was way off base.

He tried not to second-guess himself as the hours went by. He knew that the men who'd been attacked had all left by the back door of the bar before closing. He was betting they had followed someone out. Or had been lured out.

He tried to concentrate on the back door, on who would come through it before the night was over. But his mind kept going to Laney and dinner tomorrow night.

Then he would be gone. He already had a story ready to tell the sheriff's department. He would be returning home to take care of a sick relative.

Just returning to the state of California would be dangerous. Standing up in court to testify against Zak Keller would be a death warrant. That was if he even made it as far as the courtroom. Keller had friends who would die to protect him—and the truth from coming out.

No, Nick thought with a rueful smile, his life wasn't worth squat. Even a bookie wouldn't take odds on him coming out of this alive. But if he didn't testify, then Keller would go free. And if that happened, Nick was one dead SOB. Keller would hunt him down like a rabid dog even if it took the rest of his life.

His cell phone vibrated in his pocket. He swore under his breath as he heard the back door of the bar open. Music spilled out, a lot of bass guitar and drums. The phone vibrated again. The door closed with a swish, taking the music with it.

Just before the door shut, he saw the woman in the light spilling out. She wore a blue dress. He watched her walk to her car. She hesitated, standing in the darkness as if listening before she opened her car door.

His cell phone quit vibrating. He waited, afraid to breathe as she slid behind the wheel. She didn't start the car. Instead, she seemed to be watching the back door of the bar as if expecting someone.

Minutes ticked by. He saw her lean her head on the steering wheel. He could almost feel her disappointment, her heartbreak, as he watched Violet Evans finally start her car and pull away.

Nick swore under his breath. He'd been so sure that tonight was the night. And he'd had his money on Violet. The woman seemed to have no luck with men and her mother was always trying to push her off on some poor soul.

He could see where Violet might have a bad attitude when it came to men. She might take some pleasure in beating the crap out of them with a baseball bat after they'd disappointed her.

But he'd been wrong. Not about the bat belonging in that house; he'd been sure of it. Nick just didn't believe Bo had been the one using the bat. Nick could see Arlene Evans beating up men. Except, tonight she was in the hospital. Maybe that was why nothing was happening here.

Nick swore again. His patrol car was parked a few blocks over. He turned to leave when the back door of the bar opened again. He quickly melted back into the shadows.

A man stuck his head out, looked around, hesitating as if checking to make sure the coast was clear. He stepped out tentatively, glancing around, hitched up his pants and started toward an old brown pickup parked at the far end of the lot.

The darkness was complete. Nick couldn't put a name to the man, but he suspected it was the one Violet had been waiting for. The man who'd stood her up.

Just as the man neared his pickup, Nick spotted movement coming out of the dark alley. The figure came up fast behind the man. Nick didn't even see the swing of the bat, but he heard the sound of it as the bat connected with the man's back. The man let out an *ufft* sound and sprawled facedown in the dirt. The figure, wearing a black hooded cloak, moved quickly toward the man.

"What the hell." Nick was running, his weapon drawn. He covered the distance between him and the scene at a sprint.

The dark figure wound up for another whack with the bat. Nick grabbed the bat and wrenched it free, shoving the barrel end of the pistol into the back of the assailant as he yelled, "Police! Freeze!"

Nick dropped the bat and reached for his flashlight. He'd recognized the black cloak. It was just like the one Violet had worn at Geraldine Shaw's funeral. He jerked the hood down and, stepping around, shoved the light into the woman's face.

Charlotte Evans blinked blindly. He lowered the beam to the ground in shock.

Charlotte focused her gaze on him and smiled. "I had a feeling that I shouldn't come into town tonight."

It was the wee hours of morning by the time Nick got Charlotte Evans booked and locked up.

He'd read her her rights, warning her not to say anything she would regret.

"I don't regret anything," she said. "They all deserved it." She saw that he didn't get it. "Men like that." She shook her head. "They are nice to me because I'm pretty." Her expression turned sour. "But I hated the way they were with my sister. They thought they could treat her any way they wanted just because she isn't pretty. That's not right. Someone needed to do something."

He had to call her mother, wake Arlene up at the hospital and get cussed out for arresting her daughter. Nick doubted Charlotte would spend more than a night in jail. He knew she would never get to trial.

First off, the assaulted men wouldn't press charges. Not against a seventeen-year-old girl. Especially not after word got out why she'd done what she had. Charlotte Evans would skate.

But Nick had a bad feeling that it wouldn't be the last the people of Montana heard of Charlotte Evans. He'd seen the way she'd swung that bat. It gave him chills to think she'd be out on the street again.

It wasn't until the next morning, after a fitful night with bad dreams and little sleep, that Nick remembered the call he'd gotten while staking out the bar.

He checked the message. It was from the crime lab.

He returned the call to Maximilian Roswell's cell.

"I just got your message," Nick said, apologizing for calling on a Sunday.

"Thought you'd want to know that we narrowed down the chemical compound found in the poison that killed Geraldine Shaw," Maximilian said. "The compound has been off the market for quite a while now, but I can tell you what it was used for anyway. Artificial-nail remover."

Nick blinked. "What?"

"You heard me right. This particular brand had enough cyanide in it to kill."

Nick rubbed his forehead with his fingers. Arlene Evans had artificial nails. So did Charlotte, her daughter. And so did Sarah Cavanaugh, he recalled with a start. And Sarah Cavanaugh had a motive for killing Geraldine.

The dispatcher appeared in his door, motioning that he had an urgent call.

"I'm going to have to get back to you on this," Nick said and got off the line.

"It's the hospital. Someone just tried to smother Arlene Evans with a pillow. The person got away. The deputy on call is searching the area but so far nothing."

As Nick left his office, he heard the cell phone in his bottom drawer ring, but he didn't turn back. He didn't want to know that the trial had been postponed. Laney was leaving Monday. Nick just wanted it over.

Nick didn't answer the phone. It quit ringing as he walked away. He didn't hear the man on the other end of the line leave a short, succinct message: "Your cover is blown. Get out now."

Chapter 12

Laney called her sister Sunday morning to ask Laci what she should make for dinner.

"Something exotic. Something he's never had before." Laci started rattling off dishes Laney had never even heard of and she realized it had been a mistake asking her sister what to cook.

"I think I should keep it simple. Make something homey like meat loaf and mashed potatoes and fresh peas from the garden. Maybe a carrot-and-raisin salad."

"You've got to be kidding," Laci cried. "You need to wow him with your culinary capacities."

Laney would rather wow him with her intelligence, her sense of humor, her native charm. On second thought, maybe she *should* cook something exotic.

"How's Maddie?" she asked.

"Doing a lot better. The therapist let her call Bo. He

broke off the engagement. He said she was nothing but trouble and blamed her for everything. The therapist listened in on the call. After Maddie hung up, she was upset and hurt, but seemed to finally see Bo Evans for the kind of man he is."

"That's good. I hope Maddie means it."

"Enjoy your dinner with Nick. I can't believe how well you two fit together," Laci gushed.

Laney laughed. "It's just a summer fling. I'm leaving Monday to go home." She hoped neither of those statements proved true. "Have you changed your mind about staying in Montana and starting your catering business here?"

"No. But I hate the thought that I won't see you until Thanksgiving."

"Who said I was coming back to Whitehorse for Thanksgiving?" Laney asked, smiling, knowing her sister only too well.

"Of course you'll be back. You'll want to see Nick."

That much was true. She *would* want to see Nick, she thought as she hung up. For the first summer in all the years she'd been coming here, Laney didn't want to leave. She'd extended her time here as long as she could unless she was her own boss.

She concentrated on what to cook. She wanted dinner to be comfortable. Maybe she'd regret it, but she was going with meat loaf. That decided, she set about getting things ready.

What to wear was much harder. Neither with her clothing nor her cooking did she want to appear too anxious, let alone desperate. Once the meat loaf was in the oven, the potatoes boiling on the stove, the peas picked and shelled and ready to be cooked, she would get dressed. She didn't want to be rushing around when he arrived.

When the time came, she decided on her favorite sundress, pulled her hair up into a ponytail and dabbed on just a touch of lip gloss. Understated.

That was her.

She had the table set on the porch, one lantern candle at the center. She hadn't even used the good china, although she was debating going back in for it when she heard the sound of a car coming up the road.

Her heart began to pound, her palms sweat, her mouth going dry at the sight of Nick Rogers as he got out of the patrol car. He wore jeans, a button-down long-sleeved shirt and boots. He looked shy and scared and happy to see her.

She smiled down at him from the porch. "Tell me you like meat loaf."

He grinned. "I *love* meat loaf."

Laney laughed. "How about a beer before dinner?"

"You really *are* a woman after my own heart," he said as he bounded up the steps to join her on the porch. He was so close she could smell the clean masculine scent of him. She breathed him in as if taking her last breath.

He stood so closely, his look so intimate, she felt a bolt of desire shoot through her. "I can get the beer," he said softly.

She could only nod, watching him go through the door into the house before she grabbed the back of a chair to steady herself. Her nipples were as hard as pebbles and pressed tight against her silk bra—and the thin material of the dress. She felt flushed. She wanted to skip dinner altogether. She wanted him to take her here on the porch in front of everyone who happened by.

She jumped at his touch.

"You look hot," he said next to her ear.

And the next thing she knew, he was pressing the icy, sweating bottle of beer to her temple.

"How's that?" he asked softly.

She didn't dare look at him for fear he would see her answer, know her heart, cause the Old Town Whitehorse gossip hotline to burn for weeks with talk of her and Nick Rogers and what happened on her front porch— and on a Sunday.

"Laney." He pressed one of the beers into her hand and met her gaze. "Laney," he said again.

Her gaze locked with his.

If he didn't kiss her, she knew she would scream. She ached for his touch, her breasts heavy, her nipples as hard as she was soft inside.

Without breaking contact with her gaze, he took her beer from her and touched the cold, wet bottle to her hard nipple through the cloth. She closed her eyes, a soft moan escaping her lips.

Putting both bottles on the table, he circled her waist with one arm and dragged her to him. She felt the heat of his mouth, of his body, the cold wet of his hand on her breast, then snaking up her thighs, under her panties to her center.

She let out a moan of pleasure, throwing her head back, as he dropped his mouth to her breast. She'd never wanted a man the way she wanted him. Never dreamed she could feel such intensity, such desire. She'd always been careful with her heart.

But as Nick swept her up, she wrapped her arms around his neck and kissed him with a need that felt fatal if not fulfilled. The ache inside her was heart-deep.

He kicked open the screen door and took her in-side where it was cool and dim and the neighbors wouldn't see her surrender to him.

In a fever, she pulled him to her, her mouth hot on his, her hands working at the buttons on his shirt, then the buttons on his jeans as he slipped the dress over her head.

She heard his intake of breath as his gaze moved like warm honey over her body, then his fingertips followed that same path. He shoved aside one bra strap, then the other. His mouth trailed from her lips down her throat to the crest of her breasts. She leaned back, her palms against the bare warm skin of his chest.

He took one nipple in his mouth, lathed it with his tongue, then the other. She groaned and pulled him closer; her hands dropped to his hips. She could feel his need, hard against her.

"Laney," he whispered as she drew him to the floor. "Laney."

The first time was fast and furious. She cried out, shuddering against him, their bodies damp and hot, their breathing coming hard and fast.

Later, lying in his arms, she barely heard the timer go off on the meat loaf. His stomach growled next to her and she laughed as she rolled over to prop herself up on one elbow and look down at him. She thought her heart would break at the tenderness in his gaze.

After the meat loaf, mashed potatoes and peas on the porch, when the sun had dissolved into the horizon and the air cooled, he turned out the light and made love to her on the porch.

She couldn't see his eyes in the darkness, but she could feel him. He made love to her as if memorizing every inch of her. As if this night would be his last.

"Oh, my God!" Glass shattered with a loud crash.

Nick bolted upright in bed at Laney's cry and the sound of breaking glass. He grabbed his gun from his holster on the floor by the bed and raced into the kitchen to find her standing in front of the television, what was left of a pitcher in pieces at her feet and orange juice swimming on the tile.

Wordlessly she pointed at the television.

He turned in time to see the face on the screen. A candid shot of him. It was there only a heart-seizing instant before it was replaced with a shot of Arlene Evans sitting up in her hospital bed smiling into the camera.

"Well," Arlene was saying. "I came up with the idea to help young rural people. When you live in the part of Montana that we do, houses are miles apart. Towns are even farther apart. Not only do our young people have a lot of chores on the farms and ranches and not much time to date, they often don't get the opportunity to meet people their own ages. That's how I came up with Rural Montana Meet-a-Mate Internet dating service."

"No," Nick said as he laid his weapon on the kitchen counter. He couldn't believe this.

"She took photos of everyone at Maddie and Bo's

party and put them up on her site," Laney said. "But now we're all on national television."

National television. He was just as good as dead.

"I meant to tell you about this last night…." Laney let her words die off.

"You knew?" he snapped.

She froze, her expression clearly surprised and hurt by his tone, then started to take a step back.

"Don't move!" Her feet were bare and there were shards and orange juice everywhere. He grabbed the paper towels and bent down to pick up the broken pieces. "I'm sorry. It's just that…" It was just that he was screwed.

"I'm sorry, but there's glass all over," he said, trying to calm down. Seeing himself on TV had sent him into a tailspin.

"I was going to tell you and then I forgot," she said as he finished cleaning up the mess and tossed the paper towels and broken glass in the trash. "I went over to Arlene's and got copies of the photographs she'd taken at the party. I was going to show them to you because I thought there might be some evidence…"

He looked at her. She was wearing a silk robe that hugged the body he now knew by heart. Just looking at her made him ache for her.

Last night after she'd fallen asleep, he'd stared at her for a long time, desperately wanting her. And not just for a night. He'd never felt this way about a woman. It scared the hell out of him. Not just because his life wasn't his own right now. Not just because he could easily be dead tomorrow.

It scared him because he wanted Laney Cavanaugh

tonight, tomorrow night and the next night for the rest of his life. He wanted to buy her a ring, ask her to marry him, stand at the altar and promise her his love forever.

He knew this was the real thing. He was in love with this woman. He reached for her, pulling her into his arms, holding her tight. He could feel her fear, her confusion. He cursed himself for letting this happen.

"I'm sorry. I have to go," he said and stepped back to take his gun off the counter, then hesitated as he looked at her. He opened his mouth, desperately needing to tell her the truth about everything, and closed it. He had to get out of Dodge. Now. "I'll call you later," he said as he headed for the bedroom.

"I have the photographs if you want—"

"It's too late for photographs," he said as he dressed. He looked up to find her standing in the bedroom doorway.

"What is it?" she asked, her eyes narrowing. "If it's about last night—"

"It's not." He stopped dressing. "Laney, last night was…unbelievable. I've never…" Words defied him. "But it shouldn't have happened. I can't get involved with anyone right now."

Her expression turned from hurt to anger. "You don't have to explain. I get it." She walked over to the bed and dropped the photographs on the comforter, then she turned and left.

He had to bite his tongue not to call her back. *Tell her, dammit. Just tell her the truth.* He swore as he strapped on his weapon. His photo was on national television. It wouldn't take Keller any time to find him. He had to get out of town. The best thing he could do for Laney was to distance himself from her and quickly.

He started to leave the photographs on the bed where she'd tossed them. But at the last minute, he scooped them up, planning to give them to one of the deputies in the department—once he'd destroyed all traces of ones with him in them. He didn't want any trail that would lead Keller to Laney in case things went badly in California.

At the front door, he stopped to look back toward the kitchen. The very last thing he wanted was to walk out this door. To walk out on Laney. But his life wasn't worth two cents right now. He had nothing to offer her. Absolutely nothing. Being around him would only put her in danger.

He opened the door and hurried across the porch, down the steps to his patrol car. He didn't look back. He couldn't.

Laney went to the window to watch Nick go. To watch him run away. Last night had been just as he'd said—incredible. They'd been so close. Too close, she saw now. She knew he'd been afraid to let her into his life. She'd warned herself not to care too much.

Look at how he'd reacted to seeing his photograph on the Montana Meet-a-Mate site. Imagine how he would have reacted if he'd seen the two of them "matched-up" on the website. She could have killed Arlene for doing this. But she knew it wasn't Arlene's fault. Laney had known Nick wasn't ready to get involved with anyone. Maybe especially her.

There'd been sparks that first time she'd laid eyes on

him. She wasn't sure when she'd fallen for him but she had. And now her heart was breaking.

She wanted to regret falling for Nick. To curse herself for last night. But she couldn't. She would have felt much worse if she'd left town without making love with him. The memory would haunt her always, but at least she had that.

The phone rang. Laney couldn't help the way her pulse surged as she reached to pick it up. *Let it be Nick. Please let it be Nick.*

"So?" Laci said. "Is he still there?"

"No," Laney said, trying to hide her disappointment on both counts. "He had to leave."

"Last night? Or this morning?"

Laney couldn't help smiling. "This morning."

"So?"

"It was wonderful. I'll never forget it. I was going to call you. I've decided to leave today rather than wait until tomorrow and drive to Billings to catch the plane."

"Wait a minute," Laci said. "You're leaving? What about Nick? Oh no, you made meat loaf, didn't you?"

"He loved the meat loaf. It was only a summer fling. Just like I told you."

"Why don't I believe that?" Laci asked.

"Because you are an incurable romantic. Listen, I have to get going. I'll call you when I get to Mesa. Give my love to Maddie."

"I'm sorry, Laney," her sister said before she could get off the phone.

Nick planned his getaway on the way back to Whitehorse. He had to swing by his office and pick up the cell phone, then by his apartment to take what few belongings he had with him. He thought he was still safe enough to make both stops. His cover had been blown, but even if Keller had seen Arlene's interview this morning on television and Nick's photo, he wouldn't be able to get here that fast.

Unless Keller had already gotten wind of where he was. That, Nick knew, had always been a possibility since Keller was out on bail with nothing to do but look for him.

His radio squawked.

"There's been another attempt on Arlene Evans's life," the dispatcher told him.

Nick swore silently. He couldn't deal with this now. He had to get out of town before it was too late. If it wasn't already. He could only guess how long his photo had been up on the Internet. Keller would have put the word out. Everyone would be on the lookout for Nicolas Giovanni.

"Arlene's under protective custody and doing fine," the dispatcher said. "You might want to come over to the jail though."

This surprised Nick. "Are you saying they caught the person who attacked Arlene?"

"One of the nurses caught her in the act. The deputy just took her down to the jail but he wanted me to let you know. It's Violet, Arlene's daughter."

Nick couldn't believe this. They already had the younger daughter locked up—and now her older sister?

"You aren't going to believe some of the stuff she's saying," the dispatcher said. "I think you'd better get over here."

* * *

After Laney hung up from talking to her sister, she wiped her tears, angry with herself for crying, then threw herself into the physical labor of cleaning the kitchen until it shone.

Then she set about packing. She would drive to Billings and catch a flight home. She couldn't bear the thought of staying here another night alone. She'd seen the expression on Nick's face. He wouldn't be coming back.

She'd packed light to come to Montana. Unlike Laci who had four suitcases and had apparently brought most everything she owned. It didn't take long before Laney was ready to leave. She rolled her suitcase out to the porch and went back to make sure everything was turned off.

The sound of a vehicle set her heart racing. Her first thought, her most fervent wish, was that it would be Nick. He had tried to stay away but couldn't. He felt just as she did.

She ran through the house, slamming open the screen door and stopping short on the porch. She'd been ready to throw herself into Nick's arms. She didn't know why he was so afraid of this thing between them. She didn't care. As long as he didn't keep running.

But the car wasn't Nick's. Nor was the man who got out of the car Nick.

Laney looked into the face of a man she'd never seen before and knew instinctively his would probably be the last face she ever saw as he pulled a gun from beneath his jacket and pointed it at her heart.

"Let's step inside," the man said, coming up the

porch stairs and grabbing her arm before she could move. He held the barrel of the gun to her temple. "You and I need to talk about our mutual friend, Nicolas Giovanni."

Nick found two of the deputies in the interrogation room at the jail with Violet.

She was sitting at one end of the marred table looking as if she'd been invited to lunch rather than arrested for attempted murder.

He stepped into the room, and she looked up and smiled as if she'd been waiting for him. As far as he could tell she hadn't shed a tear. "Violet."

"Deputy Rogers," she said in response as he took a seat at the opposite end of the table and glanced at the deputies. They both seemed to shrug as if they couldn't quite believe this either.

"Want to tell me what's going on, Violet?" Nick asked, keeping his voice as calm as she appeared.

She met his gaze. There was a determination in hers, a resolve. "I tried to kill my mother this morning. I'm sorry that I failed again."

"So it wasn't the first time, I take it?" he asked, trying to keep his voice neutral.

"I tried before to smother her in the hospital, but I got interrupted. That time I managed to get away by hiding in a storage closet. I wasn't responsible for the other times we tried to kill her."

We? He stared at her for a moment, then pulled out his notebook and pencil even though he could see that the deputies had been videotaping her responses. He just needed a moment and this gave him the time.

"You say you were not responsible for the other times 'we' tried to kill her?" he finally asked.

"Those times it was Charlotte and Bo," she said matter-of-factly.

"Why don't you tell me about those times," he said.

And she did, starting with Maddie and Bo's engagement party. It had been Charlotte's idea to poison their mother at the party with a macaroon. Violet's job had been to bake the cookie and make sure that only the poison cookie was left on the plate when Charlotte offered it to Arlene.

"So the macaroon was intended for your mother rather than Geraldine," he said.

"I felt sorry for Geraldine. Charlotte said we'd done her a favor." Violet shrugged.

"And Bo?"

"He didn't really care that Geraldine died except that now we would have to come up with another plan for Mother," she said.

"I meant, what part did Bo play in the other attempts on your mother's life?"

"Oh," she said. "He pushed Mother down the stairs. He pretended it was an accident. Mother forgave him of course. He was always her favorite."

"I would think that would be a good reason why he wouldn't want her dead," Nick pointed out. He noticed that the deputies seemed to be in shock as they listened and he suspected they'd already heard most of this.

"Bo hated her as much as we did. He hated her hanging on him, making so much of him, he was embarrassed by it. He just wanted her to go away." Violet's tone was such that she could have been talking about the weather or what to make for dinner instead of cold-blooded murder.

"And the overdose?"

"That was Charlotte. She put the pills in Mother's coffee."

"Where was your father when all this was going on?" Nick had to ask.

"He works all the time. I think he does it so he doesn't have to come in the house except to eat and sleep."

Nick took off his hat and raked a hand through his hair. He had to get moving, but he was so shocked by this that he couldn't help but ask the question that haunted him. "Why did you want your mother dead?"

"Me personally?" She met his gaze and smiled ruefully. "Do you really have to ask? She would have married me off to Jack the Ripper if she could have. And since she couldn't marry me off to anyone, she made my life unbearable. I tried to find a husband just to get away from her but I couldn't. No one wanted me."

He heard the pain in her voice. "You know your sister has been arrested for assault," Nick said and explained why.

For the first time, Violet's eyes filled with tears. "I didn't know she was doing that." She bit her lip. "I didn't think anyone cared."

Nick didn't know what to say. He turned to one of the deputies. "Have you brought Bo Evans in yet?"

"We were waiting on word from you."

"Pick him up and you'd better call the county attorney and let him know what's going on." Nick shifted his gaze from the deputy to Violet. "I'm sorry you felt you had no recourse but to kill your mother."

She shrugged. "We did what we had to."

"Your mother is still alive," he said, not sure she knew that she and her siblings had failed yet another time.

Violet nodded. "At least for the moment."

Nick felt a chill in the room as he picked up his notebook and pen and rose from his chair. He wanted to be anywhere but in this room with this woman.

In his office, he sat down, felt the photographs Laney had given him in his shirt pocket. He took them out and tossed them on the desk, sick from what he'd heard in the interrogation room. Even sicker when he thought of Laney and the way he'd left things with her.

He glanced at his watch. He had to get moving. He should be hightailing it out of town. Keller would be on his trail. Even with Geraldine Shaw's murder solved and the after-hours bar assailant in jail, Nick felt he'd left too much undone.

One of the photographs caught his eye. He drew it closer. The snapshot was of Laney. She looked so beautiful. He wished he'd had the chance to dance with her that day.

Past Laney, he saw Charlotte caught in the act of taking something from her pocket and slipping it on the macaroon plate. Moments later Arlene would be offered the cookie, but Geraldine would take it before the murder weapon could reach the right victim. Life was so much chance. He shook his head and put down the photograph.

Soon all three of the Evans offspring would be in

custody. He wondered how Arlene would take it. He suspected she would blame Violet. He used to hear cops debate whether it was the environment or the genes that eroded a family to the extent the kids were trying to kill one of their parents.

Hard to say. The bottom line was that as horrible as the Evanses were, they couldn't hold a candle to a guy like Zak Keller, who'd grown up on the same street as Nick, practically living with Nick's family.

Nick hurriedly unlocked the bottom drawer and took out his cell phone. Time to get the hell out of town. As he turned on the phone he saw that he had a message.

He played it and felt his blood run cold.

Chapter 13

The man who called himself Zak Keller dragged Laney into the kitchen and shoved her down into a chair. He was tall and broad-shouldered with a surprisingly handsome face and a full head of sandy-blond hair cut in the latest style. He wore expensive clothing, looked like a businessman, even smelled good. On the surface, there appeared to be nothing dangerous about him.

Until you looked into his eyes.

Zak Keller's were a colorless blue and totally devoid of emotion. Soulless eyes.

"Here's the plan," he said in a voice as smooth as any pricey attorney's. "You're going to call Nicolas. You tell him I'm here to see him and that if he doesn't do exactly what I want him to, I'll blow your brains out. Can you remember that?"

It wasn't something she was likely to forget. Her

heart pounded so hard it made her chest hurt. She was having trouble catching her breath and her mind was like a caged squirrel, running too fast, going nowhere. She knew she had to calm down, had to think.

She stared at the man, absolutely positive he meant every word he'd said about blowing her brains out. "I can remember that," she said, surprised how calm she sounded.

He nodded and smiled at her. The smile of a shark just before it took a big bite.

Her logical mind argued that Zak Keller had the wrong man. She didn't know a Nicolas Giovanni. She knew a Nick Rogers, a deputy sheriff with a kind heart, a shy man, a man who was running from something.

She'd thought that something was her.

But now she had a bad feeling it was something much more dangerous. It was Zak Keller.

She fought not to show just how terrified she was. Especially of that little voice in her head that said Nick Rogers was Nicolas Giovanni. Nick had said he was Italian but that hadn't explained the last name Rogers. She'd seen the look on his face for that split second when he'd seemed to realize he'd given something away.

"You ready to make that call?" Zak Keller asked, glancing at his watch, then her.

"Yes," she said, aware that whatever Nick had been covering up was deadly serious. Otherwise she wouldn't have this man standing in her kitchen holding a gun on her, threatening to kill her.

"I left out one important point," Zak Keller said as he handed her the phone. "If you try to warn anyone before you get Nicolas on the line, I will kill you. It doesn't make any difference to me really. I just thought this way would be more fun for Nicolas. We understand each other?"

She nodded and took the phone. As she dialed the sheriff's department number, he stepped closer and pressed the gun painfully into her temple, all the time smiling.

"Deputy Sheriff Nick Rogers please," she said when the dispatcher answered. Her voice sounded too high to her but Zak Keller didn't seem to notice.

"Just a moment."

Laney could hear the extension ringing. The way Nick had torn out of her house this morning, he could be miles away by now. She recalled how upset he'd been to see his face on national television. What had he done that would make him so afraid of having his picture on the Internet, on national television? Something that had a killer after him.

She could feel the man standing over her growing impatient. He'd planned to use her, but clearly he would just as easily change that plan by killing her first and going after Nick alone if he had to.

"Hello?"

Laney almost wept with relief at the sound of Nick's voice. "Nick."

One little word. But Nick heard everything he'd feared in that one word. He'd been on his way out of the office, hurrying after discovering the message on the cell phone in the locked bottom drawer. He wasn't sure what had made him turn back to answer the phone. Just a feeling…

"Laney, what—"

Zak Keller prodded her hard in the temple with the gun.

"I have a message for Nicolas Giovanni from Zak Keller," she said as evenly as she could. "He says if you don't do exactly what he wants, he is going to blow my brains out."

Her words struck Nick like a punch. The pain seared through him, burning him to his soul. For a moment, he couldn't speak, couldn't breathe. His heart had stopped, his mind stunned by the horror of even the thought of Zak Keller near Laney.

"You there, Nicolas?" Keller asked and laughed as he took the phone.

"I'm here," Nick said. He knew better than to demand that Keller let Laney go. Just as he knew better than to pretend she didn't matter to him. Unfortunately, he knew how Keller operated.

"Good. It's been too long. You've been a hard man to find."

Nick said nothing, waiting, his heart in his throat at what Keller would do to Laney.

"You and I need to get together, don't you think?"

"Only if Laney comes along," Nick said.

Keller laughed. "She isn't your usual type, my old friend. I thought you liked brunettes."

"I take what I can get."

Keller's laugh this time said he didn't buy Nick's nonchalance when it came to Laney, making Nick wonder how long he'd been in the area and just what he knew.

"How'd you find me?" Nick asked.

"Does it matter?"

"Just curious."

"Saw your picture on the Internet. It was the damnedest thing. It appeared you'd fallen in love," Keller said. "You really are a fast worker, old buddy. You got a cell phone?"

He knew Nick did. "You want the number?" Nick asked, but figured Keller already had it.

"Sure."

Nick rattled it off, wondering if Keller was even writing it down. If Keller already had the number then he'd taken out the one man Nick had trusted with his life. And now Nick had cost that man his life. Grief twisted inside him. How many more people had to die? But he knew the answer to that one. At least two.

"I'll call you and let you know where to meet us," Keller said. "But Nick, just in case you decide to do something stupid—"

The next thing Nick heard was Laney's scream. Hot flames of anger seared away the grief and desolation as the phone went dead. Nick threw the phone across the room. He saw the dispatcher looking toward his office. He had to pull himself together.

But his brain was screaming: *Keller has Laney. Keller has Laney.* Nothing on this earth could be as bad as that.

Laney scuttled across the floor trying to get away but Zak was on her, slamming her into the wall, slapping her again, making her cry out a second time.

Then smiling, he hung up on Nick.

"You can get up now," he said, his voice suddenly

so calm it sent ice through her veins. "We're going for a little ride."

She struggled to her feet, her hand going to her mouth and coming away bloody. The bastard had split her lip—just to get a rise out of Nick.

Anger took the edge off her terror. Her brain seemed to start functioning again. She didn't want to go for a ride with him. If there was any way she could keep from getting into his car...

He had put the gun back into the holster as if he thought he no longer needed it and moved to replace the phone.

Her gaze took in the kitchen, seeing anything that she could use as a weapon. The knife rack was too far away. He'd be on her again before she could draw one, let alone use it on him, something she wasn't completely sure she could do anyway. A canister would be too awkward. Just as the large mixer or the toaster.

She staggered to the edge of the kitchen counter and stopped. He half turned to glance back at her. She curled around herself, pretending to be more hurt than she was.

He turned his back to her again as he hung up the phone.

She grabbed the coffeepot from the coffeemaker. There was almost a full pot. She'd made it while she'd cleaned and got ready to leave and forgotten all about it. But the coffeemaker had kept it hot.

She moved swiftly, but he must have heard the pot scraping across the bottom of the coffeemaker. She was already running at him, the pot raised, when he spun around faster than she had anticipated.

She swung the pot with everything she had. His arm

came up to block the blow. The pot shattered, sending hot coffee splattering across the kitchen—and the man.

He let out a bellow of pain and anger.

She never saw his other arm until it hit her, sending her sprawling backward across the room. She hit the wall; her head snapped back. Pain shot through her head just before everything went black.

Nick opened the bottom drawer of his desk, took out the cell and turned it on, then switched it with the phone on his belt that he'd been given when he'd taken the job.

He hated the way his hand shook. This was exactly what Keller wanted—him running scared.

But how could he not be terrified for Laney? Nick knew what kind of man Zak Keller was. He'd seen how callous and cold-blooded the man could be. Nick knew what kind of danger Laney was in.

His mind raced with only one thought—saving Laney. From the beginning, Nick had known he probably wouldn't get out of this mess alive. At the very least, he would never be able to be a cop in California again. Keller had friends who would make sure of that.

But Laney hadn't asked for any of this. She deserved so much better. Nick would never forgive himself for jeopardizing her life. How had Keller found out about her? Because of last night?

Nick knew that couldn't be possible. Keller couldn't have known about them that quickly. Keller had said he'd found him *and* Laney on the Internet?

On impulse, Nick called up Arlene Evans's Meet-a-Mate website. He'd been so upset this morning at Laney's that he hadn't paid any attention to anything except the fact that Arlene and her damned site had made national television.

Now as he flipped through the photographs of the possible "dates," he saw what Keller must have seen— a photo of Nick and one of Laney with a stupid red heart around the two photographs and a caption that read True Love?

There were other photographs linked as well with stupid captions.

Nick felt sick. Arlene had no idea what she'd done. Not just to him. But to Laney. Arlene also had posted information about each of them. Keller wouldn't have had any trouble at all finding Laney.

Nick wanted to break something, to destroy the office, to curse God. But he knew that would just be a waste of time and property and spirit.

If he hoped to save Laney, he had to think like Keller. He had to be cold-blooded. He had to be calm. Mostly, if given the opportunity, he would have to be a killer.

In a separate locked drawer, he took out his own gun. He didn't have to check to see if it was loaded, but he did anyway. He needed to cover every base. He knew Keller would.

He grabbed two full clips and stuck them into the pocket of his denim jacket. From the drawer he took out his sheathed knife and slipped it into his boot.

Keller would expect him to be packing. He didn't want to let him down. His sheriff department-issue pistol that he'd been given when he took the job, he slipped into the holster, put on his denim jacket and, leaving the keys to the patrol car on his desk, left.

When he'd gotten to Whitehorse, he'd picked up an

old used pickup. It was a beater, but it ran well. Since then, he'd been working so much he had barely used the truck.

But now he walked the four blocks to his apartment. It was one of a half-dozen built in a row, white with blue trim, neat as a pin.

Inside, he packed just for something to do while he waited for the call. He didn't have much. Everything fit into two duffel bags. He carried them out to the pickup and put them behind the seat.

Then he climbed behind the wheel, started the truck and drove down to Packy's to fill up with gas.

Keller hadn't called, but then he hadn't expected him to. Zak would try to drag this out as long as possible. He didn't just want to kill Nick; he wanted him to suffer.

Nick wouldn't let himself think about what might be happening to Laney. He couldn't or he would lose it. He had to keep his cool. Keller was hoping he would lose control, act on emotion rather than reason.

Not that Nick had a chance in hell. Keller would make sure of that. Nick was as good as dead. But maybe there was a chance for Laney. He concentrated on that.

On that and the thought that if he failed today, Keller would be free.

Nick couldn't let that happen. He'd had a chance once to kill Keller. He hadn't taken it. He wouldn't make that mistake again. But Keller might not give him another opportunity. In fact, Nick was pretty sure Keller wouldn't.

But maybe there was another way, he thought as he drove back to the sheriff's department. He checked out the video camera and new tape, went into his office and locked the door. It only took a few minutes to set up the camera; when the light came on, he sat down in front of the lens and began to speak.

"My name is Nicolas Giovanni. If you're watching this, I'm dead. As I make this recording, L.A. homicide detective Zak Keller has kidnapped Laney Cavanaugh. She might already be dead for all I know."

His voice threatened to break. He cleared his throat. "I was to testify against Zak Keller next week in a trial in Los Angeles. Since I don't think I'm going to be making that trial now, I'm giving my testimony by video. I saw Zak Keller kill two police officers in cold blood on May 31 of this year."

Nick took a breath and let it out and began again.

"I attempted to arrest him, but I was wounded and he got away. However, I did retrieve the gun he used and put it into evidence. The gun as well as the report verifying that his prints were on the weapon later disappeared, as did Zak. He was arrested but released on bail. After an attempt on my life, I went into hiding. Right now I am waiting for another call from Zak to tell me where to meet him." He shut off the camera and waited as the day turned to dusk, then dark.

When his cell phone rang, Nick turned the video camera back on and stepped closer. He let it ring another time, then answered it on camera.

"That you, old buddy?" Zak asked, amusement in his voice. "Took you long enough to answer. You playing games with me?"

Like you're playing games with me? "Couldn't get the damned thing out of my pocket," Nick said, wanting Zak to believe he was nervous. Hell, he was way beyond nervous.

Zak laughed. "Okay, here's the plan. You—"

"I need to know that Laney is still alive." He hoped the audio was picking up Zak's side of the conversation.

"You're in no position to make demands, Nicolas," Zak said, a sharp edge to his voice.

"Come on, Zak. Just let me hear her voice."

Silence. For a minute he thought Keller might have hung up.

"Just a minute. She's coming around."

Nick held his breath as he looked at the camera, saw the red recording light, waited to hear Laney's voice, terrified of what Keller had done to her.

"Nick, I'm all right."

She didn't sound all right.

"What has he done to you?"

"You want to hear the plan, Nick, or do you want to hear her scream? Your choice."

"Let's hear the plan, Zak."

"I'll have to call you back. Start driving north toward Saco."

"When does the killing stop, Zak?" Nick asked.

"You know the answer to that, old buddy. See you soon."

The line went dead. Nick looked at the camera, then walked over and shut it off, removed the cassette and put it in the padded envelope, addressed the video to the prosecuting attorney, Los Angeles, California. He gave the package to the dispatcher with instructions to overnight it the next morning.

Then he walked out to his pickup, climbed in and headed north toward Saco.

Laney woke to panic. She couldn't see a thing, but she realized at once that she was in a small dark place and she couldn't breathe. She tried to move but found her wrists and ankles bound, tape over her mouth.

She fought back the terror, sucking in air through her nose, as she realized where she was.

In the trunk of a car. She could hear the engine, the hum of the tires on the road, feel the rough carpet against her cheek as the car hit a bump, jostling her.

She lay curled in a fetal position. Her head ached and it took her a moment to remember what had happened. Zak Keller. She closed her eyes as fear overcame her.

Where was he taking her?

To meet Nick. Nicolas Giovanni.

Terror immobilized her worse than the tape that bound her. He was going to kill her. Except if that was all he had planned, he would have done it back at the house.

She felt the car slow, turn; the road became rough just before the car stopped in what felt like a few miles off the highway.

The engine died into silence. She held her breath as she heard the car door open, close, the sound of footsteps on gravel growing nearer.

The trunk lid popped open.

She blinked, blinded by the tiny trunk light overhead and surprised to see that it was dark outside. Even darker was the silhouette of Zak Keller standing over her.

"Laney Cavanaugh." His voice was as cold as his eyes. "Here, let me help you out."

The switchblade in his hand caught the light. She cringed as he brought it down. She heard his chuckle as he cut the tape that bound her ankles; then the blade disappeared, and he smiled and offered her his hand.

"I hope the ride wasn't too uncomfortable for you," he said.

He was just making conversation, clearly liking the sound of his own voice. He couldn't care less about her welfare and she knew it. She was a means to an end and she feared what that end was.

Her mouth was still covered with tape, her wrists still bound, as he helped her out of the trunk, then slammed the lid. They stood for a moment, him gripping her elbow.

She could make out structures, all dark. It wasn't until he led her toward the larger of the buildings that she recognized where they were. Sleeping Buffalo Resort. She'd heard that it was closed for repairs. Obviously so had Zak Keller.

At the door to the indoor pool, he shoved her into the corner. "Just stand there. We don't want another episode like back at the house, now do we?"

She said nothing, but she could see his expression. He wanted her to try to escape. He wanted to hurt her.

She watched him produce a crowbar and realized he'd had it in his other hand the entire time. Had she tried anything, she would have known about its existence much sooner.

As he worked quickly and with obvious expertise in breaking and entering, her mind raced. What were they doing here? She hated to imagine what he had planned for them. There was no doubt in her mind he would kill them. When he finished torturing them with whatever game he was playing.

Knowing that she had no chance of surviving gave her a kind of peace. Fear came with hope. She had no hope.

The wood around the door splintered. Zak Keller froze. She could tell he was listening. He knew no one was around or they wouldn't be here. He wasn't a man who left anything to chance. But he also knew there could always be surprises, unplanned contingencies.

No one came at the sound of the wood splintering. Nor when he pushed the door open and dragged Laney inside. She smelled the heavy damp scent of the mineral pool. Their footsteps echoed on the concrete floor as he led her past the desk into the huge pool area.

The ceiling was high, the echo of their footfalls on the concrete louder in here. She could hear the gurgle of the water at the inlets as they skirted the pool. It was pitch-black inside the massive room, but she could make out a faint light coming from the locker rooms.

He drew her toward the light in the women's locker room, down the narrow entry past the old-fashioned wire baskets with numbers on them, around the corner to the line of dressing rooms.

He stopped in front of one and drew back the plastic shower curtain to expose a bench. "Sit."

She sat. The switchblade appeared again. He sliced the blade through the duct tape around her wrists. She rubbed at her sore red skin, trying not to imagine what was coming next.

"Okay, here's the deal," he said, leaning over her. "You're going to call your boyfriend and tell him to come get you. But if you scream, which would be stupid on your part since there isn't anyone around for miles, but if you do, I will hurt you. We understand each other?"

Perfectly, she thought, and nodded.

He jerked the tape off her mouth. She couldn't help the small cry of pain. He smiled, taking pleasure in her pain, no matter how small. Then he took out the cell phone, dialed a number and handed her the phone.

It rang three times. She could see Zak Keller growing impatient again. If Nick was smart he would be miles away from here by now. He wouldn't come out here. Why get them both killed?

"Hello."

The sound of his voice brought both relief and regret. "Nick." She cleared her throat, her gaze on Zak. He looked ready to hurt her as if balancing on the edge of a knife blade, ready to go off at any minute. "He wants you to come out to Sleeping Buffalo."

"Do whatever he tells you to," Nick said, his voice sounding almost too calm. "Don't give him an excuse to hurt you."

"Ask him if he knows where the pool is," Zak ordered.

"Do you know where the swimming pool is?" she asked.

"I'm on my way."

Something in his voice tore at her heart. "Don't. Run. He's going to—"

Zak slammed her against the side of the dressing-room wall.

She was ready for the blow and made no sound.

The phone clattered to the floor. Calmly Zak picked it up, glaring at her, disappointed that she hadn't screamed for Nick's benefit.

"How do you inspire such loyalty?" Zak asked Nick as he spoke into the phone. "She risks my wrath to save your sorry ass. You're really something, Nicolas. But then you always did have a way with the ladies, didn't you? We'll be waiting for you." He disconnected and looked at Laney.

She could tell he wanted to hit her again. She met his gaze, held it; seconds passed.

"Take off your clothes."

Chapter 14

"I said, take off your clothes," Zak Keller ordered. "I can rip them off if you like, but then you might get more than you bargained for if that happens."

Laney looked into his eyes. She hadn't bargained for any of this and he knew it. In the depths of those soulless eyes, she saw evil as dark and sinister as the pits of hell.

"Oh come on," he snapped. "I'm not going to rape you." He shook his head and chuckled. "Don't get me wrong. I'm tempted. But there isn't time. Nick won't know that I didn't though. It will drive him crazy to think that I had you." He pulled out the gun and pointed it at her head. "Or Nick can find you slumped in a pool of your own blood in this dressing room. Your choice."

"Why are you doing this?" she asked as she slowly began to take off her shoes and socks.

"Nick didn't tell you? No, I guess he wouldn't. Nick and I were partners." He motioned with the gun for her to speed up the disrobing.

"Partners?" she asked as she put her shoes and socks aside and began to unbutton her blouse, trying to imagine what kind of business dealings Nick would have had with this man.

"Homicide detectives," Zak Keller said.

"*You* were a *cop?*" She couldn't hide her shock.

His laugh had a sharp edge to it. "I'm *still* a cop. Nick is trying to take that away from me, but it will be over my dead body." Anger made the veins in his forehead pop out. The hand holding the gun was trembling and she could see that he was having trouble controlling his anger.

She let her blouse drop to the floor. "You were partners?" she said in an attempt to calm him down.

"Partners," he repeated, and took a moment before he said, "We were from the same neighborhood. We grew up together as close as any real brothers before we became brothers in blue. Only Nicolas forgot about the code."

"The code?" She began to unbutton her jeans.

"The code that no matter what happens on the job, cops stick together. Nick broke the code."

"So you were police officers in Houston together?"

"Houston? Is that what he told you?" Zak laughed. "L.A. He hasn't been very truthful with you."

No, Nick hadn't. But if Zak was any indication, she was beginning to understand why.

She slipped out of her jeans, leaving her bra and panties on. She could feel those cold pale eyes on her.

"So he never mentioned me?" Zak asked. "I'm deeply hurt. I'll have to tell him when I see him. I used to spend more time with his family than with my own. He tell you about his family? No? A big Italian family."

So at least that much was true.

"Come on, take the rest of it off. You don't have anything I haven't seen before." He glanced toward the pool. "I'm worried about Nicolas. Calling himself Rogers. The way he loves old Roy Rogers westerns, didn't he realize that name would set off alarms with me? New deputy sheriff in town. Linked romantically with pretty local girl. That is all so Nick." Zak laughed. "He always was a sucker for those sappy happy endings."

Laney slipped out of her panties, then her bra. She shivered, crossed her arms over her bare chest, and raised her eyes slowly to meet Zak Keller's. She knew he'd be grinning. He was.

"Now that wasn't so bad, was it?"

She said nothing, holding his gaze.

"Put your arms down," he ordered.

She did, refusing to look away as she felt his gaze slide over her body like slime. It took all her composure not to strike out at him. But she knew he would have enjoyed that too much.

There was no getting past him, not with him blocking the narrow opening of the dressing room. He had her trapped. Trying to fight him would only play right into his hands.

His grin broadened as his gaze returned to hers. "I think I'm beginning to understand now what Nicolas saw in you." He reached into his pocket with his free hand and pulled out the duct tape. "Sorry, but I'm going to have to tape your wrists again."

She glared at him, making him chuckle, as she stuck out her hands.

He grabbed them, putting the gun back into his pocket as he taped her wrists together tightly.

She didn't make a sound, holding in the pain, determined not to give him the satisfaction.

When he'd finished, he ripped off a piece of tape and, staring into her eyes as he did it, slapped it across her mouth. "Nicolas will be here soon. We're almost ready." His gaze dropped to her left breast before coming back up to hers. With his eyes locked on hers, he reached over and pinched her nipple hard.

She cried out before she could stop herself. It came out a muffled sound behind the tape.

Zak Keller smiled. "*Now* we're ready."

Nick turned off the highway just south of Saco. He'd been out this way before. Next to the road was a small enclosed area like a manger. Inside was a large brown rock that some thought resembled a sleeping buffalo. The rock was sacred to the Native Americans in the area. That was why it was covered with tobacco, their offerings.

There was a story that the rock had once been moved into Whitehorse, but each morning the massive rock would be facing the opposite direction it had the night before. Spooked by this, the rock had been returned to where it had been found and later put in this shelter.

Nick drove down the road toward Nelson Reservoir and Sleeping Buffalo Resort, fear making his mouth dry and his heart ache. If Zak hadn't taken Laney, Nick would have gone in, guns blazing. But Laney changed everything. That was why Zak had abducted her. But why bring her here?

The pool was closed, the large interior dark. Nick parked next to what he assumed was Keller's rental car. As he neared the building, he saw that the door had been pried open. He pushed on it, staying to one side.

He didn't really expect an ambush. Keller didn't work that way. He preferred theatrics. Zak had always kidded him about his love of old westerns. And yet Zak had planned an old-fashioned shoot-out here in this 1930s resort.

Nick listened. He could hear the soft lap of water, a sound like a fist to his belly. Keller hadn't just randomly chosen this place. He knew about Nick's fear of water. Early in his career, he'd been in pursuit of a felon and fallen through a rotten pier to be trapped underwater until rescued by some bystanders. The incident had left him afraid of water.

Laney stood shivering in the dark beside the pool. Zak had hold of her arm, his fingers digging into her flesh. She'd heard the car drive up, heard the engine shut off, the car door open. Then there had been nothing but silence.

She could feel the tension in the cop's grip. He'd taken the gun out of his pocket again before he'd led her out to the pool. She noted the way he stood just a little behind her as if he planned to use her as a shield should Nick come in firing.

Laney thought of her sister and her grandparents. It

tore out her heart to think that she would never see them again. She feared that the news of her death would kill her grandmother Pearl and devastate her grandfather Titus. She couldn't bear to imagine what it would do to Laci. They had always been so close.

Fear threatened to paralyze her. Once they'd reached the side of the pool, Zak had taped her ankles together. She'd always been a strong swimmer but with her wrists and ankles taped together, she feared she wouldn't be able to keep her head above water. There was no doubt in her mind that she would end up in the pool. Why else would Zak Keller choose this place?

Nick crept along the edge of a short stone wall that opened into the pool area. He could hear the slap of the water against the sides of the pool, smell the hot water and feel the steam coming off the surface brush past his face.

He took deep breaths, caught between his fear and his anger. He could see the clear path of how his life had led him to this very spot, to this dark night, to this deserted pool. He'd seen things in Zak that had worried him even when they were kids. The barely concealed rage. The troubled kid from down the block with the alcoholic father, the whore mother. He'd seen the bruises on Zak, bruises his friend had always passed off as clumsiness.

Nick had known better, but he'd let Zak save face. Nick's family had practically adopted Zak, giving him a safe place to come when things were bad at his house, feeding him, even clothing him with hand-me-downs from all the cousins.

Zak had said he wanted to be a cop from the time they were just kids. Nick had fought his family legacy, but Zak had been so persuasive, telling Nick that Zak needed his head at the academy. Nick had helped Zak with his grades; Zak had helped him on the firing range.

Nick remembered the day they'd gotten hired. The picture of the two of them in their uniforms sat on the mantel at Nick's parents' home. Nick and Zak smiling at the camera. Zak so proud. It was the same year that Zak's father had taken his life and Zak's mother had run off, never to be seen again.

Nick shoved away the memories as he crouched behind a section of the stone wall. All the signs had been there. The violent arrests, the warnings, the growing distance between him and his partner.

And then the night that Nick had watched Zak kill two police officers from another precinct over a drug bust that had gone haywire. Zak had blamed the two cops for ruining his perfect bust record.

For months Nick had feared it would come to this. Laws and trials weren't for men like Zak Keller. He believed he was above the law. This was Zak Keller's idea of justice, killing anyone who crossed him. Even his once best friend.

"Zak?" Nick called, staying low behind the wall.

No answer. Water dripped nearby and lapped at the edge of the pool.

"Keller, you wanted me here, now show yourself."

A low chuckle came from the other side of the pool. "I wasn't sure you'd come," Keller said. A lie. Zak wouldn't have taken Laney unless he knew he could use her as leverage.

"Where's Laney?" Nick called.

"She's around. First get rid of your gun."

Nick pulled out his service revolver and tossed it down the concrete apron around the pool. The gun clattered across the floor, coming to a stop at the far end of the building.

"Any more weapons you'd like to be rid of?" Keller asked, then chuckled. "I didn't think so. There's a light switch off to your left. Why don't you turn it on?"

Nick could think of two good reasons why that would be a bad idea. Fear of what he would see was at the top of the list. Followed quickly by a bullet. Not a killing one. Just a maiming one.

"I want to know that Laney's all right first," he called back.

"You never had any faith, you know that? It was one of your flaws."

"Faith? I had all the faith in the world in you, Zak. I trusted you with my life." He felt anger rear its ugly head. It felt good. Better than fear. Keller wanted him to be afraid. "You betrayed me before you even betrayed yourself and every other cop."

"Nicolas, Nicolas, if I wanted a sermon I would have gone to church."

Nick heard the shuffle of feet on the other side of the pool where the locker rooms were.

"Your girlfriend is here now. Say something to him," Keller ordered.

There was the sound of tape being ripped off, then "Nick?" Laney's voice sounded tight. "What's going on?"

"Didn't you tell her, Nick? Ah, I'm disappointed in

you. All that talk about honesty and you let her walk into something like this cold?"

"It's okay, Laney. I'll give him what he wants and he'll let you go."

"I really doubt that, Nick. He—"

Nick heard a struggle. It was all he could do not to make a run through the dark in the hopes of getting to the other side before Keller could get to a light and take a clear shot at his target.

But before Nick could move, he heard a splash.

"Okay, here's the deal, Nicolas. Your girlfriend just went for a swim in the deep end of the pool. Her hands and feet are taped together. Now turn on the light, Nick, before she drowns."

Chapter 15

Laney went under. The dark water rushed around her. She'd had only an instant to grab a breath before Zak had shoved her in. She was naked, her wrists and ankles bound, the tape back on her mouth. She sank to the bottom and struggled to kick back to the surface.

The pool at this end was no more than ten feet deep. But even if it had been six, she knew she still could drown in it. She fought her way to the surface, kicking her feet in tandem like a mermaid's tail. It was awkward and tiring.

She surfaced, took a huge gulp of air through her nose and went under again. For that moment though, she'd seen Zak standing at the edge of the pool, the gun in his hand. He hadn't paid any attention to her. His gaze had been on the far wall of the pool where the entrance was. He'd been trying to see Nick in the darkness.

Laney knew she had to get to the side of the pool—
the farthest away from Zak Keller. She pushed off the
bottom, aiming herself toward the closest side away
from him—the side with the diving board, the deepest
part of the pool.

She kicked with all her might, surfaced and sucked
in air. She still had a half-dozen feet to go. Her head
went under. She sank back down to the bottom again,
knowing it was her only hope. The swimming was tiring her out. She wasn't sure how much longer she could
manage to surface.

Nick's heart was in his throat. Seconds were tick-
ing by. He could hear Laney struggling in the water.
He would kill Keller if it was the last thing he did. He
should have killed him that night when he'd realized
that Keller wasn't just a bad cop; he was the worst kind
of cop.

But Nick had believed in the law. He'd tried to arrest his partner instead. A huge mistake with Nick still
shocked by what he'd witnessed and Keller taking full
advantage of it.

Keller was convinced he could do anything he
wanted and get away with it. And so far he had.

Nick swore under his breath as he felt vital seconds
tick past. He had no choice. He had to save Laney. But
turning on the light would only get them both killed and
he knew it. He knew Keller. He knew what he was capable of. The blinders were off. It was kill or be killed.

"Okay," he called to Keller. "Let me find the light."

Nick hurriedly pulled off his boots and jacket, slipped
his own gun into the shoulder holster and, taking the

knife from the sheath, crept along the stone wall until he was near the diving board at the deep end. He'd gone in the opposite direction that Keller had told him to.

He could hear Laney thrashing in the water a few yards away. He just prayed she was managing to get to the surface enough to get a breath of air.

"I can't find the light," Nick said.

"You went the wrong way. You never could tell your left from your right," Keller said and chuckled at what a fool Nick was.

Nick had always played that part between the two of them. *Naive,* Keller used to call him. "As much crap as you've seen, you still want to believe that human nature is inherently good," Zak would say then laugh. "You're a prize, Nicolas. A real prize."

With the knife in his hand, Nick dove into the pool at the deep end.

The heavily rich mineral hot springs water was a dark tea color. He knew he had only a matter of seconds to get to Laney, cut her free and fire.

He opened his eyes under the water and saw nothing in the darkness of the pool. But he knew any moment Keller would go for the lights and, once he did, Nick would be his target.

Light suddenly shimmered overhead on the surface of the pool. Nick could see Laney just inches from him. She was fighting to surface. He came up next to her, dragging her toward the edge of the pool under the diving board as he cut the tape binding her hands and pressed the knife into her palm before reaching to draw his gun from his holster.

The gun was gone.

Nick looked up to find Keller kneeling over him at the edge of the pool, the dark barrel end of a .357 Magnum pointing at his head.

"You son of a bitch," Zak said, grinning. "That was one nice stunt. You always were one crazy mother—" He swung the barrel, caught Nick in the temple; the light overhead dimmed and threatened to go out as his head was shoved underwater.

Laney ripped the tape from her mouth with her free hand and coughed as she gasped for air and clung to the side of the pool with the hand holding the knife.

Her lungs ached. She'd swallowed too much water. Her limbs felt weak from the hot water, the terror and waning adrenaline.

She saw Zak Keller hit Nick, saw him push Nick under. She was just yards away from where Zak stood at the edge of the pool. She gripped the knife in her hand, forgetting for a moment that her ankles were still bound together.

Nick surfaced, coughing, his hand going to his head. She could see blood streaming down his face from the cut just over his left eye. He looked dazed as he made a swipe at the blood.

Hurriedly, Laney struggled to get the blade of the knife between her bare ankles to cut the thick tape. As weak as she was, it took both hands. As she finally got the blade between her ankles and began to saw, she slid down the side of the pool to the bottom.

The knife felt awkward in her hands. She was trembling, straining to cut the tape, needing air as if her lungs would never get enough oxygen ever again.

She felt Nick's hand as he reached for her and looked up to see him floating underwater just above her. The water around him was dark with his blood.

She couldn't stay down any longer. Her lungs were on fire. She had to surface. She had to surface *now*.

The knife blade slipped. She felt the blade nick her skin but she ignored the pain as she jerked the blade hard upward, cutting the heavy thick tape with the last of her strength. The sticky tape still bound her legs. She had to drop the knife to get the tape off.

As she bent, her vision starting to dim from lack of oxygen, she saw the gun. It lay on the bottom of the pool. Almost within reach.

Zak Keller grabbed Nick's shirt and jerked him to the surface. "Nicolas, Nicolas, what were you thinking? Oh, I know, you just had to play hero. Save the girl. Save your soul."

"You think killing me is going to make all that trouble back home go away?" Nick asked as he tried to catch his breath. Blood ran into his left eye. He blinked up at Zak.

He'd seen Laney underwater struggling to cut the tape. He wanted to reach for her, but knew that would only call attention to her. It would be just like Keller to shoot her now, now that Nick could watch. After all, if he knew Keller, and he did, that was exactly what the cop planned to do.

"They'll be watching you," Nick said, moving in the water to block Zak's view of Laney. "You'll always be under suspicion."

"Thanks to you," Keller snapped and pointed the

barrel of the gun between Nick's eyes. "Why didn't you leave well enough alone? What were those cops to you? Nothing." He shook his head. "Dammit, Nick, you and I were partners, hell, we were bros." He sounded close to tears. "I loved you, man. You were family."

"Yeah, but we didn't know then that you got all the criminal genes in the family."

"Funny, Nicolas. You always were a barrel of laughs." He glared down at him. "I'm trying to tell you I didn't want it to end like this. How can you still buy into all that bureaucracy bull? Justice goes to the highest bidder. You think I was the only cop on the take?" He laughed. "You have no idea."

"It wasn't just that you were on the take," Nick said. "You killed two *cops*." Next to him, a strip of duct tape floated up. Laney had managed to free her ankles. So why hadn't she surfaced?

Zak was watching *him,* not her. What was she doing down there? He could feel the water move. She was swimming but apparently not toward the surface. What the hell?

And that was when it hit him. She must have seen his gun on the bottom. Was going down for it. He wanted to scream "Don't do it!" Laney didn't know Keller. He'd shoot her before she could figure out how to fire the gun.

He swam a little closer to Zak even though he knew it was dangerous. But Nick had to be ready the moment Laney surfaced. He'd have to go for Zak before Zak could kill her.

"Go ahead, kill me," Nick said. "That is why you came all this way, wasn't it? So what's stopping you?

Oh, did I mention that I made a videotape and recounted everything? About seeing you kill those cops, about you taking Laney Cavanaugh, about you planning to kill us both. I even taped your phone call to me telling me where to meet you."

Keller's bravado slipped a little, then his eyes narrowed, but all his attention was on Nick. "And you dropped it in overnight mail? Nicolas, nice touch, but I have friends in the county attorney's office. That little package will never reach anyone who can hurt me."

He cocked the gun. "And you're right. There isn't any reason to put this off any longer. I'd hoped that I could talk you into changing your story, but I can see that I'd be wasting my breath." He aimed the gun at Nick's forehead, his finger on the trigger. "Goodbye, Nicolas."

The gun was heavier than Laney had expected it to be. She brought it up close to her face. The lack of oxygen was making her light-headed. She had to surface, but when she did she knew she had to be ready to pull the trigger.

She knew a little about guns. Her grandfather Titus had taught both her and Laci to shoot when they were younger. He said it was important to have a healthy respect for guns.

This model had a clip. She couldn't be sure there was a cartridge in the chamber. She pulled back the slide and let it go. All she had to do was pull the trigger when she surfaced. She slipped her finger through the trigger guard and looked up. Air. Her body felt like lead.

She shoved off the bottom with both feet, her hands holding the gun trembling as she shot toward the surface, her eyes open. She knew she would get only one chance. If she missed, she was dead. And so was Nick. They were probably both dead anyway.

She brought the gun up, fighting to keep her hands steady as she burst to the surface, gulped air and pulled the trigger. The boom resounded, echoing like thunder across the pool. She fired again just before she went under. Or at least she heard a shot. Then another and another.

It wasn't until then that she felt the pain and knew she'd been hit.

Nick grabbed for Zak the moment he felt the water change behind him, the moment he heard Laney surface and fire. All he could reach as he lunged out of the water was Zak's leg. He grabbed hold and jerked as hard as he could.

A gunshot boomed in the big barnlike room, echoing across the water.

Zak lost his footing, falling backward, coming down hard on the edge of the pool. Another shot rang out as Nick jerked Zak into the water and grabbed for his gun.

Zak had recovered from hitting the edge of the pool. Either that or he was running on high-octane anger. Nick didn't remember him ever being so strong as they struggled for the gun, both going under the water. Nick could see that he'd been wounded by the shots Laney had fired. But still Zak fought like a man obsessed.

Nick was running out of air. His head ached from where he'd been hit and he knew he'd lost a lot of blood. He needed to surface. He managed to wrestle the gun from Zak but as he swam toward the surface, his lungs bursting, Zak made a grab for the gun.

Zak had cocked the gun before hitting the water. His finger hooked through the trigger guard as he fought to turn the barrel end away from himself and at Nick. The gun went off. Nick felt the report and looked down an instant before he surfaced. He saw the expression on Zak's face, saw the surprise, the pain, the realization.

Blood floated on top of the water like an oil slick. Laney hung on the side of the pool, fighting for air, fighting against the pain in her side. She cupped her hand over the wound.

She had seen movement just under the water. The surface of the water was rough, the waves lapping at the side of the pool, the air thick with steam.

Her vision began to blur. She felt her hand holding on to the side of the pool slip. Her head went under. She grasped for the edge of the pool, the pain in her side excruciating. She knew she had to get out of the water, get help.

Her eyes were open. She could see something on the bottom of the pool. A body. Nick?

Laney felt hands lifting her. She was rising through the water toward the light. She could see the rough surface of the pool above her, the light growing brighter and brighter until her head burst through. She took a huge gulp of air, then another. And then she saw that the man holding her was Nick.

Relief mixed with the pain and the fear and came out in rattling sobs.

"It's okay, baby," he breathed against her neck as he

drew her through the water toward the shallow end of the pool. "It's okay. I'm here now. I'm here."

She clung to him as the light overhead dimmed, then blacked out.

Chapter 16

Nick stayed by Laney's side in the ambulance and helicopter that airlifted her to Billings. Doctors had insisted on stitching the cut over his left eye while he waited for her to come out of surgery for a gunshot wound to her side.

He was exhausted, but he couldn't sleep. He kept remembering the limp feel of Laney in his arms and Zak's body lying in the dark water at the bottom of the pool.

Nick hadn't been to church since he was a boy, but he prayed that Laney would survive. He couldn't bear the thought of losing her, even though he knew that once she regained consciousness she wouldn't want anything to do with him. He couldn't blame her. This was all his fault. He would never forgive himself.

Just before daylight, Laney opened her eyes. He moved to her side, taking her hand, relief closing off his throat, making his eyes tear. All he could do was smile down at her. She squeezed his hand, then closed her eyes again.

The doctor came into the room and told him Sheriff Carter Jackson was waiting for him in the hall.

Nick kissed Laney on the forehead and went out to face Sheriff Jackson, who he'd heard had returned from Florida to find his jail full and a dead man at the bottom of a swimming pool.

"I've got a lot of questions," Jackson said. He had two deputies with him. "And when you're through answering them for me, it seems you're wanted in California to answer a whole bunch more."

Nick nodded and glanced back toward Laney's room. He didn't want to leave her, but he could tell if he refused, Jackson was ready to arrest him.

"The doctor said it looks like she's going to pull through just fine," Jackson said, following Nick's gaze down the hall to Laney Cavanaugh's room. He eyed the stitched-up cut over Nick's left eye. "Meanwhile, you're going to have to come with me."

Nick didn't need Sheriff Jackson to tell him he was in a world of trouble. It was his word against Zak's about what had happened the night the two cops had been killed. Zak had used what cops called a "throwdown" gun to kill them. It had been untraceable to Zak and now that gun with Zak's fingerprints was missing.

The only hope Nick had was the videotape he'd made. If Zak's voice was on there, it might prove that Nick had killed Zak in self-defense.

He didn't want Laney to have to testify. Sheriff Jackson would take her statement and send it on to California.

Nick hoped that would be the end of her involvement. Zak Keller still had friends in California. Nick was determined never to risk Laney's life again.

Laney agreed to return to Old Town Whitehorse to recuperate and let her sister and grandfather look after her. What had happened still felt like a bad nightmare. When she'd awakened in the hospital, drugged and in pain, she'd been disappointed not to see Nick.

She must have dreamed it, but she thought she remembered him beside her bed the first time she'd woken up. She remembered the feel of a kiss on her forehead.

Her doctor had told her Nick had left with a sheriff from Whitehorse. She'd heard since that Nick had returned to L.A. where he was being questioned on the death of Zak Keller and two policemen killed eight months before. He was on suspension from the police force in L.A. until after the case went to trial.

The grapevine hummed with all the news. Rumors abounded. She heard that Nick was really a spy for the CIA. She also heard that he was with the FBI and had been working undercover in Whitehorse.

The publicity had been great for Sleeping Buffalo Resort, which had opened again to record crowds.

"How are you feeling?" Laci asked as she joined Laney on the porch.

"Fine." Laney looked out at the open country. It was late September. They'd had a cool spell but today was hot, the sky cloudless and a blinding blue.

"I'm baking you some sugar cookies," Laci announced. "You know the kind you like with white icing and sprinkles?"

"You keep cooking for me like this and I'll be as round as a beach ball," Laney said. The truth was she felt guilty because she barely ate. She'd lost her appetite and wondered if she would ever be hungry again.

"You sure you feel all right?" Laci asked, sounding worried.

Laney reached over to squeeze her sister's hand. "You know the doctor said the wound has healed just fine. He said if I stay here much longer it will be considered malingering."

"It's Nick, isn't it?" Laci said.

Laney turned away to look down the road, hating the tears that welled in her eyes. She had such mixed feelings about Nick. She'd gotten most of the real story from Sheriff Jackson. She understood why Nick had lied about his name, where he was from, who he really was.

Except she'd fallen in love with Nick Rogers, the man she'd thought he was. She didn't know Nick Giovanni from L.A.

"He called again," Laci said as the timer went off on the oven in the kitchen and her sister rose to get her cookies out before they burned.

Laney nodded. She hadn't felt up to talking to him. In truth, she didn't know what to say. She was sure by now that he'd returned to his job as a homicide detective. She'd heard he'd been reinstated now that everything had been cleared up. She'd offered to go to L.A. and testify if the county attorney needed more than her statement. But the video Nick had made the night she'd been abducted by Zak Keller had been crucial in ending the case.

"I think you should talk to Nick," Laci said.

"I think you'd better see to my cookies." Laney smiled when she said it.

"He's in love with you," Laci said as the timer went off again. "Any fool could see that," she called as she scrambled back into the house to save the cookies she'd baked.

Laney found herself looking down the road. She knew she would never be the same. The doctor had said it was normal considering the trauma she'd been through.

She smiled at that now. As terrified as she'd been every moment with Zak Keller, that paled next to the real ordeal she'd experienced this summer. She'd fallen in love and now her heart was breaking at even the thought that she would never see Nick Rogers again.

She knew that was why she didn't take Nick's calls. He was back in L.A., back with his family, back being Nicolas Giovanni. The trauma she'd experienced was the death of Nick Rogers, the man she'd fallen in love with one summer day in the middle of Montana.

She'd been staring down the road so long that at first she thought she'd just imagined the small cloud of dust on the horizon. She watched the dust billow up, the cloud growing larger as the vehicle approached. She told herself it was probably bad news.

Whitehorse had been rocked when the story had come out about the Evans offspring. Arlene was still in denial. At least when it came to Bo and Charlotte. She had gotten both of them lawyers. Now Bo and Charlotte were swearing it had all been Violet's idea, including the attack on the men outside the bar. Laney suspected Arlene had persuaded them to say that so she didn't lose all her children.

Violet had had to be taken to a maximum-security jail in Great Falls after she'd attacked both of her siblings in court. Word around town was that Violet would be taken to the mental hospital in Warm Springs for evaluation. No one expected her ever to stand trial. Arlene had already gotten both Bo and Charlotte out on bail.

Laney stared down the road as the sun glinted off the roof of a car she didn't recognize. Her heart kicked up a beat, her pulse a drum in her ears, as the car pulled to a stop in front of the house.

She couldn't see the driver, not with the sun ricocheting off the windshield, half blinding her.

She watched as the driver's side door slowly opened, and like a mirage, Nick stepped out.

He hesitated as he looked across the hood of the car at her. He wore a gray Stetson, jeans, a western shirt and boots. She found she couldn't speak as he closed the car door and started up the steps. Laney caught a whiff of warm sugar cookies and Nick's all-male scent, the two mixing into a smell that would be forever branded in her memory.

Nick stepped into the cool shade of the porch, pulled off his hat, turned the brim nervously in his fingers as his gaze met hers. "I'm sorry, but I had to see you."

She found her voice. "I'm glad you came." Tears burned her eyes as she pushed herself out of her chair, drawn to him like metal to a magnet.

He stepped toward her saying, "Please, don't get up." But she was already on her feet, already headed for his arms. He opened them and pulled her in, burying his face in her hair.

Nick felt the small, quiet shudders of her sobs as he held her, afraid to hold her too tightly for fear of hurting her. He'd talked to her doctors, been assured that the bullet from Zak's gun had gone all the way through her side and hadn't hit any vital organs. That she had healed just fine.

But Nick knew from experience what it was like to come back from a gunshot wound. The trauma wasn't all in the flesh. And after what Laney had been through, even as strong as he knew her to be, he worried that she might never heal.

"I'm so sorry," Nick said against her hair.

She shook her head and drew back, wiping her eyes before looking up at him. "The sheriff told me everything. It wasn't your fault."

"I should never have looked twice at you," he said, then felt himself soften. "But I couldn't help myself."

She smiled through her tears. "I know the feeling."

He heard the screen door squeak open a crack behind him. "I have Laney's favorite sugar cookies and iced tea if either of you are interested," Laci said from the doorway.

Nick grinned as he met Laney's gaze. "Maybe in a little while. I need to talk to your sister first."

"Okay, well, maybe I'll make some homemade ice cream," Laci said and shut the door.

"There's a lot I want to tell you," Nick said, thinking about his best friend, Danny O'Shay, about growing up in the streets of L.A., about Zak and everything that had happened culminating in the swimming pool the night she'd been shot.

But all that could wait. "The Whitehorse sheriff has offered me my old job. He kept it open in case I wanted to come back," Nick told her. "Amazingly, he thinks I make a pretty good deputy sheriff. He doesn't realize I had a lot of help solving the local crimes while he was in Florida."

Laney was staring up at him. "I thought your life was in California?"

"I have a huge Italian family in L.A., but none of them have ever been to Montana so I suspect there will be a constant flow of parents and uncles and aunts and cousins for years to come if I stay here," he said.

"Are you telling me you're actually thinking of taking your old job back?" She still sounded disbelieving.

"I told Carter I had to think about it. That it was contingent on you."

"Me?" Laney asked, her voice breaking.

"You said once that you wouldn't mind staying here if you met the right man. I'm not saying I'm the right man. But I sure as the devil would like to try to be that man. If it isn't too late. If you think you could ever trust me after everything that's happened. If you—"

Laney touched her finger to his lips and laughed. It felt good to laugh. Just as it had felt wonderful to be in Nick's arms again.

"Why don't you just kiss me and let's see what happens," she said.

"This from the woman with the analytical mind?" he said as he reached for her.

His kiss was everything Laney remembered and more. She opened to him, surrendering to a man named Nick Giovanni, a man she felt as if she'd just met. The woman who always looked before she leaped just jumped right in.

She told herself they had time to get to know each other, as she heard Laci in the kitchen making ice cream. Later they would sit on the porch and watch the sun go down as they ate sugar cookies and home-made ice cream together.

She remembered her restlessness at the beginning of her summer visit. As Nick deepened the kiss, she knew she would never be restless again. Not as long as Nick was around. It was good to be home. As that old saying went, home is definitely where the heart is. And her heart was right at home here in Montana.

* * * * *

SPECIAL EXCERPT FROM

HQN

Daniel went missing in a refinery explosion twenty years ago, but Kate never gave up hope, convinced her husband was somewhere out there, suffering from amnesia. Then, on a trip to Buckhorn, Montana, she sees him. Jon doesn't remember her, but his instincts tell him she's in danger from the person she should trust most.

Read on for a sneak preview of
Out of the Storm,
the first book in the new Buckhorn, Montana series
by New York Times *bestselling author B.J. Daniels.*

Chapter One

The gold wedding band came off easier than she thought it would. It had worn thin over the years and so had she. But still it left an indentation in her flesh, a reminder of so many things, including the promise she'd made all those years ago. She quickly slipped it back on.

"Kate?"

She looked up, blinking at the handsome young man on one knee in front of her. She was thirty-nine, a whole year away from forty. She had the rest of her life in front of her.

"What's going on, Kate?"

She swallowed and met his blue gaze. He was so different from Danny. Collin was younger, incredibly handsome, and he was alive and offering her a very different future. For almost twenty years, she'd been a widow, a single mother of two daughters and alone. She looked down at the ring he was holding out in the small velvet box. The diamond was big and beautiful.

She'd never had anything like it. When she and Danny had gotten married, they'd been teenagers and hadn't even been able to afford rings. He'd had to borrow the money from her father to buy them.

"I thought you were ready for this," Collin said as he brushed a lock of sunshine-golden hair back from his face. The disappointment in that face brought her out of her thoughts of the past. Danny was gone. Their daughters were now raised and on their own. It was time to think about the future.

She looked down at the wedding band on her ring finger, unable not to think of the day Danny had put it there. They'd been so young, so naive, so much in love. The ring had symbolized that amazing love all these years. She'd vowed never to take it off. For years, she'd held on to his memory like a life raft, needing what it meant to her to keep her head above water during the hard times and feeling safe during the lonely nights. But she knew it was time to let go. Danny wasn't coming back.

Over the years, she'd dated, but no one felt right. Until Collin. She met his blue gaze and felt herself smile. Slowly, she slipped the ring off again, closing her fist around it.

Holding out her left hand, she let Collin slip the beautiful diamond engagement ring onto her finger. It felt heavy and a little loose.

"It's official," he said, grinning. "We're engaged. And none too soon." He laughed to take away some of the sting from his words as if he hadn't meant to complain. She'd been putting him off for months. While she'd loved being with him, the thought of marriage had brought back thoughts of Danny. She and Collin had both wondered if she would ever agree to marry him.

Rising from his one knee, he pulled her up off the couch and into his arms. "We need to celebrate, and I have just the thing." He drew back to meet her gaze. "No, I'm not going to tell you what it is. It's a surprise. But you need to go pack because we are leaving first thing in the morning."

"Leaving?" Kate looked at him in alarm. All of this was suddenly happening too fast. She felt as if she was on the washer's spin cycle. "Wait—"

He put a finger to her lips. "No more waiting, Kate. It's time you trusted me. I'm going to be your husband."

Don't miss Out of the Storm *by B.J. Daniels,*
available January 2021 wherever
HQN books and ebooks are sold.

HARLEQUIN

INTRIGUE

SEEK THRILLS. SOLVE CRIMES.
JUSTICE SERVED.

Save $1.00

on the purchase of

ANY Harlequin Intrigue book.

Available wherever books are sold,
including most bookstores, supermarkets,
drugstores and discount stores.

Save $1.00

on the purchase of ANY Harlequin Intrigue book.

Coupon valid until February 28, 2021.
Redeemable at participating outlets in the US and Canada only.
Not redeemable at Barnes & Noble stores. Limit one coupon per customer.

52616798

Canadian Retailers: Harlequin Enterprises ULC will pay the face value of this coupon plus 10.25¢ if submitted by customer for this product only. Any other use constitutes fraud. Coupon is nonassignable. Void if taxed, prohibited or restricted by law. Consumer must pay any government taxes. Void if copied. Inmar Promotional Services ("IPS") customers submit coupons and proof of sales to Harlequin Enterprises ULC, P.O. Box 31000, Scarborough, ON M1R 0E7, Canada. Non-IPS retailer—for reimbursement submit coupons and proof of sales directly to Harlequin Enterprises ULC, Retail Marketing Department, Bay Adelaide Centre, East Tower, 22 Adelaide Street West, 40th Floor, Toronto, Ontario M5H 4E3, Canada.

5 65373 00076 2 (8100)0 12464

U.S. Retailers: Harlequin Enterprises ULC will pay the face value of this coupon plus 8¢ if submitted by customer for this product only. Any other use constitutes fraud. Coupon is nonassignable. Void if taxed, prohibited or restricted by law. Consumer must pay any government taxes. Void if copied. For reimbursement submit coupons and proof of sales directly to Harlequin Enterprises ULC 482, NCH Marketing Services, P.O. Box 880001, El Paso, TX 88588-0001, U.S.A. Cash value 1/100 cents.

© 2020 Harlequin Enterprises Limited

BACCOUP41800